Praise for the novels of Beverly Connor

"Calls to mind the forensic mysteries of Aaron Elkins and Patricia Cornwell. However, Connor's sleuth infuses the mix with her own brand of spice as a pert and brainy scholar in the forensic analysis of bones. . . . Chases, murder attempts, and harrowing rescues add to this fast-paced adventure."
—*Chicago Sun-Times*

"Connor combines smart people, fun people, and dangerous people in a novel hard to put down."
— *The Dallas Morning News*

"In Connor's latest multifaceted tale, the plot is serpentine, the solution ingenious, the academic politics vicious . . . chock-full of engrossing anthropological and archeological detail." —*Publishers Weekly*

continued . . .

DEAD PAST

A DIANE FALLON FORENSIC INVESTIGATION

BEVERLY CONNOR

AN ONYX BOOK

ONYX
Published by New American Library, a division of
Penguin Group (USA) Inc., 375 Hudson Street,
New York, New York 10014, USA
Penguin Group (Canada), 90 Eglinton Avenue East, Suite 700, Toronto,
Ontario M4P 2Y3, Canada (a division of Pearson Penguin Canada Inc.)
Penguin Books Ltd., 80 Strand, London WC2R 0RL, England
Penguin Ireland, 25 St. Stephen's Green, Dublin 2,
Ireland (a division of Penguin Books Ltd.)
Penguin Group (Australia), 250 Camberwell Road, Camberwell, Victoria 3124,
Australia (a division of Pearson Australia Group Pty. Ltd.)
Penguin Books India Pvt. Ltd., 11 Community Centre, Panchsheel Park,
New Delhi - 110 017, India
Penguin Group (NZ), 67 Apollo Drive, Mairangi Bay, Auckland 1310,
New Zealand (a division of Pearson New Zealand Ltd.)
Penguin Books (South Africa) (Pty.) Ltd., 24 Sturdee Avenue,
Rosebank, Johannesburg 2196, South Africa

Penguin Books Ltd., Registered Offices:
80 Strand, London WC2R 0RL, England

First published by Onyx, an imprint of New American Library,
a division of Penguin Group (USA) Inc.

First Printing, February 2007
10 9 8 7 6 5 4 3 2 1

To Zachary, Will, and Cassidy

ACKNOWLEDGMENTS

A big thanks to my editor, Anne Bohner at NAL; to Winterville, Georgia, Chief of Police Eric Pozen for bringing me up to speed on meth labs; and to Judy Iakovou and Diane Trap for their wise advice. I appreciate all of you.

Chapter 1

Diane Fallon jerked to consciousness. She lay for a moment, caught between waking and sleep, frightened, not knowing where she was or what she had heard. She tried to focus her eyes. On the wall next to her bed a glass-covered photograph of a chambered nautilus flickered with an orange glow. Diane sucked in a breath, rolled over, rose on her elbow, and looked out the window of her apartment. Beyond the glistening fresh-fallen snow covering the ground, the ice-covered trees lining her street were silhouetted by an unnatural orange glow. A smoky haze drifted through the light of the streetlamps. A hail of sparks, punctuated by intermittent sounds like muffled gunshots or distant fireworks, swirled and fell from the navy blue night sky. In the distance, orange and yellow flames engulfed whatever lay beneath.

Diane swung her feet to the floor and sat up, trying to clear the fog that still held on to her brain. "Oh, God," she whispered. There were houses on that street, mostly rented by students of Bartram University. She looked at her alarm clock but found it dangling off the nightstand at the end of its cord. The illuminated digits switched from 3:06 to 3:07 as she put it back in place. *Explosion. There must have been an explosion. That's what woke me up.*

Diane reached for the phone, heard a distant sound

of sirens, and drew back her hand. Garnett, the chief of detectives, would call her when she was needed. She wasn't a first responder. Like medical examiners and undertakers, forensic anthropologists and crime scene specialists are among the last to be called—when there are only the dead to help.

Watching the fire, she sat for several moments on the edge of her bed. Briefly she thought of lying back down to try for a few more hours' sleep, but went for a shower instead. When the inevitable call came, she wanted to feel alert, and she thought a shower and coffee would do the job better than sleep.

It wasn't a call that came, but a banging on the door. Diane stepped out of the shower, wrapped herself in a robe, and hurried across the living room.

"Who is it?" she called out.

A female voice, stressed and hesitant, called through the door. "Miss Fallon? We're your upstairs neighbors."

Diane opened the door. The two of them, young husband and pregnant wife, wrapped in dark blue parkas and knit caps pulled down over their ears, stood in the doorway.

Diane stood dripping under her robe, trying to think of their names. Leslie and Shane, she remembered. They'd lived here several weeks, but Diane hadn't made their acquaintance yet. She felt a pang of guilt. A cool breeze from the stairs made her shiver.

"Hello," she said, looking down at Leslie's swollen midsection. "Do you need to go to the hospital?"

"No." They both shook their heads. "We're just making sure everyone heard the evacuation announcement. The police are driving up and down the street calling out for everyone to leave this area. There's been some kind of chemical explosion." The young woman cradled her belly as she spoke.

"Oh, oh, my God," said Diane. "Thank you. That's

very kind of you. I was in the shower and didn't hear . . ."

She let her words trail off as the door across the hallway opened and Veda and Marvin Odell, the eccentric older couple who lived opposite her, rushed out with suitcase in hand and hurried down the stairs without stopping or even casting a glance in their direction. Diane and the young couple watched the backs of the Odells as they fled, Veda's vintage black rabbit-fur coat flapping behind her as if the animal were still alive and egging her onward. Diane was glad to see that with all their interest in death and fondness for funerals, the Odells were not eager to attend their own.

The young couple looked back at Diane and were about to say something when the sound of the police bullhorn reminded them of the urgency to leave.

"I appreciate your knocking on my door. Do you know if the landlady has a ride?" asked Diane.

"I called her," said Leslie. "Shane and I are taking her to her nephew's. She said she would check on the people on the ground floor."

Diane nodded. "What about the basement?"

"Basement?" asked Leslie.

"Someone lives down there?" Shane asked.

Diane nodded. "You get the landlady, I'll check on the guy in the basement."

They heard the bullhorn again and Leslie, frightened, looked over at her husband, as though they had lingered too long. Diane thanked them and watched a moment as Shane helped his wife negotiate the stairs.

She closed the door and hurried to dress quickly. *Chemical explosion,* she thought, as she threw clothes into her duffel bag. *What kind of chemical explosion do you have in a residential neighborhood? Gas leak? Chem lab? Drug lab? Damn.* Diane had seen kids playing and riding their bikes on that street. It was a neighborhood that often had several students to a house. Diane shivered at the potential catastrophe. She hurriedly slipped on her coat and went out the door, locking it behind her. The old Greek Revival house that had been converted to apartments appeared empty and quiet. Diane locked the main door as she stepped out onto the columned porch.

In the street a line of cars was leaving the area. It was calm, not frantic. No blaring horns or angry shouts, just streams of headlights, each spotlighting the car in front, a necklace of cars.

Diane trudged around to the side of the house to where the basement entrance was located, down a short flight of stairs with wrought-iron bannisters. She was about to knock when she saw a note taped to the door. It was from Professor Keith, resident of the basement apartment, saying he had evacuated and could be reached at his office on campus. She turned and plodded back up and through the thick snow to her own car.

There was an acrid odor in the air and something that made her eyes burn. She wondered what she was inhaling with each breath. She pulled the wool scarf over her mouth as if that would help keep out the invisible fumes. Popping sounds of breaking glass grew louder and the explosion of paint cans, aerosol sprays, and all the other flammable things people keep in their houses added to the noise. A string of firecracker-like sounds made her want to run for cover. It sounded like a gun battle.

Traffic was thinning considerably, but the mass exit had turned the snowy street into a river of slush. Diane had to stand in thick ice water as she used her hands to clear snow from her windshield. By the time she finished, her hands and toes were freezing. She got in the car, started the engine, and turned the heater on high, hugging her arms to herself and blowing into her hands. She wished she had some hot coffee.

Before she pulled out into the street she saw Professor Keith's Volvo several feet ahead, exhaust coming from the tailpipe. He must have just left the note before she got to his door. Diane put her car in gear and started to ease out into the street when she noticed a man standing next to a group of tall snow-covered shrubs. He was pointing a gun at the passenger side of Keith's Volvo.

Diane grabbed her cell and started to punch in 911. NO SERVICE. *Shit.* She looked up at the Volvo again. The guy with the gun looked like a kid, the way he carried himself. He held the gun sideways like punks do on TV shows. He was shaking it at the car, obviously trying to make Keith let him in. He held the gun in his left hand, and looked as though he was favoring his right side. She tried to ease forward slowly. The sound of her tires spinning in the slush caused him to turn and look at her. Keith and his Volvo sped away, leaving Diane to face the young man now coming toward her pointing a gun and dripping a trail of blood.

Chapter 2

Diane's heart beat hard and fast as the dark figure approached her. Her gaze darted around the car for a weapon. None. No gun, no knife, not a tire iron, or a baseball bat. Her mouth was so dry she doubted she could even muster harsh words for protection.

He stood in her headlights, pointing the gun at her. He was young, covered with soot, his eyes red-rimmed and swollen as though from crying. His hair hung in frosty wet ropes in his face. He was clad only in a flannel shirt and jeans. It was twenty degrees outside. He should have been shivering, but he wasn't.

In his left hand he still held the gun in the same sideways punk-ass position. His right arm, the origin of the blood, hung at his side. He tried to raise it, squinting his eyes as if trying to keep back the pain. He shook the gun at her and dipped his knees slightly, as though readying to jump up and down. The gesture made him look like a child beginning a tantrum. She started to duck, in case the gun went off. That was when she saw his right hand was missing.

He started walking toward the passenger side of her car. *Think fast.* The car wouldn't move on the ice, and he would probably shoot her if she tried. Even if she did manage to get the car moving, she knew better than to let him take her to another location. She couldn't allow him in the car with her.

Words were her only weapon. Diane swallowed hard and cleared her throat. OK, what words? *Think fast, damn it.* She couldn't reason with him. A grievously wounded kid in pain holding a gun can't be reasoned with.

What then? What words would he respond to? He was almost to the passenger door when an idea hit her. She had to act quickly.

He might listen to what he wanted to hear. She turned off the ignition, swung open her door, and stepped out of the car, almost slipping in the slush. She caught the door to keep from falling. They faced each other across the car's snow-covered roof. He jabbed the gun in her direction, skimming it through the layer of snow on top of the car, releasing flakes into the air. She spoke before he could say anything.

"You need help. Get in the backseat and hunker down so the police won't see you."

"What?" He squinted his eyes and looked confused. "I'll shoot you," he said, slurring his words.

Great, she thought, *he's probably drunk or on drugs, too.* "Can you drive like that? You need me to drive. You need help." She was very careful not to use any negative words in describing what he could or couldn't do. Something she learned from her former boss, the diplomat.

He stood staring at her for several moments. "I have a gun," he said, as if she hadn't noticed the silver-plated weapon he was waving at her.

Diane's teeth chattered—either from cold or fear, she didn't know. She was wondering if this was such a good plan after all. He was making no move to get in the car.

"Yes, I see you do. That's all right. I'll take you to get help."

"I'm not going to any hospital." He thrust out his chin, trying to look defiant, she supposed, but succeeding only in looking petulant.

"I know a private clinic where a doctor will fix you up and ask no questions."

"I'll ride in the front." He waved his gun at the car.

"If you do, the police will see you. There's not enough room to slide down out of sight. There's a blanket in the back. Cover yourself. You have your gun," she added, as if maybe he had forgotten.

He simply stared at her, not moving. The snow was falling again; large flakes caught in her eyelashes. *Just get in the car.* She looked up and down the street, worried that any approaching car might force him into rash action.

He made a move toward the back door, stopped and stared at it, then at his gun. He fumbled, trying to open it with his gun hand. For a moment she thought he was going to shoot the door. The smell of smoke from the house fire was getting stronger and it irritated her nose. A burst of cold wind swirled her hair and it stung her face like tiny whips.

He shoved the pistol into the waistband of his trousers, opened the door, slid into the backseat quickly, and shut the door.

Diane didn't hesitate a moment. As soon as she heard his door slam shut, she pressed the DOOR LOCK button on her remote, slammed the driver's door shut, and ran, thankful that just two days before she had three eight-year-olds as passengers in her backseat. The child safety locks were still on, and in his condition, by the time he managed to climb into the front seat, she would be halfway through the woods to the other street where there would be a swarm of policemen.

Twice she almost slipped crossing the road. The slush was turning to ice. It numbed her feet as it sloshed into her low-cut boots. She was passing in front of a parked van when she heard muffled gunshots from inside her car. *Shit, that was a new car,* she thought as she dove for cover, sliding to a stop behind the van. Several more shots rang out accompanied by the sound of breaking glass. For a moment she didn't know if the sounds were from the gunfire in her car or the loud roar and crackle of the house fire on the opposite street.

The smoke from the fire was growing thicker. Diane pulled the neck of her shirt over her mouth, took a deep breath, and sprang across the nearest yard past a snowman. She stopped inside an alleyway and hugged the side of a house. Out of the corner of her eye she saw a blue light flashing on the street she had just fled. She turned and sprinted back in the direction of the light as fast as she could in ankle-deep snow.

She felt reasonably safe now from the one-handed kid with the gun. It was dark and she doubted he could hit anything from inside the car. If he ran out of bullets, which she suspected he was about to, he'd have a hard time reloading with one half-frozen hand. Why would he want to shoot her, anyway? She kept in the shadows and away from the streetlights just in case.

The smoke stung her throat and made her eyes water. As she ran toward the police cruiser waving her arms, she stepped off the curb and half fell into a pothole where the icy slush completely filled her boot before she could recover herself. The cruiser slowed, and an officer rolled down the window and shined a light in her face.

"Keep your hands were we can see them . . . ," the driver said. "Is that you, Dr. Fallon? We got a report of an attempted carjacking."

"Make that two attempted carjackings," she said.

He turned off his flashlight, but Diane was left with the bright afterimage. She blinked a couple of times before she recognized the policemen as people she knew.

"He's in my car," she said, pointing in the general direction. She handed him her keys and quickly explained how she lured him into the backseat. "He's missing a hand, bleeding, scared, in pain, and may be high on drugs or alcohol. He has a gun and has been shooting."

"Dangerous combination," said the policeman on the passenger side. "How about you? You all right?"

"I'm fine. Just wet and cold. Don't worry about me."

"You stay here, out of the line of fire."

Diane was glad to let them deal with him. She heard the driver calling for an ambulance as they drove slowly toward her car. Diane moved out of the road, huddled near a pine tree, and watched the scene illuminated under the streetlight.

They stopped just a few feet from her car, opened their doors, and, their guns drawn, used the doors for shields. Diane saw the driver reach for the mike. She hugged her arms to herself and wiggled her toes in her boots. They had not been a good choice for stomping around in the snow.

"This is the police. Toss your gun out of the window and raise your"—he hesitated for a beat—"raise your hands where we can see them."

Diane waited, watching her car. Nothing. The policeman repeated the order.

"Don't make us come and get you," he added. "We don't want anyone to get hurt."

Nothing.

The two crouched policemen moved slowly toward her car, one on either side, their arms outstretched, their guns aimed ahead of them. Diane squinted against the wind, trying to see inside her car. From that distance, she couldn't see a thing. She huddled against the pine tree, partly for warmth and partly to make a smaller target.

The policemen stepped up to the car, shining their flashlights inside. They hesitated a moment, and one of them aimed the remote. She couldn't hear the click of the doors unlocking over the noise of the fire and the wind. She saw one of them open a back door, reach in, and come out with a gun. She guessed that the kid had passed out in her backseat.

The ambulance arrived just moments after the police had secured her car. She walked over and stood with the police and waited as the EMTs gently pulled the kid out and onto the stretcher. With his eyes closed and face relaxed he looked so young, still a teenager, facing the rest of his life without his right hand. She suddenly felt pity for him—now that the police had secured his gun.

"Do you know him?" One of the patrolmen asked. Ben, Diane thought his name was. He was thirtyish, about ten years older and twenty pounds heavier than his partner. Bundled up in winter coats and earmuffs, they looked very much alike.

Diane shook her head, looking at his face again. "I've never seen him before."

"Some guy—Shawn Keith—called it in," said the other patrolman. "He said something about a woman being in trouble. Didn't say it was you, Dr. Fallon."

"Keith may not have known it was me. The kid tried to stop him first."

As the EMTs worked getting him stable for transport to the hospital, Diane gave the police details on her encounter with the youth.

"You're lucky he had only one hand. Punk kids are dangerous. He's probably the meth cook who blew up the house," the patrolman added, nodding in the direction of the fire.

Diane doubted it. Whoever was cooking the meth was probably dead in the explosion. But more than likely, the kid was connected in some way.

"Could I get a ride to the crime lab?" she said. I'll have my forensic people process my car when we're allowed back in the area."

"Yeah, sure." Both of them looked in the direction

of the fire as if they had just remembered it and the evacuation order. "We'd better get out of here."

They saw the ambulance off and, after retrieving Diane's suitcase, the three of them piled into the police car. She was glad she had put her suitcase in her trunk instead of the backseat where he would have bled all over it. On the way to the crime lab, the two of them took turns admonishing her for not having snow tires in the middle of a North Georgia winter.

They let her out at the entrance to her crime lab. Diane smiled and thanked them, glad to get away from their banter. The sick dread in her stomach, which she had awakened with because of the fire and the fear inspired by the gun-wielding kid, was still with her. Instead of going up to the lab, she walked around the building to the entrance to the RiverTrail Museum of Natural History.

Chanell Napier, head of museum Security, was on night duty and opened the door for her before she had a chance to fish out her key.

"Cold night out there, Dr. Fallon," the slender, round-faced African-American woman said as Diane entered. "What you doing out here so late?"

Diane explained about the explosion of the house on the street near her apartment and the mandatory evacuation. She left out the part about the carjacker because she felt too tired for the questions that were sure to follow.

"Oh, no. There's students from Bartram living in those houses, aren't there?"

Diane nodded. "I'm going to stay in my office the rest of the evening," she said.

Juliet Price from Aquatics, who managed the seashell collection, came across the lobby toward the doors. She looked like a waif or a wood sprite with her wispy blond hair and slender figure. She fumbled in her purse and pulled out her car keys as she reached Diane and Chanell.

"You working mighty late," said Chanell.

"I don't need much sleep," said Juliet. She nodded at Diane and Chanell as she hurried out the large double doors.

"She's a scared little thing, isn't she," said Chanell.

"Juliet's a shy one," said Diane. "She's good at her job, though." Diane looked at her watch. "I wish I didn't need much sleep. Don't call me unless the museum's on fire."

"Sure thing," said Chanell.

As Diane made her way through the large double doors of the east wing and to her private conference room adjoining her museum office, she expected her cell phone to ring at any moment. It didn't. She took off her wet boots and socks and lay down on the stuffed sofa. A brown suede and cotton jacket of Frank's was lying across the back. She picked it up and folded it into a pillow. It smelled of his cologne. He'd been gone only three days, chasing a fraud lead to Seattle. It seemed like a month.

Frank was a rock—always reasonable, always logical, and always loving. She thought about calling him, but he was probably asleep—or maybe playing poker with his detective friends in Seattle. He would ask her how her day was and she would say great, but tomorrow wouldn't be a good day at all. Tomorrow she'd have to identify charred bodies. Frank would sympathize and say some right thing; then he would tell her how fortunate that the dead have her to speak for them, and he'd tell her he would be home as soon as he could. She wished he were here now. Frank liked to cuddle and she would like to have him here to warm her. She grabbed the throw at the end of the sofa, covered her cold feet, and drifted off to sleep in the middle of her imaginary conversation with him.

Diane awoke with a start. Not because there was an explosion outside her window this time. It was her cell phone vibrating and ringing in her pocket. She fished it out and looked at the illuminated display before she flipped it open and put it to her ear.

"Chief Garnett," she said, hoping she didn't sound sleepy.

"I guess you know why I'm calling."

Chapter 3

At nine o'clock in the morning the air was just as cold as it had been in the early hours before daylight when Diane fled from her home. The sky was gray-white and sunless. She stood in the ankle-deep snow just outside the yellow crime scene tape surrounding the burned-out husk of a house that was at the center of the night's events. Unlike the bright, sparkling white mantle in front of her apartment house, the snow here was an ugly blanket of black and gray. The air smelled of chemicals, smoke, and wet ashes.

Little remained of the house—its stone foundation, a few blackened pieces of wood framing, twisted shapes of water pipes, broken and blackened ceramic plumbing fixtures, the remnants of a brick fireplace, and a section of charred floor hanging over the dark pit of debris that had been the basement. She could pick out the forms of blackened disfigured bodies like a hidden picture puzzle among the rubble. She dreaded the next few days.

"The fire chief tells me it was a meth lab that exploded in the basement." Chief Garnett, well dressed as usual in a dark brown topcoat, stood beside Diane, surveying the damage. He shook his head. "There was a party going on upstairs at the time. The house was rented to a bunch of college students."

Douglas Garnett, chief of detectives, was Diane's

immediate supervisor for her position as director of the Rosewood Crime Lab.

"How many people inside? Do you know?" she asked.

White steam rose in front of their faces with each breath. Diane's nose was growing numb.

"That's what you're going to have to tell us." He paused a long moment. "The neighbors say there was loud music going all evening. They saw kids on the front and back porches. I'm afraid to guess how many."

"Dear God," Diane whispered.

"We have a few survivors. Kids who were out in the yard when the house exploded. They're all badly injured, but alive. So far, our best lead for information is the kid who tried to jack your car. He's in the best condition of all of them. I understand he's out of surgery. I'm going to talk with him after I leave here.

The cold was beginning to seep into Diane's fleece-lined jacket. She bent her knees and rubbed her gloved hands together. The cold didn't seem to bother Garnett. He stood scanning the burned-out building, his hands in his pockets.

"I've called in all the area medical examiners—Rankin, Pilgrim, Webber—we need to do this fast. Anxious parents are calling wanting to know if their child is among the victims."

At the sound of a generator motor starting, Diane looked a couple of doors down the street at the morgue tent being raised where she and the MEs would work. The white canvas structure covered the entire front yard of an empty house with a FOR SALE sign out front, which made it a good choice to occupy.

City workers were quickly erecting a forensic city in the neighborhood. They had installed blue and white Porta-Johns near the morgue tent. A command post in a small travel camper sat in the driveway. In the street they'd parked a refrigerated trailer from a semi to keep bodies, evidence, and equipment. The forensic complex looked expensive and Diane said so.

"We'll have to bring in a portable x-ray machine and other equipment to do our job. All this could be done at one of the hospitals for a lot less money and aggravation."

"Good publicity is priceless," Garnett said, nodding his head toward the local and Atlanta news media setting up their own tent city on a lawn across the street. "Nothing like seeing your leaders taking immediate action."

"I guess." Diane's attention was caught by a circular saw blade lying half-buried in the snow at the base of a thick oak tree. She squatted beside it. Garnett peered over her shoulder. Diane took a plastic bag full of orange marker flags from her jacket pocket.

"What do you have there?" asked Garnett.

Diane stuck a flag in the snow beside the saw blade. "The red color on the edge here . . . I think it's frozen blood."

Just as she was about to stand, she saw just beyond the blade something else covered in a thin layer of snow but unmistakable in its appearance. She planted another flag beside the object and stood up.

"Is that a hand?" asked Garnett.

"It is. And if I'm not mistaken, I know who it belongs to. The kid who tried to take my car. It would appear that the saw blade came flying from the explosion and caught his wrist. Looks like a clean cut. If he had had his wits about him and taken his hand with him, I wonder if it could have been reattached."

Garnett didn't say anything for a moment, but just stared at the hand with his mouth turned down in a frown. "At least he's alive," he said.

Diane looked over at the burned-out house. "At least that," she whispered.

Carefully retracing her previous steps, she walked away from the tree, back out to the road. Next to the media tent a shelter of green-striped canvas was being erected. More media? The tent city just kept growing. "Who are they?" she asked.

"Local church groups are setting up a tent to keep you guys in sandwiches and coffee. A sort of comfort station."

Diane shook her head and looked him in the eye. "You know, Garnett, this is getting too large. It's going to get out of hand."

"We'll have to see that it doesn't." He nodded at the new tent. "It's also there for the parents. You know that anyone who can't get in touch with their kid is going to come down here. This will give them a place to sit and wait and someone to talk to besides us."

Diane conceded that might be a good idea. "What about the people who live in these houses?" She encompassed the neighborhood with a sweep of her hand. "They are going to want back in their homes."

"Most of the people on the street have been given permission to come back. The houses next to the explosion suffered damage and their owners are staying in a hotel until they can return. A cordon will be put up and the police will keep people out of your way."

Diane still didn't agree with the way the city was handling the tragedy. But the decision was made. The mayor loved a good show. It looked like he was going to have one. Instead of arguing the point further, she turned her attention back to the crime scene.

"We won't be able to walk on what's left of the floor of the house. What we'll do is build a network of boards just over the floor, anchored outside. . . ."

The ambient noise went up several decibels; Diane stopped talking and looked up the street. A line of vehicles was driving through the police checkpoint. The white van she knew. It belonged to her crime lab. It and two cars approached and parked next to the curb in front of a neighboring house. The last vehicle in the line belonged to the arson investigator. Diane groaned inwardly. He parked across the street from the others, pulling up in the yard to keep the street from becoming a bottleneck. The new arrivals drew members of the news media like flies to a corpse.

Diane wanted to tell Garnett that this was going to be trouble, but she remained silent. Nothing she could do. Marcus McNair was the arson investigator, after all. He had right of access to the scene. But Garnett apparently · had his own apprehensions. His frown deepened the creases in his forehead and around his mouth when he saw Marcus emerge from the red city vehicle and grin broadly at the swarm of reporters hurrying in his direction.

"I have to cut this off," he said, and strode across the street to intercept the press.

Diane stayed and waited for her crew who, carrying their crime scene cases, were climbing out of the van. The last thing she wanted was to come between Marcus and publicity.

Marcus McNair wanted her job. He had applied for it when the city announced it was creating a crime scene unit. He thought his bid for the director's position was a certainty—he was an arson investigator; his brother-in-law was a city councilman with a lot of pull; he was athletic and handsome; and the only person he was up against was a civilian female museum director.

What McNair didn't know was that the job was wired for the director of the museum where the forensic lab was to be located. He didn't know about all the political shenanigans the mayor and police commissioner had conjured to force Diane to provide building space in return for relief from an overburdening tax assessment. He didn't know that the museum director was a former human rights investigator, a crime scene specialist, and an internationally known forensic anthropologist. Judging from the reception he gave Diane at every encounter—scowls, sarcasm, or just plain ignoring her—losing the position had been a blow.

Diane greeted her team and ignored the conversation Garnett and Marcus were having with the news media. David, Jin, and Neva stopped, set down their cases, and scanned the scene before them. They were all bundled in their dark blue winter jackets with CRIME SCENE UNIT printed in large yellow letters across the back. All but Jin wore knit caps and boots.

Jin was bareheaded and wore sneakers. He had worked in New York City as a crime scene specialist, and during the past few weeks he had tried to explain to them many times that this wasn't really cold weather; they didn't know what cold weather is. He had wanted to live in a smaller city for a while and Diane felt fortunate to have him. "I hate fires," he said. "I really hate them." He covered his straight black hair with the plastic cap that Diane had them wear at crime scenes.

Neva pushed a lock of brown hair under her knit cap and donned the plastic cap. "People are already calling my parents, cause they know where I work," she said, "and they want to know who's been killed. This is just terrible." Neva came to the crime scene unit from the Rosewood police.

David and Diane's eyes met briefly. She knew what he was thinking. This is too much like the life they left. David worked with Diane at World Accord International doing human rights investigations all over the world. They had seen too many piles of burned bodies.

"We're going to work the area around the house first. I've marked a couple of things I've found," Diane said, pointing to the orange flags—silent sentinels guarding the severed hand and the saw blade. "Work inward. After we clear the way to the house, we will have to build a scaffold over the floor. It's not stable."

Diane glanced over at Marcus. She imagined he'd

have something to say about that. He and Garnett were walking toward them, only Marcus looked like he was strutting. It was the smirk on his face that made her take a plastic shower cap from Neva's case and hand it to him. The expression on his face changed as their eyes met.

Chapter 4

Marcus McNair scowled at Diane as she held out the plastic hair cap to him. "You want me to shower?" he said, giving her his deep-throated gravelly laugh.

Judging from his expression, she might as well have asked if he wanted to wrap a snake around his head. She had heard on good authority that many women found him charming. She found him annoying.

"The hair covering is to protect the crime scene. We don't want any more contamination than has already occurred."

Diane's team grinned at McNair. He cast a quick glance at the media.

"I don't think I'll be needing that," he said.

Diane knew that he would never accept the possibility of his picture being taken in anything that looked like a shower cap. She just wanted to see him back out of wearing it, and immediately felt guilty for baiting him.

"What we got here?" he asked quickly.

Garnett responded. "The crime scene unit is going to clear a way to the house. When that's done, we need to build a low scaffold over the house site so all of you can work." Garnett gestured as he spoke, as if building the scaffolding with the movement of his hands.

"Well, what I think," said McNair, "is I can have a look at the structure. We may not need to build anything. . . ."

Garnett cut him off. "The decision is made. If you don't want to help clear the path, then you need to stay out of the way until you have access to the scene."

There was something else going on, an undercurrent of hostility Diane had been unaware of until now. She had rarely seen Garnett that short with anyone. Whatever it was, she didn't want her team in the middle of it. She unconsciously stepped back.

"Now look here, Garnett," said McNair. "The fire department was first on the scene and took control of the situation. I work for the fire department, not you. I'm investigating a suspicious fire here. This is my turf and I'm in charge. All you need to do is get out of my way." McNair all but thrust out his chin, daring Garnett to hit it.

Diane glanced at the reporters to see if anyone had noticed. They had collared Lynn Webber and were occupied. However, Whit Abercrombie, the Rose County coroner, was approaching. He winked at her.

"No, I believe I'm in charge," Whit said. McNair spun around at the newcomer just as Whit slapped him on the back. "We've had this conversation before. It doesn't matter who gets to the scene first, Marcus. State law clearly says that in those instances in which there is loss of human life, the coroner of the jurisdiction—that would be me—has prevailing authority and control of the scene of death until such time as his responsibilities are satisfied and he relinquishes control to other authority. I don't know why I have to keep telling people that."

His dark eyes sparkled as he grinned broadly, showing bright white teeth. Whit had a short black beard and it made him look devilish at that moment. Like

Jin, he must have a tolerance for cold, thought Diane. He was dressed in jeans and a white cotton shirt with a black leather jacket open down the front.

McNair felt ganged up on; Diane could see it in his eyes as his gaze darted from Whit to Garnett and back to Whit again.

"Whit," began McNair.

Again Garnett cut him off, explaining to Whit the plan that Diane had laid out. Whit nodded.

"Sounds reasonable. It's going to be a whole lot messier and more complicated to extract the remains if the rest of the floor collapses." Whit looked at the burned-out house as if for the first time and shook his head. "We need to get those bodies out as quickly and carefully as we can. If it was a meth lab, there's no telling what may still be lurking in that rubble. The hazardous waste people are on the way from Atlanta. They'll handle the septic tank. It'll be full of contaminants. This whole thing is a tragic mess and we need everyone's cooperation." He looked at each of them as he spoke and then settled on Garnett. "Any idea how many kids were in the house?"

"I've got my people making a list of possibles," said Garnett. "When we can, we'll interview the survivors, see what they can tell us. I think we're looking at one of the biggest tragedies Rosewood has ever suffered."

"Marcus," said Whit, "I think you might as well learn what you can from the firefighters for now. It's going to be later in the day before you can get access to the house."

Whit's mild, friendly manner diffused the situation for the moment, but McNair cast a mean glance at Garnett before he left.

"Do I need to know what's going on?" asked Diane when McNair was out of earshot.

For a moment Garnett watched Marcus McNair trudge to his car through the thin layer of slush still on the road.

"Albin Adler, the councilman, is trying to start an

investigation of the police department, raising a big stink, and McNair's feeding him misinformation. It's just political nonsense. It goes on all the time, but I want to keep it out of here."

Diane was more than willing to let it not be her problem.

"Adler wants to run for mayor and then governor," added Whit. "And he's got all his relatives doing his dirty work. I understand they're legion."

Diane's team had been waiting patiently, appearing to ignore Garnett and Whit's conversation as they rummaged through their crime scene cases, pulling out what they needed. But Diane knew they were soaking up everything. David would use the information to feed the basic paranoia he enjoyed nurturing; Jin was fascinated with southern local politics; and Neva would use it to wheedle more information from buddies on the police force.

Diane watched them a moment before she spoke, smiling as she thought how much she liked her staff. David looked up at her and grinned. She left Whit and Garnett to their conversations and focused on her team.

"OK," she said, "David and Jin, I want you to clear a path to the site and a perimeter immediately around it to provide a work area. Neva and I will work the area outside that perimeter."

"I can handle that," said Neva, "if you need to set up. . . ." She nodded toward the morgue tent—the place where the bodies and the body parts would be delivered—and let the sentence fade off.

"I'll work here until the medical examiners are ready," Diane said. "Let's get started."

Marking found items with flags—green flags for debris, orange for human remains—Jin and David were searching a wide path from the driveway to the burned-out house. She and Neva began a search of the front yard from the street to the house.

Most of the debris was pieces of wood and shingles from the house. Other than blood, probably from victims who were outside the house when it exploded, neither she nor Neva initially found any human remains.

Diane was setting a green flag beside what looked like the leg of a chair when she heard her name. She stood up to see medical examiner Lynn Webber waving to her from the road.

Reaching for something hanging on a limb, Neva was a few feet away near a small maple tree.

"Neva, I need to go. . . ."

Neva retrieved the object—it looked like a piece of cloth to Diane—bagged it, marked the limb with a tag, and put a yellow flag beside the tree. Yellow flags were the code for "look up."

"Sure. We can handle this," Neva said.

"Neva, I know this is a lot, but when you finish here, I need for one of you to process my car. It's parked in front of my house."

"Your car? What happened?"

That's right, thought Diane, *they don't know.* She hadn't told them about the kid with the gun.

"Someone tried to highjack my car last night."

"What?" Neva stood openmouthed. Glancing over at the burned-out house still holding the charred bodies, she said, "All this, and you had to deal with a carjacker?"

Diane gave her a quick explanation, waving off her concerns with a flick of her hand. "It turned out all right." And it had, but the kid with the bloody stump had haunted her dreams during the few hours' sleep she was able to catch before Garnett's call.

Diane retraced her steps to where Lynn Webber stood shivering in her brown suede coat. Her white earmuffs looked like snowballs against her short black hair. Her tan linen slacks appeared wholly inadequate for the weather, as did her leather fashion boots with two-inch heels.

Lynn's dark eyes were somber. "How bad is it?" she asked.

"Bad. Garnett is trying to find out how many students were involved. They're setting up a command post near the morgue tent," said Diane, gesturing for her to lead the way.

"Allen Rankin and Brewster Pilgrim are waiting in that tent." Webber pointed at the green and white striped tent. "They were offered hot coffee."

"Sounds good." Diane smiled and walked with Webber toward the hospitality tent.

"You know," said Webber, "our local hospitals are better equipped to handle this. I feel as though I've run away with the circus."

"You're preaching to the choir. Apparently, the mayor wants a very visible presence so everyone will see that he's on top of the situation."

Lynn Webber shrugged. "Maybe he's right. People do have a tendency to think you aren't doing anything if they don't see you doing it."

"Well, they'll have a ringside seat here," said Diane.

As she walked with Lynn through the slush, she scanned the crowd that was gathering behind the police barricade. Cars were parked down the street as far as she could see. Too many people, she thought. Surely, this many people don't have missing children.

"Most are rubberneckers trying to catch site of something sensational," said Lynn, as if reading Diane's thoughts. "At least, I hope this many people haven't lost a loved one."

As she grew closer to the onlookers, Diane could pick out the worried parents and friends. It was the look of desperation and fear that gave them away. The gawkers and ghouls had eyes that glittered with anticipation as they strained to get a look at the burned-out house in the distance. A man with a camera tried to get under the roped-off area, and a policeman pushed him back.

"All those people . . . ," whispered Lynn.

Diane avoided meeting anyone's gaze and was glad to duck inside the coffee tent. A young policeman was on his way out with a carton of several cups of coffee for the policemen standing duty. He nodded at them as he passed.

There were few people other than medical examiners in the tent. A long table on one side held a commercial coffeemaker and an array of pastries. Four women manned the table, setting out plastic forks and packages of Styrofoam cups. They looked up as Diane and Lynn entered and began pouring two cups of coffee.

A policewoman was arranging a desk near the entrance. Diane guessed it was to be the location to receive x-rays, toothbrushes, hairbrushes, and other objects that might hold DNA or other clues to victims' identities. Diane didn't recognize the policewoman. She thought she was learning all the personnel on the force, but apparently there had been some recent additions.

This young woman looked just out of the academy. In fact, her smooth unlined face looked like she could still be in high school. She was unloading a grocery bag, setting boxes of different sizes of Ziploc freezer bags on the desk.

Lynn Webber walked on past to a waiting cup of hot coffee, but Diane stopped at the desk.

"Hi." She hoped she sounded friendly. "Are those all the bags for holding objects for comparison DNA samples?"

"And you are?" said the young woman without looking up from her task.

"I'm sorry." Diane held out the identification that

hung around her neck. "I'm Diane Fallon. I'm head of the Crime Lab here in Rosewood."

The woman looked up and gave her a tight smile. "Yes, I'm to collect the samples from the parents."

"Plastic bags are good for transporting evidence," Diane said. "But for storage, plastic isn't right for all evidence. Let me bring you some evidence bags. . . ."

"My sergeant told me to get these." Her voice was curt; she broke eye contact and continued unloading the plastic bags.

"If a parent brings in a damp bath towel, for example, it would . . ."

"I do what my sergeant tells me."

"Of course you do. I'm sorry to have brought it up to you." Diane took her phone from her pocket, flipped it open, and called Garnett. "Chief Garnett, I would like the evidence from family members collected in the evidence bags from our lab, and I need you to talk to the sergeant in charge so he can change the orders of the patrolman at the scene here."

Diane paused. The policewoman looked at her, wide-eyed. She sat back and expelled her breath in a huff.

"I'm in the coffee tent, or whatever you call it. The police are setting up a desk here to receive the samples."

Diane paused again, listening to Garnett. "I did tell her myself. She is very into chain of command." Diane handed the phone to the policewoman. "It's Chief Garnett. He wants to speak to you."

The young woman took the phone hesitantly, eying Diane as she said hello.

"Sergeant Davis told me . . ." She stopped talking for several moments. "Yes, sir," she said and handed the phone back to Diane.

"I'll have someone bring you the proper bags and boxes," said Diane, punching Neva's cell number. She told Neva what she wanted and apologized for pulling her off the scene. Diane was thinking that things like this could be avoided if she gave workshops to the police on collecting evidence. They had resisted the notion, but she'd talk to Garnett about it again.

Diane smiled and thanked the policewoman, but she could see she hadn't made a friend. *Great,* she thought, *I'll never get on good terms with the police.*

The other two medical examiners, Pilgrim and Rankin, were in a corner, sitting on a couple of folding chairs and drinking from steaming Styrofoam cups. She waved at them and headed in their direction. They had barricaded themselves in with folding chairs held in place by their booted feet. Their bodies looked relaxed, but their faces showed deep frowns. Rankin was on his cell phone. Lynn was a few feet away, drinking her coffee with an amused expression. She handed Diane a cup as she walked by.

"It's good coffee," Lynn said, grinning at Diane. "You were so nice. I'd have ripped her a new one."

"She was only doing what she was told. It always amazes me how little influence I have."

Lynn's laugh was almost a giggle. The two of them pulled up chairs and sat across from Rankin and Pilgrim.

"I just got off the phone with Whit," said Rankin, shifting his position and putting his cell phone back on his belt. "He's thinking there may be as many as thirty bodies."

Chapter 5

Diane stood at a shiny stainless steel table in the cold morgue tent, looking down at a shock of blond hair held together by an iridescent blue clip. The hair and a small bit of scalp were attached to a piece of parietal bone from the right side of a skull.

Explosions and fires are odd. They consume or blacken most everything, but occasionally there are surprising anomalies, such as this beautiful lock of blond hair—almost untouched, somehow thrown free in the explosion, along with scalp and bone.

Diane measured the size and arc of the bone before Jin photographed it. Jin was a good assistant for this, not just because of his keen interest in DNA and his basic competence, but because, even in the worst of circumstances, he was nearly always happy. The tent would be somber without him if its only occupants were her, the MEs, the police, and burned bodies.

"Plenty of roots for DNA," said Jin as he tweezed samples of rooted hair from the scalp. He had a green surgical cap covering his straight black hair and wore green scrubs and short sleeves despite the cool temperature of the tent. Diane envied his ability to withstand the cold. She was bundled up and freezing. "You know if we had our own DNA . . ."

"I know," said Diane, interrupting Jin before he made another petition for a DNA lab. She liked the idea, but refrained from telling Jin or he would be ordering the equipment.

The problem was that Rosewood didn't want to pay for a DNA lab. Diane guessed they were holding out for her to put one in on the museum's budget. After all, the museum, which was officially not part of the crime lab, had its own DNA lab—what's one more lab, she was sure they were thinking. True, depending on how she crunched the numbers, she might be able to make a DNA lab pay for itself. But she didn't tell Jin that, either.

"You going to put in a DNA lab?" asked Lynn Webber. Diane looked up to see Lynn putting an organ—it looked like a heart—on the scales.

Diane looked sideways at Jin as he stared down at nothing in particular on the tent floor. Just as she thought, he'd put Lynn up to it.

"Jin wants to." Diane evaded answering her directly, hoping Lynn would drop it.

"It'd probably pay for itself," said Lynn, retrieving the organ from the hanging scales. Diane shot her a scowl. Lynn smiled back.

"Probably female," said Diane of the remains on her table. "It's a small skull." She looked again at the wavy lock of hair, touching it with her gloved hand. "And this is a female hairstyle and clip." She recorded the information on a form.

Jin packaged the small piece of someone who only yesterday had been alive, labeled it, and put it on a trolley to be taken and stored in the refrigerated area of the trailer. He filed the hair root sample, then selected another small box containing body parts to be examined. It was the severed hand.

"That's odd," said Jin. "It's not even burned."

As if on some kind of psychic cue, Rankin looked up from an x-ray he was examining on a light table. "Did I hear you were carjacked last night?" he said.

Diane cringed as everyone in hearing range stopped and stared at her. They had been working for three hours with little communication, other than task-oriented shoptalk—Lynn Webber commented that the victim she was working on died instantaneously, and Rankin said his might have died of smoke inhalation, he wasn't sure. A little conversation was a welcome diversion and a rest.

"Boss, you didn't tell us about that?" said Jin.

"I heard you locked him in your car," continued Rankin. Allen Rankin was the ME for the city of Rosewood. He was younger than Pilgrim, more Webber's age, and slim with brown hair, too even in color to be natural. He looked at Diane with interest, expecting the story.

"Well, for heaven sake," said Lynn, shaking her head. "What happened and how in the world did you lock him in your car?"

"It happened when I was evacuating my apartment," said Diane.

"That's right, you live near here," said Rankin.

"How did you find out about it?" asked Diane.

"I have ears in the police department," he said.

They were all still staring at her, so Diane told the story about the kid with a gun and one hand.

"He lost a hand," exclaimed Jin looking down at the one lying on the table in front of him. "This hand?"

"It would be my guess. He lost his right hand and this is the right hand of a male. I believe it was sheered off with a saw blade that came flying from the blast." She retrieved a box from the long table containing unprocessed evidence that grew by the minute. She double-checked the label, initialed it, and opened the lid.

"Ouch," said Jin when he saw the bloody circular blade.

"We'll have to take a blood sample from it to be sure this is what did it. We can match the hand and blade with the blood in my car—and the kid."

"You think he was involved with the meth lab?" said Pilgrim. He and his assistant were making noise moving a cadaver to his table. Diane strained to hear over the rustling of the body bag. At least the body bags had arrived. At first they didn't have enough and they had covered the victims with a clear plastic. Even the dieners thought it was creepy.

"It seems likely," she said. "If he was only a victim, what was he doing with a gun?"

"Exactly," said Rankin. "Ironic thing is that he has the least injuries. All the other survivors have critical internal or brain injuries. He may be the only one who can shed light on this and I understand he's lawyered up."

Diane heard several grunts of disapproval from people in the tent. It sounded like too many people. A constant parade of personnel came and went—bringing in bodies and evidence from the site, or delivering antemortem information from relatives, or paperwork from the police department. Diane hoped one of them was a gatekeeper. She didn't like the idea of a reporter listening in on their conversations, or worse. She watched for a moment—all present were MEs, technicians or police, all people she recognized, all doing a job. And there were guards at the door.

Diane focused her attention back on the hand lying on the table, palm up in a half-curled position. The thing she noticed first was that the nails were professionally manicured.

"Has his nails done," said Jin. "Not your average student."

"I wonder what the palm could tell us," Diane said, attempting a smile.

"That he has no future."

Jin responded so quickly that Diane looked over at

him and raised an eyebrow. She was joking, but the authority in Jin's voice surprised her.

"The future is in the right palm, his past in the left."

"Oh?" Diane stared at him.

"I used to date a girl who was into reading palms. That's what she said." He grinned broadly.

She measured the hand and photographed it front and back, took samples from under the nails, swabbed the skin, and printed the fingers. Jin took a sample of tissue for DNA comparison. He handed her more remains.

The squeaking sound of a cart brought her head up. Grover, Lynn Webber's morgue assistant, was wheeling a body back from the portable x-ray set up in the trailer. He maneuvered between the light table and a frame hanging with x-rays he and Pilgrim's assistant had taken so far. He bumped the light table where Allen Rankin was examining dental x-rays and muttered an apology. Diane wasn't sure if he was talking to Rankin or the body. He referred to the charred and mutilated bodies as babies.

"All them poor babies," he had said on his first glance of the scene. "Them poor, poor babies."

Grover was probably in his forties, but it was hard to tell. His dark skin was unlined and his hair had no gray. He was a big guy with big hands and a face so solemn that he looked perpetually melancholy. He had absolute respect for human remains and a good knowledge of anatomy.

"We have a match," Rankin said from his seat at his field desk.

The first match. The first "this is someone. Not just human features roughly carved in charcoal." Not a John or Jane Doe. No longer anonymous.

Rankin rose to give his report to the officer in charge of the records, a heavyset policeman with wavy salt-and-pepper hair, a bloodhound face, and a body that looked both sturdy and agile—Archie Donahue,

Diane believed his name was. As she recalled, he had been on the Rosewood police force for a long time and worked in the evidence locker. Well suited for this work, filing and cataloging the artifacts of lives that loved ones hoped would identify them in death.

Archie sat at the long evidence table and looked up from the stack of antemortem records he'd just accepted from the intake desk in the coffee tent. He was about to enter them into the computer program that kept track of all the incoming details of missing students—anything that would help identify them. Archie seemed to hesitate reaching for Rankin's report. Probably dreaded the thought that one of the dead would be a child or grandchild of someone he knew. Rosewood wasn't that big a town. And if it were true that there are only six degrees of separation between everyone in the world, then in the town of Rosewood the number of degrees was probably one or two. Many local children stayed to attend the local university. Everyone in Rosewood would know someone touched by this.

Diane saw his hands shake as he looked at the report.

"Bobby Coleman . . . I know his daddy," he whispered in a cigarette-and-whisky voice. "We go to the same church."

They all stopped, Pilgrim, Webber, Diane, even the assistants—a spontaneous moment of silence for his grief—for Bobby's family's grief.

Brewster Pilgrim broke the silence. "I need your opinion here, Diane," he said.

Pilgrim was the coroner of the county to the north of Rosewood. He was inclined toward being heavy, and looked like everyone's ideal grandfather with his white hair and white brush moustache.

"I can't tell the sex," he said. "Looks too close to call to me."

Diane changed gloves, walked over to Brewster's

work area, and looked down in the open cavity of the charred cadaver.

"We should have given this to you," he said. "Hardly any flesh left. Must have been in the hottest part of the fire. And look at this. I believe a beam or something fell on him. Look at the crushed pelvis here."

The cadaver was charred black down to the bone. There was flesh, but it had been so consumed by fire that the hard bone underneath the flesh was exposed over the entire body. The head was gone, probably exploded in the heat. Pieces of skull lay in a shallow box near the remains with blackened flesh still clinging to them. Obviously found nearby and probably from the same body.

"I believe you're right about the break." She examined the broken right ilium and left pubis. It looked like something heavy had fallen across the pelvic region and crushed the bones. "It is a rather androgynous pelvis, isn't it," agreed Diane.

She carved flesh away from the pelvis to look at the various markers for gender. What she saw was a wide subpubic angle, wide sciatic notch, and the presence of the preauricular sulcus.

"Female," she said.

"Thanks," said Pilgrim. "I'd have probably called it male. Looked like a male pelvis to me."

As he spoke, Diane teased a bit of bone away from the pubis with a pair of tweezers and put it in the palm of her hand.

"What's that?" asked Pilgrim, leaning over her shoulder to look at the delicate piece.

"Fetal bone," said Diane. "She was pregnant."

Chapter 6

Brewster Pilgrim looked for a long moment at the bone so tiny and fragile it could have come from a bird.

"Them poor babies," whispered Grover who stood behind them shaking his large head.

Pilgrim snatched off his latex gloves, threw them in the trash. "I need a break," he said, and headed out of the tent. "I don't know why we can't convince kids to keep out of drugs . . ." was the last thing Diane heard him say before he disappeared into the cold.

Diane bagged and labeled the fetal bone and went back to her station. Lying before her on the table were assorted fragments of a skull that had burst from the heat of the fire that incinerated the body. She pulled up a stool, sat down, and began her next task—fitting together the pieces of the bone puzzle. Jin was helping Lynn Webber sample the marrow of a femur for DNA profiling.

Rankin suddenly looked up from the charred and bloated remains of the corpse on his table. "We can't stop kids from getting drugs because there is an army of dealers working against us," he said. "And we'll never stop them because it's a trillion-dollar business. There's just too much money—more money than any of us can wrap our brains around." He paused for the briefest moment. "And no one can go up against that kind of money. Don't kid yourselves that we can do anything but pick up the pieces from the carnage." He stopped speaking just as suddenly as he had begun and continued his autopsy.

They had all paused to watch Rankin as he ranted. Diane had a sick feeling that he was right. They couldn't do anything. Her gaze met Lynn Webber's briefly and she knew that Lynn had the same sick feeling. Grover was still shaking his head.

Just a few more pieces of the skull puzzle and she too would go to the coffee tent and relax for fifteen minutes. It occurred to her that she wasn't that far from her apartment. She could just go the short distance through the woods and sit down on her own sofa with a hot cup of her own coffee. The thought sounded heavenly. She placed two pieces of occipital together—the thick bone that made up the back of the head. From the prominent nuchal crest, the skull looked like a male.

The morgue tent was void of conversation for several minutes. Only the sounds of work—the clinking tools, shuffling of movement, creaking trolleys—filled the silent space where Rankin's rant still hung in the air. Everyone was silent, thought Diane, because like her they realized that Rankin was right—there was nothing that any of them could do but pick up the pieces.

Archie, the policeman in charge of evidence, stood and said to no one in particular that he was also going to take a break. Diane watched him leave with two other policemen. *They must feel the weight of Rankin's words most,* she thought. They were like the little Dutch boy trying to hold back the water with his finger in the hole in the dike. They were supposed to do something, but they too were powerless against so much money.

Lynn finally broke the ensuing silence in what appeared to be a deliberate attempt to lighten the atmosphere.

"So, Jin," she said, "what do you do in your spare time?"

"I scuba dive," he said. "Diane's been teaching me caving. I'm getting pretty good, aren't I, boss?"

Both Jin and Webber's voices were muffled by the nuisance masks they wore.

"You're a real natural," said Diane.

She looked among the fragments of skull scattered on her table for a triangular shaped piece that fit on the frontal just above the orbit. As she sorted through the remains, she noticed the absence of any part of the maxilla, the bone that holds the upper teeth. Identification would be easier if she had teeth to work with.

"Diving and caving sound dangerous," said Lynn. "You don't do them at the same time, do you?"

"I was advised not to do that," said Jin, stealing a glance at Diane. "Too dangerous."

"Do you do anything relaxing?" asked Lynn.

Diane wasn't sure if she was really interested in Jin's leisure activities, or just trying to fill empty airspace. Her voice sounded strained, even under the mask.

"Diving's relaxing," he said, his eyes above his mask reflecting a broad grin. "And I've found some nice, quiet moments hanging on to a rock wall."

Lynn Webber gave a muffled laugh. "At least it gets you away from crime," she said, watching him extract the sample of bone marrow.

"I like to solve mysteries as a hobby," said Jin.

Diane looked up quickly from a broken zygomatic arch, expecting a joke, looking forward to a laugh, but it didn't sound like the beginning of one of Jin's jokes. He sounded serious. Solving mysteries as a hobby— she couldn't wait to hear what this was about.

"A hobby," Lynn exclaimed. "I'd think you would have enough of death in the crime lab."

"Disappearances," said Jin. "I'm kind of into strange disappearances."

"Strange disappearances?" asked Lynn. "Like how? Hoffa, Judge Crater? Aren't all disappearances strange until someone finds out what happened?"

Jin shrugged. "Some. Hoffa, that's not strange, I mean not the kind of strange I like. It was probably just a mob thing. Same with Crater. Probably Tammany Hall stuff. What I find interesting are disappearances like the one that Sherlock Holmes couldn't solve—you know, like James Phillimore."

Jin took the pose of someone trying to remember a quote—chin up, hands suspended of movement. " 'Mr. James Phillimore who, stepping back into his own house to get his umbrella, was never more seen in this world.' That's the kind of missing person problem I like."

"That is more intriguing than Hoffa, I agree," said Lynn. She stopped working on the cadaver in front of her and listened to Jin.

Diane paused, too, sitting back on the stool. She had a large portion of the skull pieced together. The back, the side, the frontal down to the brow ridge, and one cheek. With the right x-ray she could probably identify the body. But it was a long shot that there would be the right x-ray.

The partial skull sat in a small tub of sand looking as if it had just been revealed by a sandstorm. The sand held the blackened pieces of bone together while the glue dried. Jonas Briggs, the archaeologist at her museum, said that in his profession they reconstruct clay pots the same way. "Makes nice little Zen gardens—thousand-year-old potsherds standing in clean bronze sand," he'd said. This Zen garden looked macabre.

There was still an array of pieces to put together. She looked at them, mentally identifying the part of the skull each piece was from. Hard to believe that only yesterday this person was alive—just yesterday.

"They had a special on Court TV two nights ago about missing persons—double feature, two hours' worth," said Jin. "Great stuff. Turns out there are several missing persons who meet my criteria of interesting. A teenage girl and her family were leaving church when she went back in for her purse and was never seen again. Doesn't that sound like Sherlock Holmes? And a whole family just fell off the face of the earth. No one knew they were gone; they just weren't home anymore—but all their belongings were still in the house, their car in the driveway. And then there was the man who was last seen in the waiting room of his doctor's office. The receptionist didn't see him leave and no one knows what happened to him. All these people were normal people with no secret lives or anything—that anyone found out about," he added. "I'd like to investigate them."

"No clues at all in any of the cases?" asked Lynn.

Diane picked up a piece of nasal bone and turned it over in her hand. Even blackened as it was, a healed crack was evident. Something distinctive about this individual, she thought as she looked for surrounding pieces.

"No clues," said Jin. "But I tell you, my favorite is Colonel Percy Fawcett."

"Never heard of him," said Lynn.

"He's the coolest missing person. He disappeared with his son and his son's friend in the Amazon while looking for an ancient city inhabited by a mysterious tribe. His story is really strange, full of subterranean cities, alien tribes, psychics, with the lost city of Atlantis thrown in. Great stuff," he repeated.

"Do you ever try to solve any of the cases?" asked Diane. Jin turned to her, looking almost startled that she had been listening.

"I've helped with a couple of cold cases that detective friends of mine were working on. I'm afraid I didn't offer much in the way of a solution. Mostly I just read up on them and try to solve them—you know, like an armchair detective. I've gotten a few good hypotheses. You know, there's been quite a few missing persons north of here in the Smoky Mountains. People disappear and nothing is ever found of them," he said. "Nothing. I mean, like what's in the Smokys?"

"Wild pigs," said Diane without looking up from the piece of skull she was gluing together. "They eat everything with blood on it—bones, sticks, you name it."

"Yes, pigs," agreed Lynn. "Once you're dead, the wild boars scarf you up."

Jin looked from Diane to Lynn. "Well, thanks for ruining a perfectly good mystery for me."

Lynn and Diane both laughed.

Diane had finished gluing all the pieces of the skull she had and they sat drying in the sandbox. It looked like the pieced-together ancient skulls that she had in the museum—but this person was recently alive.

"I'm going to take a break," she said. "When I come back, I'll see if we have any x-rays of faces with broken noses. I believe I can ID this skull."

"I think I'll finish up this cadaver," said Lynn. She sneaked a peek at the table where Brewster Pilgrim left his.

Jin slipped off his gloves and put on a new pair, walked over to Pilgrim's table, and began preparations to cut the femur and take a DNA sample. Back to business.

Diane left the tent and gulped in the outside air. The cold bit her lungs. It felt good to be out of the morgue tent.

Chapter 7

Sleet was falling again. The drops felt like cold pin-pricks on Diane's face. The argon streetlights shining bright against the backdrop of the twilight sky flooded over the tent city and gave the place an eerie glow. There were searchlights and strange machines in one direction along the street, and a quiet crowd of people standing in the other. In a David Lynch movie it could have been the midway of some macabre traveling circus.

Diane looked wistfully in the direction of her apartment but did not yield to the temptation to escape to its peace and solitude. She would take fifteen minutes of relief in the coffee tent. But first she stopped at the crime scene.

The blackened rubble of the house was now criss-crossed by planks and grid strings and illuminated by a ring of large spotlights shining into it from all sides. Neva and David were stretched out on boards, sifting carefully through a grid square near the front of the site. A mobile crane parked to one side of the yard was lifting a basket of something out of the gaping hole of the burned-out basement.

Diane looked over the edge into the pit. Wisps of smoke or steam rose here and there from the dark mass into the cold night air. The bright white light of the spotlights seemed to be absorbed into the charred rubble and not reflected back. A gust of wind carried up from the basement an acrid stench that smelled like a combination of wood smoke, wet, burned garbage, melted plastic, and scorched flesh, with an assortment of chemicals thrown into the mix. Diane stepped backward for a breath of air to clear her lungs.

The house that was there only yesterday had been a yellow Victorian with an octagonal tower, high-peaked roof, fireplaces, wraparound porches, and white gingerbread trim. A long line of students had lived many of their university years in its apartments. Diane remembered scenes of them laying down a large tarp and pouring sand over it to make themselves a beach volleyball court on game weekends, or some student relaxing on the porch swing reading a book, or several sitting on the steps shouting at their friends passing in cars. And now . . . nothing but black ashes covered with the spiderweb of crime scene string and scaffolding.

Was one of those students from the porch swing in happier times now lying on her autopsy table? The thought made her profoundly sad.

Diane walked toward the front of the burned-out house through the safe path that her team had created. All the snow had melted from the path, leaving a muddy walkway covered by planks. David saw her approaching, rose, and walked on the planking toward her, readjusting his baseball cap on his balding head. Neva looked up and waved, but kept working.

The drops of sleet were getting heavier, and Diane could feel her hair getting wet. She pulled a knit cap from her coat pocket and put it on, pushing her hair underneath it.

"How's it going?" asked Diane. She could tell by the look on David's face he wasn't happy.

"Frustrating," said David. He took off his cap, smoothed down the nonexistent hair on the top of his head, and put his cap back on. "It's going fine if we can keep McNair away."

"What's he doing?"

"Mostly meddling."

"Meddling?" Diane raised her eyebrows. "He *is* the arson investigator."

"Then he should act like one." David glanced over his shoulder as if someone might be listening. "He looks through all our evidence bags—breaks the seal and paws through the contents. Says he needs to see what we're finding. I told him that the lab is the place to examine the evidence, and he told me to just tend to my job, that he's in charge. I don't know how this guy thought he would be even remotely qualified to be the director of the crime lab. He's not qualified to be an arson investigator. Any good defense attorney can challenge every piece of evidence we've collected, because of him."

"I'll speak to him." Diane felt a sudden flush.

"It won't work, unless you intend to watch him, too." David lifted his chin slightly, which was a signal to Diane that McNair was approaching.

"OK. You go back to work and I'll try and talk some sense into him."

Diane whirled around and walked to meet McNair as he approached. She watched a scowl form on his face. *Unbecoming,* she thought.

"We need to talk," said Diane. Not a good opening, but she wasn't feeling diplomatic.

"*We* need to talk?" he said, emphasizing the word *we*.

"Don't break the seal on the evidence bags. . . ."

"Listen, you can't tell me how to run my investigation. I need to see what they're finding."

Diane's flush was now a full-fledged burn. "They're recovering what's left of the human victims of this fire, and they're doing it by strict protocol. We have serious chain of custody and contamination concerns here.

This is not the time or place to examine sensitive evidence."

"People want answers fast. The slow way you and your people work won't do."

"Forensic analysis and identification of human remains is an exacting process with the most profound legal and personal consequences. It takes the time that it takes. And my people are the best in the business."

McNair gave her a dismissive snort and a snide smirk. Diane had an almost irresistible urge to hit him right in the middle of his smirky mouth.

"What do you propose we do?" she said. "Give a hasty identification of someone's child on the basis of a nose ring or a belly piercing?"

McNair glared at her. She fully expected him to yell at her or say something like, "You're not my boss," but he was silent for several beats.

"Why don't we compromise on this?" she said. "Why don't you set up an examination table inside the morgue tent where chain of custody can be maintained and the dangers of evidence contamination can be controlled?"

"That's probably a good idea," he said.

Diane thought she would fall over. He had admitted she had a good idea? Maybe he was trying to make nice after all. She glanced over to the end of the road where there seemed to always be a crowd.

"Is that mostly journalists, onlookers, or loved ones?" she asked.

He shrugged. "All of the above, and they're all looking at us. They want to know exactly what happened—and they want to know yesterday."

He walked past her to the site and immediately got on his cell phone. Maybe he was taking her advice, she thought. She hated adding another table to the already crowded morgue tent, but it was better than fighting over the evidence.

Diane walked to the hospitality tent. The sleet was

turning into snow. The weather hadn't chased away the onlookers. Inside the tent was warm, mainly due to the number of people in it. Several men and women were gathered around the police intake desk, all trying to talk at once. More people stood by the long table of refreshments, drinking coffee and eating cookies. Brewster Pilgrim sat by himself in the corner, sipping from a Styrofoam cup. He nodded when he saw Diane.

She worked her way around to the table where the coffee was being served. A slender woman with short brown hair sprinkled with gray and wearing an apron handed her a cup of coffee and a napkin. Behind the table were Diane's neighbors Leslie and Shane. Leslie was putting out a fresh box of doughnuts, and her husband was pouring coffee. They looked up and smiled when they saw Diane.

"Aunt Jere," Leslie said to the woman. "This is my neighbor, Diane Fallon. Diane, this is my aunt, Jere Bowden."

Diane smiled and nodded. "It's nice to meet you," she said. "Leslie and Shane are the ones who warned me of the danger from the explosion."

"Well, we've always taught our children to care about others." Mrs. Bowden smiled and handed Diane a chocolate-covered doughnut.

"Were you able to get hold of the guy who lives in the basement?" asked Leslie. "Who is he?"

"A professor of history. Thin man, looks like he wears Goodwill clothes," said Diane.

"We thought he was a homeless guy the landlady fed. I've seen her give him bags of food."

"That's old bread from her nephew's bakery. Keith, that's his name, likes to feed the ducks in the park."

"Oh!" Leslie's face suddenly registered uncertainty. "Sometimes I leave a sack with a peanut butter and jelly sandwich and an apple along with her sacks."

Diane smiled and Leslie's husband laughed.

"He must be mystified as to why the landlady sometimes packs a lunch for the ducks," he said.

Leslie grinned and looked embarrassed. Her aunt put an arm around her shoulder.

"He probably just thinks the landlady is looking out after him," she said.

"That is a very kind thing to do," said Diane.

Leslie's smile faded. "Diane is identifying some of the—you know."

"Oh . . . you do need a break, dear," said Mrs. Bowden. "Why don't you find a quiet corner to sit awhile and rest? Maybe with Dr. Pilgrim over there. We'll bring you some fresh coffee when you want it."

"We have hot chocolate, too," said Leslie. "And marshmallows."

"That would be nice," said Diane.

"We'll bring you some when you finish your coffee," said her aunt.

Diane took a sip of coffee just as someone carrying a tray containing extra cups and paper plates came into the tent, almost running into her.

"Sorry, oh, Dr. Fallon . . ."

It was Juliet Price, one of Diane's museum employees. Juliet stopped abruptly, almost spilling her load of supplies. Her blond hair came loose from its clip and fell in her face. She looked wide-eyed at Diane as if she'd been caught at something.

"I . . . I took vacation time to help in the tent. . . ."

"That's very good of you, Dr. Price," said Diane. "I appreciate what you're doing here. It's a big help." Diane used Juliet's title, hoping to make her feel less like a kid playing hooky from school.

Juliet was extremely, pathologically, shy. She was actually underemployed at the museum, working below her qualifications, but her job allowed her to work by herself, and Juliet preferred working alone. She had even turned down a promotion when Diane offered her the more responsible position of collection manager. From the look of fear that had been on Juliet's face at the prospect of the new job duties, Diane might just as well have told her the police were coming to arrest her.

Working in the hospitality tent with all its face-to-face interaction was a bold step of courage for Juliet. As she carried her tray of supplies to the table she nodded, and Diane thought she saw a wisp of a smile from her. *Well, at least that's progress,* thought Diane.

As Diane started in Brewster Pilgrim's direction with her steaming cup of coffee, someone laid a hand on her arm.

"Did I hear someone say you are identifying the . . . the students in the house?" The woman looked at Diane with wide blue, red-rimmed eyes. Her honey blond hair was limp and simply combed back. She wore a running suit that Diane knew to be expensive and running shoes that cost at least two hundred dollars. A mother of one of the students, Diane knew immediately.

"Yes." Diane gave her a weak smile. She wished she could say, "No, I have nothing to do with this"— especially when looking into a parent's sad eyes.

The woman thrust a folder into Diane's hands. "These are pictures of my daughter. Please tell me if you've seen her." She opened the folder and all but shoved it into Diane's face.

"The police have a place set up over there"—Diane gestured toward the intake desk—"to bring pictures and . . ." She trailed off, not wanting to say samples of DNA. Nor did she want to say the truth—that no one was recognizable.

Diane unconsciously backed up as she looked down at the picture of a beautiful young woman of fair complexion and long blond hair with a gentle wave held back from her face with a blue clip. An electric shock rippled through her and she tried not to let her face reveal anything. After all, there was no way to visually identify a person by a lock of hair . . . but it looked so much like the lock that had been on her table. Diane stepped back half a step. She was now up against the table.

"They won't tell me anything . . . please . . ."

The woman flipped through the pictures of her daughter, showing them to Diane—confirmation, ballet, prom, graduation. A life in an instant. Diane wanted to cry.

"I know waiting is painful. The process is slow. . . . We are working as quickly as we can. As soon as we know anything definite . . ."

"You don't understand," she said. Tears welled up in her eyes. "I have to know something. I can't find my daughter."

That last statement pierced Diane through her heart. How many times had she uttered the same words in the jungle when she couldn't find Ariel, her daughter who was killed with many of her friends in the mission—massacred to stop the human rights investigations her team were doing in South America. Diane dropped the doughnut as she grasped the table behind her.

"I'm sorry. . . ." Diane began fumbling for words.

"Mrs. Reynolds." Jere Bowden had appeared at the woman's side and put an arm around her shoulder. "You remember me, we are in the same Sunday school class. Waiting is so hard. Let us wait with you. Please come sit down with some hot cocoa; then I'll go with you to talk to the police officer again."

Diane watched Mrs. Bowden lead the grief-stricken mother to a chair and sit down with her. Mrs. Reynolds clutched the photographs in her lap as if she were hanging on to her daughter. Diane supposed she was. Shane took her a steaming cup of something. Diane started toward Brewster with her cup of coffee, but he was walking toward her. She took a sip. It burned her tongue.

"Here, this is more relaxing." Leslie handed her a cup of cocoa with a marshmallow floating on top, took her coffee, and put it on the table.

"Thank you, Leslie. You and your family are very kind," said Diane.

Leslie cradled her belly. "I can't imagine what it's like waiting to find out if your child has been killed. It's simply awful."

"Yes, it is," whispered Diane.

Brewster reached her and took her arm. "Why don't we walk back together. This is no place for us. We'll send out for coffee from now on. I think we need to work only a couple more hours today, anyway. We need sleep to do a good job."

Diane agreed. She looked back at the woman, who broke down in sobs that racked her body as she was being led to a chair by Archie and Jere Bowden. The short interaction with the mother had tired Diane in a way that working over human remains for hours had not. They walked quietly back to the morgue tent. Diane sipped on her hot chocolate. Leslie was right. It was more comforting.

Diane took up her station again. Rankin and Webber were still going strong. Jin had put another collection of charred bones on her table.

"You need to take a break?" she asked Jin.

"I'm good," he said.

Diane pulled on a pair of gloves and examined the bones before her and the photograph of them in the location where they were found. Just as she was about to pick up a femur, Detective Frank Duncan, her friend and lover, walked into the tent and headed for her. Back early, she thought as her heart skipped a beat. She smiled at the sight of him, but it froze on her face when she saw his handsome features creased into a frown—and the fear in his eyes.

"I can't find Star," he said when he reached her table.

Chapter 8

Diane stared blankly at Frank's face; her mind hit a wall, rejecting what he was telling her. She slumped and barely felt Jin grasp her arm and steer her to a stool just as her legs gave way. Across the expanse of the tent, the tables—Lynn Webber's, Allen Rankin's, Brewster Pilgrim's—all were laid out with bodies, any one of which might be . . . and the bones on her own table . . . *Please God, not Star, not Star.*

The MEs stopped what they were doing and looked from Frank to Diane, worry evident in their eyes as they viewed with new concern the remains of corpses and personal items on the tables before them. The officer organizing the incoming samples seemed about to say something, but closed his mouth, his forlorn expression deepening. Grover looked profoundly sad.

Only a couple of them, Jin and Lynn Webber, actually knew Star, but most knew Frank. A lifelong resident of Rosewood, he served the Atlanta police department as a detective in the Fraud and Computer Crimes unit. And all knew Star's story. The little runaway teenage girl accused of the murder of her parents and brother. She had become Frank's ward through her parents' last will and testament, and he had made her his adopted daughter. Diane had freed her of the murder accusations by finding the real killer. Star was in her first year at Bartram University partly because Diane had promised her a shopping trip to Paris if she would give college an honest try.

"What do you mean, you don't know where she is?" asked Diane as if his words hadn't made sense.

"I can't find her," he said.

That phrase again—*I can't find my daughter.* Diane didn't think she could bear it.

"I got home from Seattle early and heard about this . . . tragedy." He took a deep breath. "She isn't at her dorm. Her cell goes immediately to voice mail. It's been like that since I got home. That was three hours ago. I've checked with her friends that I can find; they haven't seen her since yesterday."

"Did anyone know her plans?" asked Diane with a shaky voice.

"They say she just wanted to study. I checked with Cindy. Star stays there sometimes to study or she goes to the museum. She isn't at either place. I can't find her anywhere."

Diane heard the desperation in his voice, and she was so frightened herself she could barely speak. She started to say something stupid like "We haven't seen her here." She knew that's what he wanted to hear. It's what that mother with the blond-haired daughter wanted to hear.

"I checked the hospitals. She's not there," he added in a voice so low that she barely heard him.

"OK," said Diane, trying to find a calm place inside her fear. "Star has tests now, doesn't she? Finals? You know she's going to study and not go to parties." She felt silly saying that. Of course college kids will go to parties, even the most studious will play hooky sometimes. Diane slipped off her gloves. "The library stays open all night. Have you checked there?"

"No." Frank looked hopeful. "No, I haven't."

"You go find Miss Star," said Brewster Pilgrim. "We're not going to work much longer. We're going home and get a good night's sleep and start fresh again in the morning."

"I'll stay and have everything organized when you come back in the morning," said Jin. "Say, does her phone have GPS?"

Frank raised a brow. "I don't know. That's an idea. I'll find out. Thanks Jin."

Jin likes to find lost people, thought Diane. How ironic that he now had someone he knows who needs finding. *Oh, God. Don't let one of these be Star.* She took off her lab coat and walked with Frank into the night.

Snow was falling heavily now, and there didn't seem to be as many people near the coffee tent—*just the loved ones,* she thought. The ones who won't leave until they know something.

Frank clasped her hand as they walked past the tent and past the journalists. Thankfully, none of them recognized her as a member of the forensics team—perhaps because she and Frank now looked like desperate parents.

Frank's car was parked well outside the cordoned-off area. She noted that he had new snow tires and she thought of her car. She wondered if Neva had had time to process it, or if it was sitting windowless in the snow. She needed to check with Neva to be sure they wouldn't lose potential evidence.

Diane grabbed the cell phone from her pocket, flipped it open, and selected Neva's number. The voice that answered was less weary than it should be.

"Hello, Diane. Anything I can do to help in locating Star?" How did she know so fast, wondered Diane. Bad news travels at light speed.

"Thank you, Neva. I'll let you know on that. I'm sorry to burden you with another matter. Have you had a chance to process my car?"

"Yes. Early on, the fire crew wouldn't let us have

access to the house site because of hot spots they were still trying to put out. David and I processed the carjacking site then. We worked the area around your car, as well as the area of the attempted Keith carjacking. Then I had your car towed to the crime lab and locked in the garage until we can get back to it."

"Thank you, Neva. If I haven't told you lately, I really appreciate the way you always come through when the going gets tough."

"You know that if I can do it, I will. Please let me know about Star."

"As soon as we know anything."

"Process your car?" asked Frank after Diane had closed her cell phone.

"Long story. I'll tell you later after we find Star."

He was satisfied with that. It was unusual for him not to try to pry the story out of her if he suspected she had some dangerous near miss. But, focused on the snowy road ahead, he was quiet now as he drove toward campus. They were almost to the library when he spoke.

"How many . . . how many bodies have you processed?"

Processed. So cold and clinical. *He's trying to keep a distance,* she thought. "Seven, maybe more. Jin and I . . ." She shut her mouth, unwilling to say Jin and I have examined many body parts. "We've only been working for a little over three hours. We think there may be thirty-two altogether."

"How many females have you processed of the seven?" asked Frank.

"Three," she answered.

Frank was a math person. She wondered if he thought he could somehow figure out the possibility that one was Star based on the math. Of course not. Silly. He was just trying not to break down by asking questions that had a definite answer.

"Three," he repeated. "If your sample is random,

then of the thirty-two victims, thirteen or fourteen of them would be female."

"We don't know if they were randomly located in the house when . . . when it exploded—or randomly recovered."

"No." He shook his head. "I'm just trying to occupy my mind. Here's the library."

He parked his dark blue Expedition and they walked up the columned entrance to the library. Since 9/11, the entrance had huge concrete planters out front so that a vehicle loaded with explosives couldn't get close to the front entrance. They walked past the planters containing spruce trees and up the granite steps.

The information desk was manned by a young woman who looked as if she might be a student herself. Frank asked if there was a way to page a patron in the library. No, there was not. From the sympathetic look they got, they were not the first to ask.

"I'm afraid you'll have to go to each floor and look," she said. "If you know what courses your . . ."

"Daughter," supplied Frank.

"Daughter is taking, you might start where those books or journals are shelved." She handed them sheets of paper stapled together. "This is a map of the library." She gave them a sympathetic smile that seemed to say, "I wish I could do more."

"Do you know what courses she's taking this semester? Isn't American History one?" asked Diane.

Frank studied the maps of the floors. "American History, Anthropology, English, Algebra, and Fencing."

"Fencing?" said Diane.

"She's pretty good. She's thinking about joining the fencing team," said Frank.

Extracurricular activities. She's getting interested in college, just as Diane had hoped. *Please, don't let her be* . . . Diane couldn't even finish the thought.

They decided to check the library floor by floor instead of going to the different subject areas. It seemed more methodical. The danger was over. There wasn't a hurry to find Star, except for their own peace of mind. They wanted to be thorough.

Bartram University's library was a rambling structure built in stages, forming an old central core and younger wings. Varying shades of red brick walls told of different periods of construction. The beige tile floors were kept shined to a high gloss. The tables and chairs were of a light-colored wood and the bookshelves were metal.

Small study areas defined by groups of tables and a few stuffed chairs and small sofas were scattered throughout the floor. Most of the patrons this evening were students who looked to be eighteen or nineteen, with a sprinkling of older people who Diane guessed were graduate students or faculty.

She and Frank split up. He searched the study areas, Diane searched the stacks—looking between rows of bookshelves for any sign of Star's short black hair with its spiky cut. As Diane passed through the stacks of books, she heard snatches of conversations. "I heard there were fifty bodies." And, "You could hear them screaming two streets over as they burned." God, students were gruesome, thought Diane, and prone to believe rumors. "I heard they are canceling finals and giving us all *A*'s—like a hardship situation." And prone to wishful thinking. "OK, tell me again how to find the area beneath a curve. Something about rhyming?" "Riemman." At least some were studying. "*The making of palimpsests was possible even with papyri.* Are you sure that's what it says? It's hard to read the writing." History? Sounds like a tongue twister. Diane looked down another of the never-ending rows of bookshelves. *Star . . . where are you, Star?* She wanted to shout her name. What kind of large public building didn't have a paging system?

Come to think of if, the museum didn't. She would have to check into that.

Diane heard Frank ask several students if they knew Star Duncan. They didn't. "A freshman? No we don't know freshmen."

At the end of another row she saw Star—black spiky hair, pixy look. Diane all but ran toward her.

"Star?" she called a little too loudly.

Startled, the girl turned at the sound. It wasn't Star. Disappointment almost made Diane sick.

"I'm sorry. I thought you were someone else. Do you by any chance know Star Duncan?"

"Star. I like the name. No, I don't know her. Sorry."

Diane mumbled an apology for disturbing her and moved on, looking. She met up with Frank and together they headed for the elevators to look on the next floor. They passed a couple walking toward the main entrance. Both wore jeans. He had on a baseball cap that said NEW YORK YANKEES. They didn't look like students and they were frowning. Diane wondered if they were looking for a lost child as she and Frank were.

The elevator doors opened and they rode up to search the other four floors—Diane the stacks, Frank the study areas. They peeked in all the study carrels. Diane looked in the bathrooms. No Star. They didn't find anyone who knew her. Finally they rode down, sick at heart and not knowing where else to look.

"You could try calling home again. She may have decided to go there and study—where it would be quiet."

Frank nodded and took out his cell. "I'll take Jin's advice, too, and contact the company that made her phone to find out if it has GPS," said Frank.

Diane nodded, trying to swallow the lump in her throat. As they passed the information desk they heard a woman asking for Jenny Baker. Frank stopped.

"Excuse me," he said. "I believe your daughter knows mine. Star Duncan. They study together."

The woman turned and stared at Frank. She had the same desperate expression the mother in the coffee tent had, that Frank had, that Diane herself must have.

"Star? You're her father? Jenny's missing. Yes, she and Star study together. I told her Star is a bad influence. Jenny would never go to a party during finals. Never. Never. Not unless someone dragged her. She is a good girl."

Diane was startled at the recriminations. She felt Frank stiffen, but his face had on his detective expression, which was no expression.

Jenny's mother started to crumble. The young woman at the information desk, distressed and helpless, looked from one to the other of them. A brass pin fastened to her blouse said SHELLEY. Like the rest of them, Shelley didn't know what to do. Just as both Frank and Diane reached for Mrs. Baker before she sank to the floor, a man rushed over from the direction of the men's room, pulled her up, and put an arm around her.

"I'm Clyde Baker. My wife's distraught. We're looking for our daughter. Someone said she might be studying in the library. Her cell's not working, but she is bad about recharging it." He sounded out of breath and as if he needed to explain why his wife was collapsing onto the floor. "Come on, Marsha." He squeezed his wife's shoulders. "We've got to look, honey. I'm sure she's here."

"You might go to the Student Learning Center," said Shelley, leaning over the desk. "It's a new building and a lot of students study there, too. It's that huge really tall building on North Campus. I think that they might have a PA system."

"Thanks," said Frank, "We will." He turned to the Bakers. "If I find Star and Jenny is with her, I'll have her call you."

Clyde Baker nodded. His wife burst into tears.

Chapter 9

The Student Learning Center was a huge building. One of the tallest on Bartram's campus, sprawled out over the hillside like a giant yellow brick dragon. Searching it would take hours, if not days. Surely there would be an intercom system.

"It would be better if I searched and you went home to get some sleep," said Frank, not taking his eyes off the building. "You have a long day tomorrow."

"I couldn't sleep, waiting to hear from you," Diane said. "We'd better get started."

They climbed the main entrance steps to the enormous carved double doors. Diane had the feeling she was up the bean stalk visiting the giant. Through the massive oak doors that opened amazingly easily, they stepped into a ballroom-sized foyer with a polished floor of what appeared to be salt-and-pepper granite. A plaque on the wall said the stone was diorite mined nearby in North Georgia. What had Mike, the geologist at her museum, said diorite is? Something like mafic plutonic rock. She remembered thinking it sounded more as if it had come from another planet than from the bowels of the earth.

Star . . . please don't have gone to that party, her mind whispered.

Beyond the foyer the floor was tile and the walls

yellow brick set at off angles, giving the same uneven effect as the outer walls. Despite the uncomfortably hard appearance of the stone floor, several students were sitting on it studying with their backs against the wall. Some were curled up sleeping with their heads on their backpacks. Frank asked one of the students who was awake where the main office was. He was greeted with a stare.

"Main office?"

The kid looks no older than sixteen, thought Diane. She must be getting old.

"Is there a main office? I mean, its classrooms."

"Yeah, there's one," said his companion, a yellow-haired kid who looked about the same age. He pointed to a hallway closed off by glass doors. "But it's closed. They'll be open tomorrow if you need to reserve a classroom or something. You wouldn't happen to know the equation for slope?" He flipped through the pages of his book. Frank kneeled to eye level with the kid, took the notebook from him, and scribbled an equation. "Oh, yeah," he said, turning it around and looking at what Frank had written.

"What kind of test are you having?" Frank asked.

"Calculus." He hesitated a moment. "I'm in trouble, aren't I? I should know slope."

"Sometimes it's better to get a little sleep than it is to keep studying all night," said Frank as he stood back up. "Let your brain relax."

"Yeah, you're probably right, but I have my Hope scholarship to think about."

It occurred to Diane that this would be ripe territory for dealers of speed. Floors and floors of kids who need to make the grade and have to stay awake all night to cram for exams. She wondered if the meth lab had supplied students here. As she looked for Star, she'd keep an eye out for dealers. She would like to take some of these kids who used drugs to the morgue and show them the consequences of the drug business.

Explain to them that the reason some of the bodies didn't have heads was because the heat from the fire caused pressure to build up in the skull until it exploded.

Let Star be somewhere . . . anywhere other than the morgue tent.

"Is there an intercom or PA system for the building?" asked Diane.

"Sure," answered the calculus kid.

"Is it open so we can use it?" she asked.

"You're asking if they put a PA system where any one of us can use it when we want?" said the other kid. "Yeah, they'd do that."

"What was I thinking?" Diane smiled at the two of them. "Thanks for the information."

"Sure, thanks for the equation."

They started walking down the hall. Frank retrieved his phone from his jacket pocket.

"I'm going to try Star one more time," he said.

"That won't work in here," called the calculus kid. "They blocked cell phone signals in this building so they won't ring in class."

"Sure enough, no service." Frank pocketed his cell.

"But isn't that a hopeful sign?" asked Diane. "I mean, surely, that's why Star's and Jenny's cell phones don't answer. They're here somewhere."

She could see in Frank's face that, like her, he really wanted that to be the case, but he was afraid to raise his hopes . . . and afraid not to.

"Yes," he said. "It's hopeful. OK, we have to find them if they're here. I suppose it's wing by wing and floor by floor again. You're sure I can't talk you into going home?" He grabbed her hand and squeezed it.

"It'll take half as long if I help," she said. "You take the right side of the building and I'll take the left." Diane lowered her voice. "Keep a lookout for other things, too."

Diane told him her thoughts about this being a good place to sell speed. He nodded.

Many of the rooms were dark and locked. The ones that were open had students studying at desks, at computers, around tables, on the floor. They studied in groups and alone. Many had brought sleeping bags and were asleep in corners with empty snack wrappers and drink cans littering the area around them like a nest. The Student Learning Center had been turned into a giant campground, and it looked like three-quarters of the campus was holed up here.

In each room that contained people Diane asked if anyone knew Star Duncan. She found two or three who knew who she was but didn't know her well and didn't know where she was. Unlike at the library, Diane didn't hear as much gossip about the explosion and tragedy. She wondered if they didn't know. It had happened on Saturday night; if they were here all weekend, they might not have heard.

Diane was only on the second floor and she was exhausted and depressed. Her back ached. She wanted to sit down and close her eyes, but there were so many rooms to go.

She pushed on, refusing to allow this search to bring the other search, the one for her daughter, Ariel, to the front of her mind. She couldn't relive that again. Not now. Not while they couldn't find Star.

She walked into a computer lab. Several students were on computers connected to the Internet. One was playing a game. None knew Star. The next room was a lounge with vending machines. There were only two people—young women who were maybe nineteen, surely not older. They could have been from the same family. Both blond, both much too thin, as seemed to be the style these days. Both were well dressed in expensive jeans and sweaters. They were sitting opposite each other at a snack table. One of them looked as if she was slipping something across the table to the other, who had folded money between her fingers. They stopped talking when they saw Diane. The one without the money held her hand flat on the table, palm down, as if hiding something under it.

"Do either of you know Star Duncan?" asked Diane, pretending to be oblivious to their transaction.

"Star who?"

"Duncan."

They looked at each other and shook their heads and looked back at Diane.

"No."

They kept their eyes on her as if suggesting that she should be leaving now.

Diane walked over to the vending machines and looked at the choices—candy, peanuts, snack cakes, beef jerky, popcorn. In the glass reflection she saw them watching her. She lingered over the selections and fished her phone from her pocket, flipped it open, and set it to camera mode.

"I'm not getting a signal," Diane said as she raised the phone and pointed it in different directions. Pausing toward them, she silently snapped their picture.

"You won't in here. They blocked the signal when they built the place. Mean of them."

"Well, damn, how inconvenient," said Diane, and flipped her phone shut, putting it back in her pocket. She fished change from her pocket, selected a candy bar for herself and a bag a peanuts for Frank, and left the room, noting the name Jessica Davenport written on one of the girl's notebook as she passed.

Maybe if they were exchanging drugs, particularly methamphetamine, the police could get a line from them on who was behind the meth lab. It was a long shot. They were probably just talking girl stuff. But if they were exchanging drugs, it would be a lead.

Garnett didn't believe the meth cook, who was probably killed in the explosion, was the only one involved with the lab. Partly, she was sure, because Garnett didn't want the guilty party to be dead and beyond his grasp. He had told her the firemen found evidence the basement was vented so as not to release the odor of the meth production into the rest of the house. And there were other signs it could have been a high-output operation with a distribution network.

Diane wanted them caught. She wanted them in prison for a long time.

By the third floor Diane was aching all over and feeling nauseated from the worry and an empty stomach. Images of searching the jungle for Ariel came unbidden to her mind—finding the murdered nuns in the mission, hearing Ariel's music playing on the tape recorder Diane had given her and that had been left along with Ariel's bloody little shoe for Diane to find.

Oh, God, don't think about that.

Diane stopped, took a breath, and closed her eyes. *No. Go away,* she whispered to her brain, *not those images now.*

She leaned against the wall and unwrapped the candy bar she had bought from the vending machine. It was a Milky Way. It was soft from being in her warm jacket pocket. It tasted sweet and melted in her mouth. She needed the sugar jolt, but not the mess it made. She ate the whole large-sized bar, crumpled up the wrapper, and put it in her pocket. She fished out a Kleenex and wiped her hands and mouth.

Down the hall was a water fountain. Diane walked to it and bent over to take a drink. In the shiny surface of the fountain head, she thought she saw a distorted image of Star.

Chapter 10

Diane spun around and came face-to-face with Star—baggy blue jean overalls, dark eye makeup, spiky hair and all.

"Star!"

Star was obviously surprised at seeing her. "Diane, what are you doing here?"

"Star," was all Diane could say. She grabbed her and hugged her tightly. She smelled like popcorn. "I can't tell you how glad I am to see you." She held her at arm's length and looked at her.

"I see that," Star said. "What's up?"

"I've been looking all evening for you. Frank got in a few hours ago and we've both been looking for you everywhere."

"I was here studying. I have a history test tomorrow." She looked at her watch. "Today. And as you know, it's real important that I get a good grade. The other kids are sweating their Hope scholarships; I'm sweating Paris." She paused a beat. "I wasn't expecting Uncle Frank until tomorrow. He knows I'd be somewhere studying."

"I'm so glad to have found you." Diane hugged her again.

"You know I love you to death," said Star, "but you are acting really weird."

It was only then that Diane took notice of a slight, brown-haired girl standing beside Star.

"Are you Jenny Baker?"

The girl nodded and looked as if she was a little afraid Diane might hug her, too.

"Your parents are looking for you. We saw them in the library."

"The library? They're looking for me? Why? I just saw them the day before yesterday." Jenny and Star looked at each other and shrugged.

"What's going on?" asked Star. "Why are you acting so funny?"

"There was a party on Rose Avenue last night," Diane said cautiously.

"I know, I so wanted to go," said Star. "It was supposed to be really cool. But you know, Paris comes first."

"That's really nice what you're doing for Star," said Jenny. "Shopping in Paris for clothes. Wow."

"It will be my pleasure," said Diane.

She smiled at the two of them—so overjoyed to find them healthy and whole—then quickly refocused her attention.

"We need to go find Frank. He's searching the other side of the building."

"What's happened?" asked Star again. "Did the party get busted or something?"

Diane took Star's hand. She reached over and took Jenny's, too. Star and Jenny exchanged glances again, Jenny's expression asking Star, "What's up with her?"

"Diane, what is it?" asked Star.

"The house on Rose Avenue . . . there was a meth lab in the basement. It exploded while the party was going on and the house burned. Many of the kids didn't make it out."

Star sucked in her breath. The two looked at Diane, wide-eyed.

"You mean, they're . . . dead?" said Jenny. She

slipped her hand from Diane's and put it over her mouth.

"Yes," said Diane. "I'm very sorry to say that many are dead. When Frank couldn't find you . . . well, you see why we panicked." Diane looked at Jenny. "And why your parents panicked when they couldn't get in touch with you. You need to call them."

"I really was tempted to go to the party," said Star. "If I wasn't doing so bad in history . . ." She let her sentence trail off.

"I knew some of the people who were going," said Jenny. "Bobby Coleman asked me to go with him," she said to Star.

Bobby Coleman. Diane hoped her face was impassive. "We need to find Frank. If there's a pay phone somewhere, Jenny, call your parents. If there's not a phone you can go outside the building." As Diane spoke, Star's gaze never left her face.

"My parents don't have a cell," said Jenny.

"Then call home. Someone is probably there waiting in case you call," said Diane. "Frank and I will be glad to take you home."

Jenny nodded.

They both looked so young—and fragile.

Diane guessed that Frank was searching at about the same speed as she, so he could be on the same floor. They crossed over to the right side of the building. The problem was that the building had so many wings. Frank was likely to be as hard to find as Star. It was little more than chance that Diane had found her. They went down the hallways, looking into the rooms. Frank would be easy to spot. He looked nothing like the students.

They passed the two young women from the student lounge. Star spoke to them. Their gaze darted to Diane's face for a fraction of a second as they walked by at a fast clip.

"Well, what's wrong with those two?" said Star.

"They are such snobs. Just wait till I get back from Paris with my new clothes."

So they had known Star after all, thought Diane. *They just didn't want me to linger so they could get on with whatever they were getting on with. Damn little witches.*

"What do you know about those two?" Diane asked Star as she peeked into a classroom.

"Jessica Davenport and Jamie Dempsey. I call them the Jersey Devils. They are so full of themselves."

Diane would wait until they were alone to question Star further. But at least now she had two names to give to Garnett as possible leads. She opened a door to the computer lab just as Frank was coming out.

"Diane . . ." Then he spotted Star. "Dear God in heaven," he said and put his arms around her. Star buried her head in his chest.

When Star had been under arrest and her parents and brother dead, she had tried to kill herself. With the desolation of her grief and the feeling that there was nowhere for her to go, she had lost hope that the world would ever be right again. Frank's asking to adopt her virtually turned her around. He had made her feel that she was worth something and, more importantly, he had believed her when she said she was innocent. Star was still a handful from time to time, but Diane knew that she was truly grateful that Frank loved and cared about her.

The four of them walked out of the building and down the sidewalk to Frank's Expedition. On the way, Jenny called home on her cell. A neighbor answered and Jenny looked surprised. But Diane knew that parents in their situation would leave someone to answer the phone, waiting for any word about their daughter.

Just as they were about to drive off, Jenny saw her parents' car turning into the parking lot. She yelled for Frank to stop, opened the door, and got out. Her mother and father saw her about the same time and came running to her, leaving their car in the middle of the road.

After seeing so many burned bodies during the past twenty-four hours, Diane was relieved beyond words to see two happy endings. She thought of Bobby Coleman's parents, and the parents of the girl with the blond wavy hair. Nothing would ever bring them closure. Diane knew there was no such thing.

Through her passenger-side window, Diane saw someone she recognized walking out of the Student Learning Center to the parking lot. It was the blond girl's mother from the coffee tent. She was alone. Diane wanted to cry.

"Bobby Coleman's dead, isn't he?" said Star. Her voice startled Diane out of her thoughts.

"The police haven't released any information, yet," Diane said.

"But he's dead. I could tell by your face. The way you had no expression. That's what you do when you don't want anyone to see you react—you set your face like that."

"Yes, honey, he is. But please don't tell anyone. I don't know if his parents have been told." Diane was silent for several seconds as the Expedition sped across the icy street toward her apartment. "He was the first one to be identified."

After a minute, Diane looked in back. Star was curled up on the seat asleep. She wished she could have found Ariel curled up somewhere in the jungle. She was so thankful they had found Star.

"What's this about your car being jacked?" Frank said in a low voice.

"Some kid running from the fire. He tried to get Keith's car but Keith sped off. He came to me next. I was stuck in the snow."

"Diane . . . ," he whispered. "I can't leave you alone for any length of time."

"Apparently not."

"How did you manage? Not anything dramatic and dangerous, I hope?"

"No. He was injured from the explosion."

She made a motion as if chopping her hand off. Frank winced.

"I persuaded him to get into the backseat and I locked him in. He couldn't get out because the child locks were on, and he couldn't climb over to the front in his condition. It gave me time to run. By that time the police came. That's about all there was to it." *Besides him shooting out my car window*, she thought.

"How is he?" asked Frank. "Will Garnett be able to question him?"

"Yes, he was going to do that today. The kid was one of the few survivors well enough to talk."

They arrived at her house and Frank walked her to her door.

"I'm so grateful we found Star," she said.

He gave her a kiss on the lips—a short kiss, then one that lingered. "I'm glad you were there to help," he said when he raised his head. "I was pretty frantic. I ran into another parent in the Learning Center looking for her daughter, too. It was scary. I hope she found her."

"Me too—and I'm glad you're home. I missed you."

Diane got only three hours sleep but felt refreshed when she awakened at eight o'clock. Finding Star had rejuvenated her as much as a full night's sleep. She showered, dressed, and made a call first thing to Chief Garnett.

"Diane, I tried to find you last night. I was told that you and Frank went looking for Star. Did you find her?"

"Yes. Yes, we did. She was studying in the Student Learning Center with another missing student. It was a good end to a very bad day."

"Good. Good. It's bad enough when it's people you don't know. . . . Everyone around here was worried."

He paused and cleared his throat. "Uh, McNair's been on the phone to the commissioner. He's trying to have you and your team removed from the recovery. Says you are tampering with evidence and compromising the investigation."

"That son of a bitch. I hope you know better than that. McNair was the one breaking the seals on the evidence bags. He's the one who compromised evidence. I called him on it. He and I had words."

"I'm not at all surprised. But he does have pull with the commissioner—at least his uncle does."

"Well, you know how paranoid David is."

"Uh, you've said that before, but what does that . . ."

"David was pretty worked up about it—as he had a right to be. It would not surprise me if he documented McNair's misconduct by snapping some incriminating pictures with his cell phone camera. We at the crime lab are prone to that behavior. I don't know that he did; he didn't say, but I know David."

"I see. I'll be sure to smile from now on whenever I look in David's direction."

"If a pic does exist, I'd want to use it only as a last resort. I'd hate to expose us as the sneaky people we are."

She heard Garnett stifle a laugh. "I'll have a long talk with the commissioner."

"There's another thing. It may be perfectly innocent. . . ." She told Garnett her thoughts about possible drug trade at the student center and about the two girls she had seen.

"When you think about it, that would be a likely place to deal. You didn't happen to get the girls' names, did you?"

"Yes, I thought you might want to talk to them.

They're Jessica Davenport and Jamie Dempsey. I also have their picture."

"Their picture? Where did you get . . . ?"

"Yes, I, well, I took it with my cell phone."

"I see," he repeated. "You people in the crime lab *are* prone to sneaky cell phone behavior, Jeez. I've never even used the camera feature on my phone."

"Well, what can I say? We all grew up watching too many James Bond movies—or Rocky and Bullwinkle. As I said, what I saw may have been perfectly innocent."

"And it may be a lead. I'll put a detective on it. And I'll talk to the commissioner. McNair's uncle has the commissioner spooked, but the commissioner doesn't like him, and he does like us, so . . ."

"I'll leave all that to you."

After she hung up with Garnett, Diane called her assistant, Andie, to check on the museum.

"We're doing OK. Did you find Star?" She sounded subdued. Diane guessed everyone in Rosewood did. She could picture Andie's usually bright, happy face masked with concern. They all knew Star, and Rosewood was a small town. They were all probably waiting to find out who among their friends were dead.

"Yes, we did find her. She's fine. She was studying on campus. She's home with Frank now."

"Whew, that's so good. I can't tell you how worried we were here."

"We all were, but she's fine."

"You know Darcy Kincaid?" asked Andie.

"Sure. One of our exhibit planners," said Diane. "Why?"

"She was at the party."

Chapter 11

"Oh, no. Oh, Andie. Not Darcy. Not anyone from the museum."

"She survived the explosion and the fire, but she's in a coma. They don't know if she'll come out of it. We're all kind of bummed out around here."

"Do Darcy's parents know?"

"They flew in from Arkansas late yesterday. Kendel met them at the airport and I found them a hotel room near the hospital. If they have to stay in Rosewood for very long, several of the museum staff have offered them a place to stay for as long as they need." Diane loved the museum and the people in it. She wasn't surprised they were so forthcoming with help for Darcy and her family.

She had taken Darcy to dinner, as she did all her employees, to get to know her, and they had consulted and worked together on planning and building museum displays. She remembered Darcy liked dolphins and worked one summer with them at an aquarium in Florida. She wore a silver dolphin charm on a chain around her neck. In all of her worry, the thought had not occurred to Diane that anyone from her museum might be among the victims.

"I'll stop by the hospital to check on her this morning."

"I heard someone tried to steal your car," said

Andie. "With all that's going on, I forgot to ask. Is that true?"

"It's true. I don't know who he was. Someone running from the fire, apparently. It ended well. He's under arrest in the hospital. I'll tell you all about it later. I'm glad you asked. My car is impounded as evidence. I need to use one of the museum vehicles. Would you have one parked out front in my space?"

"Of course," said Andie.

"I'm calling a taxi and will be over shortly. Call on my cell if you need me, but it looks like you all have things well in hand." Diane hurried to get off the phone, but Andie still seemed to need debriefing.

"How long . . . ," she asked. "How long will you be out there—at the scene?"

"I don't know, Andie."

"I guess it's pretty bad."

"It's worse than that."

"Nothing like this has ever happened in Rosewood."

"I hope nothing like this ever happens again."

Diane wished there were some way she could make sure that it would never happen again. Although she believed what Rankin said about not being able to stop the drug trade, maybe there was a way to stop it in her corner of the world.

When Diane arrived at the museum, one of the museum's SUVs was waiting in her parking space. Before she went back to the circus—as she thought of the tent city—she headed for the hospital. She stopped at a toy store on the way and bought a stuffed dolphin.

Diane was becoming an all too familiar face at the hospital—visiting Frank, Star, Mike, Neva, not to mention her own time in residence as a patient. Too many hospital visits, too many violent injuries. Maybe someone she knew would have a baby and she could come for a happier visit. She rode the elevator to Darcy's floor and walked down the stark gray corridor to the ICU waiting room. She recognized Darcy's parents right away because Darcy looked just like her mother—dark hair, dark eyes, and dimples in her cheeks and chin. The two parents sat together on a small crimson sofa. Both were looking at the clock. Waiting for another of the timed visits to ICU, Diane guessed.

"Excuse me, are you the Kincaids?" asked Diane.

"Yes, we are." Her father stood up, his wife after him. They looked to be in their fifties, fit, and terribly worried. "This is my wife, Edwina. I'm Jesse Kincaid."

"I'm Diane Fallon. Darcy works for me at the museum." She held out her hand.

"Yes, she's told us all about you," said Mrs. Kincaid. Each took her hand and shook it in turn. "Darcy just loves working for the museum. She says it's her dream job."

Her father put his hands on his belt. "You folks at the museum have been so good to us. We sure do appreciate it."

"Not at all. Anything we can do to help, just ask. How is Darcy? Do you know?"

"They won't tell us anything," said Mrs. Kincaid.

"They don't know anything, Edie," he said. "They said we might know something in forty-eight hours."

"It's just this waiting," Mrs. Kincaid said. "And they only let us in for fifteen minutes at a time. Darcy looks so swollen, I wouldn't even recognize her."

"I know the waiting is hard. It's all hard. Do you have a car to get you places?" she asked.

"Yes, we have a rental car," said Mr. Kincaid.

"We have a restaurant at the museum. It's not that far from here, and if you get tired of eating hospital cafeteria food, please come to the restaurant as my guest. Just tell them who you are."

"That's so nice. Are you sure?" said Darcy's mother.

"It's a small gesture in a very trying time," said

Diane. She didn't say, "I lost a daughter and the kindness of good people pulled me through." She removed the stuffed dolphin from the sack she was carrying and handed it to them.

Her mother took it and held it to her chest. "Darcy just loves dolphins. You all have been so kind. We don't know how to thank you."

"You don't need to. We all pray for the best for Darcy."

Diane started to leave and Mrs. Kincaid laid a hand on her arm. "We heard that the explosion was from a drug lab. Darcy wasn't into drugs; we would have known."

"She probably didn't know the lab was there," said Diane. "The house was divided into student apartments. There were lots of people going in and out. It's in my neighborhood. It's a good neighborhood. I live a street over and heard the explosion when it happened. No one knew."

"When I first heard, I thought it was a gas leak or something," said Edwina. "This . . . this is just so much worse."

"Have they arrested anybody?" asked Darcy's father.

"They're investigating," said Diane "The people in the lab were killed. We're concentrating our efforts right now on treating the injured and identifying all the victims. But believe me when I tell you, right now in Rosewood, getting to the bottom of this has top priority."

The Kincaids were decent people, but Diane was glad to take her leave. The tragedy of this event was weighing down on her and she had too many burned body parts to process. She needed to find her way back to her objective anthropologist self.

Leaving the hospital, she took a shortcut through the sunroom. Even though there was no sun shining through the windows, the room was warm and cozy.

With its open feeling and warm golden brown walls and an abundance of plants, it was one of the more pleasant rooms in the hospital. Several patients were there. Some sitting, some with their IVs, some just milling around.

One patient looked familiar, a young man sitting with two people who were probably his parents. The realization hit her who he was. The one-handed car-jacker. Then she noticed the policeman standing a few feet away. The kid was looking much better than the last time she saw him.

"Why do you have to stand so close?" the mother scolded the policeman. "Can't you see how injured my son is? I don't know why you are treating him like a criminal. He is innocent."

She was a thin woman with a tan complexion, honey brown hair, and Gaultier clothes. The father—she assumed he was the father—clothed himself in a similar expensive fashion.

"I ought to have your badge," the mother said.

"Lady, I don't think you would like the job," said the policeman.

Diane tried to recollect who he was.

"Don't you get smart with my wife."

The man stood up and marched over to the police-man. The boy just smirked and looked on. Not a nice kid, Diane thought, but she had come to that conclusion much earlier when he held his gun on her.

"When I find out who that stupid bitch is who accused him of trying to hijack her car, there'll be hell for her to pay, and you'll pay it with her for that smart mouth."

"Yeah, yeah, they all say that right before I turn the key and lock their cell. Look mister, I don't care who you are or who you know. You take one more step toward me with that attitude and you are going to be under arrest along with your son."

"What is your badge number?" The father balled

his fist by his side, but didn't take another step toward the officer.

"It's on my badge here." He pointed to it pinned to his shirt. "I assume a man of your standing can read numbers."

Diane thought he was laying it on a little too thick. It would have been her advice to keep a professional attitude. But he must have had to listen to these folks smart off to him ever since they arrived. She decided that this was not a good shortcut to take. She started to retreat when the kid recognized her. She was shocked; she didn't think he could possibly remember her face, given the condition he was in.

"That's her. The director of the museum here in Rosewood," he said.

Suddenly Diane had two angry people bearing down on her. She really didn't have time for this.

Chapter 12

Diane held her ground as she watched the two angry people coming toward her.

"Stop right there," she said when they approached her comfort zone. "If you come any closer I'll call the police. Speaking to me personally is inappropriate under the circumstances."

They took several steps forward before stopping, Diane guessed to show that she couldn't tell them what to do.

"So you're the lying bitch who got our son in trouble," the mother shouted at her. They now had the attention of all the patients and visitors in the sunroom. "Look at him, he's maimed for life, and he's not receiving the sympathy he deserves because your lies have the police believing he had something to do with the explosion. He's the victim here."

Diane didn't say anything. She merely folded her arms across her chest and let them talk. *"Sometimes when you remain quiet and just let people talk,"* her old boss from her human rights investigation days told her, *"they will reveal all sorts of things. There's a whole set of people out there who really want to confess."*

"Blake told us how you lured him into your car." The father said this as if it were some brilliant piece of evidence he had uncovered against Diane.

The kid's eyes glittered with excitement. Diane was

willing to bet he was used to this—setting his parents off against people, or each other, then sitting back to watch the fireworks. A disturbed kid with clueless parents who apparently had more money than sense. Diane said nothing.

"He was asking for help, damn you. You know he found that gun in your car. It was your damn gun, yours. He didn't have it until you lured him into your car. He was just trying to break the window to get out. How dare you accuse him of trying to hijack your car." His mother was speaking through gritted teeth now and her voice was a low growl.

"So you are the director of the museum," his father said when his wife ran out of breath. "I hope you aren't too attached to your job. I know several members of the board and I serve on three charity organizations with Vanessa Van Ross."

And you couldn't know any of them very well, thought Diane, *or you would know that particular threat is empty.*

Diane watched as her silence irritated them. The mother's eyes were dark slits, her mouth turned down in a deep frown. The father's mouth was a thin straight line. His dark eyes were full of malice.

"Well, what have you got to say for yourself?" his mother said. Diane expected her to stamp her foot.

"Nothing," said Diane. "I have said everything to the police. Anything else I'll say in court." She turned her back and walked out the door.

"Don't you turn your back on us," screeched his mother, so loud that Diane was sure she cracked the windowpanes.

Diane continued walking down the hallway, but soon heard high-heeled footfalls behind her. The woman was following her! Diane didn't know why this astonished her. She stopped and turned.

Before Diane could say anything, the woman came at her with long red fingernails on hands formed into claws. Diane dodged, but was hit with a fist in the shoulder and knocked flat against the wall. Before she could take more evasive action, the policeman who had been guarding the son was putting cuffs on the mother.

"What the hell are you doing, you oaf! You can't do this!"

"Let go of my wife. I'll sue you, the police department, and the city. Get those handcuffs off her."

Through all the yelling, Diane could hear the policeman reading the woman her rights. By the time he finished, not only were several hospital staff gathered at the scene, but hospital security had shown up, along with another policeman.

"What are you arresting me for? You stupid jerk," she spat at him.

"Attacking Dr. Fallon here."

"I didn't attack her. She attacked my son."

"Lady, I saw you hit her. She's not just the director of the museum, she's the director of the crime lab, and that makes her a member of the Rosewood police department. So you just struck an officer to boot, and I'm taking you to jail. You can call a lawyer from there."

"We didn't know she was a police officer," said her husband.

"Sir," said the policeman, "is it your belief that it's OK to assault private citizens who are not police officers?" He turned to the other policeman. "Jackson, go watch that Stanton kid. Make sure he hasn't run off. I'll be back after I book Mrs. Stanton."

"You aren't going through with this," said Mr. Stanton. "This is ridiculous."

"Louis, do something," she said. "Pay the man or something."

"Now, you wouldn't be trying to bribe me, ma'am," said the policeman who Diane now remembered was Mickey Varner. "I'd hate to be adding charges."

Mickey looked over his shoulder at Mr. Stanton. "You can see her down at the station."

He hauled her off, protesting all the way. Diane wouldn't be surprised if by the time they got to the police station, resisting arrest would be added to the charges.

The son, Blake Stanton, was standing in the doorway, looking at Diane with black hatred. She suspected that this was not the fireworks he had anticipated.

Before going into the morgue tent, Diane walked across the adjoining yard to the crime scene to see how David and Neva were doing. The sky was overcast with gray-white clouds, and the temperature was below freezing. She could see her breath every time she exhaled. Diane thought she heard on the radio that the forecast was for another ice storm this evening. It must be really hard living in Siberia, she thought as she trudged through the show. But from her experience she knew that as hard as it was working in the cold, working in the heat would be worse. The cold mutes the smell—though it's still bad enough.

Between her crew and McNair's arson team, they had made significant progress clearing away debris. In over half the area she could see the burned floor where piles of charred rubble had been before. David and Neva met her as she approached.

"How's McNair acting?" asked Diane in a low voice.

"About the same," said David. "The talk you gave him didn't do a bit of good. He's still looking in the evidence bags. I tell you what I'd like to do . . ." He didn't finish the sentence.

"David, did you happen to take pictures of him tampering with the seals on the bags?"

David stared, frowning at her for several moments.

"Diane, it worries me when someone knows me that well."

"That would be a yes," said Neva.

"It's good that you did. McNair is telling the commissioner we're compromising the evidence. I just want to make sure when push comes to shove, we have some leverage to shove really hard. I knew I could count on you."

"You should talk about me. Who took photographs on her cell phone—from her closet, yet—just a few months ago of her ex-husband sneaking into her bedroom?"

Diane smiled. "David, I like you the way you are, paranoia and all. I wouldn't change a thing."

"Why is McNair doing this?" asked Neva.

"It's a control thing. Why do control freaks like to control?" She shrugged. "In this case, probably because it's such a high-profile crime. He must think it will launch his career or his fortunes or something."

"The guys who work for him really aren't that bad when he's not around," said David. "They know their business and I get the sense that they don't like him very much."

"Do the best you can. I'm having Garnett work on the problem. That's all I can do at the moment. If he comes back and starts pawing through sealed evidence again, call me."

"Will do," said David. "We've sent you a truckload of bones. The nearer to the heat of the blast, the more loose bones we find."

Diane sighed. It still surprised her that someone who is alive and vital one minute can, in a moment, be reduced to bones.

"Then I'd better get back to work," she said.

The morgue tent looked just as it had when she left—blackened bodies on every table. Jin was at her table laying out bones. Archie was at his table sorting through boxes of objects and medical information collected from parents of missing children. It frightened Diane to think that with the slightest change of fate, he might have been filing Star's identifying information. She shivered. All of them looked up when Diane walked in.

"We were all so glad to hear that you found Star," said Lynn Webber. "It was as if she belonged to all of us."

"I appreciate that, guys. I can't tell you what a scary night it was until we found her. She was doing what she should have been, studying for finals with a friend."

She paused a moment as she took her place at her metal table. "Her friend, Jenny Baker, was asked to go to the party by Bobby Coleman. She decided to study instead."

"Bless her little heart," said Lynn.

"I know the Bakers, too," said Archie. "I'm glad I won't be going to her funeral as well as Bobby's."

"You know," said Rankin, "maybe they should have brought outside people in to identify the bodies. We're going to know so many of these students. I know the parents of one of the kids in the hospital. They're trying to save his arm."

"I know," said Diane. "One of my museum staff is in the hospital in a coma." Diane put on her lab coat and latex gloves. "But who could do a better and more careful job than we can? If it's hard on us, just think of the parents and relatives who are our friends and colleagues."

"You're right about that," said Rankin. "I guess it's what we do."

"Is there anything new here?" asked Diane.

"They found another charred body in the basement rubble," said Lynn. "That brings the total to thirty-three. Garnett assigned priority to all the basement bodies. He wants to know who was found in proximity to the lab. Brewster identified two more bodies of students from their dental charts."

Another body. Diane hoped that was the last one. She looked at the bones in front of her. Jin had laid them out on labeled trays.

"I thought this might be the best way," said Jin. "Each tray represents the grid they were found in. When you have examined them, I'll pack them up and take them to the lab to extract DNA."

Diane nodded and picked up a charred triquetral—one of the carpal bones in the wrist—and began her measurements.

"I understand you had a row at the hospital," said Rankin after several minutes.

"Who are you talking to?" asked Pilgrim.

"Diane," Rankin said. "Tell us about it."

"Not much to tell. I was visiting Darcy Kincaid, the museum staff member I told you about." Diane described for them the events that transpired in the hospital.

"What?" said Lynn. "You're kidding. She just attacked you right there in the solarium?"

"In the hallway. She hit me one good lick, but didn't do any harm. The policeman guarding the son arrested her."

"Why did she attack you?" asked Jin, who seemed to find it funny, judging from the grin on his face.

"They're saying their son is the innocent victim and for some unknown reason, I'm trying to frame him or something. Anyway, their story is that I'm the culprit and they are going to have me fired and sue the police department."

"I think they are going to have to adopt another attitude," said Brewster Pilgrim. "People aren't in the mood right now for that kind of nonsense."

"Amen," said Archie.

Diane wanted to get off the topic of her misadventure, so she tried to make light of it. "It was a minor event. I'm sure when their lawyers see the evidence they'll recommend abject contrition."

After seeing Blake Stanton's parents, she felt oddly sorry for him; then she looked at the blackened bones in front of her and her sympathy evaporated. *If he had anything at all to do with this . . . ,* she thought.

She went back to work examining and measuring. There were several wrist bones found together, suggesting that they were from the same wrist. All were from the right side. She put the bones together like a three-dimensional puzzle and found that they fit as though they belonged, and they had complementary wear patterns in the articulated surfaces. She noted a healed fracture on the hook part of the hamate.

"The size of the bones falls within the male range," she said to Jin as she recorded the information on the form. "That doesn't exclude larger boned females, of course. I think he—or she—might have been a baseball, racquetball or tennis player."

"Why is that?" asked Jin.

She showed him the healed fracture. "This kind of fracture is not uncommon among athletes in sports that involve the swinging of a club."

"Really?" said Jin. "You can take a handful of wrist bones and say this is a male baseball player? That's so cool."

"I didn't say that. I said it could be. It's suggestive. And I don't know what kind of club was swung. Could've been an ax and he cut firewood for a living."

"Anyway, it's really neat what you do with bones."

Archie shuffled through one of the boxes. He brought her a large envelope. He was limping slightly; she recalled a policeman getting shot last year and she wondered if it was Archie.

"I remember this," he said, "because Marjie, the policewoman who brought this batch in, said he's a neighbor, and the son of a Rosewood policeman. He's on the university's racquetball team. She told me this is an x-ray of his hand."

"You have a good memory. Thank you, Archie," said Diane. "This is a big help."

"Any little thing I can do." He went back to his seat just as Marjie brought him more packages containing information on more missing children.

Diane took the x-ray from the envelope and put it on the light box. There it was, a small fracture line like the healed one in the bones in front of her. She took each of the wrist bones in turn and compared it to the x-ray. There were no more fractures, but the relative sizes and wear patterns matched. She was satisfied that these were the bones of—she looked at the name on the x-ray—Donald Wallace. Now, if she could just find the rest of him.

Wallace? She looked back at the name. Then picked up the envelope and read the label. Just as she feared. His father was Izzy Wallace, a policeman, as Archie had said—and a friend of Frank's. *Damn.*

Diane dreaded telling Frank. He was so overjoyed at finding Star. Now his friend will have this dreadful news. Izzy Wallace wasn't one of her favorite people and she certainly wasn't one of his, but she would wish this on no one. She looked forlornly at the other bones in the trays and set about seeing if she could match them up.

It looked as if most of the bones found along the adjacent grid squares belonged with these wrist bones. But Jin would have to take DNA samples anyway to confirm.

As if reading her mind, Jin spoke. "We'll have to use mitochondrial DNA on most of these remains. The nuclear DNA will have been too degraded by the fire."

Diane nodded. "I think for most we'll have dental records and x-rays to go along with the DNA. There'll just be a few that we'll need to rely only on DNA."

"You know, boss," began Jin.

"I know, Jin. If we had our own DNA lab, you could have all these done tonight and we'd have everyone's identity tomorrow."

"There's that, but I was going to suggest that since I have to extract these samples when we get back to the lab, why don't I go out and help Neva and David get all the remains collected. We'll get done faster."

"That's a good idea."

Jin pealed off his gloves and slipped off his green lab coat. Just as he started out the door, David entered carrying a box.

"We found another body."

He brought the bones to Diane's table. His dark eyes sparkled. Diane waited for the other shoe to drop. There was usually another shoe when David looked like that.

"We found him among metal bed slats, and a partially consumed head and footboard," he said, "so we think he may have been in bed at the time of the fire. And get this. He was shot in the head."

Chapter 13

"Shot?" said Diane.

Allen Rankin looked up from the cadaver he was examining. "Someone was shot? In the house? Before the fire?" he said. "That puts a different complexion on the whole thing."

David set the box on an unoccupied gurney near Diane's table and handed her snapshots of the scene. "I'll get the official pictures to you when I can," he said.

Diane took the small photographs of the bones in situ. "This is how you found them?" she asked.

"Just like that. It looks like the bullet went in the left cheek and out the right side of the head," said David.

Diane opened the box and began setting the bones out on the gurney in anatomical position. Up to this point, the bones recovered from the site had been various shades of gray to black in color, depending on how burned they were. This set of bones were charred and blackened, but they didn't have any of the lighter shades of gray or white; they were mostly a dark rich brown. Nor did they have any bits of charred flesh attached to them.

Grover came to help Diane lay out the bones. The MEs left their tables to take a look at the murder victim. Like Grover, they wanted to see something that could add a whole new dimension to the investigation. She could see they were as curious as she.

Diane picked up the skull and examined the bullet wound. It apparently hit dead center in the left infraorbital foramen—a hole under the left orbit for nerves and vessels—and exited through the right side on the lambdoidal suture where the parietal and occipital meet. The bullet's exit took huge fragments of skull with it.

Diane took off her glove and touched a femur with her fingers.

"This ain't right, is it?" said Grover.

"Grover, you know your bones, don't you?" said Diane. She remembered when he cleaned the bones of a murder victim for her how he had packaged the bones with all the correct sides together, even the ribs.

"What?" asked Pilgrim. "What is it that you are seeing?"

"For one thing," said Diane, "look at the photograph. Look how the bones are arranged."

"He looks to have been in a super flexed position when he died," said David. "You think he was tied up and executed?"

"No," said Diane. She smiled at Grover. "What do you notice about the bones, Grover?"

"They're mighty brown, Dr. Fallon. Mighty brown."

"Um huh," murmured Diane. She picked up several bones and studied each. She examined the skull again and the teeth and surfaces inside the skull.

"The bones are awfully clean," said Jin.

"Aren't they, though?" said Diane.

"A dental chart isn't going to help much on him," said Rankin. "He has no fillings, and the poor fellow had more than a few bad dental caries in his molars. That one in his incisor looks like it might have been ready to abscess."

"How old is he—or she?" asked Jin.

"He. The pelvis is clearly male. He was probably in

his early twenties." She showed them the rugged surface of his pubis symphysis—where the two hip bones come together in front. "The older you get, the more worn down it is—among other things. And he's just getting in his third molars."

"So, Grover," said Lynn Webber, "what's with the brown bones?"

"I believe he's worn down to his bones in a coffin. Don't you, Dr. Fallon?" he said.

"I do indeed," said Diane.

"In a coffin?" said David. "What are you saying?"

"Bones in a coffin often get that very brown color to them. Look," she handed David back the photograph. "This fellow is far too flexed to have been put that way while he was still fleshed out—even if he were bound tight. Look at how the long bones are all parallel and the smaller bones are all in a pile. I believe the skeleton was in a box under one of the students' bed. I'll have to run some tests, but these bones are very old, perhaps a hundred years or more."

"I'll be damned," said Rankin. "I guess his killer's beyond the likes of us now. But that begs the question, just where did a student get the skeleton of a person who appears to have had a proper burial when he died?"

"Good question. If any of the house's residents are among the survivors, we can ask if they know," said Diane. "In the meantime, pack this fellow back up. I'll take him to the osteology lab and work on him later."

"All that's real interesting," said Archie. He was standing behind Jin, looking over his shoulder. "Never knew you could tell so much from just bones."

"Oh, she can tell you more than that when she gets to really analyzing him," said Jin.

"You trying to butter me up, Jin?" asked Diane.

"Every chance I get, Boss." He grinned at her.

Grover began repacking the bones in his careful way—as if the deceased could feel what was happening to them and he wanted to make sure they were comfortable throughout their journey to the afterlife. Everyone else gravitated back to their respective workstations, except Lynn Webber. She hung back. Jin went with David back to the burned-out house site.

"OK, Grover," Lynn asked her diener, "how did you know about the bones turning brown in a coffin?"

"Like Raymond was always saying," he replied, referring to his cousin who had been Lynn's assistant before him, "there are some questions it's just best not to ask." He gave her a rare smile, and Lynn laughed out loud.

Diane got the idea that this was the first joke Grover had ever made.

Diane packaged and labeled the bones, which she had tentatively identified as those of Donald Wallace, pending DNA confirmation. How awful for the parents to have raised a son or daughter to adulthood with all their hopes and dreams for that child, and in just one moment of disaster to have nothing left but a few bones—no face to look upon, nothing to see or hold. She did not envy the people whose job it was to inform the parents that their child's remains had been identified.

By the end of the day all the bodies had been autopsied, and all but eight were identified. Of those remaining eight, the forensics team felt they would be able to ID most of them when everyone had been reported missing. It was, after all, still soon after the tragedy and it might be a week or more before some people were confirmed missing and forensic evidence could be collected for comparison.

Diane had yet to determine how many individuals the disarticulated bones represented. Those would be the hardest to identify. Now that the recovered bodies had been processed, she was going to take the remaining bones back to her lab, which was a more efficient operation than this tent city and had much less distraction.

Toward the end of the day when one of the last bodies was being wheeled in by Pilgrim's diener, a reporter managed to get inside the tent by waiting until one of the rear entrances was unguarded. He crept in with his camera before anyone noticed him but froze when he saw a charred body in the characteristic pugilistic pose roll past him on a gurney. When the stronger flexor muscles shrink and contract from the fire, the arms and hands strike the pose of a boxer. It is a disturbing sight. The burned flesh is bad enough, but the posed appearance of the cadaver looks all the more horrifying. The reporter stared transfixed with his camera in his hand until one of the policemen led him away.

Diane guessed him to be new to this type of story—apparently he'd never seen firsthand a fiery accident or the aftermath of a house fire. She felt sorry for him. These were images no one wants in their head.

"I guess he'll never do that again," said Rankin, the ME the body was headed for.

"But his description of what we're doing in here is going to be worse," said Lynn.

"How could he possibly describe anything worse than this has been," said Brewster Pilgrim.

"You have me there," said Lynn. She took off her lab coat and gloves. "I'm going to sit down by Archie here and do some paperwork, go home, and soak in a hot bath for several days," she announced. "Or until we get some more dental charts and x-rays to look at."

"You know what we haven't seen?" said Rankin.

"What's that?" asked Pilgrim.

"Meth mouth. Even if most of the students at the party didn't know what was going on in the basement, which I think may be true, and were not methamphetamine users, what about the cooks in the basement or some of the residents? Or surely there were some buyers at the party. I haven't seen anybody with the diseased mouth of a serious crystal meth addict."

"Neither did I," agreed Pilgrim.

Lynn looked up from her paperwork. "What are you saying that means, exactly?" she asked.

Rankin shrugged his thin shoulders. "I guess maybe if this was just someone cooking for themselves and a few addicted friends, I'd expect to find some of those friends at the party. All I've seen is some pretty good dentition. The worst teeth I've seen are in our hundred-year-old fellow. If it was a large-scale operation and the meth was going to a distributor, then there might not be many addicts at the party. That's all. I'm just thinking out loud."

"It's a good thought," said Diane. "The teeth I've seen have only been damaged by fire—no signs of methamphetamine use."

"It's an idea," said Pilgrim. "I'm not sure I like the implications. It speaks of a much greater problem."

"It's a big problem any way you look at it," said Archie. "We're just over an hour from Atlanta. What makes anybody think that Rosewood's immune to drugs? Let me tell you, we're just like every other place in the country. I wish we weren't."

Diane didn't like that thought. But he was probably right. Right now, however, her problem was identifying bodies, not finding evildoers. She happily left that to Garnett and others. She took off her lab coat and checked out for the evening, leaving orders for all the bones to be delivered to the crime lab.

It had stopped sleeting several hours earlier and was now hard cold. Diane hurried her pace toward the crime scene to check on David, Jin, and Neva. They must be exhausted, sifting though that huge mess of charred detritus.

They were packing up the crime scene van, about ready to leave the site to the night watchmen.

"How's it going?" she asked.

"It's going as well as can be expected," said Neva. Her face was rosy from the cold. She took a Kleenex out of her pocket and blew her nose. "McNair's men took most of the evidence away in a truck. Not much we can do. David's doing a slow burn—pardon the pun."

David's features were frozen in a frown. "We were outnumbered and Neva and I were at the coffee tent when they did it. Jin didn't know about the issue, or he would have called you. They didn't get the smaller stuff; it was locked in our van."

Diane could relate to the slow burn David must be doing. Her cheeks were aflame. "I'll talk to McNair and Garnett," said Diane. "And whoever else . . ."

She was interrupted by three vehicles pulling up behind their crime scene van. Doors opened and people started piling out. Diane couldn't see them clearly for the glare of the headlights in her eyes, but their aggressive movement toward her gave her the distinct feeling she was about to be arrested.

Chapter 14

Diane blinked her eyes when the headlights finally switched off. *What in the world,* she thought. She felt David, Neva, and Jin walking up beside her. *A united front—against what?*

"Diane." One of the individuals was Chief Garnett.

She felt a silly sense of relief. "Chief," she said as he came into the circle of light cast by the streetlamps.

She could see by the set of his jaw that whatever it was, it wasn't good. That feeling was reinforced by the presence of the police commissioner and McNair with him, along with two men she didn't know who seemed to be with McNair.

The police commissioner was a small man who looked as if he would be more at home doing anything but police work. He wore rimless glasses and earmuffs. Part of a gray lapel matching his gray pants peeked out from the front of his black fur-trimmed topcoat. He was shivering. Diane didn't wonder that he was cold; he wore no hat and he had only a thin layer of hair.

McNair wore his usual smirk, but it had more of a look of triumph to it now.

"We've reached a compromise," said the commissioner.

"I'm taking the evidence you've collected," McNair said.

The commissioner cast him a scowl, but McNair didn't notice because he was looking at Diane. It was obviously a done deal. Diane was afraid that what they were going to do was compromise the evidence.

If McNair was expecting a howl of protest, he was disappointed. Diane said nothing. She decided to treat them pretty much the way she had treated the Stantons at the hospital—let them confess.

"What he means," said Garnett, "is that the arson investigation unit will handle all nonhuman evidence and your unit will handle all the bones and nontissue human remains. The medical examiners will handle any tissue samples."

"That sounds logical," said the commissioner. He made it sound as though he was asking Diane a question.

She felt like saying it might be logical if anyone but McNair were handling the evidence.

"I'll take the evidence now," said McNair.

"If I'm not mistaken, you have already taken most of it," said Diane.

"Now, I'm taking the rest of it." McNair nodded to the two strangers and they started for the van.

David stepped in front of the door, blocking their access.

"Commissioner," said Diane, "perhaps Mr. McNair needs to be reminded that we are all required by law to follow strict protocol for the transfer of custody of evidence. Each item must be individually logged out of our inventory and signed for before it leaves the custody of the crime scene forensics unit."

"She's stalling and evading, Commissioner," McNair snapped. "Giving us a lecture."

"Are you refusing to cooperate, Diane?" asked the commissioner. "If so . . ."

"No, of course I'm not. I'm simply pointing out that if Mr. McNair's men enter that van and take the evidence without following the required protocol, they will render the items unusable as evidence in any legal proceeding or criminal prosecution."

"I see what you're saying," replied the commissioner, then reconsidered. "Exactly what is it you're saying?"

"Simply that protocol requires that my crew retrieve each bag containing nonhuman materials from its storage box, enter a record of its transfer into the evidence log, and hand it over to Mr. McNair's custody as it is signed for by Mr. McNair or a legally authorized member of his staff," said Diane. "What happens to it after that point is Mr. McNair's responsibility."

"That sounds proper," the commissioner said.

McNair's men looked at him and he nodded for them to stand down. *This is ridiculous,* thought Diane. *They are acting like thugs.*

"I'll have to look inside all the other bags to make sure I get everything I need for my investigation," said McNair.

"Very well," said Diane. "The commissioner and Chief Garnett are here to sign as witnesses that the seals were broken on site when the evidence is challenged in court." Diane took a pen from her pocket and handed it to the commissioner.

"Sign?" he said. "Challenged in court, you say?"

"Yes, we all remember the O.J. trial and what happens when evidence is not handled according to strict protocol. We will need official witnesses as to who did what and when, and who authorized it, especially if the seals are to be broken for no legitimate forensic purpose in field conditions where evidence can be lost or contaminated."

Damn it, thought Diane, *if the commissioner is going to cave in, he is going to accept responsibility for the consequences.* Her statement had the desired effect. The commissioner didn't want his name on anything, and there was no graceful way to say he wasn't going to authorize the diversion from proper protocol.

"I think we can trust that Diane's crew know the difference between bone and other material," he told McNair. "It's what they do."

McNair scowled. It was a small thing, but from the look on his face, McNair wanted to win even the small battles.

Diane told Neva and David to bring out the bags of evidence containing nonhuman materials.

"I want to look at the labels on all the bags you don't hand over," McNair said.

"Don't be ridiculous," said Garnett. "The way you're acting, you'd think we aren't all on the same side. What possible reason could they have for withholding evidence? We have an agreement. My people will abide by it."

"I agree," said the commissioner.

David shot Diane a look that said, "Don't you think this is damn peculiar?"

Yes, she thought, *very peculiar.*

It took David and Neva more than half an hour to retrieve and log out all the bags they had so carefully packed in the van. Diane hated to see the carefully collected and recorded evidence go to McNair's custody. On the other hand, all he wanted was the glory, and he had many good people working for him. The evidence should be safe in their hands. He wouldn't be getting his hands dirty analyzing any of it. He didn't really know how.

"We'll be finishing up the fire scene, too," said McNair. "We'll box any bones we find and send them to you."

He turned, got in his truck with his friends, and sped away, throwing up slush on all of them, even on the commissioner's nice black topcoat.

"This is for the best," said the commissioner, brushing off his coat with a gloved hand. "He's rough around the edges and not very tactful, but the job will get done."

"That is our hope," said Garnett. "This is a high-profile event, and it will come back to bite all of us in the ass if McNair screws it up."

"He won't. I assure you, he won't." The commissioner sounded more hopeful than certain.

The commissioner got in his car with one quick look over his shoulder and drove away. *At least he didn't splatter us,* thought Diane.

"What just happened?" she asked.

"McNair's uncle got to the commissioner," said Garnett.

"Did you explain that it was McNair who was mishandling the evidence?"

"Yes, and the commissioner believed me. This is really not about logic or who's right; it's about politics," said Garnett. "We are just going to have to make the best of it. Do you have pictures?"

"Yes," said Diane.

"If McNair screws up and it becomes a public issue, we'll use them. If any perp gets off because of McNair, we'll certainly use them."

Diane was thoroughly pissed when she arrived at her apartment. She had made the short walk through the woods, trudging through snow over a foot deep in hopes that the walk would cool her down. It didn't. She took a shower, dressed in something decidedly nonforensic, and drove to the museum.

It was closed, but in times like these when she'd been ankle-deep in bodies and politicians, or just generally having a bad day, she drew peace from visiting and contemplating the exhibits in the museum. Sometimes it was the Egyptian room and the amulets that had been folded inside the mummy's wrappings; sometimes it was the rocks and gemstones; sometimes she walked among the giant dinosaur skeletons or sat and looked at the wall murals of dinosaurs with tiny fanciful unicorns the artist hid in all the paintings.

Her former boss, Gregory Lincoln, liked to look at Vermeer paintings when he was out in the field. Gregory carried postcard-sized representations of his favorites. He would look at the everyday scenes painted by Vermeer for hours—the love letter, woman with a water pitcher, the guitar player, the geographer. They seemed to put him in a meditative trance. Diane once asked what he was thinking when he looked at his pictures.

"I'm trying to figure out what's going on in them. What's the woman thinking about as she's handed the letter? What map is the geographer drawing, how many places has he been?"

Diane had adopted Gregory's habit of looking at beautiful art when she needed a break from a particularly grim assignment and had kept it up even after she gave up human rights investigations. Tonight the soothing shapes of the seashells held a particular appeal.

It would be a couple of hours before the low-level night lighting came on. Museum lighting is a science all its own. Because light is both destructive and necessary, she had staff whose only job was to tend to the peculiar needs of museum lighting. At night there's the bare minimum of lights, and most of them are low to the floor so no one trips over anything. It's good for the exhibits, but not good for viewing. She could of course override the day-to-night lighting change, but she would not do that simply for her own personal viewing.

The RiverTrail Museum of Natural History resided in a nineteenth-century three-story granite building. The interior decor contained ornate moldings, polished granite floors, wood paneling, brass fixtures, wall-sized murals of dinosaurs, and very large rooms.

Using her master key, she entered through the west-wing entrance where the Aquatic Animal section was located. The guard on duty at the information desk nodded a hello. Diane smiled at him. She cast a glance at a brachiosaurus in the dinosaur room in front of her before she turned left and walked straight to the seashell section.

Seashells are the houses and bones of mollusks—soft-bodied creatures that mostly inhabit aquatic environments. The museum had a fairly decent collection from among the more than fifty thousand possible varieties.

As in bones, if you know the code contained in seashells, you can read the history of the animal. The distinctive pattern of pigments laid down on a shell is governed mostly by DNA but is shaped by the experiences of the animal. Even among the members of the same variety, no two individuals have exactly the same pattern. A mollusk enlarges its shell along the edge, just like human bone growth at the epiphysis. On these growth edges the pigmentation pattern is laid down. Whatever happens to the mollusk—feast, famine, injury, temperature changes—has an effect and is recorded in the pattern. The mollusk wears its history on its back. A computer monitor in the shell room graphically illustrated the process, but Diane skipped that tonight. She'd seen it many times when it was being created.

She lingered a moment by the Humans and Shells exhibit to wonder at the cowrie shell necklaces from Africa, the mother-of-pearl jewelry, the carved conch shells loaned from the Archaeology Department depicting religious and ceremonial engravings of the southeastern Indians of the United States. There were display examples of kitschy souvenir shells from Florida. One of the prize specimens in this particular exhibit, acquired by Diane's assistant director, Kendel Williams, was a gilded saltshaker in the form of a rooster made from the shell of a chambered nautilus.

Just beyond the Humans and Shells exhibit was the Math of Seashells. Not a favorite with most visitors, but Diane liked it, as did all the math teachers in the area. They often brought classes on field trips to watch the video explanation of the mathematics of the spiraled chambered nautilus based on the Fibonacci sequence of numbers. The video went on to show that pinecones, sunflowers, spiral galaxies, movement of bees, and even the Parthenon contain the same mathematics. Teachers loved that. For those really into the math of seashells, there was a video of the algorithmic process involved in the laying down of the pattern. Not very popular, but Diane left it on the computer, anyway. The instructors of higher mathematics loved her for that.

The fossil shells were a favorite of visitors mainly because they loved looking at the spiral shells whose component minerals had been replaced by pyrite so that they looked like pure gold. But these weren't Diane's favorites.

What she liked best were simply the shells themselves, the spiky, shiny, swirling, spiraling, multicolored unaltered seashells. There was something very calming about just looking at them—much like the joy of looking at the Vermeers.

She was looking in wonder at the details of a particularly lovely pelican shell when she heard raised voices coming from the aquatic lab.

Chapter 15

The door to the aquatic lab was ajar and Diane moved toward the opening. Only one of the voices was doing the shouting. Diane recognized it as belonging to the new aquatic collections manager, Whitney Lester.

"I know you stole the shells. It will be easier on both of us if you just admit it now."

Diane didn't hear the answer, only a soft murmur.

"I'm tired of wasting my time with you. You are going to lose your job. That's certain. Whether or not it goes to the police is up to you. Where are the damn shells? I'm not going to have valuable articles go missing on my watch, do you hear?"

Diane walked into the lab and found Lester glowering over Juliet Price. Lester had backed her up against a table. Juliet looked terrified.

"I'm sick of your mousy ways. Tell me, damn it!" yelled Lester.

"What's going on?" said Diane, in a voice she hoped was calm.

Whitney looked in Diane's direction with the same angry look she was giving Juliet, ready to light into whoever was interrupting her. Her expression turned to surprise, then an attempt at a smile.

"Dr. Fallon, I didn't hear you come in."

How could you with all your yelling, thought Diane. "What's going on?" she repeated.

"Miss Price stole several valuable shells from the collection. I'm trying to persuade her to give them back."

Diane looked at Juliet Price. Her arms were folded over her stomach and she was bent over. Her blond hair swung forward and hid her face.

"Dr. Price, are you all right?" asked Diane.

"She's fine. She's a malingerer."

Diane ignored Whitney. "Juliet, are you all right?" Diane walked toward her and guided her to a chair.

"I didn't steal the shells," she whispered. "I need this job."

Diane heard a snort from Whitney. "You should have thought of that. . . ."

"Enough," said Diane. "Juliet, you aren't going to lose your job. Sit right here and try to stay calm. I'll be right back."

"Mrs. Lester, in the office, now," said Diane.

Whitney Lester looked as if she'd been hit between the eyes. "You're not going to leave her out here?"

"Now, Mrs. Lester." Diane preceded her into the collection manager's office and sat down behind her desk.

Whitney Lester followed and stood for several seconds as if waiting for Diane to get up from her desk. After a moment she sat in a chair in front of the desk, smoothing her brown suede skirt under her. She sat up straight and arranged her face to show her serious disapproval—or at least that's what it seemed to Diane as she watched the movements of Lester's expression go from surprise, to puzzlement, to a stern demeanor. She reached up once to smooth her salt-and-pepper hair.

"What's this about?" asked Diane.

"Juliet stole some valuable shells. I'm trying to get them back." She puffed up her chest, looking very righteous.

"What's missing?" asked Diane.

Whitney straightened up again, looking more confident. "A *Conus gloriamaris,* seven inches long and worth four thousand dollars. Eight *Cypraea aurantium,* three hundred dollars apiece." She ticked off each item on her fingers, hitting each finger firmly and bending it back as if that lent greater emphasis to the loss. "A giant whelk worth two hundred fifty dollars. That's over six thousand dollars worth of shells."

"Have you informed Security?"

"No, I like to handle things in my own department," she said.

"Did you see Dr. Price take them?" asked Diane.

"No, but she is the only one who could have. They were here last week in the vault. I saw them. Now they're gone. She's here practically all the time and the only one who has access to the vault."

"So you were browbeating her. Couldn't you see she is terrified?"

"Yes, I could see that. I was trying to get a confession. You, of all people, should appreciate that."

"This isn't a police interrogation room, nor is Dr. Price some perp you pulled in off the street. She's an employee of this museum, and no employee here will be bullied. I hope that's clear."

"My management style . . . ," began Whitney.

"Is not acceptable," interrupted Diane.

Whitney looked back through the open door as if to see if Juliet Price was listening. Diane could see Juliet sitting there where they left her, still holding her folded arms to her midsection. Diane was sure she was listening to every word. But it apparently was not giving her comfort. Juliet was one of the few employees that she had not had either lunch or dinner with— mainly because Juliet kept putting it off for one reason or another.

Diane remembered interviewing her for the job. She was dressed in a conservative dark tweed suit and had her light blond hair pulled back into a French twist.

It was one of the few times that she had seen her face. Her pale hair and skin and sky blue eyes gave her an ethereal appearance—almost like an angel. Had she chosen to flaunt it, she could have men hanging around her all the time. As it was, she was almost invisible. Juliet spent a lot of time hiding.

Diane and Kendel almost hadn't hired her, her shyness was so extreme. But in the end, her expert knowledge of marine life, and of mollusks in particular, proved to be the deciding factor. In reality, she was overqualified for her position. With her Ph.D. in marine biology she could be on a curator's track. But she wanted to work cataloging shells and putting together learning kits for the schools—which was mainly solitary work. Hiring her had been a good deal for the museum.

Until now there had been only one other puzzling event. When Juliet came to work, Andie put together a gift basket as she did for all the new employees. Andie liked to create the baskets with the theme of the new employee's expertise. In Juliet's case it was oceans and shells. The basket was filled with tropical fruit, shell-shaped chocolates, canned oysters, colorful seashells, and as a centerpiece, the mermaid Ariel from the Disney animation, all amid blue green celluloid grass and artificial plants that looked like seaweed. It was a beautiful basket. Andie had it sitting on Juliet's desk when she arrived. The gift didn't have the desired effect. Juliet saw it, screamed, and almost fainted.

Juliet had been mortified by her reaction. Kendel reassured her, telling her that on her first day she herself had screamed loud enough to wake the dead and scare the employees up to the third floor. Of course, Kendel screamed because she found a rather large adult snake coiled up in her desk drawer. The thing that sparked Juliet's fear had been a gift basket.

Andie felt guilty, everyone else was simply puzzled,

and Diane was left wondering if perhaps Juliet had a stalker who had been leaving her unwanted gifts. She asked Juliet if that was why she wanted a very low-profile job. Juliet assured Diane that was not the case, but her only explanation was that she was afraid of new dolls. Not a particularly satisfactory explanation. Which was probably why, thought Diane, she avoided having lunch with her.

Whitney Lester sat stiffly in the chair. It was a plain un-upholstered wooden chair and looked very uncomfortable. Diane wondered if she chose it because normally she wouldn't be sitting in it, but her staff would. *Then maybe, I'm reading too much into a chair,* thought Diane.

"My management was always effective in my previous positions," said Lester, her chin raised, ready to defend herself.

"Bullying is not the culture we promote in this museum."

Whitney Lester stood her ground. "The shells are gone. Everyone else in this department is off on that ship." She said it as if marine biologists are foolish to go off on a research ship. "Who else could have stolen them?"

"You," said Diane.

That stopped her cold. She sucked in her breath. Her eyes widened until Diane could see the whites all the way around her iris.

"Me? Me?" she sputtered.

"By your own admission, you were the last person to see them in the vault. You know the exact value of each item. You haven't gone to Security; instead you wanted to keep it quiet. And you weren't exactly telling the truth when you told me that Juliet is the only one who has access to the vault. You do."

"But I didn't," she said, her knuckles were white, gripping the arms of the chair.

"I don't know that," said Diane. "Accusing Juliet Price could be an elaborate ruse to deflect suspicion from yourself."

"You can't accuse *me,*" she said, emphasizing the word *me* as if she should be, like Caesar's wife, above reproach.

"Yet you accuse Dr. Price on fewer grounds than I just presented to you."

"I'm the collection manager. It's my job to know all the collection. That's why I know their value."

"And it's Dr. Price's job to be here working and have access to the vault as she needs it."

"But I *know* I didn't take the shells," Lester insisted.

"Dr. Price says she knows she didn't," countered Diane.

"This isn't right," Lester said finally.

"No, it isn't right, and neither is it right to accuse and browbeat Juliet Price. Here's what is going to happen. I am going to report the theft to Security and let them handle it. You are going to get me photographs of the missing items to give to them. They will question everyone. It doesn't mean any specific person is under suspicion. And I'm telling Andie to sign you up for a management class. They will teach you the style that we use here in the museum."

"Management class?"

"Yes. You may not buy into our philosophy here, but you will abide by it. Now, I need those photographs."

Whitney Lester stood up, looking like she wasn't sure what to do, as if obedience was defeat. Diane felt a twinge of guilt for being so hard on her, but she had been looking forward to a peaceful time amid the shell collection, and Whitney Lester had ruined it.

Diane stood and went back out to Juliet Price who wasn't bent over holding her stomach anymore. She was standing, smoothing out her gray corduroy jumper, trying not to look in either Diane's or Whitney Lester's direction. Diane walked over to her.

"Your job is safe. The security people will talk to you, so try and remember what you can about the missing items," Diane told her.

She nodded. "Yes, ma'am."

"Have you had anything to eat?"

Juliet shook her head.

"Then we'll go to the restaurant and have our oft postponed dinner."

Chapter 16

The museum restaurant had the look of a medieval monastery or ancient library with its maze of tall old-brick arches and vaulted ceilings. Four archways at right angles to each other made small chamberlike spaces throughout the restaurant. The spaces were furnished with dark rough-hewn wood tables and large padded wood chairs. The walls of the restaurant were lined with booths inside arched brick alcoves. Diane preferred the privacy of the booths. Apparently, so did Juliet.

Diane could tell by Juliet Price's demeanor that their presence in the restaurant was pushing Juliet out of her comfort zone. She said nothing, and her gaze darted around the room as if looking for some unknown thing. She scooted into the booth, looking dwarfed by the high-backed wooden bench. The dark interior and candlelight gave her an even more ethereal look. Diane would not have been surprised if she just suddenly faded away.

"I have lunch or dinner with each of the employees of the museum to try to get to know them a little better. We're long overdue. This is not meant to be a punishment or an opportunity for me to scrutinize you. I just like to know the people who work at the museum. So, tell me about yourself."

Juliet nibbled on a bread stick. "There's not much to tell. I've mostly led a very quiet life."

"Well, start with what you would like to eat. The waitress will be coming back soon," said Diane.

They looked at their menus, but Diane knew what she wanted. This late in the day she selected a vegetarian plate with portobello mushrooms, cheese, and tomatoes, and a fruit salad.

"That sounds good. I'll have the same thing," said Juliet when Diane ordered.

Diane made an effort to engage Juliet in conversation but was having little success. Juliet fingered her napkin as they waited for the food and looked like she'd rather be reamed out by Whitney Lester than eat dinner with Diane.

"I hope you are not worried about your job," said Diane.

Juliet looked up from her napkin and Diane was startled by the clarity of her piercing blue eyes. There was someone in there after all.

"Why did you believe me when I said I didn't steal the seashells?"

It was a fair question. Diane did tell her point-blank that her job was safe. Why had she said that?

"Usually, stealing on such a scale takes a bit of daring. You don't seem to be a person who takes any kind of risk."

Juliet gave a wisp of a smile. "No. I suppose I'm not. I'm a coward and I'm afraid of silly things."

Diane thought of the incident with the gift basket. Yes, that seemed to be a silly thing. She wondered what was behind it.

"Almost everyone has a fear that others might think of as silly."

"I seem to have a lot of them. They make no sense. Even I realize that. I'm afraid of new dolls, and I don't know why. I'm afraid of certain words—I see them written down or hear them spoken and they strike dread in me. That's why this job is so important to me. With so many neuroses, I need to work at something solitary. Creating educational kits and cataloging seashells is perfect."

"Have you seen a professional about your fears?" asked Diane.

"Yes. In college. They weren't very much help."

"I'm sorry," said Diane, "this is very personal and I didn't mean to force you to share that kind of information. What do you do for fun? You do have fun, don't you?"

Juliet was thoughtful for a moment. "No, I really don't." She shrugged. "I like to read."

"What do you like to read?" asked Diane.

"Biographies of historical figures. I'm reading Dumas Malone's biography of Thomas Jefferson at the moment."

Diane raised her eyebrows. "Which volume are you on?"

"*The Sage of Monticello.* Have you read them?"

"No," said Diane. "I've read about them. I read a lot of science fiction."

"Really. I also like historical romances." She smiled at the admission of a guilty pleasure.

Diane thought it was a very rare dropping of her guard.

The waitress brought their food and they ate for several minutes without saying anything. Diane felt lucky to have gotten this much out of her.

"I like working here," said Juliet. "I know I'm a little strange, but academic settings are perfect for people who are a little strange."

Diane grinned. She agreed. "I think there is a little strangeness in all of us. I like to go caving. Most people find that very strange, especially the guy I date."

"I've heard about your caving. I confess, I can't imagine going caving."

"Most people can't. But I find caves to be absolutely beautiful mysterious worlds."

"The geology curator also explores caves, doesn't he?" she said.

"Yes. He's one of my caving partners. The caving club meets here in the museum once a month, if you'd ever like to drop in. You aren't obligated to go caving. You could talk to the group about fossil seashells. We usually have some kind of educational program at the meetings."

Diane talked a long time about the caves she'd explored. She told Juliet about Mike's—the curator of the geology collection—extremophiles research. Their conversation was awkward and a little strained and certainly one-sided, but Diane felt it was probably normal for Juliet.

"They have terrific chocolate cake here," said Diane.

The waitress came and Diane ordered a piece. So did Juliet.

"I like chocolate," said Juliet. "The chocolate shaped shells in the gift basket were wonderful. I was going to buy some more but then I found out that Andie made them herself."

Diane didn't mention the gift basket event—and Juliet's screaming terror over a mermaid doll. Some things were better left unmentioned. But she was curious.

"I know Darcy Kincaid a little," said Juliet. "She's working on another exhibit for the shells. She thinks the fossil shell exhibit can stand some improving. I hope she's going to be all right."

"So do I," said Diane.

"Do you know how she's doing?"

"The doctors don't know anything yet. Maybe tomorrow."

"Darcy has lots of plans—graduate school, getting her boyfriend to propose. I've met him, too. He's a charming guy," she said.

The way she said *charming,* Diane wondered if she meant just the opposite. But there was nothing in her clear blue eyes that suggested that she meant anything other than what she said.

Dessert came—a moist triple layer chocolate cake with chunks of chocolate chips and iced with fudge frosting. Juliet raised her brow after she took her first bite.

"This is delicious."

The waitress refilled their coffee. As Juliet raised the cup to her lips, the sleeve of her sweater slipped up enough for Diane to notice several scars on her arm. She wondered if Juliet was a cutter. At the end of dessert, Diane took a card out of her purse.

"I don't intend to interfere in your business, and this is the only time I'll mention it. I have a friend. Her name is Laura Hillard and she is a psychiatrist. If you ever want to talk to her, even if it is just to learn coping strategies to deal with people like Whitney Lester, give her a call. She won't report to me, and I won't ask you if you called her. This is just for your information if you need it." Diane put the card on the table and pushed it forward.

Juliet picked up the card and turned it over in her hand. She stared at it for a long time before she spoke.

"I've been having dreams again," she said, still staring at the card. "They stopped for several years and now they've started again. That's why I couldn't cope with Ms. Lester tonight." She looked up at Diane. "I don't remember much about my early childhood. I only know what I've been told and what I looked up in the newspapers. I was kidnapped when I was seven and left for dead in a culvert. I think all my problems stem from that—even if I don't remember it." She put the card in her purse.

Diane was stunned. It was several moments before she could speak. "Juliet," she said finally, "I don't know what to say. Was your kidnapper caught?"

Juliet shook her head. "No."

"You only saw a therapist in college? Not sooner?"

"Since I couldn't remember, my parents didn't want the memories dredged up. They thought it best if the experience remained buried. My mother died a year later and my father remarried. My father and my grandmother told me I had nightmares because I felt guilty for being disobedient and 'got myself snatched,' as my grandmother used to say. She told me that if I was obedient, the dreams would stop. My stepmother thought the cure was summer camp. A benign cure, but I was never able to pull off being a happy camper."

No wonder she's skittish and prefers solitude, thought Diane. *I would be too if I had been through that as a child.* The knowledge made Whitney Lester's behavior all the more appalling.

"I'm sorry," said Diane. "Life must be very difficult for you. If I can help, I will."

"You gave me a job. Do you know how many times I lost jobs in the interview stage? That's why this job is so important to me. I'd never jeopardize it by stealing. I've never stolen anything. I'm not a thief."

Diane was glad they had dinner. It helped her understand a lot of things about Juliet. She offered her a lift home, but Juliet said she drove to the museum and her car was parked in the lot. Diane left a tip on the table and the two of them walked out together. The hostess nodded to Diane on the way out. She knew to send the tab to Diane's office. Diane found that arrangement easier than arguing with the few guests who insisted on paying their own way. The matter was a nonissue if they weren't presented with a bill.

The restaurant was about to close and there were few cars in the parking lot. Diane noticed that one of the streetlights was out. It was the one near her car. She stopped, wary. Juliet apparently sensed the change in Diane's demeanor, for she slowed and stiffened. Diane reached for Juliet's arm.

"Let's go back in," she whispered.

Juliet didn't ask why, she turned on her heel, but as Diane reached for her phone to speed dial the security desk in the museum she saw a man stand up from behind her car. He had a baseball bat and he was walking toward her. Diane turned to run, but another man was coming up behind. Juliet gave a cry and sank to the ground.

Chapter 17

Diane wanted to run—she thought she could make it to the museum—but she couldn't leave Juliet crumpled on the ground. She hurriedly dialed museum Security as the men approached. She frantically tried to think of some defense. As with Blake Stanton, the young carjacker with the gun, she had only words with which to defend herself. These men weren't going to be as easy as Blake was.

"Stop where you are and back off," she said.

She must have sounded pathetic to the huge men wielding baseball bats. Her thumb pressed the keys on her phone and she heard Security answer. As she brought it to her mouth she yelled.

"Front parking lot now!"

The men advanced, bats ready to strike. Before they got to her, the headlights from an approaching car shone on all of them. The two men stopped for only a moment; then one started to take a swing at Diane. She ducked when the car's siren blasted and the blue light flashed. It was a police car. *Thank God,* she thought, as the men took off running across the parking lot, the police car in pursuit. Just then three of her security guards came running out of the building, their hands on their guns ready to pull.

"We need to help Dr. Price inside," said Diane

when they reached her. She and one of the security guards helped Juliet to her feet.

"I'm sorry," Juliet whispered.

"It's all right," said Diane.

As she spoke, she watched the police car cut one of the runners off so that he slammed into the side of the car. The other man ran past the car and into the woods.

With the help of a guard, and flanked by the two other guards, Diane helped Juliet inside.

"Thanks for coming so fast," said Diane when they were safely inside the building.

"Sure thing, Dr. Fallon. What was that about?"

"I don't know. Can you take Dr. Price to my office and let her lie down on my sofa? And get her some water, or whatever she wants from my fridge."

The security guard nodded and walked with Juliet across the granite foyer and through the double doors that led to the offices. The other two guards stayed with Diane.

"Go outside and see that the restaurant personnel and patrons get to their cars safely. Don't make an issue of it. Just keep an eye out. Call for someone to keep a lookout on the terrace side of the restaurant."

"Yes, ma'am." As the two guards left the museum to go to the parking lot, one was on his radio.

Diane had a feeling that the men with the bats were after her, though she didn't know why, except that she was the intended target of all the other attacks that took place at the museum. Better her as the target, she thought, than the patrons. Who would want to send their kids to a museum targeted by gangs wielding baseball bats?

Diane watched the activity at the police car from the doorway. She wanted to walk over to them and find out who the hell the guy was, but she would just be a distraction. She suddenly wondered what the police car was doing here in the first place. Had someone called them? Were there other problems she didn't know about?

For whatever reason, the police were there and she was glad of it. It was clear that one guy would have gotten off at least one blow before her security people reached her.

She saw another patrol car join the first one and watched as they transferred the prisoner. The perpetrator looked to be about six feet and heavyset. The police had removed his ski mask, but she couldn't see his face.

Two policemen from the first car, her rescuers, were walking toward the museum. When they were near enough, she recognized Archie from the morgue tent and Izzy Wallace.

Dear God, she thought. *Izzy wants to talk about his son.*

Diane opened the door wide for them. "Thank God you were here," she said as they entered the museum.

"We got one of the guys," said Archie. "You OK?"

"Yes. I'm fine. I wouldn't be if it weren't for the two of you. They were about to do us some real harm, and they really frightened one of my employees."

"I need to talk with you," said Izzy.

He'd taken his hat off and he held it in his hand. Diane thought of the phrase "hat in hand." It seemed to fit. Izzy wasn't someone she got along with, but now he needed something. Something she wasn't sure she would be able to give.

"Dr. Price is in my office. Let's step into the Security office and talk there," said Diane. They nodded.

Diane led them through the same double doors that Juliet and the guard had gone through, but Diane headed to Security instead of the Personnel offices. There was a small refrigerator in the office, and she got the three of them bottled water.

"My boy," said Izzy, "could you have made a mistake?" He looked at Diane with eyes that pleaded with her to tell him it was a mistake.

"How . . . ," began Diane.

"It wasn't Archie," said Izzy hurriedly. "It was someone else. Is it true?"

"We need to have the DNA results to know for sure," said Diane. "Right now, we just have the x-rays."

"But you could have made a mistake in reading the x-rays," he said hopefully.

"Yes, I could have. Dr. Rankin, Dr. Webber, and Dr. Pilgrim also read the x-rays separately, and we all reached the same conclusion."

Izzy groaned.

"We all could be wrong. X-rays are not absolute. That's why we're trying for DNA."

Izzy shook his head back and forth. "I'd hoped you were wrong. I told Evie you were wrong. But . . . we don't know where Daniel is. We can't find him anywhere and it's not like him to just . . . We've looked everywhere. The library, the Student Learning Center, his friends, parks, the movies, the mall."

Izzy Wallace put his head in his hands. Diane felt sick at heart. Hers and Archie's gazes met, and she could see he felt the same helpless sick feeling. Izzy raised his head.

"Daniel's a good student. He's a good boy. He's going places, not like me. He's smart, always gets As in school. He's not a drug user. I'd know. I can tell a drug user."

"I know," said Diane. "I doubt if many of the kids there were."

"This is killing Evie. I don't know what we are going to do. Daniel is our only child."

Diane wanted to cry. She could see Archie did, too. How was Rosewood ever going to heal from this?

"Why couldn't they get out?" said Izzy.

"What?" said Diane.

"Of the house. Why couldn't they get out? Why didn't more of them get out?"

"I'm not sure," said Diane. "I think that the explosion . . ." She trailed off. "I'm not sure."

Izzy uncapped the water and took a sip. The three of them sat there for several minutes, saying nothing. Diane wished she could make this go away. It seemed like an eternity since she was awakened in the middle of the night to the sight of the fire reflected in her photograph of the chambered nautilus.

"Thanks for seeing me. I just . . ." He fidgeted with his hat. "I just wanted . . ." His lower lip trembled. "I just wanted you to tell me you made a mistake." He put his head in his hands again and sobbed.

"Did he suffer?" he said at last.

"No," said Diane. She laid a hand on his. "But Izzy, until the DNA comes back . . . We aren't a hundred percent certain it's Daniel."

"I know. But where is he? Why can't we find him?"

When Izzy and Archie left, Diane wanted to sit down and have a good cry. Instead, she took a deep breath and walked to her office to see how Juliet Price was. This ought to have set her back, thought Diane. If she wasn't already having nightmares, this day should surely bring them on.

Juliet, drinking from a bottle of orange juice, was sitting on the stuffed red sofa in Diane's office. The guard was sitting in the easy chair. He looked up, relief evident in his face. Diane guessed he had been trying to engage Juliet in conversation. Diane thanked him. He eagerly got up, nodded a good-bye to Juliet, and left.

Juliet set down her drink, looked at her hands a moment, and twisted her ring, an aquamarine in a gold setting. "I—I'm sorry. I disappeared on you when we were in real trouble. I'm sorry."

What an odd way of putting it, thought Diane as she pulled up a chair and sat across from Juliet.

"There was nothing you could have done. We were lucky the police and my security came when they did. This was not your fault."

She looked up at Diane, her ice blue eyes swimming in tears. "I'm useless. I just disappear when things get hard."

Diane noticed blood seeping through the fabric on the arm of Juliet's shirt.

Chapter 18

"Were you hurt?" Diane reached over to look at her arm.

Juliet pulled it back. "It's nothing."

"Did you cut yourself?" asked Diane. Juliet was silent. "Dr. Price." Diane used her title and a firm voice. "Let me help you. It looks like you need it."

"There is no help," she whispered. "I've tried."

"What if there is help to be had? Isn't it worth it to try again?"

"I'm sorry I deserted you."

"You didn't desert me. You were faced with maniacs with bats. Half the people in the museum would have collapsed in the face of that. I'm concerned about your cutting yourself. That is what you're doing, isn't it?"

Diane saw that the door to the bathroom was open. She usually left it closed. She guessed that Juliet had cut herself when she came in from the episode in the parking lot. Some kind of strange coping strategy that Diane didn't understand.

Juliet was rubbing her hands, as if washing them, almost wringing them. Her face looked panicked.

"I know that seems strange, but I have to."

"Doesn't it hurt?" asked Diane.

"Now it does. That's the point. It doesn't at first. It's as though I'm disappearing—I can't even feel anything. The cutting brings back the feeling. It anchors me back to the ground. Without it, I'll just fade away."

Odd, thought Diane. Fading away was the way she saw Juliet.

"I said it was not my intention to mind your business, but I feel like you're in this current situation because of me."

"You? How?" asked Juliet.

"The men were more than likely after me, and you were just an innocent bystander."

"Really?" She seemed surprised.

Diane wondered why. Did Juliet see everything as her fault?

"Yes, and I'm sorry. However, since I have a responsibility, I feel like I need to urge you to see someone. It doesn't have to be Laura, and your job doesn't depend on it. But for your own sense of self, give it a try."

Juliet nodded, but Diane wasn't sure she was even listening.

"Maybe," she whispered.

"That's good enough," said Diane. "Now let me drive you home."

"I can drive. I'm here now. I'm fine."

"I'll have the guards walk us out."

"I'll agree to that."

It was good for Diane to be home in her own apartment. "I need a vacation," she said to herself as she stripped off her clothes and got into the shower.

After a long shower, she slipped on a nightshirt and got into bed, hoping for no midnight phone calls or explosions. She fell asleep wishing Frank were here in bed with her.

It was her clock that awoke her and not the phone. Diane thought that was a good sign. She breakfasted on peanut butter on raisin bread and an apple and dashed off to the museum. As she was getting in the car, she looked through the woods at the tent city being disassembled. She was glad to be working in her own lab from now on. She got in the car and drove off.

After Diane checked in with Andie, she went straight to the Security office. Chanell Napier, her head of Security, was on duty.

"They tell me we had some excitement last night," said Chanell. "Are you all right, Dr. Fallon?"

"I'm fine, Chanell. Have you found out anything?"

"The police caught the second guy. They have them both downtown. I expect they'll let us know what it was about when they find out. You know how Chief Garnett hates anything to happen to the museum."

Diane did. He hated anything that might make Diane rethink her arrangement with Rosewood about having a crime lab in a wing of the museum. He and the mayor had promised that the crime lab wouldn't attract anything dangerous to the museum. They hadn't been able to keep that promise, but Garnett certainly tried.

"Keep your ears open," said Diane. "Find out if anyone else has had any problems at all going to their cars. But I actually came here on another matter. Aquatic Animals have had several valuable seashells stolen." Diane handed her the folder that Whitney Lester had given her.

"Here are pictures of the seashells. There is a sheet with the value in there, too. I think the theft amounts to over six thousand dollars."

Chanell shook her head. "Not another one. I'm sorry to hear that."

"What do you mean?" asked Diane.

"Other departments have had losses. Always rare items and always small items."

"Why didn't I know about this?" asked Diane.

"Most of the complaints have come in just recently while you were at the explosion site. The collection managers just now noticed things missing. In some cases, less valuable items were substituted for the real ones, and it took a while to discover the difference."

"What's been stolen?" asked Diane, horrified that systematic theft was happening in the museum.

"Just yesterday, the Geology manager said three gem quality stones are missing, including a diamond donated by Vanessa Van Ross."

"Oh, no, not her ten-thousand-dollar diamond."

"I'm afraid so. They also have two valuable geodes missing. Entomology reported that a rare"—Chanell got a folder from her desk and opened it—"*Boloria improba acrocnema* is missing." She pronounced the name syllable by syllable. "That's a butterfly. The curator said it's worth about seven hundred dollars."

"Anything else?"

"Paleontology reported fossils missing, including dinosaur eggs." She waved a sheet with a list of items. "We don't know the value yet, but right now we may be looking at about thirty thousand dollars worth of missing items."

"What's being done to get to the bottom of it?"

"I'm reviewing the videotapes. So far nothing stands out. The problem is we don't have a specific time for any of the thefts. I've asked all the departments to tell me, as best they can, exactly when was the last time anyone can confirm that the missing items were still here. I've been in touch with the GBI and the FBI. Right now the value is not enough for them to sit up and take a lot of notice. But they are helping me look at collectors who are known to buy stolen property. I've asked all the departments to go over their inventory. That's how Geology discovered the gemstones. The collection manager is beside herself. Someone put fake gems in place of the real ones so no one would notice anything was missing. She said Mike was going to be furious when he gets back from wherever he is."

"He's searching for extremophiles in caves in Brazil."

"Lord have mercy . . . whatever that is. It's an education every time I talk to one of these curators."

Diane smiled. "Has Archaeology suffered any losses? They have some valuable artifacts."

"I asked Jonas Briggs. He said no. I think he was a little offended." She grinned. "But you know him."

"Keep on this," she said. "Keep me informed of all developments."

"We will, Dr. Fallon. We've been talking with Dr. Williams while you've been working on those poor students' remains. That whole business is just simply awful."

"Yes, it is. It's caused a lot of profound grief. It's going to take a long time to recover—if ever. You don't really recover from the loss of a child."

"No, ma'am, you don't."

Diane called Kendel Williams and asked her to meet her in front of Aquatics. She left Security, which was in the east wing, and walked to Aquatic Animals, which was in the west wing. On the way she passed the museum store and she wondered if they had had anything stolen. She stepped into the store and asked the manager. She was putting Dora the Explorer dolls on the shelf.

"Stolen?" She ran a hand through her platinum hair and shook her head. "No. Not here. We occasionally get someone trying to shoplift, but the detector always catches them."

"Let Security know if anything turns up missing."

"Of course."

On her way out of the shop she met Kendel.

"What's up?" Kendel asked.

"Some personnel business. I need a witness. I think she's going to be a problem and I'm just being cautious."

Kendel's fine brown hair was in a smooth French

twist today. Different from the usual turned under,
shoulder length do. Her brown eyes and soft voice
fooled a lot of people when they met her. She could
negotiate for museum items with the best, and was
hard-nosed about it. She had acquired several nice
pieces for RiverTrail. Diane was glad to have her as
assistant director.

"Troublesome. That would be Whitney Lester,"
said Kendel.

Diane and Kendel continued on to Aquatics just
across the west-wing foyer. The museum hadn't
opened yet, so there was no one among the exhibits.
They passed the shells, and Diane lingered a moment
at a few of them before she went into the lab.

Juliet was there working on the educational kits. All
the kits were popular with teachers. Juliet and her
counterparts from different departments put together
examples of shells, or rocks, or fossils, whatever the
subject was, into a box, along with lesson plans, activities, and educational material. They couldn't keep
enough in stock, even though the kits were not for
keeping but for checking out and returning to the museum. Several schools in the area designed their science classes around the kits.

"Hello, Juliet, how are you this morning?" asked
Diane.

Juliet looked up, startled. "Oh, fine. I'm fine.
Really." She smiled at Kendel, tugged at her long
sleeves, and went back to work.

"Is Mrs. Lester in?"

Juliet nodded without looking up. "Yes. She's been
in about an hour talking on the phone." Juliet bit her
lip. "You should gird your loins."

"Thanks for the tip." Diane knocked on the door.

"Juliet, I'm busy. I told you when I arrived that I
don't want to be disturbed. I meant it."

Diane exchanged glances with Kendel and knocked
on the door louder.

Chapter 19

"Damn it, Juliet. . . ." The door swung open and Diane and Kendel came nose-to-nose with a red-faced Whitney Lester. "Dr. Fallon. Dr. Williams. I didn't realize. . . . Actually, I'm glad it's you. I need to talk to you."

"Then we have mutual needs," said Diane.

She entered and closed the door behind her. Diane and Kendel sat in the two chairs in front of the desk.

Diane took an index card from her pocket and handed it to Mrs. Lester. "Andie wrote down several dates and times for the management class."

"That is what I wanted to speak with you about." Whitney Lester laced her fingers in front of her. "I've talked with the state Human Resources Department to find out what my rights are."

She paused, Diane supposed to let the weight of her words sink in.

"They tell me you can't force me to take classes that I don't want or need."

"No, I can't. However, I can release you from your job," said Diane.

"They say you can't." Whitney folded her arms across her chest.

"If you want to make this a case of your lawyer versus the museum's lawyers, that's your prerogative and I won't even try to talk you out of it. I don't know, of course, how you presented your claim to Human Resources, but if I find that you aren't able to do your job according to the standards laid out in your contract and in the museum's handbook, I have an obligation to inform you of your shortcomings and provide a way to remedy your deficits. You of course can refuse. I can then let you go."

"This course"—she flipped the card so that it slid across her desk, stopping near the edge—"has nothing to do with my knowledge of marine life and my ability to keep track of the collection."

"On the contrary. First, part of your job is to manage staff, not just inanimate objects. As for the inanimate objects that you manage, had you gone to Security with the information of the theft, you would have discovered that almost all of the departments have had recent thefts similar to yours. It was your management style that stopped you from doing that and therefore stopped you from taking more effective action to manage the collection. As it is, Security was delayed getting the information. Time is an important element in recovering stolen items. Security has been looking for the stolen items. They didn't know to include the seashells."

Whitney Lester's mouth sagged. The defiant glint in her gray eyes went out. She looked defeated. Diane imagined the news of the other thefts was an unexpected blow to her carefully constructed scenario of how she had been wronged.

"Other departments have had items stolen?" she asked in a low voice.

"Yes, and Dr. Price is not a suspect in any of them," said Diane. "I can't force you to go to these classes. But despite what the person at Human Resources told you, I can and will let you go if you refuse."

Kendel sat relaxed in the chair with her legs crossed. She always managed to look elegant. Diane envied her for that. She also knew that was part of Kendel's presentation when she negotiated—looking relaxed before she pounced. Kendel reminded Diane of a lion. Here, however, Kendel was a witness; pouncing wasn't part of the task. Diane imagined she was content to watch. Kendel kept a pleasant smile on her face as if Diane were discussing the acquisition of a new collection of shells with Whitney.

Diane stood and Kendel stood with her. Whitney remained seated. "I guess I have no choice," she said.

"We all have choices," said Diane. "And we all must accept the consequences of our choices. This is not meant to be a punishment." She and Kendel left Whitney in her office, furious, from the look on her face. Juliet, still looking like she was about to fade into the ether, was working with a tray of *Turridae*.

"Thanks for witnessing, Kendel," said Diane when they were out of Aquatics.

"No problem." Kendel walked with Diane until they reached one of the stairwells. Kendel nearly always used the stairs. "I have to visit the Preparation Department," she said as she started to mount the stairs. "I think that went well. However, I would have hurt her and wouldn't have had witnesses." Kendel smiled, turned and walked up the stairs.

Diane laughed and shook her head. She took the elevator to the third floor and crossed over to the wing where the crime lab was located.

David, Jin, and Neva, sipping freshly brewed coffee, were sitting at the round corner table.

"We were just discussing McNair," said David. "What is that guy about?"

"Glory, control, following his uncle's agenda," said Diane, pouring herself a cup of coffee. "This current fiasco is about the coming election. We haven't had a crime this high profile and McNair and company want credit for bringing justice to all the families who also happen to vote in Rosewood."

"It's always politics," said Jin. "Who was it who said kill the politicians?"

"I think it was Shakespeare," said David. "And it was lawyers."

"Yeah, well, I guess I'll take lawyers over politicians," said Jin.

"How about my car?" asked Diane. "Have you had a chance to process it?"

"All done and locked in the vault," said Neva. "When he goes to trial, all the information will be there. What do you want done with your car?"

"I suppose I'll trade it again. I tell you, the guys at the Ford place must be wondering what kind of life I lead."

"Speaking of that," said David. "Did something happen last night? I've heard the security guards talking about guys with baseball bats lurking in the parking lot, and something about you and another person. What was that about?"

Diane explained briefly about the incident in the parking lot.

"So," said Jin, "you can tell the car dealer that this was a separate incident from the one that damaged your car."

"I do seem to attract maniacs," said Diane.

"Are you all right? You said the police came in time?"

"Yes. It ended well and I hear the police caught both guys. I'm just hoping that it's not something directed at the museum."

"I see," said David. "Just you."

"What about the other person?" said Jin. "Could it have been about her?"

"I don't think so. Maybe the police will have some news. I'll call them a little later."

The private crime lab elevator doors opened and Chief Garnett walked out. They watched him walk down the narrow hall past the glassed-in work areas of the crime lab to reach them on the other side. He sat down at the table, nodding at Diane's staff.

"What brings you here?" asked Diane. She got up, poured a cup of coffee, and brought it to the table for Garnett. She passed the cup of black coffee over to him.

Garnett's dark hair looked like it had more gray in it. His eyes had weary lines at the corners that she hadn't noticed before. But maybe it was her imagination.

"Several things." He picked up the coffee and took a sip. "Hot. That's nice. It's cold outside. First, I wanted to find out how the explosion analysis is going."

"You're joking, right?" said Diane. "You know we don't have the evidence."

"I mean the remains. That's really the most important. That's what everyone is interested in."

"As the MEs have probably told you, all the intact bodies have been identified. On some of the remains we are waiting on the DNA. Some samples have been sent to the GBI lab. Jin is extracting samples from the last remains to be found. I haven't finished analyzing all the bone fragments, but I'm working on it. I expect the DNA will be more important to the identification than my analysis." Diane paused. "You know, don't you, that much of the physical evidence is compromised? Any good defense attorney will ream whatever unlucky person gets on the stand to discuss the evidence. I can tell you this, it won't be any of my people."

"I agree. But McNair's people are good. . . ."

"Garnett," said Diane, "that doesn't matter. Do you want a list of all the bags he broke the seal on and pawed through?"

Garnett sighed. "I know. The DA's very upset. We are going to have to somehow work around what

McNair did. I don't have to tell you we don't need to make it public knowledge."

"No," said Diane, "you don't. But a lot of people know about it. Are you sure some of his own people won't make it public? Are all of them satisfied with his stewardship of his position?"

"Look, I know this is a mess and I know the commissioner behaved like a . . ."

"Titty baby," supplied Jin. "Wimp, weenie, chicken, sellout . . ."

Garnett looked over at him and grimaced. "I suppose that's several ways to put it." He took another sip of coffee. "However, I also had another reason for coming over. We managed to get those two guys with the baseball bats to talk."

Chapter 20

"You know who they are?" asked Diane. "Who? What was it about? Not the museum, I hope."

"No. It was about you."

"Me?" Diane received that news with mixed relief. She certainly didn't want thugs targeting patrons of the museum, but neither did she like being a target herself. "Why?" she asked.

"The two work for the Stanton Construction Company. Patrice Stanton hired them."

"The little carjacker's mother?" said Jin. "She hired hit men? God, what a family."

"I suppose I don't need to ask why," said Diane.

"No. She is really pissed at you for having her arrested and for accusing her son of trying to hijack your car. The men said she offered them a bonus if you had to have your jaw wired shut."

Diane winced. So did her staff. David rubbed his jaw.

"She's a mean woman," said Garnett. Her jailers were about ready to pay her bail just so they wouldn't be around her anymore before her husband came and got her. I just wanted to warn you. I don't think you've heard the last of her. She's the type of woman who won't let go."

"That's comforting," said Diane. "Any suggestions?"

"None legal," said Garnett.

Diane gave him a rueful smile. She could ask security to walk her to her car every evening, but when she got home she'd just have to make a run for it. Damn those crazy people.

"How bad is this problem with the councilman . . . who did you say? Albin Adler? McNair's uncle." asked Diane. She probably ought to pay more attention to local politics but she found them petty and a waste of time and energy.

"No one thing he's done is too bad. It's just that he keeps coming up with new jabs. He'll accuse you of beating your wife, then announce to the newspapers that he's going to question you about allegations that you beat your wife. He's a dirty fighter. He knows that rumor and gossip are more powerful than the truth."

"You have friends in the media," said Diane.

"That's no help," said David. "You know the media these days. They don't do their own work, and for them it's the sensational story they want, not the truth."

Jin grinned at him. "Spoken like a true paranoid skeptic."

"He's not far from right," said Garnett.

"See," said David.

"So, McNair found out you beat your wife. What else has he dug up?" said Diane, smiling at Garnett.

"That's not funny. McNair's dug up dirt on who has marks on their record, who's ever been investigated by internal affairs, who owes money—that kind of thing. Rachel and I recently bought a tiny cabin on Lake Lanier and suddenly I'm hearing whispers about where I got the money for a second house. McNair should talk. He just bought a boat, and someone said he's putting in a pool in his backyard. Councilman Adler hasn't said anything about that."

"I'm sorry all that is going on," said Diane. "I'm particular sorry it's threatened the evidence in the meth lab explosion case."

"Where *does* McNair get the money?" asked David.

"His wife comes from money," said Garnett. He rose to leave. "I just wanted to warn you to watch your back," said Garnett. "Mrs. Stanton's gunning for you. We picked her up on this latest, but she's made bail again."

"It sounds like her two hired hands are the ones who need to worry," said Diane.

"I'm sure they are worried. By the way, the judge who allowed bail for Mrs. Stanton both times for attacking you is a friend of McNair and Adler."

"So, not much hope of getting a restraining order against Mrs. Stanton from him. I guess I need to hire a bodyguard," said Diane.

"It wouldn't hurt," said Garnett.

Diane was kidding, but he sounded serious. She watched him as he walked out of the crime lab. He left through the museum entrance. He was probably going to look at some of the exhibits on the way out, she thought. He often did that. Perhaps, like her, he'd discovered peace in looking at beautiful and interesting things.

"So, Diane, do you need to hole up in your vault so no one can get at you?" said David.

"I am beginning to feel under siege." She stood. "I'll be in the osteology lab with the meth lab bones. Jin, we need all the DNA samples collected and sent to the GBI lab as soon as possible."

"Sure." He jumped out of his chair, ready to follow her to her lab.

"David, just don't let anyone kill anybody until all this about the explosion is over," said Diane.

"I'll take out an ad."

"Neva, you said you processed my car? Put a copy of the report on my desk, please."

"Your lab office desk?"

Diane nodded. She doubted that there would be anything of use other than Blake's blood, but there might be some bit of trace evidence that would help. She and Jin went back to her lab. He gathered up the bones that were ready to sample and took them back to his glassed-in lab to process.

Diane opened several boxes of bones that were collected in adjacent grid units and laid them out on the table to see if she could make any matches. Most were skull fragments, probably belonging to the bodies that had already been processed by the MEs. She moved her sandbox to the table and began piecing bones together, wondering if any of the bones she touched belonged to Izzy Wallace's son.

By the end of the day, she had parts of three skulls glued together and had matched several long bones that articulated together. In two of the partial skulls she had enough of the maxilla to compare with dental x-rays. She boxed them up and took them down one floor and over to the east wing to use the x-ray machine in the conservation lab. The x-rays didn't take long.

Back in her lab she compared the film she took with the dental x-rays of possible victims. The first one she looked at was Daniel Wallace. It was a match. She felt heartsick. Even though she was fairly sure, based on the broken wrist bones, that Daniel Wallace was among the victims, she realized she had been holding a glimmer of hope that he had just run off and didn't tell his parents. It's a horrible thing when the best hope for your child is that he ran away. Diane wrote her reports and faxed them to the police unit in charge of coordinating the identifications.

Diane went into her office and sat down behind her desk. On it lay the report Neva had made after processing her car. She picked it up and started to thumb through it, then set it back down. She was tired of forensics for the day. She turned out the light and went home.

She sat in her car and looked at the front of her

apartment building for several minutes. She scanned the street for cars she didn't recognize. None. She walked down the sidewalk and up the steps. They were clean of snow and ice, but all the ground around was covered in about a foot of the white stuff. It was still sparkling white and pretty. She was almost to the door when someone stepped out and put a hand on her arm. She jumped back, ready to fight.

"Dr. Fallon, I'm sorry."

It was Shawn Keith, her neighbor in the basement apartment. He was wrapped up in a brown sweater and muffler and was shivering.

"I didn't mean to frighten you. I saw you drive up and I was waiting for you to come in. I wanted to apologize. I . . . you see . . . I had my mother with me."

Diane stared at him a moment. What is he talking about? Then she realized—the carjacking, Blake Stanton.

"You mean that kid trying to take your car?"

He nodded. "I saw him walking to your car when I took off."

"It's all right, Professor Keith. You did the right thing. You called the police. They came and everything was fine."

"I've been worried about it ever since it happened. I should have . . ."

"Done just what you did," said Diane. "Really, you did the right thing."

"That's kind of you to say," he said.

"It's true. It looks like you need to get inside. You're turning blue."

"It is freezing out here. Thanks, Dr. Fallon." He nodded his head up and down. "Thanks."

Diane climbed the stairs to her apartment and unlocked the door, glad to be home. Just as she walked in, her telephone rang.

"Don't let it be a murder," she said to herself as she grabbed the phone and dropped to the couch.

"Diane, it's Frank."

Diane grinned to herself. She'd take Frank over a murder any day.

"Hello, Frank. It's good to hear your voice. How are you?"

"I'm OK. I heard about Izzy Wallace's son. I know Daniel. Is it true?"

"Yes. I'm afraid it is. I matched his dental records this evening. That, with the x-ray of his wrist, cinches it. But the family hasn't been officially notified."

Frank was silent a moment. "I'm sorry to hear that. I've been so grateful for finding Star. . . ."

"I know. I've had those same emotions. How is Star? How did her test go?"

"She said she thought she did well. She thinks she's going to make above a three-point this semester."

"Wow, good for her. When can I see you?" Diane hadn't meant to say that. She was just feeling very lonely.

"How about tomorrow night?"

"I'd like that."

"You sound beat."

"It's just all the bodies from the explosion and everything that goes along with it. I'm having problems at the museum. Someone is stealing some of our rare items."

"I'm sorry to hear that. Any leads?"

"No. We're just now discovering what's missing. Many of the items weren't from the exhibits, but from the vaults."

"So it's someone who knows the museum."

"It looks like it."

"That narrows it down considerably."

"I don't want it to be someone from the museum."

"I know."

"Frank . . ." The call waiting signal beeped. "Just a moment. Let me get this call."

She switched to the other call. "Diane, it's Garnett. We're at a crime scene in the Briarwood Apartments. Better get your crew over here."

Chapter 21

Briarwood Apartments were upscale dwellings catering more to the professional crowd than to students of Bartram University. Diane met David, Neva, and Jin in the parking lot in front of section C, four duplexes clustered together.

"I looked at these when I moved here," said David. "Nice apartments. I liked them. Very quiet, good neighborhood. A little expensive for my budget."

They got their crime scene kits out of their vehicles and followed the sidewalk to apartment 131. Garnett met them at the door, frowning when they saw him. Diane knew what he was thinking—Councilman Adler was going to make hay out of this. Murders in good neighborhoods scare people.

Diane sent Jin and Neva to search outside the apartment—under the windows, any nooks and crannies where someone could lie in wait or leave evidence. She and David slipped covers over their shoes and hair and walked into the room. The body was in the living room, lying face up, blood pooled under her head. She was a young woman. Long blond hair partially covered her battered face. Her blue eyes were open.

Allan Rankin was there. He was taking her liver temperature. He pulled the thermometer out and scribbled in his notepad before looking up.

"Hi. Diane. Apparently we must not see enough of each other."

"Apparently," she said. "What do we have here?"

"The name on her mail says J. Cipriano. Female, twenty-six years old. Been dead no more than thirty minutes," Rankin said.

"Sexual assault?" asked Garnett.

He had walked up behind them. Diane looked down at his feet. They were covered.

"Neva gave them to me," he said, following her gaze.

"No visible signs of sexual assault. I'll know more later." He stood and looked down at the body. She was dressed in a blue sweater and white wool skirt. "At least she's not charred," he said.

"Cause of death?" asked Garnett.

"She bled out. Took a beating, fell, and hit the back of her head on the corner of this glass table." Rankin pointed to the bloody table edge.

Diane looked around the room. It was tossed. All the books in the room were pulled off the shelves and lay on the floor in piles. Diane could see into the bedroom from where she was standing. Books were lying on the bed and floor. Odd.

"Some kind of book maniac, I'd say," said Rankin.

"What did she do for a living?" asked Garnett. "Does anyone know?"

Rankin shook his head. "A lady in one of the other apartments—I think I heard her name was something Bowden—she may know the victim. She's the one who called the police."

"Bowden," said Diane. "Where have I heard that name before?"

"It sounds familiar to me, too." Rankin thought a minute. "The coffee tent. There was a woman from the church named Jere Bowden."

"I remember," said Diane. "Very kind lady. She's related to my upstairs neighbors."

"You want to come while I talk to the witness?" asked Garnett. "Maybe it's the same woman."

Diane nodded and looked at David.

"I've got it," he said. "It's a small apartment, one person ought to do."

"I'll be back and help," she said.

Diane left the apartment and slipped off her shoe and head coverings. Garnett was asking the policemen at the scene where the witness' apartment was.

"One thirty-two," said Garnett. "It's across here."

They knocked on the door. After a few moments a woman answered. She was indeed the woman from the coffee tent, Jere Bowden.

"Oh," she said. "Dr. Fallon. We will have to meet sometime under more pleasant circumstances."

"Yes, we will," said Diane. "You know Chief Garnett, don't you? He was at the other crime scene."

Jere held out her hand. "Yes, I do. Please come in and sit down. Can I get you some coffee?" She smiled. "Or tea or something?"

"No, thank you. We just need to ask about your neighbor."

Jere nodded. "Please, come sit down." She gestured toward the living room up a small flight of steps from the foyer. "My husband is in Michigan ice fishing, of all things. I told him he should have just stayed home. We seem to be having the required weather."

Diane sat on a cream-colored love seat, Garnett on a stuffed dark blue chair. Jere sat opposite them on a sofa that matched the love seat.

"What is the victim . . . the young lady's name?" asked Garnett.

"Joana Cipriano. That's with one *n* in Joana. She teaches music at the university. Very nice young woman."

She stopped and her eyes teared and almost overflowed. Diane and Garnett waited.

"I'm sorry," she said after a moment. "I told myself

that I wasn't going to do this. You need information to catch the man who did . . . what he did."

"Man?" asked Garnett.

"It was a man at her door. I didn't see him do it and I only saw his back. I can describe his size and clothes, that's about all."

"Tell us what you know," said Diane.

"I've been here by myself all day. Resting from, well, you know. Anyway . . . these apartments are pretty soundproof, but sometimes you can hear when someone comes to the door of your neighbor. Joana, as you can see, is just across the sidewalk from me. I was sitting there reading." She pointed to a chair by the front window. "My curtains were drawn. I draw them when I sit in front of the window. I heard someone knock on Joana's door. She opened it and this male voice asked her . . . I've been trying to play it back in my mind, but it was muffled." She put an index finger to her forehead and tapped as if jiggling her thoughts. "But he said something about a book. Did she have a book. Something like that."

"A book?" said Garnett. He looked briefly at Diane. "Did he say what kind?"

"No, not that I heard." She paused. "Then Joana said, 'Do I know you?' and I didn't hear his answer, just mumbling." She shook her head. "There was something in his voice that worried me. I can't really put my finger on it. But there was something in his tone that I didn't like. I'm one to act on my instincts, so I called the police. I know they thought I was crazy—reporting a perfectly normal conversation and asking them to investigate. I thought, well, the worst they can think of me is that I'm a crazy woman, but if something is wrong, they can prevent it." She shook her head again. "I told them it didn't sound right to me. They said they would send someone, but it took over an hour."

"I'm sorry, Mrs. Bowden," said Garnett. "I'll look into that delay."

"Can you tell us what he looked like?" asked Diane.

"I looked out the window before I called the police. He was a large man in a black coat. Like a ski coat—made of that kind of material. He had on blue jeans and brown work boots and a baseball-like cap, but it was padded and sort of matched his coat. I saw some of his hair sticking out the back of his cap. It was black with a few gray streaks through it. He wasn't a young man, but he wasn't old, either. If I had to guess, I'd say early fifties, maybe a little younger. His head came to just under the fixture for her porch light."

"That's a very good description," said Garnett.

"I want to help. When I looked out the window, I made note of what he looked like. As I said, his voice didn't sound right to me."

"Could you recognize an accent?" asked Diane.

Jere thought for a moment. "His voice wasn't that clear. I had the impression he wasn't from the South, but I could be completely wrong on that."

"Did you hear anything that happened in the apartment?" asked Diane.

"No. When I came back from calling the police he wasn't at her door anymore, and it was closed. I listened, but I couldn't hear anything. But as I said, these apartments are really very soundproof once the doors are closed." She sighed and her eyes watered up again. "I should have gone over and knocked."

"No, Mrs. Bowden," said Garnett, "you should not have. You did the right thing. I'm just sorry it took so long for the police to get here."

"I'll keep trying to remember anything else," she said. "However, I have to tell you that she also has an ex-husband who was trying to get back with her. He's loud, but I don't think he's ever been violent with her. But you don't really know what goes on behind closed doors. It wasn't him that was at the door today, I do know that."

"What's his name?" asked Garnett.

"Gil Cipriano. He's in the History Department at Bartram. He's a student there getting his Ph.D."

Garnett handed her a card. "Call us, please, if you remember anything else."

She looked at the card. "I will."

Diane and Garnett left and walked back to the crime scene. The body was being removed just as they got there.

"Everyone's been working on this meth lab explosion, trying to find out if there's anyone behind it besides whatever unlucky bastard was doing the cooking. I suppose that's why they didn't take her call as urgent. You take the conversation on its face, it didn't sound urgent."

It seemed to Diane that Garnett was making excuses for the policeman who delayed sending out officers to check on Joana Cipriano—especially when it was clear that their presence might have saved her.

Diane slipped on fresh head and shoe coverings and walked inside. David was still working the living room. She went to the bedroom and stood in the doorway, surveying the room. The walls were a dusty rose color. The comforter was white with roses that matched the color of the wall. There was a bench at the foot of the bed with a rose-colored throw draped over it. The furniture and the carpet were white. It was a pretty feminine room and in perfect order except for the books thrown around. *What is he looking for?* she wondered.

Diane began at the door and examined the carpet first, making herself a path around the room. She found nothing but books on the carpet. Later when she finished she would vacuum and see if that picked up anything her eyes failed to see.

Diane dusted all the surfaces as well as the books for fingerprints. She found many. Most would probably be Joana's, but they might get lucky. The key was in the books, she felt, but what was it about the books? Most of those in the bedroom were bestsellers from the book-of-the-month club. None seemed to hold any secrets.

"What kind of books are in the living room?" Diane called to David.

"Music history, biographies, poetry . . . ," he called back.

It seemed like a normal selection for a faculty member in music history. What they needed to know was, what books were missing?

Diane's thoughts were interrupted by a commotion at the front door.

Chapter 22

"What's going on? Where's my wife? What's happened?"

It must be Gil Cipriano, thought Diane. She walked into the living room and stood beside David, who was dusting a CD player for prints. A young man was at the door trying to come in and was being blocked by Garnett and two policemen.

"Just calm down," said Garnett.

"Calm down. If you come home and find this, are you going to be calm?" he said.

"I was under the impression you and Mrs. Cipriano were divorced," said Garnett.

"Yes, we were . . . we are, but we're getting back together."

Diane scrutinized him. Gil Cipriano had dark good looks—jet black hair, black eyes, olive skin. He looked to be in his late twenties and of Italian descent. He also looked distressed, but looks can fool you. However, at this distance, she didn't see any marks on his knuckles.

"Where is Joana?" he said. "Has something happened?" He caught sight of the blood pooled on the floor where Joana's head had lain. "Oh, God, is that from her? Damn it, where is she?" He pushed on Garnett, and the two policemen restrained him.

"Calm down, Mr. Cipriano," said Garnett.

"You keep saying calm down, but you won't tell me anything and I find this in my living room. Tell me what happened to Joana, damn it."

"Where have you been all day?" asked Garnett.

"At school. I'm working on my dissertation." He stopped. "I've been in the library all day. People know me there. Now tell me what happened. Is Joana all right? Is she in the hospital?"

"No, son, she isn't in the hospital," said Garnett. "She has been murdered."

Cipriano stared at him.

"I'm sorry for your loss," Garnett added.

"Sorry for my loss? Are you trying to say that Joana's dead? She can't be dead. We're getting back together. She has a recital in two days. We have plans." He looked at Diane and David as if just noticing them. "Who are you? What happened with Joana's books? She doesn't like people messing with her things."

Diane picked her way though a safe path toward the door. As she passed near David she asked him, "Is there a clear area where we can question him?"

David nodded over his shoulder. "The breakfast nook has been cleared."

"Why don't we bring him inside," Diane said to Garnett. "Bring him this way."

Garnett nodded. He escorted Cipriano to a small alcove opposite the kitchen where he sat down at an oak breakfast table and put his head down on his arms.

"We need to find out if he has any way of knowing if any of her books are missing," said Diane, as she and Garnett sat opposite Cipriano.

"Gil, can I call you Gil?" asked Garnett.

"It's my name." He raised his head. "How did she . . . die? Did she suffer?"

Probably, thought Diane, remembering her face.

But right now, they couldn't tell him that. Garnett just said there was a struggle and she apparently fell and hit her head on the coffee table, which was right.

He was silent for a moment. "What's she saying about books?" he asked, nodding toward Diane.

"Would you be able to tell me if any of hers are missing?"

He stared at the two of them. "You're kidding, right? Who keeps a list of the books they have?"

"Are there any special books she had, any rare books, any books that were actually safes?" asked Diane.

"Rare? No. Joana reads mainly those book-of-the-month things. And poetry. She likes that. We both do. What do you mean, books that are safes?"

"You know," said Garnett. "It looks like a book, but inside it's really a box to keep money and jewels in."

"Jewels? Joana doesn't have jewels. If she did, she'd keep them in a safe deposit box, not in a book."

"There are a lot of music, history, and biography books in the living room. Are some of them yours?"

"The history and biography are mine. Why all these questions about books? We don't have any particularly valuable books. They're just books."

"Has anyone asked you about them before?" asked Diane.

"No. I keep telling you, they are just books. What's this about? Are you saying someone hurt Joana over a book? Like an overdue book or something? I know graduate students get desperate, but . . ." Gil looked from one to the other as though they were nuts.

Maybe the guy didn't say book, thought Diane. *Maybe Jere Bowden heard wrong. What sounds like book? Box—maybe. Look. Took. Rook—chess? Nook—place? Hook—weapon? Cook—meth lab? Could it be about the meth lab explosion?*

While Diane was lost in her thoughts, Garnett was

trying to nail down Gil's alibi. The library is a hard alibi to deal with. Sure, lots of people see you, but it's easy to come and go.

"Was Joana involved in drugs?" asked Diane.

"Drugs? No, of course not. She hates drugs."

"Did she know anyone who was killed in the explosion?"

"I think maybe one of her students. She called to tell me about it. I can't remember his name. Bobby something."

"Did she know anyone who lived in the apartment house that blew up?" asked Diane.

"No, not that I know of. Look, I don't understand any of these questions."

"Just things we need to know," said Garnett. "Like, do you know if she had any enemies?"

"Joana? No. She doesn't have any enemies. All her students like her. So do her fellow faculty members."

"How about socially?" asked Garnett.

"Social enemies? Like jealous wives and lovers? Joana isn't that kind of person. She's pretty, but she doesn't inspire jealousy in people. She's nice. Everyone likes her. Look, we're just normal people. She teaches music, I'm getting my doctorate in history. No one would have reason to kill her."

"How about you? Do you know anyone who might want to get even with you for some reason?"

"Me? No. I tell you. I'm just a student. No, there's no one I know who would do something like this."

"Why did you and she get a divorce?" asked Garnett.

He shrugged. "She thought I had an affair."

"Did you?" asked Garnett.

"Not exactly."

"Affairs are like pregnancies," said Garnett. "You either are or you aren't. Did you have an affair?"

"I didn't call it that. It was all over the computer. We didn't even meet in person. It was in a chat room.

Look, I don't have to go into this now, do I?" He cast a quick glance at Diane.

"I need to know the name of the woman you chatted with," said Garnett.

"Do you have to? I mean . . . I don't really know her name. She called herself Justforkicks. And that's all it was. Besides, it's over now."

"I see," said Garnett. "Doing any more online dating?"

He shrugged again. "Occasionally. Nothing serious. It's like safe sex. It's all cartoons, anyway."

"Cartoons?" asked Garnett. Diane didn't know what he meant, either.

"Webcam. It'll make you look like a cartoon character. It's the software. Like anime—the Japanese stuff."

Diane was completely lost and she suspected that Garnett was, too.

"I tell you what," said Garnett. "Will you let us have a look at your computer?"

"I don't know. This is just personal stuff. I don't even leave my room. I don't meet anyone."

"Someone might have taken you seriously and thought your wife was competition to get rid of."

"That's crazy. It's just . . ." He looked at Diane again. "It's nothing more than what it is. The people I talk to don't even know who I am."

"What's your screen name?" asked Diane.

"Do I really have to say?" he asked Garnett.

"Where are you staying?" asked Garnett.

"I have an apartment on Applewood Street, four seventy-two. I room with two other students. They just went home after exams."

"You staying in town during the break?"

"Yes."

"We may want to talk with you again," said Garnett.

"Where is she?" Gil asked. "Can I see her?"

"She's with the medical examiner," said Garnett.

"We need for you to make a positive ID. I can have a police officer take you there."

He nodded, the realization of what he was being asked to do suddenly reflected in his face.

Garnett released Gil Cipriano to one of the officers at the scene to be driven to the morgue. Diane and Garnett watched out the window of the breakfast nook as he walked down the sidewalk in the direction of the patrol car, his shoulders slumped, his hands in his pockets, his head bent down.

"What do you think?" asked Garnett.

"He always speaks of her in the present tense," said Diane.

"Yes. I noticed that," he said.

"His knuckles were clean and unmarked," she said.

"I noticed that, too," he said. "What were all those drug questions? Did you find something to link her to the meth lab explosion?"

"No, not really, just a chain of thoughts." Diane explained her results on finding words that rhyme with book. "Thin thread, I know, but worth a shot at asking."

Garnett gave a slight laugh. "Slim, indeed. But you're right. Mrs. Bowden could have heard wrong."

Garnett's phone rang. Diane stood up to go back to helping David finish processing the crime scene. Garnett put a hand on her arm.

"She's been here at this crime scene for several hours," he said. Garnett listened for several moments. "Yes, I can. I've been here, too." Pause. "I understand. We have other staff who can come." He paused again.

Diane wished she could hear the other side of the conversation. She was beginning to feel that she was the *she* he was talking about.

"Of course it won't be compromised." He paused for several seconds.

Diane could hear someone on the other end but

couldn't make out the words. She could tell they were excited.

"I don't give a rat's ass what she wants." Garnett snapped the phone shut and turned toward Diane. "Things just keep getting worse."

"I know I shouldn't ask, but how have they gotten worse?"

"Someone just murdered Blake Stanton, the kid who tried to jack your car the other night. The mother thinks it was you."

Chapter 23

"That kid? Someone killed him?"

Blake Stanton wasn't her favorite person, but he was still just a kid who had a great many decades ahead of him.

"What happened?" She asked Garnett.

"I don't know yet. The commissioner didn't give any details." Garnett shook his head at some unspoken thought and stood up. "I've got to go on this one. I'll take Jin and Neva. They can process the scene. I can't have you anywhere near it."

"I understand that. David and I will finish up here. After that, I'm going home and turning off my telephones."

"I hear you there."

Diane refocused her attention on the Joana Cipriano crime scene. David had finished the living room and kitchenette and was now working on the bathroom. It wasn't a big apartment—one bedroom, bath, living room, kitchenette with the small nook for a table. It was probably one of the less expensive apartments in the Applewood complex.

She and David went over all the surfaces in detail. They checked for fingerprints on the walls, the doorjambs, the bathroom fixtures, inside, outside, and the underside of everything that might have been touched. Thankfully, it was not a cluttered apartment. They vacuumed the entire house, using a new bag for each grid they had laid out on the floors. When they finished, Diane was confident they had all the evidence the scene would yield. They packed up the books and took them to the lab where they would be examined for any clue as to the motive for Joana Cipriano's murder or who had murdered her.

It was the early hours of the morning when Diane arrived back at her apartment. She could get perhaps four hours' sleep if she went to bed now. Jin and Neva probably wouldn't get any sleep.

Blake Stanton. What was that about? The meth lab explosion? Was someone afraid he would make a deal with the DA for a lighter sentence on the carjacking, so they killed him to shut him up?

Diane tried to put the whole thing out of her mind when she crawled into bed. Before she fell asleep, her last thought was the hope that she would be awakened only by her clock. Before she even dozed off completely, her phone rang. For a whole second she gave serious consideration to not answering it.

"Fallon here."

"Don't think you are going to get away with what you did. I will never let you go. For the rest of your miserable life I intend to haunt your every waking moment. You will never get another minute of peace, you hear? Are you listening to me?"

Diane hung up the phone. Great, now Patrice Stanton had become her stalker. The phone rang again. This time Diane looked at the caller ID. Unknown. She unplugged the phone from the wall and went to sleep.

The clock went off too soon, awakening her from a dream in which she was plummeting toward earth with no parachute. *It can't possibly be four hours since I went to sleep,* thought Diane as she struggled out of bed. She looked at her unplugged telephone and decided not to plug it in. She dragged herself to the shower and turned it on cooler than her usual setting.

"Shit!" she screamed when the cold water hit her.

Diane finished her shower and dried off, shivering the entire time. It would be warmer to lie naked in the snow, she thought as she slipped on her clothes. Well, at least she was wide-awake.

She forced herself to eat a bowl of cereal before she dashed out the door to the museum. When she got to the curb where the museum loaner was parked she stopped cold. Someone had spray-painted in bright red letters the words MURDERER, KILLER, BITCH, and assorted obscenities all over the white Crown Victoria. Diane could guess who it was. The car was left driveable, she noticed. Diane took out her cell and dialed Andie.

"Andie," she said to the perky voice that answered. Andie was always perky in the morning. Diane bet she didn't have to take a cold shower to get that way. "Are you at the museum or are you en route?"

"En route. What's up?"

"Can you swing around by my place and give me a lift?"

"Sure, something happen to the museum car?"

"Patrice Stanton, trying to work through her grief," said Diane, before flipping her phone shut.

Diane stamped her feet trying to keep warm as she waited for Andie. She called Neva to come and photograph and print her car ASAP. Then she called a mechanic she often used and asked him to pick it up after Neva finished and take it to his brother's shop for a paint job.

"Sure thing," he said. "You want flames?"

Diane could see him grinning into the phone. "No, it got those last night. I want it like it was. Can he resist making it a canvas?"

"Sure thing. Somebody vandalize your car?"

"Indeed they did. They weren't very poetic about it, either."

"I'll get it right away," he said.

"It's in front of my apartment building. You can't miss it," she said.

Andie pulled in front of the museum car, stopped and got out, and looked at it.

"Who is Patrice Stanton and why did she do this?" said Andie, her Orphan Annie curls bouncing as she shook her head.

"I'll tell you on the way." Diane got in Andie's Honda and closed the door.

"OK, what happened? Why does this woman think you are a murderer?" said Andie.

Diane explained about Blake Stanton.

"The kid with one hand who held a gun on you and tried to take your car?"

"Yes, the same," answered Diane.

"And this chick thinks you did him in and is harassing you about it?"

"Yes."

"Bummer."

When they were almost to the museum, Diane asked Andie to take the gravel access road that led around to the loading dock.

"You think she is waiting on you out front?" asked Andie.

"I wouldn't be surprised. She's a woman with a mission."

Her son was dead. Diane tried to remember that. Grief takes many forms. Mrs. Stanton's form was certainly destructive.

Andie turned in the gravel access road, drove to the back of the museum, and stopped.

"Thanks, Andie."

Diane hopped out of the car and entered the museum by the back way, which was actually a quicker way to her office. She let herself in by her private

entrance, locked the door behind her, set her coffeemaker to chugging, sat down, and began sorting
through paperwork on her desk. The phone rang and
she picked it up.

"RiverTrail Museum of Natural History," she said
automatically.

"I want to speak with that killer, Diane Fallon."

Diane recognized Patrice Stanton's voice. It crack-
led with hatred.

"May I take a message?"

"Yes, you can take a message. Before I'm through,
everyone is going to know what a cold-blooded killer
they have working for them at the museum."

"May I say who's calling?"

Patrice Stanton was quiet a moment.

*Startled by the polite response? On to me? Wonder-
ing if she should reveal herself? Thinking of a
snappy comeback?*

"Tell her it's the mother of the son she murdered,"
Patrice said. "Murdered in cold blood."

"In cold blood, got it." Diane replaced the receiver.

In a few minutes she heard Andie come into her
office. Diane rose and opened the adjoining door.

"Andie, we're going to be getting some harassing
phone calls today from Patrice Stanton."

"Can't the woman be stopped? Isn't there anything
we can do?" asked Andie.

"Yes, there is. I know she is suffering and is trying
to vent her anger, but we have to exercise caution and
protect the museum from whatever imprudent thing
she might do."

"So, what should I do?"

"I'll have Chanell make necessary security arrange-
ments. If you receive any calls from her, field them as
best you can. Keep a log and a brief summary of them
and notify Chanell. Check discreetly with the heads of
the museum departments; instruct them to let me
know immediately if any of them receive abusive calls

from her, and I'll have our attorneys get a restraining order against her."

"OK, will do."

Diane walked to the office of Chanell Napier, her chief of museum Security. She brought Chanell up to date on the situation, including calls at Diane's home and the vandalizing of the museum car.

"I feel sorry for the woman," said Chanell, "but she better get a grip on herself. I can record all the calls coming into the Director's Office in the event that we take legal action. My people will have that set up within the hour. If she's already been arrested once, I can get a mug shot of her and provide all of my security people with her picture. I think we better keep her off museum property until this whole thing is cleared up, don't you?"

"All those sound like sensible precautions, Chanell. Thank you."

"You don't need to thank me, Dr. Fallon. You know I take the protection of you and this museum seriously. We're not going to have any more of the kind of thing that's happened around here in the past. We're going to stop trouble at the door."

Diane informed Andy of the security precautions being put into place, then returned to her office, her paperwork, and her e-mail—thankfully, Patrice hadn't thought of e-mail yet. With any luck, perhaps she would be computer illiterate. Diane called the hospital and asked about Darcy Kincaid. The nurses station asked her for the family code word that would allow them to give out the information.

"Golden," said Diane, looking at the note on her desk from the Kincaids.

"She's out of her coma and drifting in and out of consciousness. Her condition has been upgraded from critical to serious."

"Thank you," said Diane. She went to the door between their offices and told Andie.

"That's good, isn't it?" said Andie

"Yes, it is. I'm going to my other office," she said. "If there are any problems, give me a call."

Andy, clearly unnerved by the situation, asked, "Is there anything else we can do about Patrice Stanton?"

"I can find out who killed her son," replied Diane.

Diane left her east-wing office and took the less visible route across the Pleistocene room, through the mammal room, and to the bank of elevators near the restaurant. Fortunately, she didn't meet Patrice. She felt silly when she got on the elevator and just a little paranoid. She got off in front of the exhibit preparation room—where Darcy worked. She went in and updated Darcy's coworkers on her condition.

From there she went to the crime lab. She hoped that Neva and Jin had found something that would lead them to Blake's killer. Patrice's harassment had just started, but Diane was already sick of it. As she passed the lounge, she ran into Madge Stewart, one of the museum board members, on her way out.

Madge was a small woman, several inches shorter than Diane. Her springy gray hair surrounded her head like a messy halo. She was quite a busybody, and Diane just knew she was in for an interesting run-in.

"I was just looking for you, Diane," she said.

"Hello, Madge. Did you try my office?"

"Oh, I just came in here to get a Coke and some peanuts." She held them up for Diane to see.

"What did you need to see me about?"

"I got this strange call. Some woman said you killed her son. Did you?"

"No, Madge, I didn't kill her son. If I did, I'd be under arrest, wouldn't I?"

"Well, I thought it might have been in the line of duty, that kind of thing." She cast a furtive glance toward the crime lab just a few feet away. Many in the museum referred to the top floor of the west wing as the dark side. Apparently Madge did, too.

"No, Madge, I had nothing to do with his death."

"Why does his mother think you did?" Madge made it sound like an accusation. It probably was. Her small dark eyes bore into Diane like she was looking for any kind of deception.

Because she's nuts, thought Diane. Her words were kinder. "This just happened to her son last night. She's in deep grief."

"How did you hear about it?" said Madge.

From the look on her face, Diane could see that she thought she had caught Diane in a slip of the tongue. *If you didn't kill him, then how did you know when he died?*—she knew Madge was dying to say.

"I was working another crime scene when the detective in charge got the call," said Diane. Madge looked disappointed and Diane wanted to laugh.

"You know, if you would get rid of that crime scene stuff, this wouldn't happen," said Madge.

"Madge, the crime lab didn't have anything to do with his death. Now excuse me, I need to go."

Diane walked across the dinosaur overlook and into the hallway that represented the border between the museum and its dark side.

Chapter 24

"OK, I need to know who killed the Stanton kid," Diane said as she came into the crime lab.

David looked up at her from his computer, Jin from his microscope; Neva was gone—processing her car, she hoped. However she saw a drawing she had been doing that looked like a picture of the back of a man. The Cipriano case, Diane guessed. She wondered about the usefulness of back view, but who knows? Someone may have seen him hanging around.

"Garnett said Stanton is a priority?" asked David. "Because they're rich, I'll bet. You know, just because Joana Cipriano's not wealthy . . ."

"Garnett hasn't said anything," interrupted Diane. "I have." She explained about Patrice Stanton and Patrice's new goal in life.

"The woman who attacked you at the hospital?" asked Jin. "Nervy."

"The woman is a bottomless well of nerve," said Diane, "She's already driving me crazy and she hasn't even gotten started. I want her off my back. In particular, off the museum's back. Tell me what you found."

"We aren't supposed to talk with you about it," said Jin. "Garnett told us not to. But I will if you ask me."

"No, I won't ask you. He's just protecting the evidence," she said.

Too bad he didn't do a better job protecting the evidence of the explosion, she thought.

"Did he tell you not to tell David?" asked Diane.

"No, he didn't," said Jin.

"Good. Tell David. I'll be finishing my reports on the explosion remains. Have any of the DNA analyses come back?"

"No," he said. "It'll be a while. Now, if we were doing it . . ."

"I know," said Diane. "We need our own lab. Find me Blake's killer and I'll go to the mat with Garnett for a DNA lab."

Jin looked at her wide-eyed. "You serious, Boss?"

"Yes."

Jin rubbed his hands together. "OK, David. Let's do it," said Jin.

"You are serious, aren't you?" said David.

"I am," Diane said.

Diane retreated to her osteology lab and began checking over all the forensic reports and filing them away in the vault with the pieces of bone.

The only skeleton not yet analyzed was the antique individual who was shot in the head. Diane laid him out in anatomical position on one of her tables. She placed the skull on a doughnut ring. She eyed the brown and black bones a moment, then began examining each one.

Most of the bones were present, with the exception of some very small ones. The tips of all the fingers of the left hand, except the thumb and index finger, were missing. All the distal phalanges were missing from the right hand. Three of the carpal bones—wrist bones—were missing from the left side and one from the right. All the foot bones were present. Diane thought that amazing under the circumstances.

The hyoid bone—the bone in the throat that supports the base of the tongue—was missing. All the long bones were present. They're harder to lose, of course, if you're keeping a box of bones. Human skeletons have twelve ribs on each side. The eleventh and twelfth—called floating ribs because they are not attached ventrally—were missing from the left side; the twelfth was missing from the right.

She checked all the ribs for nicks and cuts that might have come from a knife or gunshot wound. She found none. She measured the long bones using a bone board. The left leg bones—the femur, tibia, and fibula—taken together were shorter than the right by half an inch. He may have had a slight limp. Other than that, the long bones were unremarkable.

Two thoracic vertebrae were missing. The coccyx—the tail bone—had a small healed crack. At some point in his life he had fallen and cracked it. It probably gave him trouble the rest of his young life. Diane examined each vertebra. There were no healed breaks, nor were there any signs of lipping or degenerative disease. Other than his teeth, he was basically healthy.

In the middle of the examination David came in and pulled up a chair.

"Neva came back. She told us about your car. You have a hard time with vehicles, don't you," he said.

"Apparently," said Diane not looking up from the bones.

"I had a long talk with both Neva and Jin," he said. "I assume you would like to be filled in, as Garnett didn't tell them not to talk to me about the case and he certainly didn't tell me not to talk to you about it."

David cast a glance at the skeleton on the table. "Is that the guy who was under the bed?"

"That's him. I thought I'd analyze his bones. It's rather relaxing."

"What do you know about him?" asked David.

"Other than he is male in his early twenties? Caucasian, from the look of his skull and the indexes of his other measurements. He had a slight limp that he was born with. He was fairly healthy; broke his tailbone at one time; stood about five feet six, and was left-handed. I'm going to have a stable isotope analysis done on a sample of his bone to see what I can find out about where he grew up and what kind of diet he might have had."

"Garnett won't spring for that," said David.

"The primate lab will," said Diane. "What's the use of being director of the museum and curator of the primate lab if I can't order a SIA once in a while?"

"Who do you think he is?" asked David.

"Who do I think he is?" Diane repeated. "I have no idea."

"How long has he been dead?"

"My guess right now, from the dry feel of his bones, would be over a hundred years. We'll learn more after some tests on the bones. There's a possibility he may be a Civil War veteran. That's just a guess. Probably, someone accidently found the coffin, thought it was cool, robbed the bones, and sent him to college."

"Interesting," said David. "Poor fellow gets shot in the head and then a hundred years later gets caught in an explosion and fire. He's one unlucky dude."

"Speaking of unlucky dudes," said Diane, "Tell me about Blake." She stripped off her gloves, washed her hands, pulled up a chair, and sat down across from David and leaned forward.

"Blake," sighed David. "Unlucky is right. You know, being born rich should give you an edge, but it didn't in his case. Now, *I* should have been born rich. I wouldn't have been such a pissant."

"You would if you had his parents," said Diane. "I actually feel sorry for him."

"Yeah, so do I. OK, here's what we know. Blake went from the hospital to arraignment. The judge released him to his parents, even though he is an adult. Money does buy a lot around here. Anyway, he went home with them. Sometime in the night his father woke up. He doesn't know why. His mother had taken sleeping pills and she was zonked. The father went to Blake's room and he wasn't there. He went back to bed."

"He didn't look for him?" asked Diane.

"He said his son is an adult," said David.

"He was released into their custody," said Diane.

"I didn't say his parents were consistent." David rubbed the top of his head. "Look, these chairs aren't very comfortable. Can I sit on the couch in your office?"

"Sure." Diane rose and stretched, easing the strain in her back. Followed by David, she went to her Osteology office.

"This is much nicer," he said, dropping himself onto her stuffed sofa. "Where was I? AWOL, right. Anyway, the father thought the son leaving the house was what woke him up, so he went back to bed—thinking, I suppose, that a one-handed kid just out of the hospital could handle himself."

"Where did he go?" asked Diane.

"Not far. He was found by the maid in the boathouse, shot in the head—no stippling."

"What kind of gun?"

"Don't know. Didn't find a bullet. No exit wound, so it's still in his head."

"Could his father have heard the shot? Is that what woke him up?" said Diane.

"Then why didn't it wake the entire community? The sound of gunfire carries very well over water. We think maybe the killer used a silencer."

"Silencer. OK. Then it was premeditated. A hit maybe?"

"I'm thinking that. Someone he was involved with lured him out of the house in the middle of the night and shot him in the boathouse. The boathouse is open on the water end. The killer could have ridden up in a boat, tapped him, and left."

"Wouldn't the motor wake everyone up?"

"One would think. The police are canvassing the neighborhood."

"Was there anything on the body? What was he carrying?"

"He was dressed in sweatpants, sweatshirt, and a coat. He had keys to the house and car in his coat pocket. He had no money, billfold, or credit cards. Those were in his room. Neva found a silver charm of a ballerina slipper on the dock. His parents didn't recognize it. I don't think he was expecting to go anywhere but outside for a minute or two. He put on his shoes without socks—in this cold weather."

"It looks like a hit. The meth lab connection looks like the best bet," said Diane.

"That's what Garnett thinks. Of course, his mother thinks it was you."

"Why?" asked Diane.

"Neva says she just wants it to be you."

"Anything else?"

"His father recently cut off the kid's funds after the kid wrecked the father's car—it was a 1965 Jaguar. Personally, I would have cut off his nose for that. Anyway, Blake still had plenty of spending money."

"Did he have a job?"

"Are you kidding? No. He was a perpetual student at Bartram. He got good grades, but went from major to major, never getting enough hours in any one department to graduate. He seemed to like the collegiate life."

"That sounds like he may have been dealing to students."

"I thought so, so does Garnett, but so far they haven't found any evidence of it."

"What does the drug unit say?"

"Not much. They are new, you know. Our esteemed city councilman turned the unit upside down, like he's trying to do with the rest of the department. Most of the guys working drugs for any length of time moved on. The people there now are just newbies."

"Curiouser and curiouser," said Diane. "OK, so the best bet seems a drug-related hit."

David started to answer when Neva, who looked like she hadn't slept in a couple of days, entered, escorting Chief Garnett. The osteology lab was actually a part of the museum and it had a digital lock on the door. Diane's staff knew the combination, but visitors had to be escorted. Diane's office door was open and he entered. Neva waved and left.

Garnett sat down in a stuffed leather chair that matched the couch where David sat.

"I didn't expect to see you today," said Diane. "Is there a break in one of the cases?"

He cleared his throat. "Diane," he said, "can you give me a rundown on your activities this morning?"

Chapter 25

Diane stared at Garnett for a very long moment.

"You want to know my activities this morning? What happened? Did someone kill Mrs. Stanton?"

"This isn't a joke," he said.

And indeed from the look on his face, he wasn't in a humorous mood. But Diane hadn't been joking.

"I can see that. I've been here all morning. What happened?"

"Marcus McNair was murdered this morning while he was jogging."

Diane opened her mouth to speak, but nothing came out. David sat up straight on the sofa, equally speechless. After a moment Diane found her voice.

"McNair, murdered? My God, what is happening? We have very few murders in Rosewood, and now suddenly in less than a week we meet our annual quota?"

"I need to give the commissioner and Councilman Adler your alibi. I don't think the commissioner actually thinks you are guilty, but as far as the councilman is concerned, you are now a suspect in two cases."

"Well, hell. OK, after working the Cipriano crime scene until three a.m, I took a nasty phone call from Mrs. Stanton about how she was going to stalk me for the rest of my life. I went to sleep and got up at seven.

I had a cold shower to wake me up, ate a bowl of cereal and went outside to go to work, and found my car decorated with KILLER, MURDERER, BITCH, and WHORE written all over it in red spray paint."

"What?" said Garnett. "Who?"

"I'm thinking Mrs. Stanton. She's been calling the museum, my board members, and anyone else she thinks can give me a hard time."

"I'll look into it."

"If you're looking for her to give me an alibi, I wouldn't count on it."

"What happened after you found your car vandalized?"

"I called to have it photographed, processed, towed, and painted. I also called Andie to give me a ride to work. She did. I went to my museum office, Patrice called again, I did paperwork—Andie was in the next room. I talked to my security chief and told her to look out for trouble from Patrice in the museum; I called the hospital to check on an employee who was injured in the explosion; I went up to her department and updated her coworkers. On the way to the crime lab, I ran into a board member who had been called by Patrice. She was wondering if I am a murderer. I told her no, then went to the crime lab and said 'hi' to everyone and came to the lab to work on bones. David came in and wanted to know about the hundred-year-old bones he'd found. I told him. I'll tell you if you think the information will be helpful. David was just about to fill me in on what he's found out from the Joana Cipriano evidence; then you came in. I think that's it."

"Marcus was killed at eight thirty a.m. Do you know exactly where you were then?"

"I think I was taking the call from Patrice Stanton. I talked to Andie and my security chief and the hospital right after that."

"OK. I'll tell the commissioner. If you would write down all the people you talked to, it would help," said Garnett.

"You can pull my LUDS," said Diane, "if you need extra verification. I mean, most of my alibis are from people I employ, except Patrice. You'll have to trick her. Don't tell her I need an alibi."

"Diane, I didn't come here to make you mad."

"I'm sure you didn't, but I'm getting a little tired of being a suspect. This is twice in a row, for heaven's sake. And there is zero supporting evidence for even one accusation or suspicion. The facts of my schedule and corroborating witnesses put the lie to it."

"You're not really a suspect. I just need to tell the commissioner where you were."

"Tell him that if I were a murderer, I'd be after him and the councilman."

"I won't tell them that," said Garnett. He stood up. "I don't need to know a combination to get out of here, do I?"

"No."

"I am sorry. If it weren't for politics, I wouldn't be here talking to you. It's just gotten strange lately." He paused. "The commissioner wants the GBI to handle McNair's scene. He says it's just so everyone will know it's all on the up and up."

"Sure," said Diane.

When Garnett left, Diane and David stared at each other with a what-the-hell-is-going-on surprised look on their faces.

"We have got to get to the bottom of this," said Diane.

"I'll get with the gang and we'll come up with a plan," said David. "You know Jin is motivated; that's a big plus for us. Were you really serious about a DNA lab? You think Garnett will go for it?"

"I'm not sure, but I may ask accounting to crunch some numbers for me. It may pay the museum to have a DNA lab that's dedicated to forensics and not research. We can bypass the local government."

"Jin'll like that even better. He already tells everyone he works for the museum." David started to rise off the sofa.

"Tell me about Cipriano first," said Diane. "We still have other cases."

David dropped to a seated position again. "I didn't get much from the scene," he said. "I've been running the fingerprints through AFIS. Most, as you expect, are hers. There are a few of her ex-husband in the kitchen and bathroom. One of her neighbors said he usually did the cooking. His prints were on the books that he said were his—the biographies and history books. I've got three unknown prints, but I have to collect some more exemplars. She had a repairman in to fix the dishwasher a couple of months ago. She's had friends in and I have to get their prints. Her mother visited a couple of weeks ago and I have to get her prints. That's going to be difficult for the poor woman. I'm glad I'm not going to be the one doing it. She lives in Maryland. The authorities there are going to do it for me."

"We have nothing?" said Diane.

"Not nothing. I have foreign carpet fibers from the area rug in her living room and from the carpet in her bedroom. Gray, beige, turquoise, red, and cobalt blue. Jin has identified them as carpet fibers coming from a Saturn, a Chevrolet, two high-end floor coverings, and a cheap floor covering. Again, we need to check exemplars. I did check the husband's car. He has a 2002 Saturn with gray interior. Jin is matching the fibers now. The cobalt blue is from a 1999 Chevrolet Impala. So far, neither her mother or any of her friends have a Chevrolet Impala with a cobalt blue interior carpet. Her mother does have an expensive beige carpet throughout her house. The Maryland authorities will take a sample of her carpet, too."

"That's something. Anything else?"

"Neva sat down with Jere Bowden and has a sketch of the man she saw. It was from the back, so I don't know how much good it will be, but Mrs. Bowden said it is accurate. The police are canvassing the neighborhood and put the picture on the news. I'm sure that drew a lot of laughs from viewers—the back of a man. Right now the detectives are asking the public about the stranger and a 1999 Chevrolet Impala."

"How about the books?"

"I've looked through a number of them, and so far nothing jumps out. It would help if I had some idea what I am looking for."

"If we had the solution, we'd have the solution, wouldn't we?" said Diane.

"Cute. I'll keep you informed on all the cases," said David.

"I'll take the Cipriano case, and you three work on the rest. Garnett will probably tell you what the GBI finds at the McNair crime scene if you ask him nicely."

"You think the cases could be linked?" asked David.

Diane shrugged. "Right now I can't see how. The only commonality between Stanton and McNair is me, unfortunately. And I really can't see a connection with Cipriano—maybe Stanton and the meth lab, but you can't get too far with rhyming words."

David stared at her for several moments. "What? Did I miss something? Was there something in one of the poetry books about the meth lab explosion?"

Diane smiled. "No. I just wondered to myself, What if Jere Bowen heard wrong? She said the voice was muffled and she couldn't hear exactly what he said." Diane went over her rhyming list with him, stopping at cook. "It was just a thought."

"Interesting. Long shot, but could be true." David looked like he was going to laugh.

"OK, it was crazy, but who knows," she said. "It

will be a while before the GBI processes the trace from McNair, but maybe you can get some of the details of the crime scene from Garnett."

"I'll get to work." David stood up. "We'll solve this," he said.

Diane could tell from his voice that he meant it.

"I'm glad you're confident. I don't relish people casting wondering glances at me for the rest of my life."

"Like I said, we have Jin. I tell you, I don't think you know how you motivated him."

"Yes, I do," said Diane.

Diane sat staring at the lone wolf for several minutes after David left her office, hoping that some pattern would form in her mind. She concluded that she didn't have enough information. Blake Stanton, she was sure as she could be with so little information, was hit to keep him from talking. If the meth lab had exploded with only the cook inside, there wouldn't be near the seriousness as it exploding with a house full of young people. It would be worth killing to keep secret any connection with that—provided that there was someone behind the lab besides the poor fellow who got blown to smithereens. The meth lab connection was a good place to start, she thought.

She opened up her bone vault where her computer equipment for reconstructing 3-D facial images from skulls was stored. She turned on the computer and the laser scanner.

Three partially reconstructed skulls were sitting in boxes of sand. One was from bones found in the burned-out basement. Not much was there—the brow and top of the eye sockets, the cheek and lower socket on the right side that included part of the nasal area. Part of a maxilla—the bone anchor for the upper teeth—and a fragment of a mandible—the lower jaw. She was able to match the upper and lower parts because the wear patterns on the upper and lower molars and premolars fit exactly. Luckily, those teeth had been still in their sockets. Unfortunately, no dental records had been submitted that matched the remains she had.

Diane used clay to prop up the reassembled pieces of skull on the modeling pedestal. It looked like a strange piece of artwork. When the modeling software was up, she turned on the apparatus and watched as the pedestal rotated and the laser read the topography of the fragments and generated a matrix of points on which to construct a wire frame of the head and face.

Diane asked the software to interpolate the missing part of the face from the parts that were present. The result would be a face that looked more symmetrical than it actually was because the computer only had one side to calculate what the other side looked like. But it would be a likeness that would be useful.

When she had a wire frame on which to work, she asked the software to use the skin depth database to reconstruct the face. Building the face was a slower process. She watched it being constructed.

She felt free in the vault. At least Patrice Stanton couldn't get to her here.

Chapter 26

Diane studied the completed 3-D model of the face generated from the glued-together skull fragments. It was not someone she recognized. She didn't think he would be. But she was willing to bet that he was known to someone in the police department.

Armed with a new face to work with, Diane printed out several paper copies, put an electronic copy of the image file on a memory stick, turned off her fancy equipment, and left the vault, locking it behind her.

She looked at her watch. It was a couple of hours past her usual lunch time. She hoped David, Jin, and Neva had stopped for lunch, but they were like her in that respect—often working right though it without noticing. Diane left her osteology lab and walked over to the crime lab. She found her crew busy. Jin and Neva had their heads together over a map. David was on the phone.

"Have you guys eaten?" asked Diane.

"Eat," said Jin. "No time. We've got criminals to catch. Neva and I were just looking at the jogging route Marcus took. I'll make a matrix of the access points and . . ."

"How did you find out where he was killed?" asked Diane.

Jin gave her his "Please, I'm a detective" look.

"What have you been doing?" asked David, placing the phone back on the hook.

Diane produced the printouts of the facial reconstruction.

"This skull was one of two that I hadn't identified. The other was found on the first floor near a window. These bones were in the basement and they were the only bones found there—that is, the only bones McNair's team turned over to us." Diane was sure that there were bones in the material that McNair took that she would never see.

"You think this is the cook?" said David.

"I'm thinking that he is," said Diane.

"Let's send a copy to Garnett," David suggested. "This should make him happy. It's the best lead they've had on the meth lab thing. They're up against the wall, and that Adler person's been giving them hell about it."

Diane handed David the memory stick; he put it in his computer and e-mailed the image to Garnett.

"OK," said Diane sitting down at the table where Jin and Neva were looking at the map. "I thought you were working on the Stanton murder, Jin."

Jin looked at Neva and over at David. "We've come up with a theory—hypothesis, to be more precise."

"An *idea* would be the most accurate," said David.

"OK, an idea," said Jin. "What if McNair is mixed up somehow in the meth lab mess?"

"Mixed up how?" asked Diane. If that were true, it would be a sticky wicket, indeed.

Jin shrugged. "Not sure. He could have been investigating it on his own in hopes of cracking it and taking the glory. Found out too much and was killed."

"Or," offered David, "he's in it up to his beady little eyeballs. He's been spending a lot of money—I know Garnett said that his wife has money, but what if he's really getting money from a drug operation? What if he's the shadow the police are all looking for behind the meth cook? He went to great lengths to get all the evidence under his control, you'll have to admit that."

"OK," said Diane, "I'm buying it so far."

"We have several scenarios to look at," said Jin. "McNair might have killed the Stanton kid because he was afraid the kid would talk, and then someone killed Stanton for the same reason, or for revenge, or something. Or, there is some other person above McNair in the meth operation who wanted to protect himself. Maybe he thought McNair was being too heavy-handed in taking the evidence and we were going to catch on that McNair was trying to hide something."

"I think we're onto something," said Neva. "I really do."

"Where are we going to put the DNA lab?" said Jin.

"Let's find the killer first," said Diane. "What are you going to do now?"

"David's trying to find out how McNair was killed. We know the location was the Briar Rose Nature Trail where he jogged. And we know he was shot. David's getting the details."

"David?" asked Diane.

"His autopsy is being performed as we speak, but this is what I have so far. He was jogging along his usual trail—a place where few people jog this time of year, especially now, with twenty degree temperatures and snow on the ground. But McNair was a marathoner, always in training. About a half mile into it he was shot in the knee. He fell, rolled around a bit, got the ground bloody, probably screamed, but we won't know that until we find the killer. He managed to get up and hopped about fifteen feet back to where he came from. He was shot again in the chest and once more in the head."

"What kind of gun?"

"Don't know that yet. I imagine the GBI does. We're going to have to get that from Garnett."

"No one heard gunfire?"

"I don't know," answered David.

"Any footprints in the snow?"

"Presumably, but we don't know," said David.

"What are the points of similarity between McNair and Stanton?" asked Diane.

Jin fielded this question. "They were both shot in an isolated place, both were shot in the head, maybe no one heard the gunshots in either case. That's all we have now."

"Interesting, but not compelling comparisons," said Diane.

"I'll bet they were both shot with the same gun," said Jin.

"Do we have the autopsy report on Blake Stanton?" asked Diane.

"No," said David.

"Can you get it for me, along with McNair's autopsy report?"

"Sure," said David.

"Good. I'd like to look at the two of them together. I'd also like to know as soon as possible if anyone in the police department recognizes the picture we sent."

"I can find that out," said Neva.

Diane started to speak just as her cell phone rang. With the sense of dread that Patrice Stanton had inspired in her, she looked at the caller ID. Unknown caller. Shit. But she couldn't keep avoiding answering any of her phones.

"Yes," she said.

"Diane, Frank here."

Diane grinned. "Frank, it is so good to hear from you."

"I've missed you, too. How about I come over this evening with dinner and stay the night?"

"That would be great. It seems that I'm going to need an alibi twenty-four/seven."

"What? What are you into now?"

"That's the point. I'm not into anything. I'll explain when I see you."

"All right." There was hesitation in his voice as he let her off the explanation hook. "See you tonight. Pizza?"

"Pizza's good."

When Diane got off the phone with Frank, she asked David, "I don't suppose you've taken that ad out yet about no murders until we recover? I could really use a night off."

"Darn it. No, I haven't," said David.

"You know," said Jin. "We could be looking at this all wrong. There's another angle."

"What's that?" asked Diane.

"Someone could be getting rid of your enemies."

Chapter 27

"Someone could be getting rid of my enemies?" said Diane. She didn't like this angle at all.

"You could have a secret admirer who wants to make your problems go away," said Jin.

"Let's say for a moment that this scenario is true," said Diane. "Then it follows that Patrice is in danger. Well, hell." She fished the cell phone from her pocket, called Garnett, and relayed Jin's latest idea.

"It's just a thought," said Diane, "and I think it remote, but you might keep an eye on her."

"She's already requested that we do so. She heard about McNair and has decided that you will be gunning for her next."

"Oh, this is just great. You know, Garnett, I do have a reputation to uphold in this town."

"I know. I wouldn't worry about it."

Easy for him to say, she thought. "We e-mailed you a likeness of the individual generated from the skull fragments found in the basement," she said.

"I got it. I'm showing it around now. This is the first break we've had in the meth case. Good job."

"Marcus' men collected the evidence in the basement," said Diane. "There have to be more bone parts from there. I have a couple of long bones, a rib, and the skull fragments from the basement, that's it."

"Maybe it was all obliterated," said Garnett.

"Do you know how hard it is to obliterate bone?" asked Diane.

"I'll check on it," he said.

"Have you been able to look at any of the other evidence from the basement area?"

"No. McNair's unit is working on it. They'll let me know when they have something." Garnett thanked her again and hung up.

Diane thought he was in rather a hurry to get off the phone.

"Well," said Diane, "Patrice had the same idea . . . but she's asked for police protection from me."

The three of them laughed. She didn't think it was funny.

"I'll be going through the books we brought from the Cipriano apartment," said Diane, "while you guys work on the other two cases."

The books were stacked in boxes in one of the glassed-in workrooms of the crime lab. The ones David had already gone through were on the table. He had made a list of the titles, authors, copyright dates, editions, and subject matter. She scanned the list, looking for a title, a name, or anything that might sound like the phrase Jere Bowden thought she heard. Nothing sprang from David's page of notes.

Diane continued where he left off. She flipped through the books, looking for margin notes or anything stuck between the pages. She went through about twenty books and . . . nothing. David was right. If you don't know what you're looking for, you have a hard time finding it.

She had started on a second boxful when Neva came into the room.

"I got a call from one of my sources," she said. "I have some information." She dragged up a chair and sat down. "It was another jogger who found McNair on the path. He said when he parked his car he saw a guy walking up the road. He was wearing a synthetic black winter coat and bill cap that matched, jeans, and work boots. He had graying dark hair, from what he could see. He noticed him because he didn't look like either a jogger or hiker. Does that sound familiar?"

"That's the description of the guy Jere Bowden saw at Joana Cipriano's apartment," said Diane.

"That's what they are thinking at Homicide," said Neva.

"So the murders *are* tied together somehow," said Diane. "How? We haven't found any evidence that Joana was involved in anything criminal." For that matter, she thought, they didn't really know if McNair was involved in anything illegal.

"I suppose it could be a coincidence," said Neva. "I mean, after all, it's not like those are unusual clothes. You could go around the city and find a half dozen men dressed like that this time of year."

"I supposed they asked Joana's ex-husband if she knew McNair?" said Diane.

"They did, and he said he'd never heard of him. Neither had her mother or her friends," said Neva.

"Did the witness have any other information?" asked Diane.

"Just that he thought the hat was new or the guy was a dork."

"Excuse me?" said Diane.

"The bill on his cap was straight, not curved. You know, you have to train your cap bill to have that curve in it. Most new hats don't have it. It's dorky to not train your cap bill."

"Of course." Diane had rolled up many a baseball cap bill and stuck it in a glass to get that curve in it. "If he saw the bill of the cap, did he see a face?"

"Partial face. The guy's collar was pulled up and he had his head turtled down and his hands in his pocket as though he was cold."

"Thanks, Neva. That's a good lead. Thank your informant for me."

"Sure. The police are kind of funny on this one," said Neva. "Normally, a member of the fire department like McNair would be held in the same regard as a member of the police department. They would pull out all the stops to find his killer. But McNair was considered lower than Internal Affairs because of the way he's gotten so many good cops in trouble." She shook her head. "He was a nasty fellow and he's sure caused a lot of problems. Garnett has to report directly to the mayor every day. They said he's pulling his hair out trying to deal with all of this—and he has a nice full head of hair."

"I can imagine. When Garnett gets the report on trace from both the crime scenes, get me a copy. I'm particularly interested in the fiber evidence from all the crime scenes."

"Sure. You really think you can get Garnett to put in a DNA lab?" asked Neva.

"I don't know. The museum might do it if the numbers line up the right way."

"Jin's really excited. Boy, you know how to reward people for accomplishment—shopping in Paris, DNA lab."

Diane laughed. "I suppose I do."

"OK, Diane," Frank said after washing down a bite of pizza with a swallow of beer, "tell me about your day." His blue green eyes glittered with amusement. "Why do you think you will need an alibi?"

Diane related the entire mess as they sat at her dining table eating pepperoni, mushroom, and sausage pizza. She started with Blake Stanton trying to hijack her car and ended with McNair taking the evidence.

"Now both Blake Stanton and Marcus McNair are

murdered. A city councilman would like me to be the killer, for some reason I can't fathom."

When she finished, Frank was no longer smiling; his eyes didn't have that wrinkle in the corners they got when he was amused.

"Why didn't you tell me about the attempted carjacking?" he asked.

"It paled in comparison to finding Star," said Diane. She cleared off her oak dining table and threw the pizza box in the trash. She put the other pizza he brought in the refrigerator. Frank always brought more food than they could possibly eat. A consequence, he said of coming from a family with two older brothers and an older sister.

"You are also important to me," he said when she returned to the table with coffee.

"I know, but it was over, and there would be plenty of opportunities to tell you."

"It must have been terrifying, facing a crazed kid with a bloody stump and a gun."

"Scary perhaps. He looked mainly pathetic, except for the gun. But what I really need is to find out who killed him and who killed McNair—and Joana Cipriano. You know, everything we've found out about her doesn't point to a person involved in criminal activity. Actually, I don't know that McNair was involved in anything criminal. It's just that I wouldn't put it past him."

They moved to her living room. She turned on some music—jazz violin played by Stephan Grappelli—opened up her drapes so they could watch the falling snow, and snuggled up with Frank on her large burgundy and gray striped sofa. She had liked the colors when she got it, but now she wasn't sure.

"Why don't you leave it to Garnett and his detectives?" asked Frank, kissing her temple.

"Because they aren't being accused of murder—twice," countered Diane.

"Neither are you, really. Just by some crazy woman and a councilman of questionable motives. I know Adler. He's not aboveboard himself."

Diane turned her head to face him. "You think he could be involved in something illegal with his nephew?"

"Wouldn't surprise me. But he's smart enough to make sure nothing leads to him."

"Would he have his own nephew killed?" asked Diane.

"That I don't know. Some days I'd say yes. But hiring a hit is dicey. More often than not, it backfires."

Diane put her hands to her temples. "I've got book titles swimming in my head, and I'm not even sure that Joana's death had anything to do with books. I'm just at a loss. I've been locked out of the information on McNair's crime scene. I need more data."

"Now, tell me again why you are not leaving this to the detective in charge of the case?"

"Because I have this crazy woman calling me every time I turn around telling me she is going to stalk me the rest of my natural life, and calling my board members and God knows who else and accusing me of murder."

Frank kissed her lips, then moved his mouth just a hairsbreadth away from hers. "Are you sure you want to talk about crime right now?"

"What crime?" she whispered.

It had been four days since Frank talked her out of investigating the murders and into simply handling the trace evidence from the crimes they themselves processed. She had to agree that this was far more relaxing. However, Jin, David, and Neva were still on the case. Jin was determined to get his DNA lab.

McNair's murder had an unexpected effect. Patrice Stanton stopped harassing her by phone. Apparently, she actually thought Diane had killed two people already and she didn't want to be next. *Well,* thought Diane, *whatever works.*

Today, Kendel sat in front of Diane's desk with several sheets of paper in her hand and a large box under her arm.

"We have a researcher who says he is going to petition the Egyptian government to ask for the return of our mummy if we don't allow him access," said Kendel.

Diane sighed. "That's a new tact."

"I'll write a letter to the legal affairs department of his university," Kendel said. "Maybe they have some influence on him."

Diane nodded.

"I'll also see if he's tried this with other institutions."

"Do that," said Diane.

"I wouldn't worry," said Kendel.

"I'm not," said Diane. "Lately I've had people threatening worse."

Kendel smiled. "I guess you have. By the way, Whitney Lester's starting her management training today."

"I hope she learns something," said Diane, eying the box. "What else do we have?"

"Mike sent you a gift. He wanted me to give it to you in person." Kendel handed Diane the box.

Mike was the curator for the geology collection at the museum and her caving partner, and he had on more than one occasion suggested that he would like to be more.

Diane smiled. "What is it? Do you know?" She weighed the box in her hands. "It's heavy."

"It is," said Kendel. "Open it." Kendel sat back smiling. "It's something you'll like."

Diane cut the tape on the box. Inside was filled with Styrofoam peanuts. She stood and put her hands down in the box, spilling the peanuts all over her desk. She found a roundish object wrapped in bubble wrap. She pulled it out and cut off the wrapping.

"Oh, my," said Diane, "this is lovely. You're right, I do like it. I love it."

She turned it around in her hand and looked at it. It was something Diane had wanted for a long time— a crystal skull carved out of quartz.

Chapter 28

Diane set the skull on her desk under a lamp and watched the light play off the surfaces. She placed her fingertips on the top of the skull and caressed it. It was as smooth as glass. The sutures etched into its surface were perfect. It was a beautiful piece. She opened the card that came with it.

> *If you look into its eyes you will be*
> *transported away.*
> *I miss our caving.*
> *—Mike.*

Another thing she and Mike had in common was a love of science fiction. In particular, they both liked *Stargate-SG1*. His note referred to an episode in that series. He was right. Staring into the eyes, she was transported.

"Aren't you tempted just a little?" asked Kendel.

Diane was startled out of her reverie. Kendel's voice abruptly transported her back from wherever she was.

"Tempted?" Diane asked.

"Mike."

"I'm seeing someone that I like very much. Mike is younger than I, and he works for me."

"That wasn't what I asked," said Kendel.

Diane smiled at her. "That is all the answer you're going to get."

"Well, I'd be tempted. And I'm dating a great guy whom I like very much. Just one of Mike's crooked smiles in my direction and I'd melt."

"I like the skull," said Diane, evading any talk of Mike and his crooked smile. "Did you help him find it?"

"I did. It wasn't easy finding one that nice and that large, but I managed," she said.

Diane imagined she did manage. Kendel was the best at finding things.

"I understand you've been visited by headhunters," said Diane.

Kendel had not tried to hide the fact that other museums had contacted her. Diane knew it would happen. She had been lucky to hire Kendel. Now that other museums were seeing her work, Diane knew they would be interested in her.

Kendel nodded. "Still have my head." She grinned. "The Illinoisan and the Smithsonian are looking for upper management."

"Kendel, you are well qualified for a director's position. I don't want you to stay here out of a sense of loyalty if something good comes your way."

Kendel shook her head. "They weren't looking for a director."

"Even so, those are big museums."

"The thing I liked about RiverTrail from the beginning was the quality of the collections and the physical facilities. The collections here may be small, but they are good and the potential for this museum to grow is tremendous. You have the space and the resources. That's not true of other museums."

Diane agreed. Good quality space is something they had in abundance, and they had strong financial resources.

"I can make a substantial contribution to a museum

like this one," continued Kendel. "The effect of my work would have much less impact at a really big museum. The geology collection here is already one of the best in the Southeast and it keeps growing. On each of Mike's excursions he sends back a unique selection of rock and mineral specimens and their petrogenesis. More and more of Bartram's graduate students in geology are coming to the museum to use our reference collection in their research. I've been working closely with the Geology Department on their exhibits. They're one of our strengths."

Diane knew that was true. The geology exhibits alone had raised the museum's ranking in the eyes of neighboring universities.

"I'm pleased to hear that you're happy here. I just want you to feel free to consider options when the headhunters come to you."

"Not a problem. That's another thing, they can't offer me the freedom I have here. Another quality I like about this museum is the lack of politics—and that's mainly your influence. I can concentrate on the collections and not constantly worry about sensitive egos and political agendas. Other museums aren't like that. This is a good place."

RiverTrail was indeed a good place. Diane counted it as one of her major jobs as director to keep it always a good place.

Kendel was summoned back to her office for some pressing matter, and Diane went to her other job—the one in the crime lab—for a different kind of pressing matter.

"We have the autopsy reports for Blake Stanton and Marcus McNair," said Neva.

"Bring them to my osteology office," said Diane, as she passed through. Even though she was more relaxed taking a hands-off approach to the investigations, she had had enough. It was not in her nature to avoid the thick of things.

Neva, David, and Jin followed on her heels. When Diane sat behind her desk, Neva handed her all the reports, including crime scene and autopsy photos.

Diane started with McNair's autopsy report. The cause of death was the gunshot to the head. He might have survived the hit to the chest. She flipped through the photographs of the scene. It was strange seeing McNair lying dead—the smirk finally gone from his face, permanently and forever wiped away.

She searched for the autopsy photos of McNair and Stanton, the head wounds in particular. She laid them side by side. Both bodies had a similarly sized hole in the middle of their forehead. McNair's had a large inflamed area around the wound. Neither had powder tattooing. Rankin noted the lack of tattooing, but made no conclusions. Rankin rarely went beyond what he knew.

"Did I hear you guys say the detective in charge thinks all shots were fired at a distance?" asked Diane.

"Yes," said Neva.

"Rosewood detectives don't get much experience with bullet wounds made by a gun with a silencer," said Diane. "And since no one in either scene heard anything, I believe a silencer was used."

Diane turned the photos around so they could see them. "Look at McNair's. The detective thought it was not a contact wound because of the lack of tattooing. But you often don't get tattooing with a silencer. This red ring is the muzzle imprint. Notice that it's erythematous—red and inflamed looking—and not abraded, as the muzzle imprint of a gun without a silencer would be. If we find the silencer, it will probably have the victim's tissue inside it."

Neva picked up the photograph and examined it. Jin looked over her shoulder. David hung back. Examining autopsy photos was not his favorite thing to do.

"If you look at Blake's wound," said Diane, "there's no stippling or muzzle imprint. He was shot from a distance. The bullet was found in his head—which may mean that considerable energy was lost before impact—also a factor with silencers, but that doesn't prove a silencer was used. It's just suggestive.''

"So what do you make of it?" asked Neva.

"McNair's murder was personal. The shooter hits him in the knee first. That hurts. Then they shoot him in the chest, and for good measure they come right up to him and shoot him in the head point-blank.''

"It sounds personal to me," said Jin.

"It was also someone who knew his schedule," said David. "You would have to know McNair or shadow him for a while to know his habits.''

Diane agreed. "With Blake Stanton," she said, "it wasn't as personal—or maybe the shooter couldn't get any closer." Diane shrugged. "Or maybe it was a different killer altogether.''

She looked at the report again. "It says here that McNair was probably killed with a Beretta—same type of gun as Stanton. I think both murders were executions and probably done by the same person.''

"What about Joana?" asked Neva. "She wasn't even killed with a gun. Besides, it looks like her death may have been an accident.''

"At least an accident that it happened before the killer got the information he wanted," said Diane. "But you're right, it doesn't have the same feel to it as the others—despite the fact that similarly dressed individuals were spotted at both scenes." Diane thought a moment. "Find out for me if the guy who found the body, the second jogger, also has regular running habits.''

"You suspect him?" asked Jin.

"The killer would know when someone was likely to come along if he'd been casing the trail where McNair was ambushed. That's the thing about dedicated joggers—you can set your clock by them.''

"I don't see the connection," said Jin.

"Maybe the killer wanted to be seen. Assume for a moment that both Stanton and McNair were killed by the same person. He seems to be professional; he left very few clues. Why then would he show himself at a time and place where he knew he was likely to be seen?"

"Good thought," said David. "You thinking he disguised himself as another suspect? Could happen; the description was in the news as well as all over the neighborhood. In that case, there might be no link between Joana Cipriano and Marcus McNair. The detectives are just running in circles trying to make a connection."

"All of this is conjecture," said Diane. "But it is something to think about."

"We need to look at each crime scene with a fresh eye," said Jin. "Just look at the evidence and build from there. . . ."

As Diane listened to Jin, she picked up Neva's report on the processing of her car that had been lying on her desk for days. She absently thumbed through it and stopped abruptly, stood, and stared at the page.

"Where is the evidence you gathered from my car?" said Diane.

Jin stopped in the middle of what he was saying. "What?" he asked.

"Which one?" asked David.

"The first one, the carjacking," said Neva, looking at the report Diane was holding. "It's all in the evidence locker." She pointed in the direction of the crime lab.

Diane rushed out of her office, through the osteology lab, and into the crime lab. She made a beeline for the evidence locker, keyed in the digitized combination, opened it, and walked in. The box she was looking for was right up front. It was labeled with her name, the make and model of her car, Blake Stanton's name, and the date and time, written in neat black lettering on the end. She pulled it out and set it on the table.

Jin, Neva, and David had followed her. They stood looking at each other quizzically and shrugged.

"Is something wrong?" asked Neva

Diane ignored her as she searched through the box for the evidence bags. She found the bag she was looking for, initialed it, opened the seal, and poured out the contents into her hand where she examined them closely before placing them on the table.

"These are *Cypraea aurantium,* " she said, eying Neva.

"Sorry, I thought they were seashells." Neva creased her forehead in a worried frown.

Chapter 29

"They look like those shells that you see in African motifs," said Neva. "That's what I thought they were.

"Cowrie shells," said Diane. "Golden cowries—they are worth about three hundred dollars apiece."

"Three hundred dollars for one of those?" said Neva, pointing to the eight shells, each the color of a deep yellow sunset.

Jin whistled. "Wow, Boss, you sure know your seashells."

"I know these because they belong to the museum," said Diane. "You found these in my car, Neva?"

"In the backseat. They were in that Ziploc bag with the blood on it. The blood is his. We sent it off to be tested. The shells have his fingerprints—from the hand that was cut off. He had a scar on his thumb that shows up in his prints. So he had them before he got in your car."

"I'm not following this," said David, standing with his hands in his pockets, staring at the cowrie shells. "These are your shells?"

"Not mine personally. The museum's. We've had a series of thefts. Among them, six thousand dollars worth of rare seashells. So far we've discovered the loss of rare items valued at a total of over thirty thousand dollars missing from various departments in the museum—including Vanessa Van Ross's ten-thousand-dollar diamond that she gave to the museum's gem reference collection."

David, Neva, and Jin glanced at each other, eyebrows raised. David shrugged.

"Why weren't we called?" asked Jin.

"Museum Security is tallying the loss. We just discovered the items were missing. The thief substituted imitations or cheaper items in place of the missing ones, so it's taken a while for all the thefts to be discovered."

David pulled up a chair from one of the tables in the room and sat down. He stroked the fringe of hair that still grew around the back and sides of his head.

"What does this mean for all the theories of the crime that we've been positing?" he said.

"I don't know," said Diane. "This adds a new wrinkle, doesn't it?" She sat down, too, and the others followed.

"Does this mean Blake Stanton's extra money was coming from thievery and not drugs?" asked David.

"Or both," said Jin. He leaned forward with his forearms propped on his thighs and hands clasped between his knees. "I don't think we have to throw away all the theories of the crime just yet."

"Campus police will probably cooperate with museum security better than they will with us. I'll have Chanell call them and find out if the university's been having similar thefts."

"You think maybe that's what he's been getting out of his perpetual student status—plenty of places to pilfer?" said David.

"Maybe," said Diane. "Just look at the hunting grounds—all the departments, the library, the campus art museum."

"Not to mention money," said Jin. "If you're any kind of good thief, there's lots of opportunities around university departments to swipe money."

"It might be a good racket," said David. "If you

don't steal too much from any one source, it may take a while before they even notice anything's missing, or that there's a larger pattern."

"But you have to have a place to sell it," said Diane.

"He has to be selling to collectors for most of it," said David. "That's where you'll get a premium price for those kinds of items. And collectors often don't ask probing questions."

"How did he get access to so many departments in the museum?" said Neva. "I mean, the Van Ross diamond isn't even on display. It's in the reference collection."

Jin and David looked at her with the same question on their faces.

"I know because Mike showed me the diamond, OK?"

"How is Mike?" said Jin. "We haven't seen very much of him lately."

"He's away searching for those strange organisms," said Neva. "All our dates lately have been over a webcam. Right now he's caving in South America."

"Webcam dating," said David. "That sounds like me. Only, I usually don't know the girl at the other end."

Jin laughed; Diane rolled her eyes.

"Just kidding," he said. "Although I understand you can have some pretty good remote kinky sex with a webcam. Joana Cipriano's ex-husband apparently gets lots of cartoon action."

"I'm not even going to ask," said Neva.

"I wouldn't." Diane shook her head.

"You can tell me later," said Jin.

Diane replaced the seashells in the evidence bag, resealed it, and had Neva, Jin, and David sign as witnesses. Just as she put it in the locker, her cell phone rang. She looked at the display. It was Laura Hillard, psychiatrist friend and museum board member.

"Hi," said Diane. "You call to tell me I'm a murder suspect?"

"I guess you know that some crazy woman's been calling all of us," said Laura. "I tried to set her straight, but it's awfully hard to set someone straight who's nuts—I know. Actually that's not why I called. It's about your employee, Juliet Price."

"Juliet? Is she all right?" Diane walked back to her office as she listened to Laura.

"Nothing's happened. Don't worry. She's been coming to see me. You know how I like to work—I have my patients come every day for a couple of weeks before I go to a weekly appointment schedule. I think the initial intensity gives them a lot of security up front and lets me get to know them better. Of course, I've had a few who think it's just a money-making scheme." She laughed. "Anyway, she gave me permission to speak with you. I thought you could help."

"Me? How?" asked Diane.

"Her problems stem from that one tragic event in her life. She remembers only snatches of it. I'm working with her on that, but I have to be careful of creating false memories, so it's going to be a slow process. But I think something happened recently that's triggered post-traumatic stress reactions. She doesn't know what it could be."

"And you want me to find out? I don't think . . ."

"No, no. I want you to take a look at her kidnapping. She has all the files in her possession. If you could solve it . . ."

"Solve it? Laura, what makes you think I can solve a—what is it—twenty-year-old case?"

"Isn't that what you do?" asked Laura sweetly.

"Not exactly. Any bones involved?" said Diane.

Laura laughed. "None that I know of. How about it? I think it would help her to know what happened. All her life her parents shielded her from the information. Her stepmother meant well, but she wasn't any

help, either. Her father and maternal grandmother
blamed her for her mother's death. It wasn't until she
was an adult that she was able to find out much at
all. Until then she only had strange memory fragments
that frightened her. You might be the only one who
can shed light on what happened to her."

"OK, I'll have a look at her files," said Diane.

"Good. I'd like you to listen to the tape I made of
her talking about her memories. She thinks it's a good
idea, but didn't want to ask you herself."

"All right," said Diane.

"I knew I could count on you. Isn't this more fun
than going on a killing spree?" said Laura.

"That's not funny, Laura. I suppose you heard
about the McNair murder."

"Of course. That's the advantage of being 'old
Rosewood.' We get to hear everything. I understand
that addlebrained Councilman Adler is trying to take
political advantage of these tragedies. Did you see him
on the news, weeping over his nephew? He didn't care
a flip for his nephew. You can't when you're a sociopath, and Adler's one if I've ever seen one."

"No, I didn't see him. For some reason he wants
me to be the killer. I'm not sure I understand that."

"Because you are part of the Rosewood police department, and he's been gunning for them. He'll stop
that in a hurry. He's made Vanessa mad and you know
what she's like when she's mad. Attacking you is like
attacking the museum, and that's like attacking Milo,
and she won't have that."

"Send me the files and tape," said Diane.

"They should be on your desk. I sent them by courier. I knew you'd say yes."

"You are awful, Laura," said Diane.

"I know. But I get things done. I'll talk to you later.
I'm eager to see what you make of it all. Juliet's having a hard time right now. Thank you for helping."

"Sure, as you say, it beats going on a killing spree."

Diane looked accusingly at her phone after Laura hung up. "I can't believe I said yes. As if I don't have enough to do."

Diane closed her office and went back to the crime lab where Jin, Neva, and David were bouncing ideas off each other.

"Any new theories on the crimes?" asked Diane.

"Nothing that makes any sense," said David. "I think the kid just had his hand—pardon the pun—in too many pots."

"You know, David," said Jin, "I've been counting the number of times you've used a word that starts with *p*, and it's a lot."

David glared at Jin for a long moment. "You what? Jin, that doesn't make a bit of sense. Why would you do that? Why not the number of words that start with *f*?"

"Because you use *p* more often," said Jin. "Statistically, you use it more frequently than the occurrence of *p* words in everyday language."

David looked at Jin, amazed. "To know that, you would have to count all the first letters of all the words I use when I talk. Why do you have so much time? And why in the hell would you care?"

"That's just something I notice," said Jin.

"He's right," said Neva. "And they tend to cluster. That's called something."

"Alliteration," said Jin. Then he grinned. "Or is it onomato-pee." Both he and Neva lauged at what Diane thought was a rather lame joke. Diane rolled her eyes and shook her head.

David looked from one to the other, then at Diane. "See what I have to put up with? They have far too much time on their hands."

Diane laughed, too. She had a slight feeling of déjà vu, but couldn't put her finger on the source. It was odd that she would, because this was such an unusual conversation. She shook her head as if she could shake out the feeling.

"As much as I'd like to continue this conversation," said Diane, "I've got work to do. I'm going to my museum office. Remember, Jin, you have a DNA lab riding on your work."

"Gee, no pressure, Boss."

David went back to his computer, still shaking his head and casting glances of consternation at Jin and Neva.

"Now you've made him paranoid," said Diane. "He'll never again use another word that starts with the letter *p*."

Chapter 30

Laura Hillard's package had been delivered by the time Diane got back to her museum office. Andie had put it on her desk. Diane opened the envelope and spilled the contents out on her desktop. There were copies of police reports, newspaper clippings, and a tape. She picked up the yellowed pages of the newspaper clippings. They were arranged in chronological order and held together with a paper clip. The first thing that occurred to Diane was that they needed to be treated with a deacidifier. She smiled to herself. First thoughts are of preserving the paper—a consequence of working in a museum.

The lead article, dated September 29, 1987, was the first news account of Juliet's disappearance. It contained a school photograph of a young Juliet. A smiling little girl, she looked happy. Diane wondered if that picture was the last time Juliet looked happy. She read the article over a couple of times. Not much information in it other than Juliet's description, that she had been missing since the day before, and was last seen playing in her backyard. Diane wondered if it was fenced in or not. How much trouble had the kidnapper gone to to take her?

The second clipping, dated October 2, 1987, described Juliet being found. A group of kids discovered her when their basketball rolled down an embankment

and into a concrete culvert. She was stuffed in the
culvert with mud and rocks as if she'd washed in. The
preteen boys pulled her out. One ran for the police.
There was a picture of a row of smiling boys, one
holding a basketball. There was a picture of the
empty culvert.

The article said she had been drugged and strangled.
When she passed out, the kidnapper apparently
thought she was dead. He'd put her in the cement
pipe and left her. A light autumn rain had washed
mud, rocks, and leaves around her body. She was
lucky she hadn't drowned.

What a terrible story, thought Diane. She wondered
how Juliet had felt reading it. No wonder she was
having post-traumatic stress issues. Anyone would,
having gone though such an ordeal.

The third clipping, dated November 7, 1987, was a
follow-up. It simply said that after a month, the police
had no leads as to who had kidnapped Juliet and left
her for dead, and no information as to the motive.

Diane looked at a copy of the police report. It was
sketchy. It included the missing person's report, the
school picture of Juliet, a doctor's report, which said
that she wasn't molested but had a bruised trachea,
arms, and ribs.

The police had interviewed the parents, grandpar-
ents, teachers, neighbors, and friends. They found
nothing. The interviews were included in the report
and Diane read through them. Only a couple of items
jumped out at her. One was a report of a woman who
had fallen while jogging on the road in front of Juliet's
home at about the time of Juliet's abduction. Several
neighbors saw her, including Juliet's mother. Two
neighbors went to help her up. The police were unable
to find her even after an appeal in the newspaper. The
other item of interest was a report from a child who
lived next door and was a year older than Juliet who
heard her say, "I don't know you," an hour before

she was reported missing. That seemed to suggest that Juliet hadn't recognized whomever she was talking to. Then was it a stranger? Was it the kidnappper?

What if, Diane thought, the woman was a ruse whose purpose was to keep the neighborhood eyes to the front of the houses and not the backs where they might see Juliet being snatched? Diane wondered if the police had a composite sketch made of the jogger. She searched and didn't see one among the papers.

She picked up the tape, weighed it in her hand, and looked at it before inserting it into a player. She felt really reluctant to listen to Juliet in one of her sessions with Laura. It was as if she would be listening to something she had no business hearing. However, if Juliet thought it was a good idea . . . Diane slipped on the earphones, and pressed the PLAY button.

"Juliet, tell me what you remember." This was Laura's voice.

There was no introductory conversation. Laura had edited the tape. Diane felt better.

"Dark and hard to breathe. I'm afraid of being closed in," said Juliet. Her voice was low and soft.

"Just tell me what you remember. We'll talk about your fears later," said Laura.

"I remember dark, and something in my eyes that hurt. I do remember that. I don't know when that was—I could have been playing outside, for all I know," said Juliet.

"That's OK. We just want to look at your conscious memories right now," said Laura. "Do you have any other memories that frighten you or that you find mysterious or simply can't connect up with anything that your parents remember about your childhood?" asked Laura.

There were a few moments of silence. "I had a doll that Gramma said I must have stolen. I didn't, but I don't know where I got it," said Juliet. "Gramma was a strict woman, but she could be fun sometimes, especially when she baked or when we collected seashells on the beach."

There was a pause, and Diane could hear Juliet breathing.

"I remember being in a dark room with new dolls. I remember a baby doll, and I remember being afraid in the room." She paused again. "The room had hardwood floors." Juliet laughed. "I'm not afraid of hardwood floors."

Diane heard Laura laugh, too.

"I remember running from something," continued Juliet, "just running. I remember someone saying, 'She said you took it.' I don't know if any of these memories are connected to the same thing, but they all give me the same fear when I think of them. I have very few memories before the age of seven. That's when it happened, and I don't really remember getting kidnapped at all. I don't know if any of these memories are from the kidnapping. I used to have this dream of rows and rows of new dolls. The dreams stopped for a long time, and now they've started back. I don't know why. And I don't know why I'm afraid of them."

"What do you mean by new dolls?" asked Laura.

"Dolls still in the box," said Juliet. "What does it mean?"

"I don't know, yet," said Laura. "But we'll find out. Memory is funny. I have a friend who associates the name *Louise* with *vinegar*."

Diane smiled. That was her. It was something she told Laura when they were kids. Talk about memory.

"Vinegar?" said Juliet.

"The word *Louise* sounded like *vinegar* to her—that's the best she could explain it to me. It may be that when she was little she met someone named Louise who spilled vinegar, and the association stuck. But most probably, when she learned the words *Louise* and *vinegar,* they somehow got stored in the same place in the brain. Or there could be some other reason entirely."

"My memories are so frustrating," said Juliet. "They don't make sense to me."

"Early memories are not always accurate," said Laura. "There was this book that I liked as a young child—it was one of the Golden books. In the book there was a red ball and red wallpaper. To this day when I see a certain kind of red wallpaper, it reminds me of that book. The same with a certain kind of ball. Not long ago I was sorting some stuff in the attic and came across that book. I looked through it for that ball and wallpaper and, to my surprise, the drawings were much cruder and the colors much less vivid than my memory of them. The drawings were childlike in the book, but in my memory they were more polished—finished."

"How does that happen?" asked Juliet. "I thought memories were written in stone once they get stored."

"No. Your memories change over time as the brain develops, or as people and events influence them. Some memories are only memories of something that was told to you, and your brain filled out the image. If all your life your parents and relatives tell you a story of how you fell in the creek and almost drowned, you will likely have a memory of it, especially if you've ever seen the creek where you were told the event occurred. That happened to my cousin. Years later, she found out it happened to another cousin, not her at all. Yet, by the time she got to be an adult she remembered the event—and it never even happened to her. Sometimes people confuse dreams with memory. That's why we are going to talk about your dreams another time."

"How will we ever figure this out?" said Juliet.

"Wading through early memories is tough," said Laura. "But we'll get though it. I have some ideas."

That was all that was on the tape. Diane was glad it was over. Hearing Juliet talk about her memories was uncomfortable. She could hear the pain in Juliet's voice. A person's deepest fears are such a private thing. Diane took off the earphones and sat thinking.

"I don't know how Laura expects me to solve a twenty-year-old crime with this scant evidence," she whispered to herself. "I must have been nuts to agree."

Diane looked at her watch. It was about time to go home. She locked Juliet's information in her desk and went to tell Andie good-bye.

"We haven't been getting any more harassing phone calls," said Andie. "Whatever you did worked." She smiled brightly.

Diane smiled back ruefully. *Patrice Stanton thinks I'll kill her,* she thought. *What a reputation I'm getting.*

Before she left the building Diane stopped by the crime lab. David, Jin, and Neva were sitting at the large round table looking at reports.

"We don't have anything, guys," Jin was saying when Diane walked in.

"I don't want to hear that," said Diane. "We have to have something. What are you looking at?"

"We have some of the trace back from the GBI," Jin answered. "They've accounted for all the fibers found on McNair. The only thing interesting is a blond hair about seven inches long. It could be his wife's; they don't know yet. So far, we can't find any link between Joana Cipriano's scene and the other two. In fact, there's no common trace evidence between McNair and Stanton."

"Everything we found in Stanton's boathouse belonged to the family," said Neva. "I don't think the killer ever got inside the boathouse."

"I agree," said David. "I think he came by boat, shot him, and left."

"What about the noise?" asked Diane.

"Electric trolling motor," said David. "Just a little hum."

"But aren't they slow?" asked Diane.

"As fast as walking. Fast enough to get you to one of the little coves where you have a car waiting," said David.

"That sounds awfully chancy," said Diane.

"This is a lake where people do night fishing," said David. "Nothing unusual about a small boat being out on the water."

"In the middle of winter?" asked Diane. She shrugged. "It's as good a theory as any we've had. But where does it get us?"

"Where you came in," said Jin. "We don't have anything."

"What do the detectives have?" asked Diane.

"Less than we do," said Jin. "We got hold of the GBI report first."

"They must have more," said Diane. "They've been investigating McNair's life, his friends and enemies, his family. Same for Stanton. Surely, they've come up with something."

"They say they have nothing," said Neva. "It could be that my sources have been told not to talk."

"I'll talk to Garnett," said Diane. "They have to have something."

"You want my opinion?" said David. "It was the uncle—he's got enough clout to dry up the investigation. And I'll bet he's behind the drug operation."

"Go home and get some rest. A fresh idea may occur to you in the morning. I'm leaving."

Diane left through the museum exit of the crime lab, crossed the dinosaur overlook, and took the elevator down to the first floor. She walked to the east-wing exit where yet another museum car was parked for her use. The museum store was closed and dark except for the floor lighting. She looked in at the row of Dora the Explorer dolls lined up on the shelf and was reminded of Juliet's dream. What was it about dolls? Diane continued past the primate exhibits, feeling guilty for not putting enough time in the department for which she was curator. An idea of an exhibit had been forming in her mind for several days and she had done nothing about it. She walked through to the lobby and out the doors.

She was home in bed when an idea hit her. She looked at the clock. *One o'clock, shit.* She picked up the phone anyway and called Andie.

Andie answered, obviously wide awake.

"I'm sorry to call you so late," said Diane.

"It's not late," said Andie. "What you need?"

"You know that basket you made for Juliet Price?"

"How could I forget it?" answered Andie.

"The mermaid doll, was it in a box? I seem to recall that it wasn't."

"No, it wasn't. Is that why you called?"

"Yes. Thanks for the information."

"Anytime," said Andie.

Interesting, Diane said to herself. *I'll wait until morning to call Laura.*

Chapter 31

It was the first good night's sleep Diane had since the explosion. She woke up feeling good—no midnight calls, no murders, no bad dreams. She made herself scrambled eggs, the kind of bacon that's already fried and just needs to be microwaved, the kind of toast made in the broiler and not the toaster, and orange juice. She didn't know exactly why she felt so good.

Her mind had certainly been working overtime while she slept. Besides an epiphany she was experiencing about Juliet Price, her head was buzzing with questions about the cases that needed to be solved. Uppermost in her thoughts today was the question of how Blake Stanton had gained access to her museum holdings. How did he manage to get into every department in the museum and how did he know so much about what they had and what was valuable?

She enjoyed her breakfast and then dashed outside where she found, to her relief, her car unmarked by the mad graffiti artist, Patrice Stanton. She drove to the museum and parked in her usual place. The weather had been warmer the past few days, but the temperature was dropping again and the wind was strong. She wrapped herself in her coat and hurried up the steps to the warmth of the museum.

She met Juliet in the lobby. Juliet's platinum hair

was pulled back and out of her face. Diane thought
that was a good sign—becoming visible.

"Dr. Fallon," said Juliet, "I want to thank you for
everything you're doing for me. You and Dr. Hillard
are really being great."

"I'm not sure what I can do, but I'll try." Diane
didn't mention the idea she was having—she wanted
to talk it over with Laura first.

"Whatever you do, I appreciate it." She looked at
her watch. "I'm waiting for visiting hours at the hospital," she said. "Darcy is in her own room now and
can have limited visitation. This is terrible for her."

"Yes, it is," said Diane, "but it looks as if she is on
the mend."

"Her parents can't decide whether they should tell
her that her boyfriend was killed," said Juliet.

"Oh, no," said Diane. "Was he in the explosion,
too?"

"Yes, but he survived that." Her voice went down
to a whisper. "But later he was murdered."

Diane was so shocked it caught her breath.

"Murdered?"

Some of the museum staff came through the doors,
bringing with them a gust of cold wind. Diane shivered.

"Come to my office where we can talk," she said.

She hadn't meant it to sound like such a command,
but Juliet followed her back to her office. Diane took
her into her lounge area and plied her with orange
juice.

"What was her boyfriend's name?" asked Diane.
Still trying hard not to sound like she was interrogat-
ing her.

"Blake Stanton," said Juliet.

If Juliet was disturbed by Diane's questioning, she
didn't show it. Diane hoped she was successful at
looking casual. She remembered how Blake had told
his parents at the hospital that she was the director of

the museum. She just assumed he had seen her in the newspaper or something. But it was clear now, he knew who she was because he had been to the museum, probably on more than one occasion.

"Darcy's crazy about him," said Juliet, sipping on her orange juice. "She doesn't like his parents much. She said his mother's a real nut job."

"Was he at the museum often? I don't recall seeing him here," said Diane.

"He was here with her a lot. He said he was thinking about going into a career in museum work, so Darcy showed him around all the departments and let him watch her plan some of the exhibits. Some people actually thought he worked here. He was really helpful to everyone."

I'll bet he was, thought Diane. A little con artist in training—gain their trust and raid their pantry.

"He was a student." It was a statement, but Diane made it sound like a question.

"He's one of those students who never graduates." Juliet sighed. "Darcy is going to be devastated. She was really in love with him."

"I get the feeling you didn't think too much of him."

"I don't—didn't really," she said. She put her juice on the table. "I got the impression he didn't really like her as much as she liked him. You know when a guy likes you, he looks at you a lot, even when you aren't looking at him. He never looked at her. He looked at other women, but rarely at her."

Interesting observation, thought Diane. "I appreciate you talking to me about Darcy," said Diane. "We're all hoping she recovers quickly. I met her parents. They're nice people."

"Darcy's crazy about her parents. She really cares what they think of her. A lot of people my age don't. Myself, I have much lower expectations. I only care that they don't think I'm crazy." She smiled.

Diane smiled with her. "They can put their minds

at ease if they think that. There's a big difference between coping strategies and crazy."

Juliet picked up her orange juice and stood up.

"That's what Dr. Hillard says."

She smiled again as she headed for the door.

"Maybe she'll give me a certificate of saneness that I can frame and hang on the wall."

"Say hello to Darcy for me," said Diane. "By the way, how is Whitney Lester treating you?"

"She sort of gives me the cold shoulder, which I accept gladly."

After Juliet left, Diane sat on the couch for several minutes thinking. The problem had been solved of how Blake managed to gain access to the back rooms of the museum, and she didn't like the answer. It presented a new and more difficult problem. Did Darcy know what he was doing? Was she helping? Diane didn't want to interrogate Darcy while she was recovering, but she wanted to get the museum's property back. *Damn.*

Of course Diane had known it had to be someone on the inside, but she'd been rejecting the idea. She got up from the couch and headed for Security.

"Chanell," she said as she knocked on her open door.

"Dr. Fallon, I was just about to come and see you. We found Mrs. Van Ross' diamond, along with several other stones from the geology exhibit." Chanell's black eyes glittered with triumph.

Diane closed the door and sat down in the chair near her desk. "You found them? Where?"

"Actually, it was a fourth grader on one of the tours late yesterday. He was digging in the potted palms near the entrance and came up with a bag of jewels. His teacher saw him pocket them and brought them to the information desk. It turned out to be the missing stones. And I'm sorry, I haven't a clue as to how they got there."

Diane could only imagine. Had Blake gotten cold feet?

"I found out who the thief is," said Diane. "His name was Blake Stanton. He's the young man who was murdered."

"That boy?" said Chanell. "I'm sorry, Dr. Fallon, I don't know how he got access to the museum. But I'll sure be looking into it."

"Unfortunately, I know that, too. He's the boyfriend of Darcy Kincaid."

"Oh, no, not Darcy. That's a shame. Is she in on it with him, do you know?"

"I don't know and I'm reluctant to ask right now," said Diane.

"I understand. Now that we know who's behind it, we can get a line on the other stolen items. How did you find out it was him?"

Diane explained about the shells being found in her car with his prints on them.

"So, you've recovered the shells?"

"Just the golden cowrie shells," said Diane. "I don't know where the others are."

"I've instituted a search of all the plants," said Chanell. "In case that's where the items were stashed for later pickup or something. Darcy Kincaid." She shook her head. "I hope that child isn't involved."

"Me too," said Diane.

Diane wasn't feeling as perky as when she awakened this morning. Finding out about Darcy had depressed her. She didn't believe there was any way Darcy couldn't have known what Blake was doing. At least, some things were falling into place. She went back to her office and called to make an appointment with Laura Hillard.

Chapter 32

Before going to her appointment with Laura, Diane walked upstairs to the crime lab. It was early and she didn't expect anyone to be there, but she would leave a note. To her surprise, all three of her crew were in the lab working.

"Do you guys spend the night here?" asked Diane.

"Just about," said Neva. "You can get only so much warmth from a webcam, so I might as well work. By the way, Mike told me to go by and have a look at the crystal skull he got for you—do you have it yet?"

"It's in my museum office on my desk. It's very nice. I like it a lot."

"Crystal skull? Like the Mayan skull, the Mitchell-Hedges skull?" asked David. "Really? Are you going to display it?"

"It's similar to the Mitchell-Hedges skull," said Diane. "Jonas Briggs wants to put on an exhibit on archaeology and legend or false archaeology, something like that. The provenances are suspect on all the crystal skulls, but there's a lot of myth and superstition surrounding them. Jonas said he's been working up an exhibit. Apparently everyone but me knew I was getting one."

Before Mike began dating Neva, it was no secret he was interested in Diane, an interest she made it plain she could not accept or reciprocate. Even now he played at flirting on occasion but never seriously. Diane sometimes felt uncomfortable with his faux flirtations because of Neva, but Neva seemed to recognize it as no more than teasing. Mike appeared always to be up front with Neva in everything he did. Diane was relieved to know that. They were all caving partners, she, Neva and Mike—and Jin, too, now. Because of his skills in rock climbing and caving, Mike was the best caving partner she'd ever had. She was loath to lose that. In any other instance she would never accept such a gift from someone she was not involved with, but this was, after all, a crystal skull.

"Enough about the skull," said Diane. "I just found out something I need to talk with you about."

"What's that, Boss?" said Jin.

"I'd like to go see the skull," said David. "You know they are all supposed to communicate with each other?"

"Who?" asked Jin.

"All the crystal skulls," said David.

"Are you serious?" said Jin, giving David a sidelong look. "You don't believe that?"

"Why not? Transmitters are made from quartz crystals," said David. "And it makes more sense than that white noise you listened to trying to hear dead voices all last month—driving us all crazy. I still hear white noise in my sleep."

"Any dead voices?" asked Jin.

"Seriously, the skulls are supposed to possess an aura," said David.

"Jonas Briggs is going to love talking with you," said Diane. "The skull's in my office. You can go ask Andie to let you in. In the meantime . . ." Diane jerked her thumb to the round table where they debriefed and discussed matters of crime. When they were seated she told them about Darcy Kincaid and Blake Stanton.

"Well, that clears up one mystery," said Neva. "How Blake got access to the museum."

"I think there are a lot of things we have to re-think," said Diane. "Darcy was at the ill-fated party. So was Blake. I think we can assume it was a date. We'll know more when we can talk to Darcy. But it's possible he may have known no more about the meth lab than the other victims."

"His and McNair's murders may not be related," said David. "Is that what you are saying?"

"I don't know," said Diane. "I just brought it to you guys to think about. Blake Stanton's murder may have had to do with his thievery and not be related to McNair at all. Maybe someone was supposed to meet him to purchase something, but killed him and took the item instead—or something along those lines."

"Maybe McNair was involved with him in his steal-ing," said Neva. "Maybe he had nothing to do with the meth lab, either. Maybe the thefts are the connec-tion and why they were killed in a similar manner."

"I know," Diane said, "This raises more questions than answers."

She told them about Vanessa Van Ross' diamond being found in the dirt of the potted palm.

"Maybe buyers were expecting Blake to have the stones, and when he didn't deliver, they killed him. I don't know. Think about it." She looked at her watch. "I have an appointment. You guys come up with something."

Diane left them sitting at the table reworking their theories. On her way to Laura's she stopped and bought a vanilla milk shake. *Nothing like gluttony to make you feel better,* she thought. The frozen drink made her shiver. She wondered how many shakes they sold in the dead of winter.

Laura's office was a small cottage with a picket

fence and a flower garden. Right now the picket fence was capped with snow and the flower beds were covered over and glistened white. But in the spring and summer it was awash with colors and butterflies. It didn't look like you were heading to a psychiatrist's office when you came through the gate and up the walk to the door.

Inside, the cottage was as cozy as the outside. There was even a fire in the grate. The receptionist told Diane to go on into Laura's office. It also had a fireplace with a warm and gentle fire. The room looked more like a snug den than a doctor's office. Diane imagined that the atmosphere must put everyone at ease.

Laura's blue eyes twinkled as she greeted Diane. "I knew you would find something," she said.

She was dressed in a lime green silk suit. Her blond hair was shoulder length and turned under. Laura always looked so well groomed, thought Diane. She and Kendel would make a pair.

"I'm not sure I have," said Diane. "I wanted to bounce it off you first."

"Bounce away. Can I get you some coffee first? Tea?"

Diane shook her head. "Just had a milk shake."

"How do you do that and stay so slim? I have to watch everything I eat," said Laura.

"I burn it, I suppose. Nervous energy."

Diane sat down on a small sofa next to the warm fire. Laura sat opposite her in a comfortable looking wingback chair.

"I looked over the information you sent. Only two things caught my attention in the reports. One was the jogger who fell, and the other was the kid next door who heard Juliet say something suggestive to someone."

"I agree about the child next door, but what about the jogger?"

"I think the jogger's fall was a ruse to divert attention while the kidnapper grabbed Juliet. I'll call the authorities in Arizona where she was kidnapped and find out if a composite sketch was ever drawn of her. But the main thing I wanted to talk with you about is this: Listening to the tape of her talking about her memories of that time, I had an epiphany."

"What's that?" Laura leaned forward, her elbows on the arms of her chair.

"I don't think her memories are of one crime, but are of two separate crimes," said Diane.

Laura sat back in her chair, shocked.

"How in the world?" said Laura. "Two crimes? Tell me."

"Remember, it's a tenuous thread I'm working with here," warned Diane.

"It would have to be. If it were obvious, I'd have seen it. This is why I asked you to look at it. Please, go on. I'm all ears."

"In what Juliet was saying on the tape, she is having a hard time separating her dreams and her fears from her memories."

Laura nodded. "That's common, especially in early memories."

"Sometimes those memories are in code," said Diane.

"OK . . ." Laura was more tentative in her affirmation this time.

"When you asked Juliet what she meant by new dolls, she said "dolls in boxes." I don't think she meant that. I think her brain has combined memories."

"Combining memories is common even when a person is an adult," agreed Laura.

Diane was trying to explain her reasoning in a linear fashion to Laura, but the idea had come to her all at once and she wasn't sure where to begin.

"Juliet said her grandmother accused her of stealing a doll. I think this was real and occurred near the time of Event One—Event Two being her kidnapping. And because the grandmother's accusation was close in time to the two major traumas and held some visual similarities, the doll became the code for the rest of it.

"When Juliet first came to work at the museum, Andie made her a gift basket, as she does for all new employees. Because seashells were a speciality of Juliet's, Andie used that as a basis for the theme of the basket. The centerpiece was a doll—Ariel, the mermaid from Walt Disney."

Diane saw the frown that briefly creased Laura's forehead. Ariel was the name of Diane's adopted daughter, who was killed. Ariel had named herself after the Disney character because she wanted to start a new life with a new name—Ariel Fallon. Diane continued.

"When Juliet saw the basket on her desk, she freaked. I mean really freaked. It was much worse than when Kendel found the museum snake coiled up in her desk drawer—and that was an event we will all remember for some time to come. Juliet was very embarrassed at her reaction and muttered something about being afraid of new dolls. Andie had taken the doll out of the packaging when she made the basket. It wasn't in a box."

Diane stopped to let it sink in.

"I'm sorry," said Laura. "I don't see the significance of that, and I can see by your face that it is significant, but I need a little more."

"Juliet said, 'I remember being in a dark room with new dolls.' You asked what she meant by new dolls, and she said, 'Dolls still in the box.' But we know from her reaction to the welcome basket that she was scared witless by a doll that was not in a box."

"OK," said Laura, still sounding unsure. "So what did she mean?"

"There is something else common to new dolls besides the cardboard box they often come in. I saw it last night when I passed the museum store and saw all the Dora the Explorer dolls lined up together on the shelf. It was really very eerie. In the low nighttime lighting of the gift shop, each of the little dolls was peering out at me from behind the cellophane window in its box. Andie's basket didn't have the doll in a box, but there was cellophane around the whole basket—and Ariel the mermaid was peering out from inside the plastic."

Diane could see from the puzzled look on Laura's face that this really cleared it up for her.

"Are you saying Juliet would be afraid of an old doll if it was wrapped in cellophane?"

"Yes."

"And this means?"

"The room of dolls she saw in her memory weren't dolls; they were murdered people wrapped in plastic, and this was the first psychological trauma for her and may have led to Event Two—her kidnapping."

Chapter 33

If Laura was shocked before, she was stunned into silence now. She sat back in her chair, staring in disbelief at Diane.

Diane pulled out the tape that Laura had sent her.

"Here, play the part where she is telling you what her memories are. Instead of it being a room full of dolls, think mass murder scene and listen to how the rest of her memories sound."

Laura put the tape in her recorder, found the right place, and played it. At the end of the sequence she stopped the tape.

"It is scarier, hearing it from the perspective you describe, I'll grant you that," said Laura.

"The sequence also makes more sense," said Diane. "The fear she has of the room makes more sense and the running makes more sense."

"Yes, it does," agreed Laura. "But . . ."

"I know. I said it's tenuous. But I think it is worth investigating."

"What in the world made you think of murder victims?" asked Laura.

"A couple of things. In the morgue tent, we were short on body bags and had to cover the victims with plastic until bags arrived. Looking at the burned bodies through the plastic was eerie, to say the least. It reminded me of a murder in Atlanta recently where the killer used plastic to wrap the victim and hid him in a wall. Plastic is popular with killers because if you wrap the victim up just right, the blood doesn't leak out."

"My God." Laura shook her head as if shaking the image out. "Can you investigate this?" asked Laura. "Would you even know where to begin? I really don't want to hit Juliet with this, especially since at the moment it's no more than speculation."

"I agree. And, yes, I can investigate it. First, there are some things I'd like to know. We know she was kidnapped from her home in Arizona, but what was she doing in the weeks before the kidnapping? Was she at home in Arizona or was she somewhere else? You can ask her that, can't you?" said Diane.

"Where she was?" asked Laura. "What makes you think she may not have been at home?"

"Because of something else that struck me on the tape," said Diane.

"I must say, Diane, you got a lot more out of the short conversation than I did," said Laura. "What else did you notice?"

"Andie's basket had the mermaid doll that we think was the trigger that set off Juliet's fear attack, but the basket also contained a lot of seashells. Even though Juliet likes seashells—she's made a career of mollusks—the juxtaposition might be important in her memory."

"How's that?"

"Do you know where her grandmother lives?" asked Diane.

"No. Is that important?"

"Along with all her fearful memories are also good memories of her grandmother and memories of collecting seashells on the beach. She didn't collect seashells on the beach in Arizona," said Diane.

"You think all of these memories are connected in time," said Laura. She got up and walked over to a small refrigerator and took out a couple of Dr. Peppers and gave one to Diane. "I need something to drink, and they won't let me drink and take care of patients at the same time. And I don't like to drink alone." She glanced at her watch.

"Do you have an appointment coming up?" asked Diane.

"In about fifteen minutes. Go on," said Laura.

Diane opened the drink and took a sip. It was ice-cold. "I think the memories are connected by fear, at the least." Diane took another drink.

"Look, Laura," said Diane. "I'm not really saying anything, except that it's something to investigate. I agree, you shouldn't mention this to Juliet. Right now it's just a flight of fancy of mine, but I'd like to look into it."

"Well, I must say, you've surprised the hell out of me," said Laura.

"I could be completely wrong and probably am. I've certainly not been able to do much with the other cases I'm working on now," said Diane.

"And why are you working on them at all? I thought your job is to analyze bones and collect evidence from crime scenes. Is Rosewood having a shortage of homicide detectives? Come to think of it, I wouldn't be surprised, the way Adler has been attacking the police."

"I got interested in solving those crimes when Patrice Stanton vandalized my car," said Diane.

"The woman's obviously crazy. She really thinks you killed her son? I know she said that, but I thought she was just sticking it to you for turning the little carjacker in."

"No, she actually thinks I killed him. The only bright spot is that she's stopped her harassment because she thinks I also killed McNair and she's afraid I'll come after her."

Laura threw her head back and laughed out loud.

*   *   *

It was getting colder outside. Diane was glad to be back in her office and warm. She reached for the phone to call Garnett when Andie knocked on her door and stuck her head in.

"You have some visitors from the dark side," said Andie.

"Send the creatures in," said Diane.

David, Jin, and Neva all came into her office, pulled chairs away from their places against the wall, and sat down. Jin turned his chair around so that he sat straddling it, resting his arms on the back.

"Is this some kind of protest?" said Diane. "Have I been working you too hard?"

"We came to see the skull," said David.

"OK." Diane picked up the crystal skull and handed it to David.

"Wow," he said. "This is nice." He turned the skull over in his hand and caressed the surface. "Is it ancient?"

"No way to tell," said Diane. "All quartz is ancient, so there's no help there. And there's no way to effectively analyze the tool marks. They could have been made a thousand years ago or yesterday using tools of ancient design. That's part of the mystery of crystal skulls."

"This is just about the neatest thing," said David. He handed it to Neva.

"It'd be pretty with a light shining through from the bottom," she said. "Pretty mysterious, too."

"Yes, it would," agreed Diane. "Did you guys come just to look at the crystal skull, or was there some other reason?"

Neva handed the skull off to Jin. He turned it over and looked at it from all sides. Then he held it up to the light and looked deep into it.

"We're just stuck, Boss," he said when he finished looking through the skull. "We thought if we sat in the skull's aura . . ."

"We thought no such thing," said Neva. "We just thought getting our mind off the cases for a while, some idea might surface."

"I've had the same problem," said Diane. "I was just about to call Garnett when you came."

She lifted the phone and dialed his number.

"Garnett," he answered.

"It's Diane. Do you have anything you can share with us? What's going on with the Stanton and McNair cases?"

"I can tell you this. The meth lab evidence didn't make it to the arson lab and I don't know where it is."

"What? Did McNair steal it? How was he expecting to get away with that?"

"Maybe he'd say his truck was stolen. I suppose his plan was to say someone came into the dock at the arson lab and took it."

"He left it in the truck? Why wasn't it transferred?" asked Diane. Her three criminalists stared at her.

"The evidence is gone?" mouthed David.

Diane nodded.

"I don't know," said Garnett, "but the meth lab explosion is pretty much at a standstill, and guess who's getting the heat?"

"I hope the commissioner," said Diane.

"He is. I think he's feeling betrayed at the moment," said Garnett. "And we are taking some pretty heavy hits ourselves."

"We have some information on Stanton that might be of use to you."

"Oh? Tell me," said Garnett.

"Why don't you come over to the crime lab here? Perhaps we can share information."

"Share?"

"I want to wrap the cases up as much as you do. I feel like Councilman Adler is going to have something to hold over me if I don't. I realize that I'm not a credible suspect, but the guy deals in rumor and innu-endo and not facts," said Diane.

"I'll be right there," said Garnett.

"We'll be waiting for you." She hung up the phone. "OK, guys, maybe this will break something loose."

Diane and her crime scene crew stayed busy in the lab catching up on work while they waited on Garnett for over an hour. Still no sign of him. Diane looked at her watch.

"I think we've been stood up," she said.

As she pulled her cell phone out of her jacket pocket to call him, it vibrated in her hand. She looked at the display. Garnett.

"Traffic bad?" said Diane.

"They found Marcus McNair's truck and the evidence—such as it is—in a warehouse off Nowhere Road. You and your team get up here."

Chapter 34

The old redbrick warehouse looked like it was built when cotton was still king. It should surely be on the list of historic sites. She remembered it from when she was a kid as a place where no one—meaning kids—was supposed to go. Naturally that was a challenge, but attempts to investigate the building or use the place as a make-out spot were met with a series of ill-tempered night watchmen. It now stood like a derelict from another age, overgrown with weeds and invasive plants, the red bricks weathered and crumbling.

Diane parked the crime scene van beside one of the police cars and she and her crew piled out. They left their kits in the van and walked to the warehouse, entering through the large open doors. Pools of the fading sunlight shined through high broken-out windows, illuminating little. The flashlights carried by Garnett and the police were the only other effective source of light. The large truck Marcus used to haul away the evidence was parked in the middle of the room.

"What do we have here?" asked Diane, looking around at shadowy piles of twisted metal and rubble dumped on the ground.

"Jeez, what a mess," said Jin. "Is this our evidence he hijacked?"

"Looks like it." Garnett was all smiles. Diane would

have thought he'd be thoroughly pissed at finding the meth lab evidence in such a state.

"Apparently McNair wanted to have a look at the evidence before he turned it in." Garnett played his flashlight over a pile of bones. Diane winced at the blackened and broken fragments that had been cast aside.

"He was making sure we couldn't identify the cook, wasn't he," said Diane. He was going to remove all the bones, repackage the other evidence, and then take it to his lab."

"That's what it looks like, but somebody shot him first," said Garnett.

"Why are you so happy about this?" asked Diane.

"Because this warehouse and property belong to Councilman Adler. Oh look," he said as another car drove up and parked outside the warehouse. "I think it's the media. I wonder how they got wind of this?" He grinned and went out to meet them.

Diane and her crew looked at each other, eyebrows raised. "Payback's a bitch," said David. "Wow, did I use another word that starts with a *p*?"

"OK," said Diane. "David, you and Neva take the truck and warehouse. Jin, I want you to scout the whole area around the warehouse to make sure that there isn't some ravine he's been throwing bones in. I'll have a look at this pile of bones over here. Do we have lights in the van?"

"Yes. I'll hook them up," said David.

Diane left the others to do their work and, going over to the pile of bones, squatted beside them to take a look. She pulled on a pair of gloves and picked up one of the bones—a fragment of skull. The bones, like the others in the greatest heat of the explosion, were badly burned. Some were almost white, others were blackened and cracked. However, there was one thing she saw immediately even in the dim light of the huge warehouse. In the pile of bones there were two left femora. There had been another person in the basement with the unknown victim whose skull she partially reconstructed.

Diane retrieved a flattened box from the van, put it together, and began packing the bones carefully inside. She was about to pack the last few bones when suddenly the section of warehouse was awash with light.

She stood and gave the scene another look. The entire floor was filled with piles and piles of rubble from the fire. He had brought all of the evidence here to go through himself before taking it to the arson lab to be processed. What was he looking for? Anything else beside the bones, or just anything that might incriminate him? Looking around at the compromised evidence, Diane had no doubt that McNair had been up to his eyeballs in methamphetamine dealing.

She finished packing the bones just as Garnett brought several members of the media in to take pictures of the dumped evidence. Diane ducked out before anyone could get a picture of her. Outside, David was standing near the van staring up at the ridge that overlooked the warehouse site.

Diane loaded the box in the van, then followed his gaze. "What are you looking at?" She held up a hand to shield her eyes from the sun.

"I'm trying to figure out what Jin is up to," said David. "He's been up on that ridge, taking pictures and walking back and forth."

Diane looked up on the ridge at Jin, who was squatting, looking at something on the ground. "He must have found something," said Diane.

"Looks like it," said David.

"Let's go see what it is," said Diane.

"You'd better go. If we all disappear, the media will get suspicious and follow us," said David.

"Good thinking." Diane got a flashlight from the

van and walked alone up the rocky snow-covered ground to the ridge where Jin was taking pictures.

"What did you find?" asked Diane.

"Hey, Boss. Look at this." Jin showed her a place among the weeds and bushes that was disturbed. There were no footprints, but the ground and vegetation were flattened.

"I found these." Jin held up a bag with cigarette butts. "We can get some DNA from these."

"Did you find any bones or evidence?" asked Diane.

"No, but this is interesting." He gestured toward the warehouse.

Diane viewed the brick structure looking more and more like an ancient ruin as the sun's rays faded into twilight. She saw nothing unusual. "Why were you photographing the building?"

"Look for yourself." Jin gave her the camera. He had screwed on a telephoto lens.

Diane looked through the lens of the camera at the warehouse. Through one of the upper windows she had an almost perfect view of the lighted inside. She saw clearly McNair's truck and the piles of defiled evidence.

"This is interesting. You think someone was up here spying on McNair?" said Diane.

"Yeah, I think so. There was a light snow the night McNair was murdered and there hasn't been one since. The butts I found had a light covering of snow. They are recent, but not after the murder."

Diane looked through the lens again. She could see the reporters photographing the scene; she saw Garnett standing by watching. She saw Neva open the door to the truck. It was a good vantage point for spying.

"Continue to scout around," said Diane. "See if you can find any tracks. If we could get a line on a vehicle, that would be great. When you finish, help David and Neva. I'm going to hitch a ride back to the lab and work on the bones we found."

"The rest of the cook?" asked Jin.

"I'm not sure now that the guy I reconstructed was the cook, or was the only cook. There was at least another person in the basement when it exploded."

"That's good—I mean the more clues we have, the faster we can solve this thing," said Jin. "Not that we have another dead body from the explosion."

"I'm hoping I have enough facial fragments for another reconstruction," said Diane. "Carry on."

Diane worked her way down the embankment, slipping a couple of times in the snow. When she got back down she went inside, pulled Garnett away from the media, coaxed him into the van, and told him about the other person in the basement—and about Jin's find.

"This is good. I can tell the media how valuable information could have been lost if we hadn't found where McNair hid it."

Get your mind off payback, thought Diane. "Have you found anyone alive who lived in the apartment house," she asked. "What about the landlord? Who was renting the basement?"

"No one was renting the basement, according to the landlord," said Garnett. "I've got some men sitting on him. I can't believe someone could have a lab in his house and not know about it. We've pushed him pretty far, but so far he's not budging."

"How about residents? One of them could have allowed someone in the basement," said Diane.

"Most of them were killed in the explosion. There's a kid who does have an apartment in the house. He went on vacation to Europe with his parents just before this happened. We're hoping when he returns he'll have some answers to your questions. I've got your drawing out there, no hits. I've sent it to the old members of the drug unit. I'm waiting to hear. Now, what do you have on the Stanton kid?"

Diane told him about the museum thefts, his relationship with Darcy, the possibility that they were on a date and neither had any idea that there was a meth lab in the basement.

"I'll be damned. That puts a new face on it. Why did he try to jack your car?"

Diane shrugged. "He was hurt and dazed after the explosion. He panicked. Maybe he really didn't know what he was doing. He probably carried a gun as a macho thing. I don't know and probably never will. But we have found no trace connection with him and McNair. Have you found any links?"

"No," Garnett confessed. "None whatsoever. They were both shot with Berettas, but not the same one. The two murders are so similar, but at the same time there are some important differences. This museum theft makes me think the similarities are simply coincidences."

"Look, Garnett, don't lock me out of this. I need to know what you know. We can help and I'm very motivated."

"I'm telling you all I know. This find in the warehouse here puts you back in the game. Right now I need to get back to the media. I'm hoping for some press that'll stop Adler in his tracks. He's hurt a lot of good men."

"Would you get one of the patrolmen to give me a ride back to the lab? I'd like to start working on these bones."

"Sure," said Garnett. "Izzy's here; I'll get him to take you."

"He's working? I thought he'd be off mourning his son."

"He's due time off, but he wants to find out who did this, and I'm letting him help. I think he needs to be involved."

"Poor guy," said Diane. They emerged from the van and Garnett went to get Izzy. Diane got the box of bones and, hoping to look inconspicuous, stood behind the van. She looked up on the ridge and saw a beam of light extending from the ground upward like a small spotlight. She watched it for several moments. It didn't move. *Jin!* she thought.

Chapter 35

Diane opened the van, shoved the box of bones in, and raced up the hill. She slipped on the snow and scraped her knees through her pants.

"Damn!" she exclaimed, picking herself up and hurrying up the embankment.

At the top of the ridge she saw the flashlight leaning against a rock. She searched the ground quickly with the beam of her flashlight. Just as her light played on a hiking boot at the bottom of an embankment on the other side of the ridge, she heard a groan.

"Jin!" she shouted.

She ran down the embankment, half sliding on the rocks and snow, fortunately not falling.

She knelt beside him as he struggled to his knees. "Jin, what happened?" she asked. "Did you fall?"

"Fall?" He said confused. "No. I don't think so." He sat up. "Damn, my head hurts. He rubbed his hand on the back of his head. "Ouch!" He brought his hand back around. "It's wet," he said.

"Let me look." She aimed her flashlight at the back of his head and parted his hair. "You have a cut and it looks like you're going to have a sizable bump. You're sure you didn't fall? What's the last thing you remember?"

Jin tried to stand up.

"Just sit there for a moment, and tell me what you remember."

"I was kneeling down, digging at something I found," said Jin.

"More evidence?"

Jin shook his head. "An arrowhead."

"An arrowhead?"

"Yeah, milky quartz, looked like, from what Jonas called the Old Quartz Culture, about eight thousand years ago. There's a zillion of those kinds of points in Georgia. Don't you visit your own museum?"

"Yes, I know what the Old Quartz Culture is. That's the last thing you remember—digging out the arrowhead?"

"Yes."

"Someone hit you," she said.

"Hit me?" Jin stood up suddenly and checked his pockets. "The cigarette butts are gone. Someone stole my cigarette butts. It had to be the killer. He was right here with me and I let him get away."

"We don't know it was the killer . . . ," began Diane.

"Who else would give a shit about cigarette butts? Jeez, I don't believe this." Jin retrieved his flashlight and began searching the ground.

"You all right up here?"

Diane looked up at the top of the ridge. It was Izzy Wallace. He was followed by Archie, the policeman from the morgue tent, and another patrolman Diane recognized as one of the two who helped her when Blake Stanton was locked in her car. The three of them came down the slope.

"We saw you running like a bat out of hell up the embankment," said Izzy. "What happened?"

"It looks like someone hit Jin over the head and stole some evidence," said Diane.

"Here?" said Archie. "While we were all down at the warehouse? Somebody was up here?"

"Looks like it," said Diane.

Izzy saw Jin searching the ground. "What do we need to be looking for?" he asked.

"An evidence bag with cigarette butts," said Jin. "Maybe I did fall and it just fell out of my pocket."

"From the bump on the back of your head, I think you were hit," said Diane. "You were unconscious for a while. You need to see a doctor."

"I'm fine."

"You need to do what she says, son," said Archie. "We'll search up here. If there's anything to be found, we'll find it."

"Let them look, Jin." She saw something on the ground and picked it up. It was the quartz arrowhead. She handed it to Jin.

"I'm sorry, Boss," he said.

"That's all right, Jin. None of us expected anyone to be up here, with all the police around."

"There's all kinds of roads and paths around here," said the patrolman.

"He could have come and gone up any one of them," he said.

"He was sure quiet," said Jin.

"This snow," said Archie. "It cushions your footsteps."

"Come on, Jin," Diane said. "I need to get back with the bones and you need to see a doctor."

"Really, Boss . . ."

"That's an order, Jin," said Diane.

She, Jin, and Izzy worked their way down off the ridge by the light of their flashlights.

"I'll be back for you, Archie," called Izzy.

"No problem, Izzy," he called back.

"You and Archie riding together?" said Diane.

"Yeah, temporarily. I'm not really back officially, and Archie usually works in the evidence locker. We're just a couple of old guys waiting for retirement, trying to make a difference."

Izzy wasn't that old; neither was Archie for that matter—perhaps in their early fifties at most—but Diane imagined Izzy felt old right now. The death of a child puts the weight of the world on you.

Diane put Jin in the front, and she rode in the backseat.

"How are you and your wife doing, Izzy?" asked Diane.

"Not good. Her sister's come to stay with us for a while. I need to find out who did all this. I'm supposed to protect people, and I can't even protect my own son from the people I should be arresting."

Diane could relate to that. She couldn't protect her daughter from the man she'd been trying to bring to trial for the atrocities he committed. To say it makes you feel like a failure doesn't even begin to describe the impact it has on you.

"Bobby Coleman's mom tried to kill herself," continued Izzy. "They're saying it was an accidental overdose, but we all know different. You don't plan on outliving your kids. It's just too awful."

It is, agreed Diane silently. *Just too awful.*

Izzy dropped Diane and Jin off at the museum and she drove Jin to the emergency room. She stayed in the waiting room until he came out.

"Nothing to it," said Jin. "The doctor put three stitches in my head and told me to call if I have pain, nausea, or dizziness—usual stuff."

"Didn't he say to go home and rest?" said Diane.

"Well, yeah, but they always say that. They're just covering themselves. I'm fine."

Diane drove him home and watched as he went into his apartment building. She headed back to the museum, but just as she was about to turn the corner, she saw his car backing out of his parking space. He was going back to the warehouse. She shook her head, reached for her phone, and dialed David.

"How's Jin?" said David.

"He's fine. Got three stitches. I just called to tell you that I think he's headed back to you guys. Watch him," said Diane.

"We will. Neva will get on his case. That usually works."

"Finding anything interesting?" asked Diane.

"The basement of the apartment house had a kitchen, so we've got lots of metal. We're looking for anything we can trace back to a person, but mostly it's just stuff that's part of the house. We've found some bone. One looks like a piece of one of the long bones. But it's slim. Has kind of an oval cross section."

"Sounds like it might be a radius."

"We'll bring all the bones to you. We're thinking we'll leave the other evidence here with a guard. Garnett's bringing in an arson investigator whom he trusts to have a look."

"Keep me informed." Diane hung up the phone and drove the rest of the way to the museum. She parked by the outside elevator dedicated to the crime lab.

The night guard was already in the small first-floor reception room that contained the elevator. She spoke to him and rode up to the crime lab, keyed in her code, and, carrying the box of bones, walked through to her lab.

Her cell phone vibrated in her pocket just as she set the box down on the table. The display said LAURA HILLARD.

"Hi, Laura," said Diane.

"I just called with some information. Juliet's grandmother's name is Ruby Torkel. She's still alive and lives in Glendale-Marsh, Florida. She's lived there all her life."

"Just a minute, let me get a pen."

Diane fished a pen from her purse, uncapped it, and looked around for a piece of paper. She found a pad in a drawer and wrote down the information.

"I don't suppose you have a number."

"Sure do." Laura gave Diane the phone number. "Juliet says she's rather cranky."

"I deal with cranky every day. How is Juliet?"

"She's good, considering the crime spree we've been having. I'm getting a lot of calls from people just needing to debrief and, unfortunately, from people needing help with their grief. Poor Juliet's trying not to freak out over the murder in her apartment complex."

"Her apartment complex? Where does she live?" asked Diane.

"Applewood Apartments. You know, where the Cipriano girl was murdered."

"Juliet lives at Applewood? The poor girl. As if she doesn't have enough problems."

"Yes. She says it has everyone in the apartments calling locksmiths. All the people with a 131-something address similar to the victim's are a little upset, including Juliet. She lives in 131 H. It was several buildings away from the murder apartment, 131 C, but it's still spooky to have an address so similar to the murder victim's."

"What a coincidence," said Diane.

"Yes, that's what I told Juliet. When they ran out of the alphabet on those buildings, they started designating them AA, BB, and so on. Imagine how spooked the people are in 131 CC. Anyway, I know you're busy, I just wanted to give you the info on her grandmother."

"Thanks. I'll get on it tomorrow," Diane said. She flipped her phone shut and just stood in place for a moment. *That's odd,* she thought. She slipped on a pair of gloves. It was an odd coincidence, too, that Joana Cipriano had blond hair and blue eyes—not as light as Juliet's, but still, it was an odd coincidence. Diane felt a sense of unease as she started laying the bones out on the table.

Chapter 36

Among the bones from the warehouse, a lot were missing and most were broken, either from the explosion and fire or from McNair's handling. None of the carpels or tarsal bones were present, nor were the terminal phalanges of the hands and feet. In fact, all the smaller bones of the skeleton were missing.

There were more than one of several bones—two left femora, two first, ninth, and eleventh thoracic vertebrae, two right ulnae, four innominates, and three scapulae. Diane didn't try to separate out the skeletons, but laid duplicate bones beside each other. It was a strange and sketchy skeleton, an incomplete bony overlapping of two victims.

Diane went into the vault, retrieved the bones collected from the apartment house basement, and laid them out on another table—not mixing bones that had a clear provenance with those that did not. She also brought out the partially reconstructed skull, fully expecting to find some of the missing parts among the new batch of bones.

She selected out all the skull fragments from the warehouse bones and began piecing them together. It was another long, painstaking process, but one she hoped would come close to putting the whole picture together. She had the back of the second cranium assembled when she looked at the clock on the wall and saw that it was in the wee hours of the morning. Time to quit. She left everything in place and locked the door behind her.

Because of the late hour and her exhaustion, she decided to stay the remainder of the night in her museum office. She'd slept on her couch before and had blankets and pillows for that purpose. She had a full bathroom, and a change of clothes in the closet.

The staff lounge was on the way to her office and she stopped to raid the vending machines of candy bars and peanuts to make up for missing dinner.

"What are you doing here so late, Dr. Fallon?" said the third-floor night security guard.

"Working. I think I'll just stay the night here in my office," she said.

"I don't blame you; it's too late to go home now," he said.

Diane made her way back to her office, locked all the doors from the inside with the locks that only she had a key to, and settled in.

It was hard to get Izzy out of her mind. They'd never gotten along, but she felt great sympathy for him and his wife. Losing a child is something you never get over. This whole episode was just too tragic.

As she threw away her candy and peanut wrappers, she became aware of a chain of thought that had been trying to surface from somewhere deep in her mind. All along, she and Garnett had assumed the most likely motive for the murders was to shut Stanton and McNair up, to protect the kingpin behind the meth lab. Everyone assumed Blake Stanton was involved with the meth lab because when he tried to hijack her car he was obviously fleeing from the scene of the explosion. Then when the museum thefts came to light, the likely motive for Stanton's murder changed and appeared to have something to do with his thievery.

But there was another, more compelling motive

they needed to consider seriously—revenge for the killing of all those students.

The explosion touched a lot of people in ways that they would never get over. She could understand the righteous anger that would lead someone to want to wipe out the people behind it.

Jin was right, it probably was the killer's cigarette butts. He—or she, but probably he—had suspected McNair and tailed him. The killer spied on McNair in the warehouse, saw how he was destroying evidence, and became convinced of his guilt.

Why did the killer suspect McNair in the first place? Because he spent more than he could afford on an arson investigator's salary? If everyone thought his wife had money, why would his spending raise a red flag? There was something else, or perhaps a lot of little things, that pointed to him. Someone knew more than the police investigation about what was going on with McNair and, rather than revealing that information, they killed him.

Diane made up the couch, slipped on a sweat suit, and snuggled under the covers. She drifted off into a restless sleep and awoke in the morning with a feeling of anxiety. In the shower, she realized it was the Joana Cipriano murder that was bothering her—and the coincidence of the house numbers. And even though Juliet and Joana didn't look alike up close, their descriptive similarities—same age, blond hair, and blue eyes—were disturbing. From a distance they would be very similar. However, there were many blond-haired, blue-eyed young women in the city. Half of them, thought Diane, worked in the museum. She tried to shake the feeling, but it wouldn't go. Mainly because she didn't believe in coincidences.

She got out of the shower, dried off, and dressed. The clothes hanging in her closet were a brown linen pantsuit and cream-colored silk blouse. The clothes weren't as warm as she would have liked, but the suit had been in the closet since fall, and she hadn't thought to change it for warmer clothes. She finished dressing, folded up her bed clothes, and unlocked her doors. She was at her desk working when Andie came in, followed by Garnett. Good.

Garnett pulled up a chair and sat down. Several seconds ticked by before he said anything. Diane noted that he looked more rested than she felt.

"The GBI's going to be investigating Councilman Adler and the meth lab business," said Garnett. "He's in a frenzy, hollering about scurrilous politically motivated accusations. But at least he has something to keep him busy for a while."

"Have you identified the face from the first basement victim?" asked Diane.

Garnett nodded. "One of our former drug unit detectives recognized him as Albert Collier. He was collared many times for drug possession, dealing, using. He was also a former student at Bartram. We're talking to his associates, trying to discover who the second person in the basement might have been. I'm hoping we can tie the whole thing to Adler and get rid of the son of a bitch once and for all."

"How is the commissioner taking all this?" asked Diane. She thought of him in his long black fur-trimmed overcoat, standing out in the snow, trying to make decisions that would appease everyone.

"I told him that if he visits the museum, he should wear sackcloth and ashes and crawl up the steps. Right now he's worried about the fallout affecting his chances of reelection.

It certainly affected my vote, thought Diane. "About the murders," she said—lest the human cost of all this get lost in the politics. "I think the motive may be revenge for the student deaths."

"Murders? You including Blake Stanton?" asked Garnett. "We're thinking now that he wasn't involved in the meth lab. Just an innocent bystander like the rest of the students. The university has had some rare books taken from the library, and several departments have reported money missing from petty cash amounting to quite a bit. What they all had in common was Stanton. That's what he was involved in. Why do you still think the same person that killed McNair killed him?"

"We all assumed that because he tried to hijack my car while fleeing from the fire, he was involved with the meth lab. His killer may have made the same assumption. At the time of Stanton's murder, we weren't aware of his role in the museum thefts. Perhaps neither was the killer. By the time we discovered what were perhaps his true crimes, the deed was done, he was already dead."

"How have you come to the conclusion that it was revenge-motivated?"

"By seeing how profoundly everyone who was touched by this tragedy has been affected. One mother tried to commit suicide, all are devastated. It's easy to see how someone could hold a great desire—perhaps an overwhelming desire—to make the guilty pay. Among many there is a great need for justice. And among a few there may be a righteous outrage growing from the perception that justice may not be served and the guilty could go unpunished for a horrendous crime."

Garnett sighed and bent his head, staring at the slate floor between his feet. "You're talking about a vigilante. I can't say I haven't had the same suspicions. I don't like it. I would hate having to arrest someone for doing something that in the right circumstances I might do myself," said Garnett.

"I know," said Diane. "I have similar feelings. That's why I've decided to simply collect evidence and turn it over to you. But there's one thing to remember. If I'm right and someone's desire to bring vengeance on the guilty was the motive, they were wrong with Blake Stanton. He was probably innocent of those deaths. He was simply a thief."

"Yeah, I'd thought of that, too," said Garnett.

"I'm reconstructing the skull of the second basement victim with the bones we got from the warehouse. I'll let you know when I have a face."

Garnett nodded. "I've been so caught up in sticking it to Adler, that I've"—he stood up and shrugged—"I need to get back to work. I'll keep you informed."

Diane started to ask him not to, but she didn't. After he left, she went to the crime lab to check on things there. Only David was in.

"How did things go last night? Did any of you get any sleep?" asked Diane. From the bags under his eyes, she thought not.

"No," he answered. "Neva followed Jin home this morning. She said she was going to make him get some rest."

"How was he last night?"

"Good. He seems OK. He's pissed that someone stole his cigarette butts. He's convinced they would have broken the case," said David.

"I think the perp was convinced also."

David nodded and yawned.

"Why don't you go home and get some sleep?" said Diane.

"You didn't get any sleep. I saw the reconstruction you were doing in your lab last night."

"Actually, I did get a few hours. I stayed the night in my museum office. Nice and comfy. Why don't I take you down to the restaurant for breakfast and send you home?"

"That sounds great. Yeah, I can get behind that idea. By the way, I put some more bones in your lab. We concentrated on retrieving bones last night because we thought that would yield the best results," said David. "Early this morning Garnett told us that the GBI will be handling the evidence from here on out. So, our plan worked out well. I'm glad to hand it over to them. I wasn't looking forward to going through all the junk."

"I'm glad they are involved, too," she agreed. "I'll work on the skull today. I have a feeling that Jin is going to get his DNA lab."

"There's something he wants to know but is afraid to ask," said David.

"What's that?" asked Diane.

"Does he still get the lab if the police are the ones to break the case?"

"They'll probably break it on our evidence, so yes," said Diane.

"You've already decided on a lab haven't you?" said David.

"If you tell Jin, I'll transfer you to taking care of the dermestid beetle colony for the rest of your life."

"He won't hear anything from me," said David.

Diane treated herself and David to a big breakfast in the restaurant. She wished her personal choices weren't always centered between either food or sleep lately. And she hadn't even had a run in the past week and a half. Maybe this evening.

After breakfast she sent David home, and she went back to the museum office to call Juliet's grandmother.

Chapter 37

Diane dialed the number that Laura had given her. After seven rings, an older woman answered.

"Who is this? I don't know anyone at a museum."

Mrs. Torkel obviously had caller ID. Diane started to speak, but Ruby Torkel started again before she could get a word out.

"Unless it's Juliet. Is that you, Juliet? What are you doing calling me from work? Does your boss know you're calling me from there?"

Diane smiled. "Mrs. Torkel, I'm Diane Fallon, the director of the RiverTrail Museum of Natural History."

"Well, what are you doing calling me?"

Good question, thought Diane. *How am I going to approach this?*

"I'm also the director of the crime lab in Rosewood. . . ."

"Crime lab? Juliet's not in trouble is she? She's not a bad girl," Mrs. Torkel said, concern evident in her voice.

"No, Mrs. Torkel, Juliet is not in trouble," said Diane. "I'm helping to find out what happened to her in 1987."

There was silence on the other end of the phone for a long moment.

"She got snatched, that's what happened."

"She was a child and it was a great trauma for her. She is very frightened by what little she remembers."

"It's best not to remember," said Mrs. Torkel.

"Her fears are very real. She wants to know what happened so she can get rid of those fears once and for all. What she does remember is blurred and fragmented."

"She never remembered anything before. Lord knows the police tried to get something out of her."

"Juliet is a lovely young woman now, but she's haunted by this incident from her past. I'd like to help her; she is a good employee."

"What does she do there exactly?" asked Mrs. Torkel.

"She takes care of our seashell collection and she makes kits to teach schoolkids about seashells," said Diane.

"She always did like to collect seashells with me. She calls them mollusks now. I don't know what that is. What do you want to know?"

"She told me about a doll that you said she stole," said Diane.

"You thinking that had something to do with her kidnapping?"

"Maybe," said Diane.

"I don't see how. She was kidnapped in Arizona. She got that doll here in Florida."

"I thought it might help her remember that time in her life," said Diane. "Didn't she get that doll just before she was kidnapped?" It was a guess on Diane's part, but she had a feeling she was right.

"Why, yes, she did. She was visiting me just a month before she got kidnapped. She came home with that doll. She was playing with some child she met on the beach. That's where I live, here on the beach, here in Glendale-Marsh. It was a nice doll and people don't just give away nice things."

"Do you know where the doll is now?" asked Diane.

"Sure. I got it. I took it away from her. I told her she couldn't play with something she stole. I was going to give it back to the child she took it from, but I never was able to find out who she was playing with. I asked some of the little girls on the beach, but they didn't know Juliet. The child might have belonged to a tourist family. We get a lot of them here. They come and rent cottages on the beach. Lots of people come and go here. Will it help Juliet if I send you the doll?"

"Yes, I think it will help," said Diane.

"I want to help Juliet. I don't see her often enough. She thinks I blame her for her mother's death. Maybe I did at one time, I don't know. Anna Marie was my only child, and it's awfully hard to lose a child. No matter how old they are, they never quit being your child. When Juliet was kidnapped, it just killed Anna Marie—the worry. She never got over it. She wasn't a strong girl."

Mrs. Torkel was silent for a long while. Diane waited.

"I'll send you that doll. Let me get a pen and take your address."

Diane heard rattling noises as though she was searching in a drawer.

"Here . . . no, the ink's dried up. Just a minute."

Diane heard her lay the phone down. The television was playing in the background. It sounded like a soap opera. After a minute she was back.

"Here, this one writes. Go ahead."

Diane gave her the museum address.

"Mrs. Torkel," Diane asked when she had written down the address, "this question may sound strange, but around the time Juliet was there, did any murders take place?"

"Here in Glendale-Marsh? Why, no. I don't know

that we ever had a murder. We're just a small tourist town. People come here with their families. The folks who live here year-round all know each other. No, we never had any murders. Did Juliet say we did?"

"No, she didn't. It was just an idea. Thank you for talking with me," said Diane.

"Tell Juliet to call me sometime. Georgia's not that far from Florida. Maybe she can come down to visit me and we can go collecting shells on the beach like we used to."

"I'll tell her," said Diane. "Thanks again."

She hung up the phone and sat in her office thinking. She was expecting to hear that there had been a murder in the Glendale-Marsh area just prior to the time Juliet was kidnapped. She had it so neat in her mind what had happened. She was disappointed that she was wrong. But she would double-check with the Florida crime records.

Diane went back to her lab to continue her work piecing together bone fragments. The bones were as she had left them—laid out and waiting. The sandbox she used to keep the pieces upright sat on a nearby table holding what she had pieced together so far. Another sandbox holding the first partially reconstructed skull sat next to it.

David had set the box he brought from the warehouse on the counter. She opened it and laid all the bones out on the table, filling in many of the missing parts of the strange double skeleton. The warehouse evidence contained many of the bones and fragments that were missing.

The fragmented skull was like a puzzle, but instead of a picture, she looked for diagnostic details—foramen, canal, fossa, margin, crest—all the road signs that told what bone the fragment was from, and where it should be on the skull. Most of the pieces came from the bones that David, Neva, and Jin had collected at the crime scene. She doubted that McNair could identify small bones, certainly not burned small bones.

She found several fragments that belonged to the first face and glued them in place. It was almost complete now. On the second skull, in addition to the back of the head, she pieced together the entire left cheek, eye socket, and bridge of the nose. She stepped back and observed her work—definitely taking shape. She worked on the reconstruction through the afternoon. By the end of the day she had a significant part of the face complete. By tomorrow it would be ready to scan. She looked at her watch. It was still a decent hour. Tonight she was going to get a good night's sleep in her own bed.

When Diane arrived at her apartment, she smelled Italian food before she even opened her door. *Frank,* she thought. She smiled as she put her key in and opened the door.

"God, that smells good," she said.

"It should," Frank called from the kitchen. "It's my famous Frank Duncan Spaghetti Supreme."

"I'm ready for it. I had a great breakfast in the restaurant, but I skipped lunch," said Diane.

In the kitchen Frank was stirring a skillet filled with bubbling spaghetti sauce. He was dressed in a casual maroon sweater and tan slacks. She kissed him on the cheek.

"You get home early today?" she asked.

"I did. I finished a big case and figured you probably skipped at least one meal. And I was right," he said grinning at her. "It's ready now; you'll just have time to change and wash up."

"Then I'd better hurry." Diane changed into sweatpants and shirt and bare feet, washed her hands, and sat down at her dining table, waiting to be served. He had already poured a glass of red wine. Diane took a sip.

"I could get used to this," she said.

"So could I. I love getting off early. Can't wait for retirement." He kissed the top of her head as he put the plate in front of her. He brought out a salad and Italian bread and sat down.

"I don't know what to say," said Diane.

"I expect I'll reap some benefits." He grinned at her.

Diane asked about his case as they ate. It was a complicated embezzlement in a large company in Atlanta and reached as far away as Seattle, Washington.

"Getting enough for court is always the tricky part," he said. "I think we're ready."

Diane told him about the explosion case, filling him in on everything that happened since she last saw him.

"David said the GBI is handling the meth lab case now. We're all relieved they are," she said.

"They have more clout to subpoena records. That's the only way they're going to find out who's behind the lab—follow the money." Frank took a sip of wine. "So the thinking now is it's someone out for justice for the victims?"

"Yes, which is why I told Garnett that I am through investigating. I'm sure he was relieved. I do tend to stick my nose in too much occasionally. Although, what we've been doing lately is more armchair detective work."

"I can see how Garnett would not be enthusiastic about the latest theory of the crime. But it looks like the perp did kill the wrong person and he did hit Jin on the head. That's the problem with being a vigilante. You skip all the checks and balances."

"I know," agreed Diane.

"Why don't we talk about anything but crime? It seems that's all we ever talk about. You want to go away for a weekend with me?"

"Love to, but I'm saving all my money for Paris," said Diane.

Frank laughed. "We could go to the mountains—maybe Gatlinburg. I'll spring for it."

"Maybe. That sounds good. Let me get through these cases first. We're still processing the material from the Cipriano and Stanton murders. And I'm still looking for the items stolen from the museum. I'm out a four-thousand-dollar seashell, among maybe thirty thousand dollars' worth of other items."

"Someone would pay that much for a seashell?" said Frank.

"It's big," said Diane.

"I know, but . . . four thousand dollars?"

"It's also rare."

"Is it gold?" asked Frank.

"That would be the cowrie shells," she said.

Just as she was about to reach for another piece of bread to dip in the small plate of olive oil, the phone rang.

"Well, damn," she said. "I guess I'd better get it."

She got up and went to the living room. The caller ID said it was the hospital. Diane answered it.

"Dr. Fallon, this is Jesse Kincaid."

"Yes, Mr. Kincaid. Is Darcy all right?"

"She's coming along well. She asked me to call. Seems she needs to talk with you about something important and wonders if you could drop by tomorrow morning. She's told us about it and I advised her to come clean. It's the only way to make things right."

Chapter 38

Darcy Kincaid's room was filled with bouquets of flowers from well wishers.

"Many are from people Darcy doesn't even know," said Mrs. Kincaid. "There were so many we gave some away to other patients so there would be a little space in her room. People really like Darcy." She rubbed her hands together nervously.

She is probably suggesting that I should like her, too, thought Diane.

"The flowers are all beautiful," said Diane.

Darcy was sitting up in bed. Her mother held her hand. Her father stood just behind Mrs. Darcy at the head of his daughter's bed.

Darcy's face was black and blue still, with a hint of green and yellow. Her eyes were swollen, but not as much as they had been, Diane imagined. Her dark hair was neatly combed and fell like a curtain around her shoulders. Diane imagined her mother had combed it for her.

"How are you feeling?" asked Diane.

"Pretty good," said Darcy. "A lot better than a few days ago."

Diane pulled up a chair and sat beside the bed. "Everyone at the museum is thinking of you."

Darcy closed her eyes. Diane could see she was trying not to cry. Her father caressed her hair.

"There are some things I need to tell you," said Darcy, after a moment.

"I'm listening," said Diane.

"I don't know where to begin," she said.

"Just start at the beginning," said her father. "We're right here."

"I met Blake on campus," said Darcy.

Not that far back, thought Diane. But she listened.

"I was giving a presentation at the library about exhibit planning. He was just . . . just so nice. I've never met anyone like him before. He was so interested in what I did, in the museum."

Her father cleared his throat in a derisive manner. Darcy threatened to tear up again.

"Go on, honey," said her mother.

"I thought he was really interested in a museum career, I really did. I took him to all the departments and introduced him to all the collection managers. He asked all kinds of questions. I just thought I was so lucky to have met someone like him who was interested in the same things I was."

Diane could see from the way her father's lips were pressed together in a grim frown that he was having to make an effort to keep from commenting.

"I didn't know about the dinosaur egg, I really didn't."

"When did you find out?" asked Diane. *Dinosaur egg?* Diane wondered if that was the first item he stole.

"About a month ago. The collection manager for the dinosaur fossils said she was missing a fossil raptor egg. I had taken some up to the preparation room where we were working on a fossil exhibit. I returned them all and hadn't been back down, but I knew Blake had, so I asked him if he'd seen them."

Darcy stopped talking and Diane thought she was going to cry.

"You need to go on and get this done," said her father.

Darcy's lips trembled. "I loved him so much, I really did. I've never loved anyone like that before."

"What did he say when you asked him about the egg?" prompted Diane.

"He confessed. He said I'd caught him, but he hadn't meant any harm. He said it was just one egg that a collector friend wanted and the museum had so many. I told him he had to get it back. He said he couldn't. The collector had already paid him for it and that he was connected with some bad people. They would beat him up if he tried to get it back."

Darcy's father shook his head. Her mother rubbed the back of the hand she held on to. "It's all right," she said.

"Go on," said Diane. "Did you believe him?"

Darcy's eyes grew wide. "Yes. He wouldn't lie to me."

"Darcy . . ." Her father couldn't hold it in any longer. "He was lying to you the whole time. Why can't you see that?"

"You didn't meet him, Dad. You didn't know him like I did."

"Darcy . . . ," he said again and shook his head.

Diane could see his frustration. Darcy still didn't know what Blake was. Her father had probably been trying to tell her.

"Continue your story," said Diane. "Can I get you something to drink?"

Darcy shook her head. "Just a week before the party he said the collector wanted some of the gemstones from Geology. He threatened him if he wouldn't get them. Blake said he tried, but Dr. Seger had put some really strict protocols in place while he was gone. He couldn't get near the vault. Shelly, the geology collection manager, is a stickler for carrying out Dr. Seger's orders."

Diane noticed that she sounded a little resentful of
Shelly, possibly because in her frame of mind right
now, she saw Shelly as putting Blake in danger.

"What did he do?" asked Diane. Though she knew
what was coming.

"He asked me to get them. He said he had to get
the Van Ross diamond and several other gems or he'd
be in real trouble. He was really scared. He said I
could put some of the other gems in their place and
no one would find out for a while. He said that would
give him time to make things right."

Jesse Kincaid gave a derisive huff.

"Daddy, it's true."

"Then what happened?" asked Diane.

"I did what he said. I was so afraid for him. I was
supposed to bring them to the party and he would get
them from me there."

"What happened?" asked Diane.

"I got what he wanted, including the Van Ross diamond. I put them in a Ziploc bag . . . but I just
couldn't take them from the museum. When I was
leaving I put them in a planter—the one with the
really tall palm. They should still be there. I was going
to tell him that I would go with him to the police or
to his father to get help. They have a lot of money and
if he was in trouble, I know they would help him out."

"Darcy, the guy was using you. Why can't you see
that?" said her father.

She looked up at her father. "Daddy, I know you
think that, but you didn't know him."

"Darcy," said Diane. "Listen to your father. He
knows Blake Stanton far better than you."

Her eyes widened. "What do you mean? Dad's
never met him."

"He knows his type," said Diane. She saw her father nodding his head.

"You don't understand . . . ," began Darcy.

"Darcy, besides being director of the museum, do you know what else I do?"

"Yes, we all do. You're director of the crime lab." Her parents exchanged shocked glances.

"Yes, and in that capacity we investigated Blake Stanton's murder."

"The man who was threatening him killed him. He did it, and it's my fault. If I had just given him the gemstones." She started to cry.

"Darcy." This time Diane used her stern voice, the one that scared the herpetologist and the mayor. "I want you to listen to me. There was no such man. He didn't exist."

"He must. Blake wouldn't lie to me." Her voice sounded in genuine anguish.

"He didn't just steal the dinosaur egg and the gems," said Diane. "A *Conus gloriamaris,* eight *Cypraea aurantium,* and a giant whelk from Aquatics are missing. A *Boloria improba acrocnema* is missing from Entomology. You know how rare they are. In all, over thirty thousand dollars' worth of museum items were stolen."

Darcy's eyes grew wider and her mouth dropped open. "No. That can't be."

Her parents were clearly stunned. Probably wondering now if it was a good idea for them to encourage their daughter to confess and take her medicine.

"That's not all. He was doing the same thing to the university. Rare books are missing, as well as money from the petty cash drawers of several departments. Darcy, your father is right: Blake Stanton was using you to gain access to valuable items. I know this hurts, but you can't defend him. For your own sake, when the police question you, don't defend him."

Darcy started sobbing. Diane felt guilty for being so harsh. Both her parents looked very concerned.

"Darcy didn't know about the other things," said her mother.

"You can see this guy was using her," her father said. "The police will be able to see that."

Diane nodded. "Darcy, Blake's behavior was typical of a sociopath. One of their special gifts is to get trusting people to believe them. He was a seriously disturbed young man and not worth the emotions you have invested in him."

"You didn't know him; he was so nice to me," said Darcy.

Her father looked at the ceiling in frustration.

"Darcy, honey," said her mother.

"Darcy," said Diane, "after the explosion, all of us who lived near the house had to evacuate. While I was trying to leave, Blake came up from the explosion, pulled a gun on me, and tried to hijack my car. I was able to escape on foot, but he fired shots at me from a pistol he was carrying."

Her mother sucked in her breath.

"Oh, God," said her father. "I knew he was no good, Darcy."

"Is that true?" said Darcy.

"Yes, it is. He was not a nice boy."

Darcy started to cry. Diane hoped she had gotten to her.

"What are you going to do?" asked her father. "I believe my daughter didn't know about the other thefts."

"So do I. What do you want, Darcy?" asked Diane.

"I don't know. I love working in the museum, I do. I'm sorry about the diamonds. They are in the planter, they really are."

"I know. They have been found. Darcy, I know you loved working at the museum, but you still broke not only my trust, but the trust of the people you work with."

"I know," she said.

Her mother patted her hand again. She looked so sad for her daughter.

"However," continued Diane, "if you are willing to become a docent, where you don't have access to the museum vaults or exhibits, you can work your way up again and salvage your career in museums."

"You mean you won't fire me?" said Darcy. She looked stunned.

"No, I'm not firing you. You can work as a docent. If you choose to quit, you won't get a letter of recommendation."

"Does everyone have to know?" asked Darcy. She looked around at all the flowers.

"No, you can tell them you want to work with kids, if you want."

Darcy looked at both her parents. They smiled at her.

"Thank you," she said to Diane. "I appreciate a second chance, I really do. Why are you giving me one?"

"There has been enough tragedy in the last couple of weeks. It needs to stop."

Diane bid Darcy good-bye and left her room. Her parents followed her out.

Her father hitched up his pants by the belt and put his hands on his hips. Her mother laced her arm through his.

"You've been more than fair with Darcy," said her father. "Her mother and I thank you for that. She really is a good girl—I don't understand how she could fall for that guy." He shook his head.

"Guys like Blake Stanton are good at conning people," said Diane.

"He certainly did a number on my little girl," he said.

"I hope Darcy continues to recover," said Diane.

"The doctors said she's doing well. We're real grateful for that. We'd like to take her home to convalesce when she's released. Will that affect her job?" he asked.

"No. She doesn't have to come back until she's well."

Diane left the hospital and drove to the museum. It was a relief to have the talk with Darcy over with. She had been dreading it ever since she found out that Darcy was Blake's girlfriend. It had been a welcome surprise that she wanted to confess and showed true remorse. That made Diane's job easier—and made it easier to give her a break. Now, if the other stolen items could just be recovered.

The museum was opening for the day when she arrived. There were two big tour buses sitting in the parking lot. Diane liked seeing that, especially in this weather. Inside there was a long line at the ticket counter. Chaperoning a line of schoolchildren were several teachers and parents whom she recognized as having visited many times. And there were others who were vaguely familiar. She was glad to see so many repeat visitors.

She crossed the lobby and headed for Aquatics. She wanted to tell Juliet that she had spoken with her grandmother.

Chapter 39

"Dr. Fallon."

The voice was one of the chaperones standing in line with a group of children. *Damn.* She didn't want to be delayed right now. She smiled and walked over to him.

"Dr. Thormond."

Diane held out her hand to the man standing with twenty or so third graders. Martin Thormond was a history professor she'd met on campus at one of her presentations for the museum. She knew he was angling to be one of the curators she recruited from the university, but his area of expertise wasn't represented in the museum. The closest museum area to his expertise would be archaeology, and she already had an archaeology curator in Jonas Briggs.

It was odd. When she first presented the idea of university professors serving as curators in exchange for providing them office and research space, it was met with a great deal of skepticism and downright snobbery in some cases. Now, apparently, curator at the RiverTrail museum had become a plum assignment.

"It's good to see you again," said Diane. "I see you've been tagged for chaperone duty. One of these yours?"

"Michael over there."

He pointed to a blond-headed kid making faces at two little girls, apparently seeing how wide he could stretch his mouth with his fingers.

"Yep, that's my pride and joy," he said.

He laughed and, at the same time trying to keep the rest of his wards in a straight line, caught a dark-headed boy about to make a break for it.

"I tell you, I now have much more respect for a mother duck."

Diane laughed and muttered some comment about their energy. The level of noise was getting louder as more children arrived. Diane wondered where the docents were.

Some girls in another line were saying tongue twisters to each other.

"Say this," one said. "She sells seashells at the seashore."

It was answered by another little girl with perfect pronunciation.

"Now say it real fast."

That was harder and ended in a fit of laughter.

"Try this real fast. Black bugs blood, black bugs blood."

That twister erupted in a tangle of words and laughter. The teachers joined in—"Around the rugged rock the ragged rascal ran."

It sounds as if they have a tongue twister for every department in the museum, thought Diane.

Someone started the old favorite, "Peter Piper picked a peck of pickled peppers."

An alliteration of p's *again, thought Diane. Why did that tug at her brain?*

". . . totally unexpected and just so much more work."

Dr. Thormond was talking the whole time, and Diane didn't have any idea what he was saying. She nodded, hoping a nod made sense.

"None of us had a clue Dr. Keith was leaving," he continued.

Dr. Keith . . . history.

"Are you talking about Shawn Keith?" asked Diane.

"Yes. He's left us in just the worst time. I'm having to take his classes," said Dr. Thormond.

"He lives in the basement of my apartment building," said Diane. "I didn't know he was moving."

"He caught everyone by surprise. I can't believe he was job hunting all this time and none of us knew," he said.

While Dr. Thormond expressed annoyance at Dr. Shawn Keith's abrupt departure, Diane was thinking about when she first saw Blake Stanton aiming his gun at Professor Keith's car. All along she'd thought it was just an opportunistic encounter. Maybe it wasn't. Maybe Blake had run to someone he knew and they got into some kind of argument and Blake pulled a gun on Keith. Someone at the university end had to help grease the way for Blake to steal things there. What if it was Keith?

The docents in charge of the groups of children came and they started on their tour. Diane waved at Thormond as he left with his baby ducks, and she detoured up to her crime lab.

Her crew was there. David was at the computer— Diane didn't know if he was working on a case, one of his databases, or algorithms for working with databases. Neva was at a microscope and Jin was sitting by himself looking glum.

"Those cigarette butts. I could've had my DNA lab," he moaned.

"Jin," said Diane sharply, "Stop feeling sorry for yourself and get to work. Not everything is high-tech."

Jin jumped at the sound of her voice. "What do you mean, Boss?" he said.

"You photographed the cigarette butts before you picked them up, didn't you?" she asked.

"Of course, I did," he said, a trifle indignant.

"Look at the photographs and find out what kind of cigarettes they are." Diane stood over him, folding her arms over her chest.

"How will that help us? You can't nail down a single person with a brand. Hundreds . . . thousands, maybe millions of people will smoke the same brand."

"Jin, with those thinking skills, I'm not sure you deserve a DNA lab."

"Boss!" he cried.

"Right now we don't even have a list of suspects—forget about a perfect match. Get us a pool of possibles to work with."

"OK, I find out what kind of butts they are and then I get a list of everyone in Rosewood who smokes that brand?"

"Jin, I've never seen you feeling this sorry for yourself," said Diane.

"I let someone sneak up on me," he lamented.

"You weren't meant to hear, that's why they were sneaking. Find a suspect population and then narrow it down. For example, we're thinking the motive for McNair's murder might be revenge for the deaths of the students. Who felt the deaths the most?"

"The parents," he said.

"Who else?"

Jin thought a minute. "The people who had to deal with it. Us."

"And I'm sure there are more. Where would members of those pools of suspects have been found lately . . . for long periods of time . . . smoking cigarettes?"

Jin thought again. "The crime scene. Tent city," he said.

"Then why don't you get your sorry self out to where the tent city was and look for cigarette butts?"

she said. "In the tent where we were, I noticed several people stepping out to smoke. I'm sure that was true where the coffee tent was also, and where the crowd of onlookers waited, and where the media were set up. If you're lucky, the cigarette butts you found at the warehouse will be distinctive or uncommon in some way. If you find a match at the tent city, then at least we will be on a trail of clues again."

"Boss, that's a good idea. But they will be trampled by now; the DNA will be degraded; they will be mixed in with the butts thrown out by the people dismantling the tents."

"Right now we are just looking for clues that might point us somewhere; we are not necessarily looking for evidence we can take to court."

"I'm with you, Boss, but still, there's a possibility that everyone will have been smoking the same brand."

"Not necessarily," said David. "If the brand is Marlboro you're in trouble; about half the smoking population smokes them. However, that diminishes with age. You get in the twenty-six-plus age group and the percentage falls considerably. Look at your photographs and see if you can figure out what brand you have and go from there. Diane's right. Get off your sorry butt and do some old-fashioned detective work."

They all stared at David. Neva spoke first.

"You have a cigarette database, I take it?"

"Of course, I do. Do you know how may perps smoke?" said David.

"But you've memorized it," said Neva.

"No, I looked it up while Diane and Jin were talking."

Jin jumped up and fetched his photographs and sat down by David. He took a magnifying glass and began examining the images.

"Here's something. Is that a logo?" asked Jin.

David looked at the picture.

"OK," he said and clicked through his screen. "I

was just looking at these. You're in luck. Those are Dorals. They're generic brands—as opposed to the premium brands. They're smoked mostly by the age group twenty-six and older, and then only by about 5.4 percent of them. You find a Doral smoker at tent city, and they're definitely someone who needs to be looked at more closely. To qualify as your possible attacker, they will also have to be physically fit. Probably someone who is addicted to tobacco. Look for someone who has to watch their budget or is just frugal by nature—but not so tight as to have to buy the cheaper value brands. And is most likely white."

"How in the world do you know all that stuff?" said Neva.

"Both the smoking interests and nonsmoking interests keep reams of data on the demographics of smokers," said David.

"Wow," said Jin. "This might work. I'll get on my deerstalker and go collect some more butts."

"I'll help," said Neva.

They left, Jin obviously in a happier frame of mind.

"Good idea," said David. "It's a place to start, and something might actually come of it."

"At least it will get Jin to thinking again. He hates feeling that he made a mistake," said Diane. "Now, I need to call Garnett. I just found out something that might change our thinking yet again."

Diane called Garnett from David's workstation. David sat listening to her as she explained about Shawn Keith and his quick departure from his job.

"I can't pick him up simply because he's changing jobs," said Garnett. "But he did witness a crime and called 911. We interviewed him once as a witness. I'll bring him in for a reinterview."

"I know it's a long shot, but if he was the one helping Blake Stanton steal from the university, he had a motive for killing him."

"Would Shawn Keith really kill the Stanton kid over a matter of petty theft?" asked Garnett.

"Keith was a faculty member in the History Department. If he were linked to theft from the university, his career as a college professor would be over. He could never work at a college or university again. He had a lot to lose."

"I guess you're right about that. So, you're changing the theory of the crime again?" said Garnett.

"I'm not changing anything. This is a process. I'm looking at all possibilities," said Diane.

"OK, I'll see if I can find him. You say he lives in your building?"

"In the basement," said Diane.

"Well," said David, after she had hung up with Garnett, "that's interesting."

"It is, isn't it? We'll see what Garnett comes up with. In the meantime, I was on my way to Aquatics."

Diane started out the door, then suddenly turned back to David. "I need to find out if there was a mass murder in either Glendale-Marsh, Florida, or Scottsdale, Arizona, in the summer or fall of 1987. The victims may have been wrapped in clear plastic."

"What's this about?" asked David. "A new case?"

"Something private I'm working on," said Diane.

"Will do," he said.

Diane left the crime lab and went back down to the first floor and across to Aquatics. When she arrived, there was a commotion going on. A thin older woman with tanned leather-looking skin and blond brown hair up in a bun was arguing with a security guard in front of the fish exhibits. Fortunately, there were only a few people in the room.

"I'm not giving you my package, young man. I don't even know you."

Diane recognized her voice.

"Ma'am. I just need to look at it."

"Mrs. Torkel?" said Diane. "Are you Ruby Torkel?"

The woman and the guard turned around at Diane's voice. The guard looked relieved.

"Yes. And who are you? How do you know my name?" she said.

"I'm Diane Fallon. We talked on the phone yesterday. Did you come all the way from Florida?"

"I'm here, am I not? You said you wanted to see the doll."

Diane motioned for the guard to leave. "Is that the doll?" asked Diane.

"It's not my lunch," she said.

"I didn't mean for you to have to bring it," said Diane.

"If I sent it, there's no telling how long it would take, and I thought, I haven't seen Juliet in a while, so I'll just bring it. But this building is so big."

"Yes, it is. I was on my way to see Juliet myself. She's probably in the lab."

"Gramma, is that you?" Juliet had just come out of the shell room into the fish room. "What are you doing here?"

"I've come to see you. This woman—Diane Fallon—wants to see that doll."

"The doll?" said Juliet, looking confused.

"You know, when you were a little girl. The one I took away from you," said her grandmother.

"You brought it all the way from Florida?" said Juliet. She guided her grandmother out of the way of tourists and toward a corner.

"Of course, from Florida. I didn't come from Europe. Aren't you glad to see me?" Juliet's grandmother said.

"Of course, I am, Gramma." Juliet gave her grandmother a hug. "I'm just surprised, that's all. How did you get here?"

"I took a bus. It wasn't that bad. I slept most of the way. Changing in Atlanta wasn't fun."

"Well, I'm glad to see you," said Juliet. "Have you had anything to eat?"

"Nothing to speak of," she said.

"Why don't you take your grandmother to the restaurant?" said Diane.

Juliet nodded. "I'll do that."

"First," said Diane, "I wanted to ask you something. Actually, I came to tell you that I talked with your grandmother and asked her to send the doll. But there is something else I've been meaning to ask. When we had dinner the other day you said you are afraid of certain things like new dolls and certain words. What words?"

"It's silly, really. One of them that absolutely fills me with anxiety is a word I ran into quite by accident in my museum work. It's the word palim . . . palim . . . I'm sorry, it's very difficult for me to even say it. It is the word . . . palimpsests. How strange is that?" Juliet laughed nervously.

"Palimpsests? That's the second time I've heard that word lately—where?" said Diane. Then she remembered, that's why the alliteration of *p*'s kept tickling her brain. "I remember. *The making of palimpsests was possible even with papyri.*"

Juliet's eyes grew round in a look of sheer terror; her face drained of color, she backed up against the wall and screamed before she slid down and held her knees, sobbing.

Chapter 40

"What in the world did you say to her?" said Mrs. Torkel as she hurried over to her granddaughter.

"I'm not sure," said Diane. She knelt beside the stricken girl, who now seemed to have fallen into a trance or a seizure. "Juliet, can you hear me?" No response. Juliet was breathing very fast.

"My husband, God rest his soul, did this sometimes. It was after the war and I'd find him out in a field hiding from the enemy, he said. He'd pull me down with him and we'd both hide there in the weeds," said Mrs. Torkel. "She's having a flashback. That's what it looks like to me. God in heaven, we thought she'd just forget and it would be all right."

"Can we help?"

Diane glanced up briefly and several of the tourists were gathered around. She didn't know which one had spoken.

"Thank you, but no. Please go ahead and enjoy your tour of the museum."

Juliet sat there for several minutes with no change. Diane and Mrs. Torkel said nothing. Juliet's breathing slowed and Diane thought she was coming around from wherever it was she had gone. After another couple of minutes, she tried to stand. Diane and Mrs. Torkel got on each side of her and helped her up and into the lab, away from the tourists. Mrs. Torkel, Diane noticed, elbowed a few of them out of the way.

The two of them guided Juliet to a chair where she sat and put her head down. Diane got her some water from the fountain in the corner. As she handed it to Juliet she caught sight of Whitney Lester in the doorway of her office with a satisfied smirk on her face.

"Don't just stand there; call the nurse," said Diane. Lester's smile faded, and she disappeared into her office.

"What's the matter, child?" said her grandmother. "Where were you?"

"I don't know. I was just suddenly running through the brush and a man was chasing me to your house, Gramma. It was so real."

Mrs. Pierce, one of the museum's nurses, arrived quickly, and Diane explained what had happened. Mrs. Pierce had a motherly bedside manner with a knack for comforting hurt and sick children. She took Juliet's pulse and felt her skin.

"Your pulse is a little rapid, but your skin isn't clammy." She shined a light in her eyes. "You're OK. It looks like an anxiety attack. Have you had these before?" she asked.

Juliet nodded.

"Are you seeing someone about them?" she asked.

Again Juliet nodded.

"Good," said Mrs. Pierce. "I recommend you take a rest for the remainder of the day. You'll be fine. Be sure and call the person you're seeing and tell him or her."

"I will, thanks."

"Thanks, Mrs. Pierce," said Diane.

"That's what you pay me for." She smiled and left the aquatics lab.

"This is just so stupid of me," said Juliet.

"No, it isn't," said Diane. "Can you answer some questions?"

"Sure."

"Did you see what the man chasing you looked like?" asked Diane.

"He was mean. He had a black goatee of a beard and straight black hair."

"Do you know why he was chasing you?" asked Diane.

"No. That thing you said, why did you say it to me?" She looked up at Diane in anguish, as if Diane had done it on purpose.

"You mean the sentence with the word you feared?" Diane was careful not to say the words again. "I heard it while I was looking for a friend in the library. Students were studying and it was just a phrase I heard. It stuck with me, I suppose because it was a kind of tongue twister. That word is so unusual, it was odd to hear it twice in so short a time. Why did that throw you into a flashback?"

"Flashback . . . like Grampa? I don't know." She looked confused. "The man said it," said Juliet.

"To you?" Diane thought that would be an odd thing to say to a seven-year-old.

"No, but . . . I don't know who he said it to. I just heard him say it. It was scary when he said it. I don't remember anymore. I'm sorry," said Juliet.

"Did he just say the word, or the whole phrase?" Diane thought that highly unlikely, but why did she freak out so when Diane repeated the sentence.

"The phrase. He said the whole thing the way you said it, and he was looking at me," said Juliet.

"Looking at you? Directly at you?" asked Diane.

"No, I'm not sure . . ." Juliet looked like she might panic again.

"That's all right. Why don't you take your grand-mother to the restaurant? Sit in a quiet booth, have something cool to drink, get some nourishment," said Diane. "I'll walk with the two of you."

"I think we both could use some food," said her

grandmother. "I'll bet you've been skipping meals, haven't you, dear?"

Diane walked them to the elevators and they all went down to the restaurant. Diane told the hostess to seat them in her place, which was her code for the bill to be put on her tab as well.

"Have a good meal. When you finish I'll have someone drive you home," said Diane.

"I can drive. I'm fine, really," said Juliet. "It's just that darn word." She tried to smile.

Ruby Torkel turned to Diane. "You keep the doll. Don't let anybody take it away from you."

"I won't."

Diane didn't even try to explain to her that the security guard was just making sure that nothing dangerous was being brought into the museum.

"Is that the doll you said I stole?" asked Juliet. She touched the package with her fingertips. "I don't even remember what it looks like."

"Do you want to see it?" asked her grandmother.

Juliet grabbed her hand back as if the package had turned into a snake. "No . . . I think I've freaked everyone out enough for one day. Maybe when the museum is having a slow day." She smiled again.

"Do you remember anything Juliet said when she showed you the doll?" Diane asked Mrs. Torkel.

"Oh, she didn't show it to me. I found her playing with it. She said it had something . . . a secret, that's what it was. You know how kids are, making stuff up. I asked her where she got it and she wouldn't tell me; she just said it was a secret. I told her she had to give it back, but she said her friend gave it to her. That's when I took it away and told her she couldn't play with something that wasn't hers and people just didn't give away toys that nice."

Juliet stood listening to her grandmother with a frown. "I don't remember any of that."

"Well, honey, you were seven," said Mrs. Torkel.

"I'm going to leave the two of you to eat and catch up on news. Juliet, you can have the rest of the day off," said Diane. "Oh, would you mind if I open the package in my office?"

"Go ahead," said Juliet. "I don't care."

Diane left them and, carrying the package, went to her office.

"Hey, Andie. Anything going on?" asked Diane as she walked through Andie's office.

"Usual stuff. Someone said there was a commotion in Fish?" she said.

"News travels fast. It was nothing. I'm going to be in my office for a while."

"MOF?" asked Andie.

MOF was Andie's abbreviation for Museum On Fire, which meant she would only disturb Diane in a dire emergency.

"Not that drastic, but field everything you can," said Diane.

She sat down at her desk and looked at the package a moment before she unwrapped it. The doll was in almost-new condition. It was a pretty doll with a porcelain head, feet, and hands, and a soft body. It had a head full of black finger curls and an ornate green satin bonnet and satin green dress trimmed in white fur. Her feet were covered in high-top patent leather shoes and white stockings. She carried a white fur muff in one hand, attached by a piece of elastic sewn into the muff and looped over the wrist. It was a nice doll, but not an expensive one. Diane's sister collected dolls, so Diane had a passing familiarity with them.

Diane leaned back in her chair and focused her eyes on the table fountain and the water running over the rocks. *The making of palimpsests was possible even with papyri.* That was such an odd phrase. What exactly did it mean—other than the obvious literal meaning? Diane knew what a palimpsest was, but she grabbed her Webster's dictionary anyway and looked it up:

> **Palimpsest:** writing material as a parchment or tablet used one or more times after earlier writing has been erased.

Diane knew that it was a practice in ancient times to erase the work of an earlier author and reuse the parchment to pen another piece of work. Sometimes the earlier work can still be deciphered. Korey Jordan, her head conservator, had revealed the earlier writing on a medieval parchment that was a palimpsest.

Why would a kidnapper or killer use a sentence like that? What was the meaning in that context?

But the more important mystery in her mind was why had she heard it in the library—apparently the exact sentence. Was it actually more common than she thought? She got on her computer and flipped over to the Internet and Googled the sentence with quotations. No hits whatsoever. She removed the quotations and tried again. She got a lot of hits, but none that contained the words in any combination even close to the sentence she heard. She clicked on her bookmark of the Gutenberg project and searched the offerings. Nothing.

So, it didn't seem to be a common quotation. Then who in the library said it? She closed her eyes and tried to remember the voice. Female? That's what she thought she remembered.

It seemed to stretch the imagination that it could be the same person who had said it in Florida twenty years ago, here now—in the university library. But it was quite a coincidence. Her thoughts were interrupted by her intercom.

"Sorry, Dr. Fallon. It's David. I thought you might want to talk with him."

"Thank you, Andie. Put him through."

"Diane, I did the search in Arizona and Florida and found no such murders. I increased the dates and increased the area of search—still nothing that fit your criteria. Sorry."

"Thanks, David. If I get any more variables, I may ask you to search again."

"Sure."

She hung up the phone.

"Well, damn," she said out loud. "I was so sure."

She picked up the doll again and looked into its dark eyes. *So this doll has a secret?* To Diane, that meant one thing. She lifted the dress and examined the stitching.

Chapter 41

When they were children, Diane's sister had collected Madame Alexander dolls, pushed baby dolls around in strollers, and dressed and undressed her extensive assemblage of Barbie dolls. Diane, on the other hand, had played with hers in a wholly different manner. Her dolls were couriers, adventurers, and spies. She often used them to carry secret messages. A message might be hidden in their clothes, inside the hole of a dislocated arm or leg, or sewn up in their torso.

Diane examined the stitching of Juliet's doll with a magnifying glass. No sign of the legs being detached and reattached, nor were there any repaired tears in the torso. She carefully undressed the doll and checked the arm attachments. Nothing at the right arm, but the left arm had been restitched by hand. Diane smiled with delight as she took fingernail scissors and snipped the thread.

She pulled the stuffing from the arm. The result was a pile of fluffy white fill on her desk, but nothing else. She stuffed the fill back into the arm with a pencil eraser and turned her attention to the torso. She began pulling the fill out of the armhole. This produced quite a large pile. The doll was now flattened in the middle. She saw nothing but stuffing. She pulled it apart to see if there was something in it she missed when she was taking it out. She hadn't.

She really hoped that Juliet and her grandmother did not come to her office right now.

With a penlight from her desk drawer she looked inside the empty sack that was the torso of the doll. Still nothing. She stuck the tip of her little finger up in the doll's head.

There it was.

It felt like a slip of paper. Diane grinned broadly. There is nothing like the thrill of discovering a hidden message. She managed to tease the edge of the paper through the opening in the doll's head far enough that she could grasp it with her fingertips and pull it out.

It was a piece of newsprint, yellowed with age, rolled up when it was put inside the doll, and now lying in a loose coil. She unrolled the strip of paper on her desktop. After all the trouble she had gone to, she expected it to say something like *Inspected by #12*. But it did not.

Printed on the paper was a series of capital letters in groups, like words in an enigmatic foreign language.

KVQ PEZJMTR WOYIYP QQMRKSDY BW
XMMRJ JMNA CZQWRCZKN VE HTE
PZHK OS XZQNQRZQMNIGT FYFFUDN
KVDER WSQT HERQR GYS TENUGFOAV
CR LRRBPEE CZQWRCZKN

It looked like a code if Diane had ever seen one. She was so gleeful she laughed out loud. OK, it was a code. Was it child's play, as hers were? Someone could take apart a few of her old dolls today and find notes still inside them containing lines of scribbled letters and numbers that stood for nothing more or less than a child's adventurous imagination at work. This could be like that . . . or it could mean something important. No way to tell at the moment.

Jin liked to do puzzles and ciphers. He frequently

contributed his logic puzzles and cryptograms to puzzle magazines. This would be a job for him.

She keyed the lines of code into her word processing program, double-checked it, and saved it under a password—then immediately felt utterly silly. She was a kid again playing games with dolls. She cut a thin piece off the scrap of paper and put it in a vial, then locked the code—or whatever it was—in her safe.

When the fill was back in the torso, she took a needle and thread from a small emergency sewing kit in her desk drawer and reattached the arm with fine stitches. That done, she redressed the doll. Thank goodness, it looked as good as new. She wrapped it in the paper Mrs. Torkel brought it in and put it in her drawer. Just as she closed the drawer, there was a knock on her door.

"Come in," she called, and Kendel entered her office.

"Hi. Andie said you wanted to see me. Sorry I'm late, I was up talking to Korcy about courses he wants to teach."

"That's fine. I have something I need you to find."

"Oh, a new acquisition?" Kendel smiled, showing a bright white set of teeth.

"No, this is something different and will surely test your abilities," said Diane.

"OK, I'm intrigued," said Kendel.

Diane turned to her computer, typed in the palimpsest phrase, printed it out, and gave it to Kendel.

"The making of palimpsests was possible even with papyri," she read, then looked up, her eyes wide and eyebrows raised.

"I want to know where it's from. I've looked on Google and Project Gutenberg. I heard it spoken in the university library recently, but it goes back at least twenty years."

Kendel smiled and tapped the piece of paper on her hand. "I'll accept your challenge."

"Thanks, Kendel. Would you take this to Korey for me? I would like to know if he can give me a ballpark figure on how old the paper is."

Kendel took the vial and looked at the piece of paper inside it.

"Looks too modern for C14," she said.

"He'll probably just have to do a chemical analysis. Something quick."

Kendel gave her another smile. "And you thought I might want to work at other museums."

When Kendel left, Diane printed out the string of coded letters she had found in the doll and put them in her pocket. Before going back to the crime lab, she called Laura.

"Diane. How is the Juliet investigation coming?"

"Interesting," said Diane.

"It always scares me when people say 'interesting.'"

"Funny you should talk about words scaring people," said Diane.

"I know. Juliet has a few that scare her," said Laura.

"I discovered, firsthand." Diane explained about Juliet's breakdown in the aquatic room. "I assume she'll be calling you about it."

"Wow," Laura said. "It's obviously associated with her trauma. But how in the world? She said a scary man said it to her? When she was seven?"

"She was unclear. At first she said he was talking to her; then she said she didn't know."

"I know what papyri is. What is a palimpsest?" said Laura.

Diane explained what it was and gave her a short history.

"What could it mean in this case?" she asked.

"I have no idea. I asked Kendel to track down its origin. She's good at finding things."

"She's the one who found the snake in her drawer, right? I heard about that."

"That was Kendel," said Diane.

"Have you had any luck finding a mass murder around the time of Juliet's kidnapping?"

"None whatsoever—not in Arizona or Florida."

"So that's a dead end," said Laura.

"For now."

"You aren't letting go of that notion, are you?"

Diane could imagine Laura's amused but stern face on the other end of the phone.

"I'm putting it aside until I have more evidence. When you talk to Juliet, ask her where she was in her flashback. It didn't sound like Arizona. I've been to Arizona, and there's not a lot of vegetation."

"There's plenty of vegetation," said Laura. "Just not the kind you're used to."

"At any rate, see what you make of her description," said Diane.

"You're determined, aren't you?" said Laura.

"I'm thorough," said Diane. "There's something else I need to tell you. I called her grandmother. She told me Juliet had visited her the month before she was kidnapped."

"Really?" said Laura. "That is interesting. It's just what you suspected."

"That's also the time she acquired the doll her grandmother accused her of stealing."

"OK, that's interesting, too. What else?"

"I asked her grandmother to send the doll to me. She delivered it in person. She was with me when Juliet had her flashback."

"Maybe the doll is what triggered . . ."

"She didn't see the doll. It was wrapped up. My original idea was to give you the doll to integrate into her therapy, or whatever. But her grandmother said something about the doll that reminded me of things I did as a kid. She said the doll had a secret."

"And?" prompted Laura when Diane didn't say anything.

"Do you remember how I used to play with my dolls?"

"You mean tear their heads off?"

"Funny. No, those were my sister's Barbies. I hid secret messages inside mine."

"I remember now. You were a cross between Dr. Frankenstein and Mata Hari," said Laura. "That's probably why I went into psychiatry—to understand *your* childhood, rather than mine."

"You're really full of yourself today, aren't you? Well, wait until you hear."

Diane described her dismemberment of Juliet's doll and what she found inside.

"You're not kidding? You actually found something?"

Diane smiled with satisfaction at Laura's amazement.

"Now I just have to decode it, provided it's not a meaningless string of gibberish—which it most likely is."

"You have surprised me again. Send the doll to me and I'll keep it here and talk with Juliet about it," said Laura.

"OK. I'll bring it by." Diane hung up the phone, put on her coat, and took the package out of her drawer.

"Andie," she said as she walked through her office, "I'm going to drop a package by Laura Hillard's. I'll be back within the hour. Call the crime lab and tell David to expect me."

"Sure."

Diane walked to her car, clicking open the locks on the way. It was still cold. She thought she heard on the weather forecast that it was going to warm up. She was about to open her door when she felt the point of a gun barrel stuck in her back.

Chapter 42

Diane's first emotion was disbelief. Here in front of the museum with so many people coming and going, someone was holding a gun on her? It had to be a joke. Then came the voice—a throaty blend of age and years of smoking cigarettes.

"Just give me the package," he said. "If you don't, I have no problem opening fire on the line of tourists unloading from that bus over here behind us."

Diane had seen the tour bus arriving when she walked out. She handed him the package over her shoulder.

"Now, that's good. All you have to do now is stand here looking inside your car for five minutes while we get out of here. Same thing applies. You move or try to get a look and I'll open fire. Nod your head if we have an agreement."

Diane nodded. She felt the pressure release from her back and she heard the footfalls walk away. She didn't move her head; she couldn't risk the safety of the visitors. But she shifted her eyes looking for a reflective surface somewhere in her car to perhaps see something of the gunman. There was none. She waited for several minutes until the passengers from the bus were inside the museum. It was another field trip of schoolchildren. She watched as they passed her car and filed into the building.

She closed her car door and went back into the museum. Fear wasn't her strongest emotion at the moment. It was anger. It was one thing to threaten her, but to casually threaten a busload of children. She went straight to the Security office. Chanell was in her office on the phone. She hung up just as Diane walked through the door.

"Good news, we've got a line on several of the stolen items," she began before Diane interrupted her.

"I need to see the security tapes for the last ten minutes. Start with the camera near my parking space.

Chanell's coffee-colored face went from a bright smile to a frown. "Is something wrong?"

"Someone pulled a gun on me at my car and stole a package I was carrying," said Diane.

"What? Here? Now?" Chanell made a beeline to the room with the video monitors.

"Stefan! What have you been watching?" said Chanell.

She stood with her hands on her hips next to a young man with brown hair with blond highlights who was wearing a brown museum security uniform. He looked up at Chanell with startled hazel eyes.

"The tour buses, you told me to always make sure to keep an eye on them."

"Where was your other eye?" she asked.

"Huh?"

"Dr. Fallon was robbed at gunpoint at her car in the parking lot," said Chanell.

His eyes grew wide with what looked like fear. "Where was she?" he said.

"At her car, in her parking space." Chanell tapped the center of the appropriate monitor with each syllable.

"I . . . I was looking at the schoolkids getting off the bus," he said.

"Call up the video for the last ten minutes," said Diane.

Stefan punched the keyboard, and a video came up showing the area of the parking lot that included Diane's car parked beside Kendel's Mercedes convertible. He sped forward for several seconds to the point the video showed Diane coming out of the museum and going to the driver's side of her car. A man several inches taller than Diane walked between Kendel's car and Diane, reached in his pocket, and pulled out a gun. He looked around for the first time, as if to see if anyone was watching.

"Stop it there," said Diane. "Give me a close-up of his face."

Stefan selected the face and enlarged it. It didn't really help. It was a profile: He had on sunglasses, his collar was pulled up, and his stocking cap was pulled down over his ears. The clearest view was of his nose.

"Enlarge the gun," said Diane.

A picture of a gun showed up on the screen. "That looks like a 1911 Army automatic," said Diane.

"Sure does," said Chanell. "That's an old gun."

"Let the video run," said Diane.

She watched as the man held the gun to her back and as she handed over the doll. He walked away with the package tucked under one arm and the gun in his pocket. There was an instant that showed his face and Diane asked Stefan to isolate it, save it, and send it to her crime lab.

"The gun, too," she said.

She watched the gunman walk out of the picture.

"Follow him," said Diane.

"Huh?" said Stefan.

"What is the next camera that has him in sight?" said Chanell.

"Oh." Stefan called up the same time on another camera.

Diane watched a view from the back of him walking away and getting into a blue Chevrolet Impala.

"Try for the license number," said Diane, as she picked up the phone.

Stefan zoomed in on the rear of the Impala, but the best they could see from the camera angle was a blurred partial.

"Send that partial of the plate to David in the crime lab. He may be able to enhance it. And see if you can get the car's interior and send it to the crime lab, too," said Diane.

"You won't be able to see his face at all," said Stefan, "even in the mirror."

"Don't go second-guessing Dr. Fallon. . . . Do what she says," said Chanell.

Diane dialed 911.

"This is 911 Emergency. What is the nature of your emergency?"

"This is Diane Fallon. I'm director of the crime lab. I was just robbed at gunpoint in the parking lot, in the past ten minutes."

"Are there injuries, ma'am?"

"There are no injuries. No medical attention is required."

"Is the perpetrator still on the premises, ma'am?"

"No. No one is in immediate danger here. The perpetrator escaped the crime scene in a late model dark blue Chevrolet Impala, possibly a 1999 year model. We don't know his direction of travel. There was probably one or more other persons in the car with him."

"Do you have a license number for the vehicle, ma'am?"

"Not at this time. We may be able to get one from the security tape."

"Hold on just one minute, ma'am. I'll get right back to you. Stay on the line."

Diane was put on hold, and almost immediately

they heard the police alert on Chanell's police radio monitor. Then the operator was back.

"Ma'am, are you there?"

"Yes, I am."

"Officers have been dispatched to your location and should be there within ten minutes. Will you be there when they arrive?"

"My chief of security, Chanell Napier, will be our point of contact here."

"Yes, ma'am, we know Officer Napier. Officers will be in touch with her in the next ten minutes. Can you give me a description of the perpetrator?"

"He was a male Caucasian, approximately six feet, appears to be middle-aged, husky voice, wearing a black ski cap, a dark blue bulky winter coat, and sunglasses. He was armed with what appears to be a model 1911 .45 caliber Army automatic pistol, silver finish, which he was last seen carrying in his coat pocket."

"Just one moment, ma'am. Please stay on the line."

Diane was again put on temporary hold, and again they heard the description broadcast over the police radio, and the warning—Armed and Dangerous. Then Diane was connected back with the emergency operator.

"We have security videos showing the incident," said Diane. "Please see that Chief Garnett is notified immediately that the perpetrator may be the same suspect sought in the Joana Cipriano murder."

"Yes, ma'am. Chief Garnett has been notified. I will transmit that information to him. Do you need any other assistance at this time?"

"No. We are fine here. Thank you for your help."

"Yes, ma'am. An officer is at your location now."

They looked up to see a Rosewood police officer entering through the doors of the museum Security office. Diane thanked the operator again and hung up the phone.

"Thanks, Chanell," said Diane. "Will you handle this with the police, please? I have to go see someone right away. Tell them the package he stole contained a doll, approximately twelve inches high, dark hair, dressed in a green satin dress with white fur trim. The perp may have it with him if he is caught. Call me if you need me."

Diane left the Security office and walked briskly to the restaurant, hoping that Juliet and her grandmother were still there.

"Do you want to be seated, Dr. Fallon?" the hostess asked.

"I'm looking for someone, thank you." As Diane's eyes grew accustomed to the darkened interior, she spotted Juliet and her grandmother getting up from the booth. She walked over to them.

"Juliet, why don't you and your grandmother sit down a moment."

Diane drew up a chair from another table and sat down at the end of their booth. *Where do I start?* she asked herself.

"Someone just stole the doll," said Diane.

"What?" said Juliet. "Stole the doll? Why?"

"I told you to hang on to it," said Mrs. Torkel. "Someone tried to get it from me when we were helping Juliet, and I had to elbow them out of the way."

"You mean someone besides the security guard?" asked Diane.

"Yes. When we were helping Juliet into the back room," said Mrs. Torkel. "Did they snatch it from you? You should have given them a good elbow."

"No, I was taking it to Laura Hillard and a man pulled a gun on me," said Diane.

Both of them looked at Diane with open mouths.

"A gun?" said Juliet. "Here in the museum?"

"In the parking lot," said Diane.

"What's the world coming to?" exclaimed her grandmother.

"Don't worry about the doll," said Juliet.

"It's not the doll that I'm worried about," said Diane.

She took a deep breath. This wasn't going to be easy.

"Juliet, I want you and your grandmother to stay in a hotel. The museum will pay for it."

"Why?" Juliet looked alarmed.

"Because of the doll?" said Mrs. Torkel. "It was just a doll."

"Juliet, I'm trying very hard not to alarm you."

"I don't think you're doing a very good job of it," said Mrs. Torkel.

"Gramma!" said Juliet.

"It's OK," said Diane. "She's right. Juliet, you know someone was murdered in your apartment building."

"Oh, goodness gracious," said Mrs. Torkel.

"Yes. They had an address similar to mine and it frightened me."

"I know. Did you know the murdered woman?" asked Diane.

"No," said Juliet, "I never met her."

"Joana Cipriano, the murdered girl, didn't look like you, but her general physical description was the same—blond hair, blue eyes—living in your apartment building. Someone who hadn't seen you for a long time or perhaps had an old picture might mistake one of you for the other," said Diane. "We have reason to believe that her murderer drove a blue Chevrolet Impala. The man who stole the doll also drove a blue Chevrolet Impala."

"Oh," said Juliet. She drew a deep breath. "I'm not crazy, am I?"

"No," said Diane. "You are definitely not crazy."

"I've always been afraid that someone was after me, even though I couldn't remember the kidnapping. But still, why would he come back after all these years?"

"Juliet, when you played with your dolls, did you ever hide messages inside them?"

Juliet looked at Diane with a blank stare. So did her grandmother.

"Why in the world would she do that?" said Mrs. Torkel.

"Just for fun," said Diane, hoping not to have to explain her own childhood play.

"No," said Juliet. "You mean like cut them open? I'd have to tear up the doll to do that."

"Not really. They can be put back together fairly easily—most of the time." Diane paused a moment.

Juliet and her grandmother looked at her as if they were beginning to doubt her sanity.

"Your grandmother said you told her that the doll had a secret," she continued.

Juliet shrugged. "I don't remember."

"That's what you told me, dear," said her grandmother.

"To me that meant one thing," said Diane. "There might be a message inside the doll."

"Well, how the heck did you get here from there?" said her grandmother.

"It was the way I played with my dolls. I won't get into that now, but I found that your doll had been restitched at the arm . . . so I took it apart."

"Took it apart?" said Ruby Torkel.

"I put it back together," said Diane. "It's as good as new."

"Did you find anything?" asked Juliet.

She was wide-eyed at this point. Diane didn't know if it was from Diane's effrontery, the odd way she played with dolls as a child, or the fact that there might have been a message hidden in the stolen doll.

"Yes, I did," said Diane. "There was a roll of paper inside with some kind of code written on it. I asked if you hid messages in your dolls because I wanted to know if it might have been something that you left, and not be of any importance to recent events. But since someone stole the doll, perhaps this is connected. . . ." Diane pulled the paper from her pocket. "This is what was printed on a strip of yellowed newsprint."

Both of them looked at the letters.

"Surely this is not about Leo Parrish," said Mrs. Torkel with a snort, sitting back in her seat.

Chapter 43

"Who is Leo Parrish?" asked Diane.

"That name sounds familiar," said Juliet.

"It should, dear. It's an old legend that's hung around Glendale-Marsh for years."

The waitress came by and asked if they wanted coffee. Diane was at the point where a beer would have been nice, but the effects of caffeine would work just fine, too. The three of them ordered coffee.

"Leo Parrish was this young man . . ." Ruby Torkel stopped. "I need to start before Leo. I need to start with the hurricane. In 1935 or thereabouts, a hurricane struck the Florida Keys and killed an awful lot of people. I was just a little baby then. They called it the Labor Day storm. They didn't give hurricanes names back then. Anyway, a train was sent to rescue people stuck on the Florida Keys. Legend has it that a man in the path of the coming storm talked someone at the railroad into letting him stash his gold on the train. Now, this is what don't make sense to me. The train was going *to* the Keys when the gold was loaded onto the train—going *into* the path of the storm, not *away* from it—that's the story. Why would he put his fortune on a train going into the hurricane?"

"Maybe he had to leave town or had to protect his fortune for some reason," said Juliet. "He had only one chance to put the gold on the train, and he believed the train would weather the storm and eventually get to safety. He probably figured the railroad company knew what they were doing and would not send a train into a situation it couldn't come out of. They had more to lose than he did."

"Maybe," conceded her grandmother. "Now the details change depending who's telling it. Some say the man's gold came from a Spanish treasure ship. Some say it's gold from the Civil War. I say it's a load of malarkey." She took a sip of coffee. "You think I could have another piece of that chocolate cake? It would go real good with this cup of coffee."

Diane called the waitress over and ordered Mrs. Torkel another piece of cake.

"Anyway, the train never made it to the Keys. It got washed off the tracks, and the money, or gold, or whatever it was, supposedly got washed away in the ocean, or the river, or covered up by mud. Like I say, the story changes."

"I never heard this story," said Juliet.

"Oh, sure, you did. You must have. Everybody in Glendale-Marsh knows the story," said Mrs. Torkel.

"What about Leo Parrish?" asked Juliet.

"I'm getting to that," said her grandmother. "You never were a patient girl. Leo Parrish lived in Glendale-Marsh in the late 1930s. I don't know much about him or where his folks were from, but he was—I guess—in his twenties about then. He was one of these boys always looking for the quick buck. The story is, he got interested in the tale of the missing fortune and, as he was a fellow with a head for numbers, he somehow figured out where the loot had to have ended up."

The cake came and the waitress brought one for each of them. Diane realized she had missed lunch. Well, what the hell, she thought, if cake was good enough for the peasants of France, it was good enough for her. She took a bite.

"I usually don't eat so much," said Mrs. Torkel after

a big bite of cake. "But, I'm on vacation." She took a sip of coffee. "Now, where was I?"

"Leo Parrish figured out where the treasure was," said Juliet.

"Oh, yes," said her grandmother. "He found it—the legend says. And he brought it to Glendale-Marsh in secret and hid it. Not long after, he went off to war—that's World War II. He was worried about the treasure, so he wrote down where it was in some kind of fancy code that nobody could decipher—and sent the code home in a book. I don't know anything about what kind of code it was, but since the thirties, we've had tourists coming to Glendale-Marsh looking for the book with the code and for the treasure. It was a real popular thing to do back in the fifties and sixties. I reckon poor Leo Parrish's family land has been dug up from one end t'other looking for that treasure."

"What happened to Leo Parrish?" asked Juliet.

"He went missing in action. Nobody ever heard from him again. If there ever was a treasure, it got lost with him," said her grandmother. She stopped talking and ate several bites of her cake.

"The treasure hunters have slacked off for several years. Occasionally, we get a few now and again, but not like we did in the fifties."

"That's an interesting story," said Diane. "You think this might be the code?" She tapped the paper in front of them.

"Who knows?" said Mrs. Torkel. "I don't know of any other code, but I can't say how it got in that doll. The doll's not that old."

"Maybe some treasure hunter found the code and hid it in the doll," said Juliet.

"Do the Parrishes still live in Glendale-Marsh?" asked Diane.

"No, they been gone from there for about thirty or forty years. Died out, mainly."

"Wow," said Juliet. "Treasure right there and I didn't know about it?"

"We found lots of treasure in our shells," said her grandmother. "They seem to have served you well. I imagine you've made more money from your interest in shells than you ever would from looking for treasure."

Diane finished the last bite of her cake. "Juliet . . . ," began Diane.

"I really don't want to stay in a hotel," said Juliet. "I will if I have to, but . . ."

"I'll have museum Security watch your apartment," said Diane.

"You think the guy who held you up for the doll is my kidnapper, don't you?" said Juliet.

"Yes," said Diane, "I do. I don't know how it all fits together, but I'm working on it. I really don't want to alarm you, but I think he may be afraid you remember him."

"Why?" asked Juliet.

Why? A good question, thought Diane. It was something else that had been nagging at the corner of her mind. Then, like the slow movement of molasses, it simply flowed into her brain.

"I think it has something to do with what you said before you were kidnapped. In the newspaper articles, neighbors were quoted as having heard you say, 'I don't know you' to someone near your backyard. Just before Joana Cipriano was murdered, she was heard to say to a man at her door, 'Do I know you?' The phrases are so close, I think her murderer was convinced he was recognized. Joana turned out to be the wrong person, but the conviction that you would be able to identify him carried over."

"You think it is about the treasure?" asked Juliet.

"He wanted the doll. A code was in the doll. That's the only story we've heard so far that contains a code.

So, yes. It may be just a treasure story, but he may believe it to be true."

"So he was trying to get the doll when he kidnapped me twenty years ago?" said Juliet.

"Maybe. We won't know that until we find him. But the police are on it. We are taking precautions, so don't you or your grandmother worry."

"Maybe we should stay in a hotel," said her grandmother. "A nice one."

"Why don't you do that?" said Diane. "I'll have someone from museum Security stay next door."

"That sounds just fine," said Mrs. Torkel. "They can follow us over to your apartment to get some things, Juliet. I'll get a chance to see where you live, then we'll stay in a nice hotel."

Juliet smiled at her grandmother. Diane got the idea that Mrs. Torkel had mellowed considerably since Juliet was a little girl.

When they finished eating their cake, Diane took them to the Security office and arranged for an escort and guard. From there she went to her office and removed the evidence bag with the original code from her safe, put it in her pocket, and walked up to the top floor of the east wing to the museum library and archives.

Beth, the museum's librarian, was a slender middle-aged woman with snow white hair whom Diane had hired when she was eased out of the university library in favor of younger employees. Age discrimination was against university regulations, but being passed over for promotions, and other passive-aggressive measures, were hard to prove and to defend against. She was clearly Bartram's loss and the museum's gain.

The door issued a gentle jingle as Diane opened it. Beth, holding a book, was standing on a tall library ladder. She looked down to see who had entered, placed the book on the shelf, and climbed down.

She looked warm in her navy pantsuit. Diane shivered. Beth kept the library slightly cooler than Diane liked, but she apparently found it very comfortable.

"Dr. Fallon," she said, "what can I do for you?"

Among Beth's abilities as a librarian and archivist, she was an outstanding genealogist and taught several community classes at the museum. Genealogy wasn't in the domain of natural history, but it was history and it was in the domain of classes people would pay to take, and that made it good for the museum.

"Beth, I have a task for you," said Diane.

She smiled. "I hope it's not as difficult as the task you gave Kendel."

Diane smiled, too. "I don't think so. I have someone I want you to trace for me. I would like to know his ancestry at least one or two generations back, but mainly his descendants—and not just his direct descendants."

Beth went to get a pen and paper. She held the pen poised over the pad. "What's his name?"

"Leo Parrish. I don't know the exact spelling. He was in his twenties in the late 1930s and lived in Glendale-Marsh, Florida, at that time. He enlisted in the Second World War, but I don't know which branch of service. He was listed as missing in action. He wrote to relatives while he was in the service, but I don't know who they are. I know that's not much to go on."

"Actually, that's quite a bit. When do you want the information?"

"Yesterday, if you can manage it," said Diane.

"Time travel's my speciality. I'll see what I can do."

Beth smiled, and Diane thanked her and walked downstairs to the conservation lab and into the head conservator's office.

"Korey," said Diane, "do you have a minute?"

"Dr. F.," said Korey, "I'd be a bad employee indeed, if I didn't have time for my boss. I've got that analysis Kendel asked for. It's not newsprint, but paper used in books circa thirties and forties."

"Book paper. Interesting." Diane took the evidence bag from her pocket and removed the original paper containing the code.

"What you got here, Dr. F.? Looks like some kind of cryptogram."

"This is the paper the sample came from. What I want you to do is duplicate it—it doesn't have to be exact, just look old. And I want the printing changed to simple random letters, but basically the same format and near the same handwriting as you can get it."

Korey put a hand on the back of his dreadlocks, raised his eyebrows, and grinned. His brown eyes sparkled.

"When you get finished with whatever it is you're doing," he said, "I'll buy you a steak if you'll tell me what this is about."

"You've got a deal. Can you do it?"

"Sure. When do you need it?" he asked.

"As soon as you can get to it," said Diane.

"You got it," said Korey.

"Put the original in your vault for me," said Diane. "And don't talk about it to anyone."

"Sounds like a serious scrap of paper," he said as he held it up to the light.

"Deadly serious," she said.

As she left his office, her cell phone vibrated. The display said it was Garnett.

"Diane," he said, "just called to tell you we have a line on the Impala."

Chapter 44

"You've found the Impala? That's a relief," said Diane. She climbed the steps to the third floor.

"We don't have it yet. It's been sighted and we have a lead on it. I just thought I'd let you know, so when we find it, your people can process it," said Garnett.

"I'll give them a heads-up," said Diane. "I'm really eager to find this guy. He told me that if I didn't give him the package, he would open fire on the busload of children visiting the museum."

"This is somebody we need to catch soon," said Garnett.

"You won't get an argument from me."

"So, it's your thinking that the Cipriano murder was a case of mistaken identity?" said Garnett.

"I believe so. The perp was after the doll all along. The woman I think was the intended target is named Juliet Price, one of my employees. The doll belongs to her. She lives just around the block from Cipriano in the same apartment complex and has a very similar address, 131 H. They are both blue-eyed blondes of similar age—their descriptors are close enough that they could be mistaken for each other. Plus, there's the Impala present at both crime scenes. The one used today was dark blue, so it's likely to have a blue interior. If we can match carpet fibers found at the Cipriano murder, we'll have him connected to both crimes."

"Napier said there was a doll involved. What's that about?" asked Garnett.

"I'm not sure. I think it's a hunt for lost treasure," said Diane.

"Lost treasure? You've got to be kidding," said Garnett.

"I'm not kidding, but I may be wrong," she said. "It's kind of a long story. I'll give you the complete rundown later."

"In your 911 call, you said there may have been two perps?" said Garnett.

"Two or more. He told me not to move for five minutes while '*we* get out of here.' "

"You may have found us the break we needed," said Garnett.

"I wish I could take credit, but he came to me," said Diane as she walked across the museum in the direction of the crime lab.

"That was a dangerous experience for you. Are you all right?" asked Garnett.

"I'm fine. He got what he was after," she said. "I was more mad than scared."

Diane walked past the lounge and across the dinosaur overlook and came face-to-face with Darth Vader. She stopped in her tracks.

"I have to go," she said. "Something's come up. Let me know if you find him." Diane flipped the phone closed.

A life-sized cardboard cutout of Darth Vader stood holding a sign that read:

STOP HERE
MUSEUM PERSONNEL ONLY

He stood just behind one of the museum's velvet covered chains used for roping off nonpublic areas. Kids sometimes break away from their group and decide to make their own tour of the museum. Some get lost in the huge building and require rescuing. So, the docents post Authorized Personnel signs in various places. Today was an especially busy day for tours of schoolchildren. One of the docents must have wanted to keep the kids out of the west wing and thought this particular sign was a funny inside joke. Diane stepped over the rope past Darth Vader and went to the dark side.

Jin and Neva, counting cigarette butts, were in one of the glassed-in rooms with their booty spread out on a long table.

"Hey, Boss," said Jin. "You all in one piece? We saw the video image of the guy with the gun on you."

"I'm fine. How are you doing here?" she asked.

Jin gestured to a table full of evidence bags. "We got a lot of butts."

Also lying on the table was a large piece of white butcher paper with a map drawn on it showing the relative locations of the morgue tent, the coffee tent, the media tent, and where the onlookers stood. Jin and Neva wore gloves and were sorting through the butts looking for Dorals. Apparently they hadn't found any yet, for there was nothing on their map.

David entered the room just as Diane donned a pair of gloves to help with the sorting. It looked like hundreds of them.

"I got the photos from museum Security," said David. "That was a big gun he had trained on you. Must have been scary."

"Made me more mad than scared. All he wanted was the doll. Were you able to clarify the photographs?"

"I got a partial plate. AXE and it looks like a Georgia plate."

"AXE," said Jin. "You think that was on purpose?"

"I doubt it. What criminal has vanity plates?" said Neva.

David shook his head. "I also got the interior. The seats look blue. I imagine the carpet is, too."

"Garnett's chasing down a lead to the car right now," said Diane. "If he finds it and them, I'm going to need you guys to process the car and their clothes too, ASAP."

"Sure thing, Boss," said Jin.

"What about the face?" asked Diane. "Could you do anything with that?"

"Not really," said David. "He had on sunglasses. My face recognition software needs to see the eyes. But I cleared it up as much as I could and sent it to the police department. They can use it to show around. Someone might recognize him."

"OK, I'm going to finish the facial reconstruction. David, do you mind helping Jin and Neva sort the cigarette butts?"

"Not at all," said David, putting on a pair of gloves. "By the way, why did the guy steal a doll? Was it valuable? And what did it have to do with Cipriano?"

"Because of what was inside the doll," said Diane. "Cipriano, I think, was a mistake. I'll tell you more later. Right now we've got evidence to process."

Diane left them sorting cigarette butts and went to her lab where the bones were still waiting for her. She had already pieced together most of the face the last time she worked on them. There weren't that many pieces left. She made quick work of it, and when she finished she had two complete skeletal faces.

She took them both to her vault, put each in turn on the pedestal, and scanned each with the laser scanner. She asked the software to reconstruct the unknown victim first, then do another construction of the first victim. Now that she had a more complete face, there would be fewer extrapolations and a more accurate rendition of the face. Even though the first reconstruction was already identified, a more accurate picture would be helpful to the police in tracing the guy's steps before he got blown into tiny pieces.

As the software worked its magic—growing a face—

she went back out to the bones and began the tedious task of trying to separate the two skeletons. She accomplished that through measurements and articulated surfaces. The task was made easier by the fact that the two individuals were of different heights. One had been athletic, as indicated by large muscle attachments on his arms and legs and pelvic bones. The other individual had been more sedentary.

The athletic individual was about ten years older than the other, as shown by the sternal end of his ribs, various epiphyses, and the condition of the pubic symphysis. He had a healed wound in his scapula—probably a gunshot wound. It would have reduced the range of motion in his arm and shoulder. From the size of the muscle attachments, he compensated by strengthening his arm and shoulder within the range of motion he had. Gradually she separated out the two skeletons until each lay on a separate table.

She went back to have a look at the faces. The image on the screen when she walked in was the re-scanned face of the identified victim from the basement. It was similar to the first version, but looked more realistic. Faces aren't actually symmetrical. There are always slight variations from one side to the other. Duplicating one side and flipping it to substitute for missing bones creates a rather strange looking facsimile. This face no longer had that odd appearance.

She flipped it over and looked at the next face—and sat stunned. He could have been Marcus McNair's brother, he was so similar.

Chapter 45

Diane stared at the reconstructed face on the computer screen. Was this what Marcus McNair didn't want them to find? A relative? Why wasn't he reported missing? Didn't he have other family who missed him? Parents, wife, children, girlfriend, friends?

She reached for the phone and called Garnett.

"I'm afraid you're going to be disappointed," said Garnett, answering her call. "We found the car down a ravine ten miles outside of town. It's been burned out. No bodies."

"I'll send David out," said Diane. "Maybe he'll find something useful."

She was disappointed, but not surprised they ditched the car. She was willing to bet it was a stolen car, anyway. She wrote down the directions to it before she addressed the reason for her call.

"Did McNair have a brother or cousin, midthirties, who was shot in the shoulder, and looked a lot like him?"

Garnett was silent for a few seconds. "He has a cousin Eric McNair who fits that description. Why are you asking?"

"I finished reconstructing the skull on the second basement skeleton. Imagine my surprise when I looked at the computer-generated face and saw a facsimile of McNair."

"Hmph. Kind of puts a new light on things," said Garnett. "I imagine that was a shock. So, that's where Eric got to."

"Who is he and what's his story? And why didn't anybody report him missing?" asked Diane. She stared at the face rotating on the screen as she spoke with Garnett.

"Eric's one of those family members you kind of hope will go off and not come back. Always in trouble. Spent time in jail for dealing, assault and battery, spouse abuse, you name it. He was shot in a drug deal that went sour. His family had hoped that cured him, but he was a hard case. I guess he's cured now."

"Must have been what McNair was trying to hide," said Diane.

"Probably so. Discovering Eric's involvement with the meth lab would definitely have implicated Marcus. They were tight. Marcus was the only relative Eric was close to."

"How did Marcus get to be arson investigator?" asked Diane.

"Marcus kept out of trouble himself. He also had a benefactor," said Garnett.

"Who?" asked Diane.

"Guess."

"Adler?" answered Diane.

"First try. It's looking worse and worse for Adler. The more we find on McNair, the more we have on Adler. I don't know if you've seen the news. He's been trying to distance himself from McNair. But his political career is circling the drain. I'd love to arrest the bastard. That would be icing on the cake."

What did David say about payback being a bitch? thought Diane. Adler had no friends in the police department. He should have thought of that. You'd think a politician would have.

"Can I get dental records on Eric McNair or x-rays of his shoulder?" asked Diane.

"The guy may never have gone to a dentist. The hospital should have x-rays from the shooting injury. I'll get them sent over to you," said Garnett.

"That'll confirm the identification," said Diane. "I don't guess there's any line on where the occupants of the Impala went," she said, jumping subjects.

"None. They obviously ditched the car. They're probably in another vehicle by now and long gone."

"They'll hang around," said Diane.

"How do you know?"

"Because they didn't get what they wanted," said Diane.

"You mean the secret code thing you were talking about?" asked Garnett.

From the tone of his voice and the ambiguity of his understanding of what the *secret code thing* represented to the gunman, Diane could see that Garnett wasn't buying the looking-for-treasure motive. It didn't matter. She bought it. And she knew they would return to get the coded message.

"You'll let me know if he's sighted?" she said.

"You know I will," replied Garnett. "But I think you can relax."

She hung up with Garnett. The face of Eric McNair rotated in three dimensions on her screen. What a tragic life to have gotten as far as his midthirties and have no one miss him. She printed out both faces—the two men who died together in an instant in the basement of the house—and saved them to a portable memory stick.

Jin, David, and Neva had made significant progress sorting through the cigarette butts. The map was full of small x's, each representing a Doral. But she didn't like what she saw. The vast majority of the x's clustered near the morgue tent and the coffee tent.

"Doesn't look good, does it?" said David.

She looked up and caught him watching her.

"We'll need to find out what the people at tent city smoke," said Jin.

What the people at tent city smoke, thought Diane. None of them wanted to say that who they were looking at as a murder suspect was one of the medical examiners, their assistants, or a policeman. Those were the only people allowed in the area.

"I hate this," said Neva, "but I'll find out what the policemen smoke."

"I'll do it," said David. "They're your friends."

"Neither of you will do it," said Diane. "We're going to give the information to Garnett and let him investigate. That's what we do: We supply objective information from the scene and he uses it to investigate the crime."

"Since when?" said Jin.

"I'm not willing to alienate the police department any more than I have to. I'm taking the coward's way out of this one. It's up to Garnett now."

"That works for me," said Neva.

Diane didn't hear Jin or David objecting. *Good.*

"This is something for you to mull over," said Diane. She laid down the printout of the face she had reconstructed.

"Why did you have the computer draw Marcus McNair?" said Neva. She looked at Diane with a puzzled frown.

"Yeah, Boss," said Jin. "You testing your software?"

"Is this McNair?" asked David, picking up the page and examining the printed picture.

"We're waiting for confirmation, but it appears to be Eric McNair, Marcus McNair's cousin," said Diane.

Jin grabbed the page out of David's hand to look at it again. "His cousin? Was he the second guy in the basement?"

"Yes, he was. I'm having x-rays sent over for confirmation," said Diane.

"What does this mean exactly?" asked David.

"Garnett believes that it connects Marcus McNair to the meth manufacturing. He's hoping that proving McNair was involved will mean he can prove Adler was involved. Failing direct proof, I suppose Garnett hopes the insinuation that Adler was involved will forever ruin Adler's political career," said Diane.

"You sound like you don't approve," said Jin. "I wouldn't waste any sympathy on Adler."

"I'm not," said Diane. "I have no sympathy for him. I . . . It's just that . . ."

"You like a clean kill," said David.

"Blunt way of putting it, but I suppose that's true. Anyway, that's not our problem. Our problem is to recover the best evidence we can from the crime scenes. Speaking of which, David, I need you to go meet Garnett at a crime scene. Here are the directions. He found the Chevrolet Impala in a ravine and burned to a crisp."

"Were the suspects in it?" asked David

"No, it looks like they just got rid of the car. Probably got another one. It's my feeling they're still in town."

"Why would they hang around?" asked Neva.

"Because they were after the coded message, and I removed it from the doll before they got it."

The three of them gave her a blank stare. "Coded message?" said Jin.

"I think you skipped a chapter," said David.

"I guess I did. The doll had what may be a coded message inside." She briefly told them the story of Leo Parrish and the missing loot.

"And these guys are looking for it?" said Jin.

"I'm guessing," said Diane. "I don't know for a fact."

"That's just a weird story," said David, as if it offended his sensibilities. "How did Juliet get involved?"

"That I don't know. I have only vague guesses." Diane didn't want to give them Juliet's life history just yet. She turned to Jin. "I have a job for you. I know how you like to solve puzzles." Diane pulled the printed copy of the code from her pocket and handed it to Jin.

"That was in the doll?" said David. "How did you know to look?"

"Long story," said Diane.

"It must be," he said. "It just keeps getting longer."

"This looks like a cryptogram," Jin said. "I can do these in my sleep. See, all you have to know is the frequency with which each letter of the alphabet occurs in everyday language—a few other things too—but it's easy."

"Good. Do it tonight when you get home. Right now, you and Neva get the cigarette information to Garnett. And David . . ."

"I know, I'm going," he said. He grabbed his case and headed for the elevator.

"I'll meet you out there," she called after him. "I have some things to do here first."

"I can do it myself," he said.

"It'll be faster if I help," she said.

The elevator door opened and David stepped in.

"When you guys finish your report, go home," Diane said to Neva and Jin. "I'll see you tomorrow."

Diane left them and walked downstairs to the conservation lab. She met Korey on the Pleistocene overlook near his lab.

He grinned and his eyes twinkled when he saw her. "I have your forgery, Dr. F.," he said.

"That's great. I was just coming to get it. I'm going fishing and I need bait for my hook." It was in a glassine envelope. She took it out and examined it.

"This looks just like the original," said Diane.

"I went down to the thrift shop and bought some

old books," he said. "I tore a piece from one of them—they weren't valuable, I checked. I wrote the message with vegetable ink. It all looks pretty old."

"Thank you, Korey," said Diane. "This is excellent. If I decide to go into a life of crime, you're my man." She slipped it back in its envelope and put it in her pocket.

"I'm glad to know that's not what we are doing," he said still smiling. "Tell me, the jobs you gave to Kendel and Beth, are they related to this?" He gestured to her pocket.

"Yes," said Diane smiling.

"I really can't wait for this," he said.

"I'll tell you when it's over, all three of you," she said and left by the overlook elevator and rode down to the main lobby.

She looked at her watch. Shortly, the night lighting would come on. Andie was probably already gone. She waved at the guard at the information desk and went to her office.

Korey really did a good job, she thought as she moved open the door to the safe. After that, everything went black.

Chapter 46

"Dr. Fallon! Are you all right?"

Who is that talking? Diane was confused and had a pounding headache—and she was on the floor. But someone was helping her to a chair. She sat down and put her head in her hands for a moment, then looked up.

Clarice, one of the night cleaning crew, her long hair in a high ponytail, wearing jeans and a museum sweatshirt, was standing over her with a look of fear on her face.

"You need to go to the emergency room, Dr. Fallon. Your head's bleeding."

"Bleeding?" Diane touched the back of her head. It was wet. *What is going on?*

"Diane?"

The new voice sounded like David.

"What happened?" he asked.

"I just found her on the floor like this," said Clarice.

"I need to take you to the hospital," said David.

What I need, thought Diane, *is to just sit right here until I feel better.*

"I'm fine," she said.

"No, you're not," said David. "I'll go get the car. Clarice will walk you to the door."

"What happened?" asked Diane.

"It looks like someone attacked you," said Clarice. "Here in your office."

"Don't clean her office," said David as he hurried out the door.

Clarice helped Diane toward her door. They were met by a security guard who took Diane's arm and assisted her the rest of the way.

"I'm sorry, Dr. Fallon. Chanell is going to rip us a new one," he said. "She's on her way down here to try and find out how this could have happened—twice. I'm really sorry. We didn't see anyone."

"What?" said Diane.

"I was saying that I don't know how this could have happened," he repeated.

"Check to see what classes are meeting tonight. Someone could have come and gone with a group that is meeting here," said Diane.

David appeared and escorted her to his car and helped her in.

"You can take me home," said Diane.

"No. We are going to the hospital," he said as he buckled himself in. "What was the last thing you remember?"

Diane thought a moment. Her head seemed to be clearing some. "I saw Korey. He gave me the forgery."

"You've lost me already," said David. "What forgery?"

"The code. Didn't I tell you about the code?"

"The one in the doll?" asked David.

"Yes. I asked Korey to duplicate it for me, make it look just like the original, but scramble the letters so they don't make sense."

"It doesn't make sense now. None of this does. When did we make this giant left turn? You said this was about the Cipriano case and lost treasure."

"David, you know, I don't feel like explaining it all now. How about in the morning? I'll get everyone up to speed. Before I forget, I stashed Juliet Price and her grandmother, Ruby Torkel, in a hotel. Museum Security is in an adjoining room, though I'm kind of losing faith in my security of late."

He drove to the same hospital that stitched up Jin when he was hit on the head. They took Diane immediately and examined her. The doctor looked at her pupils, tested her reflexes, and tended to her head wound, giving her five stitches.

She had the same doctor that Jin had. To Diane he didn't look old enough to be a doctor. He had one of those baby faces that would probably carry him well into his sixties still looking like a kid.

"Is there an epidemic?" he said when he finished stitching her up.

"Possibly," she said.

"How do you feel? Headache?"

"Yes, I definitely have a headache."

"How about dizziness? Weakness in your arms or legs?"

"No," she answered.

"Have you vomited?"

"No."

"Do you have any memory loss?" he asked.

"I don't remember what happened."

"What's the last thing you do remember?"

Since David had asked that same question, she had had time to think. "I talked to an employee, went to my office. . . . That's the last thing I remember."

"Do you know how long you were unconscious?"

"No. The night lighting in the museum was already on. It comes on at nine thirty. But I don't know how long it had been on. Actually, I have no idea how long I was out."

"Have you noticed any irritability?" he asked.

"I'm really pissed at whoever did this."

He smiled. "I'm going to order a CT scan. Do you know if you're allergic to contrast dyes?"

"I'm not," said Diane.

"I'm going to keep you overnight, just to watch you. I think you're fine, but we need to be sure."

"You didn't keep Jin overnight," she said.

"I suspect you were out longer. I'm just being cautious. It's nothing to worry about."

"Just as long as you don't say it's because I'm older," said Diane.

After the CT scan, Diane was taken to a semiprivate room. No one was in the other bed. She was glad of that. The last thing she wanted right now was a roommate. David came in to see her.

"I'm fine," said Diane, as he walked in the door.

"I talked to the doctor," said David. "He said if everything looks good tonight you'll be going home in the morning. Do you want me to call Frank?"

"I will. If you call him, he'll worry. How was the Impala crime scene?"

"I didn't find much. It was rocky and there weren't any tracks. The car is pretty much a burned mess. I had it hauled to our impound, anyway. Maybe something escaped the flames. Who do you think attacked you?" said David.

Diane gave him a blank stare for a moment. "Damn. Hand me my jacket."

He got her jacket from the tiny closet on her side of the room and handed it to her. She searched the pockets.

"It's gone," she said. "Did you find a glassine envelope in my office with a fragment of paper in it?"

"I haven't been to your office. Was it valuable? Was that what Korey gave you?"

"Yes," she answered. "It was Korey's forgery. No, it wasn't valuable."

"Can he make you another one?" asked David.

"Why?" said Diane.

"To replace the one stolen, I don't know. What was it for, anyway?" he asked.

"It was bait. I wanted whoever stole the doll to get it—just not in this way. They worked faster than I had planned."

"What did you have planned?" said David.

"It wasn't completely worked out yet. I was maybe going to plant a story in the paper about the doll and finding the code. I was trying to think of a way to contact them so they would know I had the message from the doll. I thought they would contact me—I really hadn't thought it out completely."

"I guess they did contact you," he said.

Diane felt her head. "They did indeed."

Diane awoke early and felt much better than she had the evening before, except that the whole back side of her scalp was painfully tender. The nurse came in and checked her temperature and blood pressure.

"Can I go home now?" she asked.

"The doctor didn't leave instructions for you to be dismissed. He'll be making his rounds soon," she said.

The nurse left and a woman with a breakfast tray came in. Scrambled eggs, bacon, toast, orange juice, and cereal. *Big breakfast,* she thought. As the breakfast lady left, a policeman came in. He was one of the young policemen she had seen guarding the morgue tent. He had a pen and pad in his hand and a cigarette stuck behind his ear.

"Hi, Dr. Fallon," he said, grinning.

Diane wondered if she looked that funny sitting in a hospital bed wearing the terrible hospital gown.

"It's good to see you again," he said. "Though, not like this. I need to get a statement."

He pulled up a chair and as he sat down, Diane sneaked a peak at the cigarette behind his ear.

"You really shouldn't smoke," she said, taking a bite of bacon. "It's bad for you."

Chapter 47

"I know smoking is bad, ma'am," he said. "I quit for a long time, but with all this explosion tragedy, I started up again."

"Do you know that none of the three medical examiners, Webber, Pilgrim, or Rankin, smoke?" said Diane. "You know why?"

He shook his head.

"Because they've all seen firsthand what smokers' lungs look like," said Diane.

"Well, I'll probably quit again. Right now I need to take a statement," he said.

Diane gave him a brief version of what happened to her, not going into treasure hunts, dolls, secret codes, or historic hurricanes. She'd tell Garnett, but she didn't really want to go into the whole thing right now—especially while her mind was focused on something else.

"Did he take anything?" asked the policeman.

"I haven't been back to my office to check my safe. I'll notify the police if anything's missing. Why do you carry your cigarette behind your ear?" she said, trying to bring the conversation back to the Doral held in place between his ear and his brain. He looked under twenty-six. So much for David's statistics.

"Cause it'll get crushed in my pocket, ma'am. I've been trying not to start back, so I bum cigarettes instead of buying them. That way, I have only one at a time." He took the cigarette between his fingers and looked at it. "Actually, I prefer a Marlboro, but beggars can't be choosers."

"Who did you bum that from?" asked Diane.

"Archie Donahue," he said.

So, perhaps David's statistics were right after all.

"Well, I wish you luck in your efforts to stop smoking," she said.

"Thank you, ma'am."

He folded his pad of paper and put it in his pocket with his pen. He stuck his cigarette back behind his ear and left.

Diane finished her breakfast, pondering what she'd learned. Which was what? Archie smoked Dorals? Not much. Hardly anything. There were probably others in the department who smoked them. Certainly not an indictment. She closed her eyes to think.

What did the person who attacked Jin hit him with— butt of his gun, nightstick, rock? I should have stayed up on the ridge to look for blunt instruments. Instead, I left the policemen there to look while I took Jin to the doctor. Ample chance to move the weapon to a new location. Damn. But if the weapon was something he carries, he may have only wiped the blood off. We could still find blood and bits of Jin's flesh. But everybody knows about blood nowadays, especially policemen. He'd have cleaned it with kerosene or bleach. We might at least be able to detect that. And that would still leave us nowhere.

"I need to get out of here," she said out loud.

"Not until the doctor says you can go."

She opened her eyes and looked at Frank. She had forgotten to call him. *Damn.* He pulled up a chair and sat down.

"Why aren't you at work?" she said.

"I had business in Rosewood today. It doesn't happen often that there's a Rosewood connection with a case I'm working on, but when it does happen, I take advantage of it. Why didn't you call me?"

"I meant to, but I got conked on the head and forgot—really," she said.

"David told me what happened this morning when I called the crime lab," he said. "I'll take you home. When are you being released?"

"As soon as I see the doctor," said Diane.

Just as she said it, the doctor entered her room.

"Your CT scan was fine. You can go home. Get plenty of rest and sleep. We'll give you a list of symptoms to watch for. If any of them occurs, call or come back here immediately."

"Thanks. I'm ready to get out of here," said Diane.

He smiled, handed her a prescription for pain pills, and went off to see other patients.

Diane got dressed and was still waiting thirty minutes later for someone to come and get her, tell her she could go, or . . . something.

"Be patient," said Frank.

"I really don't like hospitals," said Diane. "And I don't like waiting. I think I'll start charging for my waiting time. Maybe it'll get my bill down to some reasonable amount."

"Isn't irritability one of the signs you're supposed to watch out for?" said Frank.

She was about to retort when the nurse came with the paperwork and a wheelchair. Diane signed the paperwork.

"I don't need the wheelchair," she said.

"Everyone leaves in a wheelchair. It's hospital policy," said the nurse.

"It's not mine," said Diane and walked out ahead of Frank and the nurse.

Frank caught up with her. "Diane, don't you think you'd better slow down? What's up with you?"

"I just want out of here. Do you know how much

time I've spent in the hospital—either visiting people I care about or being a patient myself?"

"Yes, but something besides your concussion has you irritated," he said.

"Right now, one of the suspects I have in mind for the killings of McNair and Stanton is someone I like. And I absolutely hate that. My gut reaction is to just let him go, and I don't like that feeling, either. I'm at odds with myself and it's damned uncomfortable. Plus, it pisses me off when a fish steals my bait."

After Diane had insisted on being taken to the museum instead of home, Frank insisted on an explanation of what happened to her. She fumbled through an account of her intention to use the code to catch the doll thief—and probably Joana Cipriano's murderer.

"Tell me again, how was this plan supposed to work?" asked Frank as he drove toward the museum.

"I told you, I hadn't thought it out enough to implement it. He struck too soon," she said.

"You know, you come up with some of the worst plans," said Frank. "Remember that one in your museum vault?"

"I wasn't finished with this one—there was no plan being played out. They just came and attacked me. The result would have been the same had I not been thinking of a plan at all. As it is, they do have the wrong code."

"You may have delayed them, but how does that get you closer to catching them?" asked Frank.

"It doesn't," said Diane. "I was going to use the forged code as bait *to* catch them. How many times do I have to go over this so that you understand it? There was nothing I did, no plan I put in motion that caused them to come after me. They did this on their own."

Frank pulled into the museum parking lot and Diane

got out. The first place she headed was to Security. Frank followed and started to open the door for her, but she beat him to it. Everyone stopped what they were doing when Diane walked in.

"Dr. Fallon." The receptionist, a student in criminology from Bartram, smiled meekly. "It's good to see you. I hope . . ." She hesitated and smiled, looking embarrassed. "I'll get Napier. She's in the video room reviewing recordings." She left to get Chanell.

I must look a fright, thought Diane. *Everyone looks scared.*

Chanell came hurrying out of the video room.

"Dr. Fallon, I hardly know what to say. Please come into my office and I'll fill you in on what we've found so far."

"I'll hang around out here," said Frank.

Diane went in the office with Chanell and sat down.

"What have you found?" she asked.

"Like you suggested, we looked at the people who were in the building for classes. We cross-referenced the security recordings to the class rolls. We've found a couple of people to look at. However, Dr. Shane— she's teaching the bird watching series—does not keep good records. We had her in here telling us who all of her students are. There are a couple of new ones she didn't know." She stopped and took a breath. "So far, that's all we have."

"Do you know how my attacker got in this section?" Diane asked.

"We're thinking he or she—it could have been a woman—got in during museum hours. There was a period of time when some of the docents and exhibit specialists were away from their usual stations visiting Public Relations. We think he or she stayed—maybe in the bathroom or a storage closet—until closing. No one is on the video slipping in or breaking in the front or back entrance of this wing."

Diane rose. "Let me know when you have more."

"Yes, ma'am," said Chanell.

Diane left and headed for the crime lab.

"You don't have to babysit me," she told Frank.

"Tired of my company already?" he said.

"I don't want to keep you from your appointment," she said.

"I've already had my appointment—early this morning. I'm all yours all day to watch your six."

They rode the elevator to the third floor and crossed over to the west wing. Darth Vader was still on guard.

"I probably need to put him at the front entrance," said Diane as she crossed over the rope and went toward the door to the crime lab.

"You think you need to slow down a bit?" said Frank.

"Why?" said Diane.

"Because you just got out of the hospital and you have a concussion?"

"I'm fine," she said, keying in her code and entering the lab.

David looked up from his computer when she entered.

"You're looking better than when I left you," he said. "I just called the hospital and they told me you had been released. I figured you'd be back here."

Diane sat down at the round table. David and Jin joined her while Neva was on the phone. Frank sat off to one side.

"Archie Donahue smokes Dorals," Diane said. "Those are probably his you picked up at tent city. There is nothing to connect his Dorals with the ones you found on the ridge."

"But . . . ," said David.

"But nothing . . . that's it," said Diane.

"That's not all of it," said Neva, joining them. "I was talking to someone at the station. Archie Donahue left right after he checked in this morning. No one knows where he went."

"So it's in the hands of the police," said Diane. "Neva, call Garnett and tell him about the Dorals and leave it with him."

Neva left and made the call to Garnett. It was quick. Diane heard Neva say they didn't know what it meant; it was just information. None of them wanted the murderer to be a policeman, and if it was, they all had the uncomfortable feeling of not wanting him caught. Not a good philosophy for criminalists.

Neva sat back down at the table. "Garnett asked about you," she said. "He said he'd drop by later today."

Diane saw a paper rolled up in Jin's hands.

"OK, Jin," she said, "what do you have on the code?"

Chapter 48

Jin looked at the paper in his hand and turned red. Neva and David laughed.

"You don't have anything, do you?" said Neva.

"It's not a cryptogram," said Jin. "It can't be. I don't think it's anything."

"May I see it?" asked Frank.

Jin handed him the paper, and Frank unrolled the page and examined the letters.

"This is the code that was in the doll you were telling me about?" asked Frank.

"Yes," said Diane.

"Have you tried other decoding techniques? If it's not a simple cryptogram, it might be another kind of cipher."

"Do you think you can decode it?" said Diane.

"Don't know till I try," said Frank.

Jin looked more depressed than when the cigarette butts were stolen from him.

"Jin," said Neva, "you can't know everything. Don't look so glum."

"It's just, I'm really good at codes," he said. His entire face was turned down in a frown as he watched Frank studying the string of letters on the wrinkled paper.

"Do you know anything about the guy who wrote it?" asked Frank.

"A little," said Diane. She related the story of Leo Parrish, the treasure train, and the Labor Day hurricane of 1935.

"So," said Frank, "this whole thing may be a hoax."

"That's what I think," said Jin. "It's just a string of random letters."

"Could be," said Frank. "You know it's not a cryptogram because the frequency of occurrence of the letters didn't lend itself to an answer, right?"

"No," said Jin. "Nor does looking at the two- and three-letter words or the endings or beginnings of words. Nothing makes sense."

"Then we need to look at another type of encryption method. You say Leo did his thing in the 1930s?"

"Yes," said Diane.

"OK, so it's not modern. No computer to help him with it. Maybe it's something popular among coders of his time, like Vigenere's method," said Frank. "Where, for example, the cipher letter for *e* in one word isn't necessarily the same cipher letter for an *e* in another word."

"Well, you've completely lost me," said Neva.

"Wow," said Jin, leaning forward, his eyes now sparkling with interest. "No wonder I couldn't decipher it. How do you know about this stuff, Frank?"

"It's only what he does for a living," said David.

"No kidding. I didn't know that's what you do," said Jin.

"It's part of what I do," said Frank. "A lot of cybercrime involves hiding things by use of encryption."

"Can you decipher it?" Diane asked.

"Probably. It will be easier if I have the keyword," he said.

"Keyword?" they all said in unison.

"Several of the early ciphers required a keyword. Even without the keyword, there are other ways it can be deciphered and a good computer program can work it out, but if I have the keyword, I can do it fairly quickly. Are there any possible keywords from this story of yours?"

"How about a key sentence?" said Diane. "*The making of palimpsests was possible even with papyri.*"

Frank raised his eyebrows and she explained about the amazing coincidence of hearing that phrase in the library, Juliet's fear of the word *palimpsest* and her dramatic reaction to hearing the complete sentence.

"Well that's certainly odd," said Frank.

David, Neva, and Jin stared at her with their mouths open.

"Wow," said Jin again. "We hadn't heard that story, Boss."

"There's been so much going on lately," Diane said. She turned back to Frank. "Do you think *palimpsest* could be the keyword?"

"Could be. I'll give it a try. Can I use a computer?" said Frank. "You do have word processing programs on your computers, don't you?"

"Of course," said David.

He led Frank to his computer and called up Word-Perfect. Frank sat down and started typing.

David moved an empty chair next to Frank, and Diane sat down. She was feeling a little weak, and her headache was back, but she didn't want to mention it. David probably guessed, she thought. Frank reached over and squeezed her hand. *He probably senses my weakness too, damn it.*

Frank made a grid twenty-seven by twenty-six. On the top row he keyed in each letter of the alphabet in lowercase. Under the *a* in the first column, he repeated the alphabet starting with an uppercase *B* and putting the uppercase *A* on the bottom of the column after *Z*. He did the same thing in the next column—under the lowercase *b* he put an uppercase *C* and put the uppercase *A* and *B* at the bottom of the column after *Z*. Each successive uppercase alphabet was shifted one letter with respect to the previous column.

"This is called a Vigenere square," said Frank when he finished. "The lowercase letters across the top represent the plain text. The uppercase letters in the columns represent the cipher text."

Neva made a gesture with her hand going over her head. "This looks too much like math with letters," said Neva.

"Not far from wrong," said Frank.

"This is great," said Jin. "Where have I been that I didn't know this?"

"I don't know," said Frank grinning. "This is Secret Code 101."

"How does it work?" said Diane.

"Let's say the keyword is DIANE. In the left column I will use only those letters." He used the word processing program to highlight the letters of DIANE and continued the shading all across the row in the table for each letter.

"Now, suppose we have the message, *'The house that Jack built.'* So, we have to make another table . . . ," began Frank.

"OK," said Neva. "You mentioned something about a computer program that would do this?"

"Yes, but I don't have it," said Frank. "Let's have a little patience. Think of this as fun. Jin does."

"You betcha," said Jin. He pulled up a chair and leaned forward, staring at the screen. "You said you use a second table?"

"Yes," said Frank. "If the keyword is DIANE, on the header row of this table I write the word DIANE over and over again until I have used up all the letters in the message to be encoded.

"Oh, I get it." Jin jumped up and sat down again. "That's brilliant. No wonder I couldn't make heads or tails of it."

"Explain it to those of us who don't get it," said Neva.

"To encrypt *'The house that Jack built,'* " said Frank, "I go to the new table and see that the first letter in the message is *t* and it is under the letter *D* in the keyword DIANE. I go to the Vigenere square and use it like the coordinates of a map to find the encryption letter I need. Go to *D* on the left most column and find where it intersects with *t* in the top row. The letter where the column and row intersect is *W*. Do the same thing for the second letter. The *h* is under *I* in the keyword Diane. Go to the square and we find that *I* and *h* intersect at *P*. Keep going and you can encrypt the whole sentence. You do the reverse process to decode the message."

"That is so cool," said Jin. "You'll have to show me how to decode it the other ways you were talking about."

"Sure. It's more time-consuming. As you see, if you have the keyword, it's a piece of cake."

"Yeah," said David, "I'd like to see the computer program. That would be an interesting algorithm."

"How about our message?" said Diane.

"OK, we're hoping the keyword is *palimpsest*." Frank took the first word in the doll code and tried it out with his square. KVQ = vvf. "*Palimpsest* isn't the keyword," he said.

"Try *papyri*," said Diane.

"Won't work," said Frank. "*Papyri* and *palimpsest* start out with the same two letters. We'll end up with vv again."

"So we're nowhere," said Neva.

"Or an alternative method for decoding it," said Jin.

"Maybe the keyword is his name," said Neva.

"That would be too easy to decode," said Jin. "If you are going to the trouble to have an elaborate code, you won't have such an easy keyword."

The phone rang and Diane answered. She was expecting Garnett, but it was Beth, the museum's librarian.

"Beth," said Diane. "You have something for me?"

"Yes, I do. I can bring it to you. I thought you'd like to know that I did find some descendants of Leo Parrish that you might be able to contact. I don't know where they are now, but I have info on the last-known locations of some of them."

"Great. Can you come to the crime lab?" Diane asked.

"Yes. I'll walk right over," said Beth.

Diane explained to the others that she'd enlisted the help of a genealogist to discover any relatives of Leo Parrish.

"That was clever," said Frank.

"And fast," said Diane. "Librarians are much speedier than private detectives."

It took only a couple of minutes for Beth to cross from the third-floor east wing to the west wing where the crime lab was. David was at the door to let her in. She entered, looking around at all the glass walls and high-tech equipment as though she'd just stepped onto another planet.

"Well," she said, "this is certainly different from the rest of the museum." She was carrying a folder, which she held close to her. They all moved to the round table to learn about the family tree of Leo Parrish.

"OK," Beth said when they were all seated. "I'll start with the Glendale-Marsh relatives. She pointed to each person on the chart as she named them, going from generation to generation. "Leo Parrish had an uncle, Luther Parrish, who lived in Glendale-Marsh in the thirties. He had two sons, Martin and Owen. Owen Parrish had a son. The son married and had a daughter—Oralia Lee Parrish. They all left Florida when Martin and Owen lost the family land. The daughter, Oralia Lee, married one Burke Rawson. They had no children that I can find a record of."

"We should be able to locate the Rawsons," said David.

"The last address I had for them was Ohio fifteen years ago," said Beth. "Now, you mention that Leo Parrish wrote to someone when he was in the service. That was his sister, Leontine Parrish Richmond. She lived in Upstate New York."

"Were they twins?" asked Diane.

Beth nodded. "Leontine had a daughter who was eleven years old in 1935." She pointed to the chart with their names. "The daughter grew up, married, and had a son named Quinn Sebestyen," said Beth. "He married a woman named Allie Shaw. And they had two children."

"Christian and Melissa," said Jin.

He was seated across the table from Beth and they all looked over at him, surprised.

Jin looked as if he had seen a ghost.

Chapter 49

All of them stared at Jin who slid the family tree toward him and studied it. "This is amazing," he said.

"What?" said Neva. "You look like she just uncovered your relatives."

"Do you know these people?" asked David.

Jin looked at Diane. "Do you remember when"— he snapped his fingers a couple of times—"when Dr. Webber asked me what I was interested in outside of work? It was in the morgue tent."

Diane thought back to the time in the morgue tent. It seemed so long ago now.

"After Dr. Pilgrim took a break, after you found the fetal bones, and Dr. Rankin talked about how all we could do was pick up the pieces," Jin said.

Diane remembered. She wondered if that moment was the trigger for Archie Donahue, realizing as Rankin did that they could never make a dent in the drug trade because the money was too great. All they could do was pick up the broken bodies and mourn the broken lives. Was that the thing that pushed Archie to "try to make a difference," as he had said—if he was indeed the murderer of Blake Stanton and Marcus McNair?

"Yeah," said Jin. "Remember, I was saying I was interested in strange disappearances. I was talking

about that Court TV program about missing people—
Judge Crater, Jimmy Hoffa, and some ordinary people
who had disappeared mysteriously. Like that whole
family that vanished. Their belongings were still in the
house and even their car was still in the driveway."

"What are you saying?" asked Diane.

"This was them—Quinn and Allie Sebestyen and
their seven-year-old daughter, Melissa, and their ten-
year-old son, Christian."

"Oh, my, this is getting strange," said Beth. She
looked uneasily around her as if that's what happened
here in the dark side—strange things.

Diane needed a moment for the information to
sink in.

"When was this?" she asked.

"About twenty years ago—1987, I think. Yeah, it
was 1987," said Jin. "Nothing was ever heard from
them again."

They all fell silent.

"Why don't I leave this with you?" said Beth, rising
from the table. "Shall I continue looking for information on these people?"

"As long as it doesn't keep you from your other
work," said Diane.

"All of this was in records that I accessed via the
Internet or by calling and asking some willing person
to look up a marriage or death certificate," she said.

"This is excellent work, Beth. Thank you," said
Diane.

David rose, escorted Beth out the door of the crime
lab, and returned to the table.

"Nineteen eighty-seven," said Diane. "The year Juliet was kidnapped. And they had a seven-year-old
daughter—the same age as Juliet. She and Juliet could
have been playmates."

"I still feel like I'm missing something," said David.

"I thought it was just me," said Neva. "I've had a

hard time keeping up ever since I got here. First, the code, and now it feels as though I'm missing part of this story."

"I know," said Diane. "I've been dribbling out information about Juliet—mainly because at first I didn't know it was related to the Cipriano murder. It was just something I was doing to help one of my employees. Also, there's some sensitive personal information on Juliet involved. But now it's something we need to solve, because I think she is in danger."

Diane went over the whole story of Juliet with them. She told them about Juliet's memories and how Diane thought the fear of new dolls sprang from another crime Juliet had witnessed, and that being a witness had led to her kidnapping.

"Those are the crimes you had me look for in Arizona and Florida?" said David.

"Yes," said Diane.

"You've been working on this mystery while you were working on the other crimes in Rosewood?" said Frank. "And running the museum?"

"Yes, and I haven't been doing a very good job of any of it, but that's going to change. Jin, did the TV program give any personal information on the Sebestyens?"

"Some. Not a lot. As I recall, Quinn Sebestyen was a math professor at a community college. His wife was a schoolteacher. The kids were good students. Everyone liked them. They were, by all accounts, an ordinary couple, an ordinary family. No marital problems that anyone was aware of, no great debt, no vices. The police couldn't find any reason they would disappear on their own or why anyone would do them harm. The best they could come up with was that someone kidnapped them or murdered them for some unknown reason."

"Did they ever vacation in Glendale-Marsh?" asked Diane.

"I don't remember that town being mentioned in the TV program," said Jin.

"Call the detective in charge of the case and ask him. See if he'll send us more information," said Diane.

"You think the Sebestyens are the dead people Juliet saw?" said David.

"Yes, I do," said Diane. "How's this for an hypothesis: Juliet was visiting her grandmother who lives at the beach in Glendale-Marsh, and she struck up a friendship with a little girl, one of the tourists. The little girl was Melissa Sebestyen. The genealogy chart Beth just provided to us shows that Melissa's father, Quinn, was the grandnephew of Leo Parrish; Quinn's grandmother was Leo's twin sister. In the letters Leo sent home to his sister he probably sent the code and maybe even a book. It probably became a family heirloom. When Leo didn't come home from the war, no one could crack his code. Quinn grew up with the story about Granduncle Leo and his hidden fortune in Florida. Quinn taught mathematics at a community college. Perhaps he inherited a family trait for being good with numbers and codes. He deciphered Uncle Leo's code and went to Glendale-Marsh to find the treasure."

"Where does the doll come in?" asked Frank.

"I'm not sure. Perhaps Quinn, being of a fanciful frame of mind, hid the code in his daughter's doll for safekeeping, or perhaps the little girl hid it there."

"Why would a kid do a thing like that?" said Jin.

Frank laughed.

"I'm just hypothesizing," said Diane. "Maybe she knew the code was important. Maybe the doll was a courier. Anyway, Melissa knew it was there because she told Juliet the doll had a secret. That's something a kid tells another kid. None of the adults would have told Juliet that."

"I'm with you," said Frank.

"Someone besides Quinn knew about the hidden fortune—actually, a lot of people did—but this someone knew that Quinn had a line on where to find it," said Diane.

"Maybe Quinn told someone," said David.

"Not if Quinn's the one hiding the code in the doll," said Neva. "That sounds like secretive behavior to me."

"OK, maybe someone who was looking for the code tracked down Leo Parrish's descendants—like Beth did," said David.

"That's a good possibility," said Diane.

"Other relatives must have known about the treasure," said Frank, "The ones who stayed in Glendale-Marsh. Even if they weren't close to the sister, they knew Leo would confide in her—they were twins. And they could have passed down the story from one generation to the next just like Leo's family did."

"Oh, I like that," said David. "It's very neat."

"Whoever it was," continued Diane, "followed Quinn Sebestyen to Florida, tried to get the information from him, and ended up killing his entire family. Juliet came over to her new friend's house and found them dead and wrapped up in plastic. She ran home to her grandmother, perhaps being chased by the killers."

"How did Juliet get the doll?" asked Jin.

"Her grandmother thought she stole it. When she asked Juliet where she got it, Juliet said a friend gave it to her. Juliet doesn't have much memory of that time," said Diane. "We may never know. But the killers did not get Juliet or the doll in Glendale-Marsh, and she went home to Arizona. They followed her there to get the doll, not knowing that the grandmother back in Florida had kept it. They were probably afraid that Juliet recognized them. They kidnapped her and when they didn't get the information they wanted from her, they left her for dead."

"Why did they suddenly resurface now?" asked Neva. "It's been, what, twenty years?"

Diane thought for a moment. She looked at Jin; then it dawned on her.

"I think," she said, "for the same reason that Juliet's nightmares began again after all these years. The television program. I'm willing to bet that Juliet watched the program or at least caught some of the advertising for it and it triggered the nightmares."

"And you think the killer saw the same program and was afraid the cold case squad had a renewed interest in the disappearance of the Sebestyen family, and that Juliet might remember something?" said Neva.

"Yes. And it also renewed the killers' interest in getting the doll and the code they never found," said Diane.

"You keep saying *they*," said Frank. "You think there was more than one?"

"I think there were and are at least two," said Diane. "A man and a woman. In the very moments before Juliet was discovered missing, a jogger was reported to have fallen in front of Juliet's home. I think the woman was a decoy to attract the attention of the adults to the front of the house while the man kidnapped Juliet from her backyard. In the library when I heard the odd phrase about palimpsests, I believe it was a woman's voice. It definitely wasn't the voice of the man who took the doll from me."

"It's a good story," said David. "It might be true. I think the first thing we need to do is track down the other relatives of Leo Parrish. What were their names?"

"Oralia Lee and Burke Rawson," said Neva looking at the genealogy chart.

"I'll start with Juliet's grandmother," said Diane. "She may know them, or she may know someone I can call in Florida who knows them."

Just as Diane was about to get up to call Ruby Torkel, there was a knock at the door. They all looked over at it as if it might be the cardboard cutout of Darth Vader. No one ever knocked at that door.

Chapter 50

"Who could that be?" said Neva. She got up, walked over, and looked out the peephole.

"Kendel," she said and opened the door.

Kendel, looking tall and sleek in her fur-trimmed chocolate brown cashmere sweater, matching wool slacks, and high-heeled brown leather boots, walked in carrying a package.

"Hi. I wasn't sure of the protocol for entering this place. I suppose people usually call first. I see Anna found a Darth Vader. She's been looking for one for a month."

David brought a chair from one of the workstations and Kendel sat down at the table with them.

"So, it's Anna I need to thank for that," said Diane.

"The docents think it hilarious," said Kendel. "They're also hoping that the kids will pay more attention to Darth Vader than to the ordinary signs. From what I hear we need to put him in Security. How are you? How is your head?"

"Sore scalp, but otherwise fine," said Diane.

Kendel winced when Diane touched the back of her head.

"I found the book you were looking for," said Kendel, smiling and opening the package.

She pulled out a small, very old, blue clothbound volume no more than four by six inches in size. It was frayed around the edges, and the spine was so faded that Diane couldn't read the lettering. Kendel opened it up.

"It's volume nine in a series," she said. *"Wonder Book of the World's Progress, Art and Science."* She handed the slim volume to Diane. "Page fifteen. Second paragraph."

Diane's face lit up as she turned to page fifteen. There it was. *"The making of palimpsests was possible even with papyri."* Diane flipped through the pages, glancing at the black-and-white pictures of paintings. She looked at the copyright date in the front—1935.

"How did you ever?" Diane asked.

Kendel's smile broadened into a grin. "I started with a linguist friend of mine. He parsed the sentence and analyzed the content. From him I found out it was probably in a book of the twenties, thirties, possibly forties, maybe earlier, but probably not later. He also suggested that it would be in a book that covered art, technology, and science because of the content and the syntax. From there I called on a few librarian friends. We found a list of authors who wrote in that domain in the right time frame and looked at some of their work. The style seemed most like the work of a man named Henry Smith Williams. We looked at a collection of his books. His main work was a history of science, but we didn't find the sentence in those volumes. Then we found a series of Wonder Books. It was in the ninth volume, about art and science."

"I'm impressed," said Neva. "You had to read all of those books?"

"There were several of us and we are all fast readers—we mainly scanned the pages looking for the word *palimpsests.*"

"The index didn't help?" asked Jin.

"Didn't have one," said Kendel.

"Kendel, this is a great job," said Diane. "I'm absolutely amazed. I thought it would be a long shot."

"I'm glad I can keep my reputation intact. Really, it was harder finding the crystal skull."

Kendel stood. "I just got back in, so I'm going home to rest on my laurels for a while before I come back to work. Oh, one of my librarian friends said that someone in the Bartram library was looking for books about palimpsests and became quite cross when the librarians couldn't find the book she wanted. Interesting coincidence, I thought."

"It is, indeed," said Diane. The voice she heard in the library, she thought.

David escorted Kendel to the door.

"I'm impressed with the people you have working for you," said Frank.

"So am I," said Diane. "Kendel has headhunters after her all the time. One of these days they're going to be able to lure her away. I hope that's not for a long time."

David came back and sat down and sighed.

"What?" asked Neva.

"Nothing. I just wish I could get a woman like that to date me," he said.

"Have you asked her out?" said Neva.

"No. I just told you, women like that don't go out with guys like me," he said.

"I'm not even going to go there," said Neva. "She puts her panty hose on just like the rest of us. Ask her out. You may be pleasantly surprised. If she says no, then you get to complain to us for the rest of the year—it's a win-win situation for you."

"May I look at the book?" said Frank.

Diane handed it over to him. She had been flipping through the pages, looking for inspiration. The key was in the phrase, she was sure, but *how* eluded her.

Frank took the book and turned to page fifteen. Diane watched him reading the entire page. While Jin and David were explaining to Neva how some women are just unapproachable, Frank took the book to the computer. From her vantage point it looked like he was trying out a couple of words—with no success. Then she saw the familiar twinkle in his eye. She watched for a moment before she spoke up.

"You have it, don't you?" she said.

The others looked at her, then Frank.

"What?" said Jin. "When we weren't looking?"

He jumped up and started to go over to the computer for a look, but Frank was already printing something out. He brought it to the table.

"What was the word?" asked Diane.

"Roman," said Frank.

"Roman? How did you come up with that?" said Jin. He took the book and looked at the page.

"It was actually the simplest part of the cipher. The sentence has nine words. I went nine lines down from the key sentence and nine words over. The word was *Roman,* so I gave it a try and . . . here we are.

With a flourish he tossed the printout on the table. It spun around and slid almost off before Jin caught it. He read it out loud.

The private family cemetery of James Vann Llewellyn in the city of Glendale-Marsh Florida Three feet under the headstone of Leander Llewellyn

A cheer went up from all of them and Jin patted Frank on the back.

"It's real, then?" said Neva.

"The message is decipherable," said Frank. "Whether or not there is a buried treasure there is anyone's guess."

"Now what?" said Jin. "We go look for the treasure?"

"No," said Diane. "The treasure isn't our concern. We need to find the murderers. Jin, you call the authorities in—where did the Sebestyens live?"

"Indiana," said Jin.

"Call them and see if they'll share information. I'm sure they'd like some new leads. I'm going to call Ruby Torkel and hope that she's in the nice hotel room I put her in."

Frank caught her hand as she was about to get up. "Why don't you go home for a while? Get some rest. Call her from there."

"Why don't you?" said Neva. "We can handle things here. I know it's hard to tell sometimes by our intelligent conversation, but we're really pretty reliable and on top of things."

Diane smiled. She was feeling tired. She supposed she could call Mrs. Torkel from her house just as easily as she could from her office.

"OK. But let me know if anything develops," she said.

"Of course," agreed Neva and David together.

Diane called Andie and told her that she was going home for a while and that, since Kendel was also at home, Andie was in charge of the museum.

"Great," said Andie. "I've got some really cool things I want to order for the Dino room."

Diane smiled as she hung up. "OK, I'm gone."

Frank drove her home. He pulled in just behind her car with its new paint job—her mechanic had delivered it while she was gone. She gave it a brush with her hand as she passed. Nice.

On the way into her building she ran into her landlady. She was a kind and good-natured woman, but Diane hated running into her. She loved to talk.

"Did you hear what happened to poor Dr. Shawn Keith?" She didn't wait for an answer. "The police arrested him. Can you beat that? A nice man like Dr. Keith—so good to the ducks in the park. I help him feed them, you know. The police wouldn't tell me why, but I can't imagine what a man like that would do to get arrested. I don't know where I'm going to find another tenant like him; he always paid on time, he was never noisy, and he didn't smoke. You know, a lot of people say they don't smoke when I tell them it's a nonsmoking building, but then they try to sneak and smoke with the window open, but I can always tell—the smell you know, it permeates everything, and that poor Marvin Odell, he hates cigarette smoke and he always complains if he thinks someone is smoking. Between you and me, I don't know why *he* can't be arrested, but they are good tenants, too; they always pay on time and they don't smoke, though Veda Odell burned a turkey one time and we had smoke all over the place; that was before you got here. . . ."

Diane was wondering if the woman ever took a breath. She started to tell her she had to go in. Frank grasped her arm and started moving her toward the staircase.

"Of course, some guests think they can smoke, and I have to tell them they can't. I don't like to, but I do . . . like that policeman who came to see you today, he was smoking and I told him he had to stop or go someplace else. I'm sorry, but I can't have . . ."

Diane put a hand on her arm. "Who came to see me today?"

"A policeman. I didn't think they were allowed to smoke on duty. . . ."

"Did he give a name?" asked Diane.

"No. He just said he wanted to see you. He waited for a while; then he left when I told him he couldn't smoke. I don't know why he didn't go to the museum; everyone knows that's where you are in the day. . . ."

"Can you describe the policeman?"

Interspersed with more monologue about how smoke permeates the draperies, carpets, and upholstery, and how the policeman smelled of cigarette smoke, the description she gave Diane of a middle-aged police officer in uniform fit Archie Donahue perfectly, down to his bloodhound face.

"Thank you. I believe I know who it was. I need to go up to my apartment now and give him a call to find out what he wanted."

Archie, she thought. *He came to see me. Why?* Diane started up the stairs. Frank followed.

"It's just awful the things that go on," said her landlady. "I just don't know what the world is coming to. That business with the explosion and the fire and all those poor students, and now that councilman's gone missing. . . . Of course he wasn't no good no way."

Chapter 51

Diane stopped on the staircase and turned back to look at her landlady—the kindly elderly lady who wore her gray hair in a bun, dressed in running clothes, and who made sure that no one smoked in her building. She was smiling up at them.

"What councilman?" said Diane.

"That moron Adler. He's gone missing. It was on the news. I hope he's gone far from here." She turned around and went back into her apartment.

Diane and Frank exchanged glances and walked the rest of the way to her apartment. Inside, Frank told Diane to get comfortable on the couch and he would heat her some soup. Warm soup sounded good. Soup was about all she felt like eating. She curled up on the couch, pulled a zebra throw that Star had given her for Christmas over her lap, and reached for the phone. She dialed Garnett's cell.

Several rings went by and she thought it was going to roll over to voice mail when Garnett picked up.

"I know you're busy, but my landlady just told me a policeman was here to see me. From her description, there's little doubt it was Archie Donahue," she said.

"Archie was there? When?"

"This morning. He must have known I was in the hospital last night and thought I would come straight home, but I went from the hospital to the museum."

"I could have told him that," commented Garnett. "How are you feeling?"

"A little sore in the back of the head."

"I'm sorry not to have sent a detective over to interview you at the hospital, but . . . we're stretched a little thin here—ironic for Councilman Adler at the moment, considering his cutbacks in the department's budget."

"The landlady told me the news about Adler. You think Archie is connected with his disappearance?"

"I don't know, but if you see anything of Archie, call me," said Garnett.

"I will. My landlady said you arrested Shawn Keith. Is that true?"

"We took him in for questioning and he became a regular magpie. Couldn't shut him up if we wanted to. Obviously eager to get everything off his chest. He was helping the Stanton kid steal from the university library's rare book room. Did find out something interesting. That night, when the kid tried to jack your car, he was having an argument with Keith. Keith thought he was high—didn't realize he was hurt. Keith was trying to get himself and his mother out of the blast area and he saw you behind him. He told the kid you had found out he was stealing from the museum and you were going to turn him in. That's why Blake came to your car. I don't like to think about what he might have done if you had driven off with him in the car."

"That wouldn't have happened. I know better than to go to a second location with someone holding a gun," said Diane.

When she got off the phone, Frank came from the kitchen with chicken noodle soup and crackers.

"Your landlady's a talker, isn't she?" said Frank.

"She is. She doesn't even stop for periods. But she is observant. The policeman she described had to be Archie Donahue. I wonder why he came to see me."

"Forget about that whole business for a while. Eat your soup before it gets cold," said Frank.

"Did you fix yourself something?" she said.

"I did. I'm heating leftover pizza," he said, disappearing back into the kitchen.

The hot soup felt good going down. There is something about chicken noodle soup that is soothing—good comfort food. It made her relax.

Diane was surprised to hear what a rat Dr. Keith was. No wonder he was feeling so guilty when he approached her the other day. He should have been feeling guilty. The little pissant Blake Stanton could have had it in his mind to shoot her.

Frank came out with his pizza and Coke—the foundation of the food pyramid as far as he was concerned—and as they ate, she told him about Dr. Keith and his connection to Blake Stanton.

"Keith, your neighbor? The one who feeds the ducks?" said Frank.

"That's the one. You never know how people really are. Unless you told me, I'd have never guessed you know how to play the accordion."

"I know, and who would ever guess that you enjoy hanging over bottomless pits on the end of a rope?" said Frank.

They talked about Star and her grades. So far, she was making good enough grades to earn her trip to Paris.

"She's even doing pretty well in math," said Frank. He was very proud, since that was his best subject.

Star's good grades were a relief. Diane finished eating and put her empty soup bowl on the coffee table.

"I need to call Ruby Torkel," she said.

"Why don't you lie down and rest a few minutes? You just got out of the hospital and if I remember correctly, the doctor told you to rest."

"I'm resting now." She pointed to the throw across

her lap as if that was clear indication she was in rest mode. "I'm just going to make a few phone calls."

She was interrupted by Frank's cell. He fished in his inside pocket and looked at the display.

"Work," he said as he answered it.

"Duncan here," he said.

"Now?" he asked

"OK." He flipped the phone closed.

"It's the Rosewood case I mentioned. I have to take care of some stuff. I suppose it would be demeaning of me to ask if you'll be OK by yourself?"

"Yes, it would. I'm a law enforcement professional. Plus, I have connections with influential people," she said smiling, and put a finger through a belt loop on his trousers.

He leaned down and kissed her on the ear, which produced an instant shiver in her.

"I'll be back when I can. I expect to find you here resting under your zebra blanket."

Frank took another swallow of Coke and left, telling Diane again that she'd better be good and take a nap.

As soon as he was out the door, she called the hotel where Juliet and her grandmother were staying. The number was busy. She lay back and closed her eyes for a few moments. Her head throbbed, but the pain seemed to be coming more from the cut than from her concussion. She decided not to take anything for it. She hadn't even filled the prescription the doctor gave her. After a few minutes she opened her eyes and tried the number again. Still busy.

It would be easier in person, she thought. She got up, grabbed her purse, and went out the door, mentally thanking her mechanic for bringing the car to her. This was the first good look she had had of the new paint job. It looked just like the original before Patrice Stanton took a paint can to it. Diane keyed in the combination and opened the door. The keys were in the ashtray. The bill was lying on the passenger side. She left the bill there, grabbed the keys and put them in the ignition, and drove off to the hotel.

As Diane knocked on the door to Ruby Torkel's room, the security guard from the museum stuck his head out of the adjoining room's doorway.

"Oh, hi, Dr. Fallon, just checking," said the guard.

"I'm glad," said Diane.

Diane heard somebody on the other side of the door.

"Who is it?" Ruby Torkel asked.

"Diane Fallon," she said.

"I thought it looked like you. You can't be too careful. These peepholes distort things." She unlocked the door, unlatched the safety chain, and opened the door. "Had any luck finding who's behind all this? I'm getting kind of tired of being cooped up in a hotel room. It's nice, we have a bedroom and a little sitting room and two bathrooms, and room service is just real nice, but I'd like to get out and go shopping."

"We're trying," said Diane. "I came to ask you some questions about Leo Parrish and his relatives."

"I told you about all I know. I don't know the family at all," she said. "Can I get you something to drink? This little refrigerator is full of all kinds of drinks."

Diane didn't want to even think about how much all this was costing.

"No, thank you. I'm fine. I wanted to ask if there is anyone back in Glendale-Marsh who might know Leo Parrish's relatives?" she asked.

"Well, I expect Elnora St. James would know. She's in her nineties, but is sharp as a tack. She lived by the Parrishes growing up. She likes to talk to people. Her hearing's not too good, but like I said, her mind is still with us. You want me to call her for you?"

"Yes, please," said Diane.

Ruby went to her suitcase and got an address book. "She lives with her great-granddaughter."

Ruby seemed to have developed some skill in the procedure for making a long-distance call from the hotel. In just a few moments she had someone on the line.

"Arybeth, is Elnora there? I have someone who wants to know about the Parrishes."

"Yes, it's about that, but mostly it's about the Parrishes themselves. She's a museum lady."

Ruby Torkel put her hand over the mouthpiece of the phone. "She wants to know if it's about the treasure. Lots of people have called to ask Elnora about the treasure. Sometimes she gets tired of people wanting her to tell them where to dig—if she knew, she'd have dug it up a long time ago."

She directed her attention to the phone again. "Elnora, how are you feeling today? That's good. I got someone here who wants to speak with you about the Parrishes. She's a real nice lady. My Juliet works for her at the museum here in Rosewood, Georgia."

Ruby handed Diane the phone. "She's feeling real good today."

Diane took the phone and settled herself down in a chair. "Mrs. St. James . . ."

"Call me Elnora, dear. I prefer it. So you want to know about old Luther and his boys? They were the devil's own."

Chapter 52

Mrs. Elnora St. James had a clear voice and an equally clear mind—and a strong opinion about the Glendale-Marsh Parrishes. This was a topic in which she was well versed. Diane found it easier just to let her talk about the family at her own pace and to interject a question only occasionally.

"The two brothers, Luther and Henry, couldn't have been more different," Elnora began. "Henry was smart and kind. Luther was dumb and mean. The land belonged to Henry. Their father left it to him. Luther was allowed to live in a small cottage near the north boundary marker, and he was bitter about that. He made Henry's life miserable. Henry left the land to his son, Leo Parrish, and Leo let Luther work it while Leo traveled. Leontine, Leo's twin sister, married and moved to New York. Stop me if I'm going too fast for you."

"You're doing fine," said Diane, glad that Beth had provided her with a Parrish kinship chart or she'd have a hard time keeping up.

"Leo Parrish was supposed to have found some treasure—I guess Ruby told you about that?" she said.

"Yes, she did. But I'm more interested in the family history," said Diane.

"You'd be about the only one," said Elnora. "Now, where was I?"

"Leontine moved to New York," said Diane.

"Yes. Leo lived with her for a while there, I think. He didn't like coming back to the family farm, and I can't say as I blame him. We sure didn't like being neighbors with Luther and his boys."

"Did Leo will the land to Luther?" asked Diane.

"Why no. Leo willed it to his sister, Leontine. Luther just took it," said Elnora.

"Took it?" said Diane.

"Stole it," declared Elnora. "Wrote Leontine and told her it was his land, should have been his land all along, and if she didn't like it, that was too bad. Though his language was probably more colorful."

"She didn't do anything about it?" asked Diane. So far the history of the Glendale-Marsh Parrishes wasn't getting her anywhere, but she kept hoping, and Elnora was interested in talking.

"Not anything direct, she didn't. She was afraid of her uncle. Isn't that a shame, being afraid of your own kin, especially an uncle? But Luther was mean, so was his sons. They'd have as soon killed her as look at her. So Luther took the land, but in the end Leontine got the last laugh."

"How was that?" asked Diane.

"Leontine was the owner of record, so the tax bills for the land went to her home in New York. And she didn't pay them; nor did she tell Luther they weren't paid. You'd think the fool would have realized he had taxes due. But he might have thought Leontine was too scared of him not to pay them herself. Anyway, the unpaid taxes built up over the years. And one day when Luther was an old man, the sheriff came and ordered him off the land. Said it had been sold on the courthouse steps for nonpayment of taxes. I would like to have been a bird in a tree when the sheriff came to the door. I understand ol' Luther was fit to be tied. He died a year later, probably from stewing over losing the land. Him and the boys tried to pro-

test, but the tax people told Luther it wasn't his land
and he had no interest to protest. I bet that made him
mad all over again.

"His boys, Martin and Owen, was living with him.
They thought the land was their inheritance and now
they had nothing. It was kind of sad for Owen. He
had a family."

"Do you know what happened to his family?"
asked Diane.

"They lived around Glendale-Marsh for a while.
Every now and again you'd hear about one of them
getting into trouble. Owen's boy was in trouble a lot.
He got some girl pregnant and had to get married. I
don't know how long that lasted. In the end, ol' Luther died and the two boys drifted away. We were
glad to see them go. They were a mean bunch. They
were always coming around and stealing stuff from us,
like they was entitled."

"Did they ever look for the treasure?" asked Diane.

"I'm sure they did. Martin tried to contact Leontine
one time, but she wouldn't have anything to do with
them." Elnora started laughing. "That treasure was
like a curse from Leo, too. Luther was always running
treasure hunters off his land. I believe he had more
potholes dug on his property than we had in the entire
state of Florida."

"What do you think of the treasure story?" asked
Diane.

"I don't know. Leo was a smart boy. I'm sort of
thinking he had something buried somewhere. Too
bad he went missing. A lot of boys went missing in
the war. That was a sad time."

"Have you ever heard of a Llewellyn family?"
asked Diane.

"Well sure, everybody knows them. James Llewellyn founded the town of Glendale-Marsh. Their
house is on the historic registry. It's a ruin—the

house was built of shells and cement. What do they call that?"

"Coquina," said Diane.

"That's it. Coquina and tabby. I guess being from a museum you'd know about that stuff," said Elnora.

"We have a display of coquina and tabby with our shell collection," said Diane.

"All that's left standing of the old house is some of the walls. I visited it once. You can still walk inside the old ruins. The rooms were tiny. I think the people must have been smaller back then. I know lots more about Glendale-Marsh, but you was asking about the Parrishes. Was I any help to you?"

"A tremendous help," said Diane.

"I'm glad to do it. It's nice that someone is interested in the family for a change and not the treasure."

"Have you ever heard of a family called Sebestyen?" asked Diane.

"Sebestyen, that's an odd name, isn't it? Why does that sound familiar to me?" She paused for several moments. "I know why—that was Leontine's daughter's married name. Do you know them?"

"I've just heard of them," said Diane.

"I think maybe I talked to their son once a long time ago. What was his name? Glen, or something like that? Let me think."

She paused for a long time. For a moment Diane thought they had been disconnected.

"His name was Quinn. That was it. He was here. I think he was looking for the treasure. He was asking about the Llewellyn's, too. His wife taught history, he said, and they wanted to take some pictures of the house and the graveyard. I remember thinking at the time that he looked a lot like Leo. I don't know when was the last time I thought about that."

"Do you remember how long ago that might have been?" asked Diane.

"Oh, I don't know, fifteen or twenty years maybe? That's a guess. It was quite a while ago," she said.

"I've kept you long enough. Thank you again, Elnora," said Diane.

"I was glad to do it. It's so nice that Ruby's visiting Juliet. She's missed her so. That child has had a hard time. I guess you know."

"Yes," said Diane. "I know."

"Did you find out what you need to know?" asked Ruby when Diane hung up the phone.

"I found out a lot. I'm not sure it will lead to who's doing this, but I have some ideas. I'm making progress."

Diane could see that Ruby was dying to know what her friend Elnora said, so she gave her a rundown of the conversation.

"Well, what does Leo's relatives and the Llewellyns have to do with Juliet's kidnapping?"

Diane realized that Ruby and Juliet didn't know anything about the investigation so far, and the story was much too long and complicated to go into now. Besides, she had to get back before Frank found her missing. The last thing she wanted was to listen to him lecture her on taking care of herself.

"I promise, I'll tell you all about it when I can. Right now, just sit tight and you and Juliet enjoy pay-per-view," said Diane.

She opened the door and almost ran into Juliet and the security guard. When museum Security picked Juliet up to take her to work in the morning and brought her home again in the evening, it was also shift changing time for them. The new guard went to the adjoining room and the old guard was leaving.

"You want me to walk you to your car, Dr. Fallon?" he asked.

"That would be nice. Thanks." She wasn't expecting trouble, but as long as he was here, she might as well make use of him.

"Dr. Fallon," said Juliet, "How are you? All we talked about at the museum today was the attack on you in your office."

"Attack?" said Ruby. "What attack?"

Diane gave them a short version.

"It was nothing, really. Just a few stitches."

"You had to stay all night in the hospital," said Juliet.

"Just a precaution," said Diane. She was inching out the doorway, trying to make a clean escape.

"You mean you got something else stolen from you?" said Ruby. "It sounds to me like that museum is a dangerous place to work."

"Oh, no, it's not, really. I can't go into any of the details of what happened right now. You and Juliet have a good evening. I'll talk with you tomorrow."

Diane didn't want to talk about the code with them, either. She wanted to go home. When she finally got away, the security guard walked her down to the parking deck and to her car. She was glad to have him for an escort. She had an aversion to parking decks. They were always dark and usually devoid of people—a place with few witnesses. She was relieved to get in her car and drive home.

Unfortunately, when she got to her apartment, Frank's car was there. He had beaten her home. *OK, this isn't going to be fun,* she thought as she got out of her car.

Chapter 53

Frank opened the door when Diane knocked. She expected a scowl. Instead, his expression was one of amusement.

"You know, I bet myself that you'd be gone when I came back, and damn if I didn't win a bunch of money," he said.

"I'm sorry, but I couldn't get Ruby Torkel on the phone and I thought it would be quicker if I just went to her hotel," said Diane.

She came in and crawled back in her space on the couch.

"Can you stay the night?" she asked.

"Sure. Someone's got to try to keep track of you. Are you in for the evening?"

"Yes. I'm here. I won't be going out again."

"Good. Tell me what you found out," he said.

Diane gave him a history of the Glendale-Marsh Parrishes.

"They sound like a pretty bad bunch," she said. "I'm thinking that you were right. The disappearance of the Sebestyen family is connected with their Parrish relatives. Martin Parrish, of the Glendale-Marsh Parrishes, contacted Leo's twin sister, Leontine, in New York and asked her about the treasure. They expected that she had information on where her brother hid it.

Descendants in both branches of the Parrish family knew about the legend of the buried treasure and the secret instructions for finding it. The Glendale-Marsh Parrishes probably believed that their New York relatives had the secret information. When Quinn, a direct descendant of Leontine, came to Florida to look, it alerted his relatives there and they ended up killing him and his family to find the secret. I think young Juliet stumbled upon the aftermath."

Diane grabbed up the phone and called Jin.

"What did you find out from the authorities in Indiana?" she asked when he answered.

"Hello, Boss," said Jin. "How you feeling?"

"I'm fine, just hungry for information."

"They were very interested in what we have," he said. "They weren't quite as forthcoming with their info. I didn't know how much you wanted me to tell them, so I kind of played it close to the vest."

"What did you find out?" she asked again.

"If you believe what they told me, they don't know anything beyond what was reported on TV and in the papers. They had completely hit the wall. When they learned that there might be a witness, they got excited. I told them she was a little girl at the time. I didn't give them her name. They're coming down to talk with us. I handed them off to Garnett, so I guess you'd better give him a heads-up so he'll know what the heck these guys from Indiana are talking about."

"I'll call him tomorrow. I think he has his hands full right now with Councilman Adler missing."

"So I guess everything is at a standstill again," said Jin.

"Until tomorrow," said Diane. "All of you go home and get some rest."

She hung up the phone and turned to Frank. "At least we've made the Indiana cold case squad happy," she said.

"I'll bet," said Frank. "It's early. Why don't we have a quiet several hours of rest, maybe a little TV, and who knows what else? Maybe a little cold pizza."

"That sounds good to me," she said, grinning at him.

As soon as the words were out, the phone rang.

"Don't answer it," he said.

"I'd like not to, but . . ." She picked it up.

"Diane, this is Cindy. I'm sorry to bother you. Is Frank there?"

"Yes, Cindy. He's right here," said Diane.

"Your ex," she mouthed to Frank.

He frowned and took the phone.

"Is Kevin all right?" he asked. As he listened, his frown deepened. Finally he said, "I'll be right there."

He hung up and turned to Diane.

"It's Kevin. He got his collarbone and arm broken playing hockey and he's in the hospital. They have to operate on the arm. I have to go."

"Of course. I'm fine here. I'm going to sleep and won't wake till morning," she said.

He kissed her. He smelled like aftershave—the kind that smelled so sexy to her and she could never remember its name. She wished he could stay. A day off for him was such an unexpected gift. She wished she had been here when he got home.

"I'm sorry," he said.

"Don't be. I understand," she answered. "I'm sorry Kevin's hurt. Give him my best."

He kissed her again and left. Diane watched as he walked down the hallway and down the stairs. She sighed, locked her door, turned off the lights, and went to bed.

Sometime during the night she awoke. She didn't know what had awakened her but she had an uneasy feeling. She looked at the picture of the chambered nautilus on the wall. No reflection of fire. That was a relief. What then? A dream? She got up for a drink of water and looked out the window. The reflection of the streetlights sparkled off every surface. Ice. It had been sleeting again. Maybe that's what it had been, the sound of limbs breaking under the weight of the freezing rain. Maybe, but something else tugged at her mind. Something she was forgetting, that was just now making its way to the surface.

In the distance through the barren trees a spot of light shined brightly at her and then was gone. As she watched, the light flickered bright again, and again, moving back and forth in some pattern of activity. She was certain it came from the direction of the burned-out house. Her stomach knotted. Who could be at the crime scene in the middle of the night, and what were they doing?

She dressed quickly in warm clothes and boots and left her apartment building. She considered taking her car but decided not to. Sleet was falling, icing over the streets. She walked across the street, past the darkened houses and into the small copse of trees. Except for her, there was no one about. She stopped just before coming out of the woods and looked across the next street at the charred rubble of the meth house. She could now see moving shadows cast against the surrounding trees by a light shining up from the blackened hole in the ground that used to be the basement. How perfectly odd.

She took her phone from her pocket and called the police station. She told them who she was and what she saw. They said they would send someone to investigate. She would stay here and wait.

In the darkness, as she looked at the sad rubble of so many lives, a realization flashed through her mind like someone flipping pictures. She understood what the evidence meant—the evidence she and her team had overlooked because they didn't understand it. The silver charm and the blond hair. They were planted on the bodies of Blake Stanton and Eric McNair as memorials to one of the victims killed in the explosion and fire. She knew who murdered Stanton and McNair, and why—and she knew where Adler was. She took her phone again and tried to dial out. This time she had no battery. She had forgotten to plug in the charger.

Diane looked around for anything to use as a weapon. She found a broken branch. Perhaps not heavy enough, but it would have to do. She walked across the street to the blackened house site. The charred wood creaked as she knelt down and looked inside the burned-out basement. She saw Adler tied to a chair, his mouth bound with duct tape. In front of him someone had lined up photographs leaning against a log of charred wood. She knew who they were—not a name, but she had seen them before.

Diane took a step back, but she was jerked backward. She fell; the back of her stitched and tender head hit the snow-covered ground. She was dazed. She tried to get up, but was pushed back down. Her weapon was gone. Diane tried to focus her eyes. When the momentary blur went away she was staring down the barrel of a gun.

The sad-faced woman looking for her daughter held it, the woman who had appealed to her in the coffee tent and showed her pictures of her daughter—the same pictures now in front of Adler. The woman she saw walking to her car alone from the Student Learning Center when they were looking for Star.

"You aren't going to take this away from me," she said. "This is all I have left."

"Catherine, don't do this. Dr. Fallon's not the bad guy here." It was Archie Donahue.

"Archie," said Diane, "I was so hoping you weren't part of this."

"I know you were. I came to see you today to explain," he said. "Catherine's my sister. Kimberlyn was her daughter, my niece. She was the girl who was pregnant. We didn't know, but the baby would have been Catherine's only grandchild." He stopped and almost cried from the pain. "That was her hair you looked at. That was our Kimberlyn's hair."

"I am so sorry," said Diane.

"Catherine, let's get out of the cold. Let's talk," said Archie. "Please."

"Get up," Catherine said.

"The police are coming," said Diane.

"No, they aren't," said Archie. "I knew you'd call for back up. I used my partner's car number and cancelled it. They'll figure it out sooner or later, but it'll be too late."

Too late for what, wondered Diane. Archie helped her up off the ground and led her toward the adjacent house, the one that was empty because of renovations from the fire damage. So, this was where they had been hiding out.

Inside the house was barely warmer than the outside. The only lights were from the glow of lanterns. Catherine pushed Diane down in a chair.

"It's not too late to stop this," said Diane.

"I don't want to stop it," said Catherine. "I want that son of a bitch to know what he's done. I want him to sit down in that burned-out shell that my baby died in and know what he did to her."

"You think he was involved in the meth lab?" said Diane.

"I know he was," said Archie. "McNair and his cousin Eric were up to their necks in the business. His wife doesn't have money. Catherine lives next door to them. She knows the wife," said Archie. "McNair was in Adler's pocket. Adler isn't clean. Why do you think he gutted the drug unit?"

"I know this is hard . . . ," said Diane.

Catherine slapped Diane across the face. "You don't know anything," she spat at her. "You don't know anything."

"Catherine!" said Archie.

Diane looked into her hate-filled eyes. "I know exactly. Someone worse than Adler and McNair killed my daughter, so don't you dare tell me that I don't know."

Catherine was taken aback. She stared at Diane, stunned. For a moment Diane saw the humanity come back into her face.

"Then how can you try to stop me?" she whispered.

"You can't let yourself become like them," said Diane.

"I'm not like them. How can you compare what I'm doing with what they did? I'm just getting rid of what you people can't. Archie told me what you people talked about. How you can only pick up the pieces."

"Blake Stanton wasn't a part of the meth lab," said Diane.

"I tried to tell her," said Archie. Diane could see tears in his eyes. "I tried to tell her."

"Why did he try to hijack your car? I heard about that." Catherine's gaze darted toward Archie.

"Because he was stealing from my museum and he thought I knew about it. Like your daughter, he just happened to be at the party. He was completely innocent of the meth lab crimes. And he has a mother just like you who is in unbearable pain because someone killed her baby," said Diane.

Diane saw it in her eyes, the sudden flash of guilt. *She is the one who killed Stanton. And Archie killed McNair.* McNair was probably guilty, but Stanton didn't have anything to do with her daughter's death.

"No, you're lying," she said.

But Diane knew Catherine believed her.

"If he . . ."

There was a pop, like a lightbulb being stepped on, and Catherine stopped talking and stared; a dot of red dripped in the center of her forehead and she fell to the floor.

"What?" said Archie.

Another lightbulb bursting, and he went down, too, the back of his head blown out.

Chapter 54

Diane stared at the two dead bodies for a second before she dove from the chair and skidded across the linoleum. Get away from the windows, her brain told her. She crawled across to the door into another room. It was a dining room that opened onto a deck. She saw a shadow on the deck from the moonlight. She crawled on her belly from the dining room into the carpeted living room.

What is this, she thought? *Payback for McNair or Stanton? Drug dealers looking for revenge? SWAT team? Adler loose from his bonds?* She crawled across the floor looking for a place to hide. She saw a partially open door and a stairway. She slithered through the door and ran up the carpeted stairs. *OK, now what.* The gunman would be coming in, she knew it. Why hadn't she gotten at least one of the guns that Catherine and Archie had? She always yelled at the people in movies who didn't pick up dropped guns in situations just like this one. *Damn.*

She ran into a bedroom and looked out the window onto the deck below. Someone was there. A hulking guy, not a ninja type. He was in a shadow. She eased over to the dresser, pulling out the drawers and looking for any kind of weapon. Foolish, the owners would have taken their guns with them. No. She felt the barrel of a gun. Pure joy. She grabbed it and pulled it out. It was a vibrator. *Shit.*

She went into the bathroom, looking for something. Nothing but shampoo, conditioner, and Band-Aids. *Come on, there's got to be a razor blade—something.* Nothing. She heard whoever it was trying to break in. Archie must have locked the doors behind him. *Thank God for that.* Her heart was pounding out of her chest. She ran to the nightstands and looked for anything.

There was a photograph on the night table. She grabbed it and fumbling, took out the glass. She went to the bathroom and put a towel around it and broke it into several long pieces. She put three together, found some tape bandage, and wrapped it around one end of the pieces. She took a washcloth and wrapped and bandaged it up so that she had a soft handle. OK, now she had a piss poor weapon. But it was better than no weapon.

Diane went back in the bedroom and started to rummage through the other nightstand. Suddenly it struck her. She was in the parents' room. She needed to go to the kids' room where there would be all kinds of sharp and dangerous things. She slipped out of the bedroom. She heard a downstairs door crash. Damn, he was in the house. She slipped into another room. Bingo. A kid's room. She looked in the closet for a weapon, hockey stick, baseball bat, rocket, anything. Baseball bat. Wonderful. A metal baseball bat was leaning against the wall. Now she was armed and dangerous.

Diane was about to come out of the closet when she noticed that the bedroom had a slanted roof. Her eyes were accustomed to the dark now, and she took time to examine the room and the inside of the closet. In the back of the closet under stacks of sports gear was a small access door into the extra space made by the eaves. She bet the kids used it all the time. It should be easy to open.

She shut the closet door and slid the small access door open and crawled in, carrying her glass knife and dragging her bat. The kids had put a latch on the inside of the door. Not a strong one, but a latch. She locked it. It was a tiny room. Nice for kids, but definitely cramped for adults. The room was partially lit by a small round window. She looked out into the front yard, watching for movement. The snow reflected varying shades of blue under the moonlight. It was pretty. How odd that it was pretty.

There beside a tree, a flicker of movement. A shadow figure sheltered itself against the trunk of the tree. It was a slim figure, not hulking like the other one she heard walking from room to room below. There were two of them. She knew who was after her now. They must have been watching her, waiting. Why didn't they get her when she came out of the house, or through the woods? Didn't see her in time? A car passed? She tried to think back to what she saw when she left her apartment. She was amazingly unobservant. She resolved from this day forth to be more observant.

There was a creak on the stairs. Diane's heart hammered harder. Her throat burned from the bile that came up from her stomach. She was praying that he'd look for her and decide she had left the house, found a way out, and run for cover in the woods. She could outrun them. She was younger. And she was willing to bet she was in better shape. Why hadn't she picked up the gun and why hadn't she run out of the house? *Because you were scared shitless,* she told herself. *Two people were just shot in front of you and you thought you were next and you just panicked.*

Diane heard the floor squeak. He was in the kid's bedroom. *Stay still, don't cough, don't sneeze, just breathe slowly.* She wanted to scream. Her heart was pounding in her ears now. Damn, why was she such a coward? She was braver than this when she was hanging by her fingernails off a ledge in a cave.

OK, pretend you are in a cave. A nice cool dark cave. Take slow breaths. She gripped her knife tight in her hand as she heard him open the closet door. *Don't make any noise.* An eternity passed. What was taking him so long? *Close the door and go look someplace else, damn you.* She waited. The door closed. She waited. She heard him leave the room. *Just stay here until morning,* she told herself. *Stay until morning.*

She listened to him go into another room. Thank God for creaky floors. He searched the entire upstairs. She heard him go downstairs. She peeked out the window. The shadow was gone, moved someplace else. Or she came inside to help search.

Diane listened and heard low garbled voices. She couldn't make out the words. They grew louder. Why? Were they arguing? Or were they talking to her?

They mounted the stairs again, but she didn't hear any more creaking. They had stopped in the hallway.

"Diane."

So they knew her name.

"We know you're in here."

It was a woman's voice. The voice from the library, the jogger of twenty years ago, and Diane was willing to bet her name was Oralia Lee Parrish Rawson.

"Diane, we know you're somewhere in the house, and we will take it apart to find you. We don't want to kill you. We need information from you."

They were silent. Waiting for an answer, she supposed.

"Diane Fallon. We know who you are. We know where you stashed Juliet. We can't get to her now, but we will. We know you saw the code. You have resources that we don't. You have computers. We just want to know what it says. It belongs to us. It belongs to my family. We won't kill you, because we want the information from you. Come out. Don't make this any harder."

Diane wasn't even tempted to answer. She stayed

where she was and prayed they wouldn't find her. She listened as they searched the other rooms, the closets. They called out to her several times. Then they came back to the kid's room. She gripped her bat in one hand and her knife in the other as she heard the closet door open again. The sports equipment and toys banged against the wall as they rummaged through the closet.

"Here's a little door," said the female. "I think we've found her. Diane, are you in there? I betcha are."

Diane heard them trying to get the door open. "It's stuck." This was a man's voice. There was a loud pop; the wood splintered around the door and floor. Diane screamed.

"Burke, you fool, we need her alive."

Diane heard them rip away the rest of the door. She was rolled up in a ball as they reached in, grabbed her legs, and began pulling her from her hiding place into the closet. Diane screamed again.

"Shit, Burke, you've killed her."

"She ain't dead, screaming like that."

While they argued, Diane summoned all her strength and hit Oralia Lee in the nose with the heel of her hand and stuck at Burke with the glass knife. He hit her hand away. She dropped her makeshift knife and it shattered. Useless weapon. In the confusion, she lost her grip on the bat.

"Damn you, woman. You could've cut me." Burke dug his fingers into Diane's leg and pulled her out into the bedroom. Diane kicked at him and he twisted her leg. "Oralia Lee, get up off the floor and help me if you want this bitch alive."

Oralia Lee didn't answer. *One down*, thought, Diane. She kicked hard at Burke and hit him in the knee. He howled and fired his gun, splintering the floor near Diane's head. Diane scrambled toward the door. He caught her around the waist and pulled her back into the room.

"I'm gonna kill you, you keep giving me trouble. The hell with the treasure. I'm gonna kill you." He shoved Diane down and her head hit the floor with a thump. Burke aimed his gun at her. "Now, give me one reason why I shouldn't just kill you right here and now."

Diane didn't move, feigning unconsciousness, trying to think. A moan came from the closet and Burke looked away from Diane.

"Oralia Lee, you . . ."

Diane didn't hesitate: As he spoke she rolled toward him and grabbed both his legs and pulled. He hit the floor hard and lost his gun. Diane scrambled for it, but he reached it first and fired at her. Click. He fired again. Click.

Diane jumped to her feet and ran for the door, down the hall and down the stairs, and to the living room to Archie. His gun was just under his body. She pulled it out just as Burke came down the stairs.

"I got bullets now," he said as Diane fired, hitting him in the neck.

She jumped up and ran out the door, leaving the two of them behind her. She thought she killed Burke, she didn't know, but Oralia Lee could possibly be coming to by now. Diane sprinted through the woods toward her house as fast as she could run. It was dawn and the light was welcome. She was tired of the dark.

When she got to her apartment, she fumbled with the keys in her pocket. Her hand was bleeding where the glass shards of her knife had cut her. She managed to get the door open and closed it behind her. She ran up the stairs to the safety of her apartment and called the police.

Garnett sat in her living room on the couch with her while a paramedic bandaged her hand.

"Did you find them?" asked Diane.

Garnett nodded. "Archie and his sister are dead. I guess you know that. I know both of them. I would never have guessed it."

"We all have our breaking points. Archie was sitting in the tent while we processed the charred remains. They turned out to be people he knew—Bobby Coleman, Izzy's son, his own niece, for God's sake. That's hard. His sister lost her daughter—and grandchild—for what? Nothing. I understand their desire for revenge. I could have been there. What about the Rawsons?"

"Burke Rawson is dead. You were true with that shot. It hit the jugular and he bled out. Oralia . . . is that her name? She's in a coma."

Diane was afraid of that; she almost hesitated when she hit her. She had broken her nasal bone and had probably rammed a piece of bone up into her brain. She felt sick.

"You can wait and give your statement later this morning," he said. "Get some rest."

"I guess we'll never know what they did with the bodies of the Sebestyen family—if they were the killers, if the Sebestyens were even killed."

"Maybe the woman'll come out of the coma—who knows," said Garnett.

"How is Adler?" she asked.

"We looked in the basement. No sign of him. We're thinking he got himself free and escaped," said Garnett.

Diane nodded, leaned back, and closed her eyes. She sat back up so suddenly that Garnett jumped.

"What basement?" she asked.

"What do you mean?" he asked.

"Which basement did you look in?" said Diane.

"The basement of the house." he said.

"The meth house?" asked Diane.

"The meth house? No, the one last night . . . where Archie and Catherine were killed," said Garnett.

"No. He was in the burned-out basement of the meth house next door."

"Holy . . ." Garnett jumped to his feet.

Damn, she hadn't been clear when she spoke with the 911 operator, and when the police arrived there was too much daylight to see the light in the basement of the meth house.

"My God, he was there all night in this weather. He'll be frozen to death," she said, rising from her sofa.

She grabbed her coat and rode with Garnett back to the scene of the crime. The paramedics were close behind.

They all ran from their vehicles to the edge of the gaping burned-out hole in the earth. Adler was still sitting with the ghosts of the dead students.

Epilogue

Diane ran along the nature trail behind the museum. She stopped when she got to the bridge and walked out on the small dock to watch the swans gliding in the water. The sun felt good on her bare arms. It had been a hard winter—too many funerals to attend, too many broken lives, too many unanswered questions.

Adler hadn't died. But in the cold he lost two fingers, three toes, and his spirit. He resigned his council post and quit politics. His family wanted to blame Diane for his being left out in the cold, but the 911 tapes cleared her. Garnett never got to the bottom of the mix-up in directions.

The Indiana cold case squad traced the lives of the Rawsons. They were in Florida at the time the Sebestyens disappeared. There was evidence the Sebestyens rented a house on the beach near Ruby Torkel in the summer of 1987. But the detectives never got even a hint of where the bodies might be buried. Diane believed they were taken out to sea and dumped into the deep. Jin hoped that Juliet's memories involved only dolls and that the Sebestyens found the treasure and were living happily and quietly somewhere mysterious.

The treasure. Diane shook her head and continued her run. To Diane, the treasure had been one of the most malignant aspects surrounding the tragedies.

It had taken months to work out all the legal details. At first, the State of Florida didn't want to relinquish any rights to a possible treasure—which they believed likely to be Spanish gold. They tried legal maneuvers to force Diane to give them the code, but the doll and the code belonged to Juliet Price and Ruby Torkel and they couldn't be forced to give it up.

Finally Florida made the deal with Juliet and her grandmother and after using ground-penetrating radar and three stout grave diggers, they discovered nothing but the remains of Leander Llewellyn.

Whether there had ever been a treasure, or a new code had been substituted much the same way Diane had done, or someone had already found the treasure years ago, or Leo Parrish was simply a prankster, no one knew. All those people—the Sebestyens, Archie Donahue, Catherine Riverton, Burke Rawson—died for nothing. Just like the thirty-four people in the house with the meth lab. They all died for nothing. Diane ran faster, trying to outdistance all the ghosts. She hoped Jin was right.

Dead End

The bite of the black widow can be deadly. Diane Fallon discovers just how far a particularly cunning black widow will go to get her revenge on Diane for putting her in prison. When she escapes from the lair of her prison cell, the black widow leaves Diane entangled in a web of deception and deadly consequences.

Coming from Onyx in February 2008

About the Author

Beverly Connor is the author of the Diane Fallon Forensic Investigation series and the Lindsay Chamberlain Mystery series. Before she began her writing career, Beverly worked as an archaeologist in the Southeastern United States specializing in bone identification and analysis of stone tool debitage. She weaves her professional experiences from archaeology and her knowledge of the South into interlinked stories of the past and present. *One Grave Too Many* was the first book in the Diane Fallon series. Beverly's books have been translated into Dutch and German and are available in countries of the European Union.

DEAD SECRET

A DIANE FALLON INVESTIGATION

by

Beverly Connor

When forensic anthropologist Diane Fallon
discovers a trio of decades-old skeletons, she also
unearths the key to a mystery that reaches back
seventy years in a legacy of love, greed, and
murder—and a family secret that still holds the
power to kill.

0-451-41192-7

ALSO AVAILABLE

DEAD GUILTY
0-451-41150-1

ONE GRAVE TOO MANY
0-451-41119-6

ANNE FRASIER

SLEEP TIGHT

A female FBI profiler is up against a killer who may have ties to her own tragic past.

"A riveting thriller...laced with forensic detail and psychological twists, Anne Frasier's latest intertwines the hunt for a serial killer with the personal struggles of two sisters battling their own demons and seeking their own truths. Compelling and real—a great read."
—Andrea Kane

0-451-41077-7

O042/ Frasier

USA TODAY BESTSELLING AUTHOR

ANNE FRASIER

PLAY DEAD

Discover the dark side of Savannah, where a female homicide detective must confront the truth about her own past to stop a twisted killer.

"ANNE FRASIER DELIVERS THOROUGHLY ENGROSSING, COMPLETELY RIVETING SUSPENSE."
—LISA GARDNER

"A MASTER."
—*MINNEAPOLIS STAR-TRIBUNE*

0-451-41137-4

Available wherever books are sold or at
penguin.com